THE
TRICKSTER,
MAGICIAN &
GRIEVING MAN

THE
TRICKSTER, MAGICIAN & GRIEVING MAN
Reconnecting Men with Earth

GLEN A. MAZIS

BEAR & COMPANY
PUBLISHING
SANTA FE, NEW MEXICO

LIBRARY OF CONGRESS CATALOGING-IN-PUBLICATION DATA

Mazis, Glen A., 1951–
    The trickster, magician & grieving man : reconnecting men
to earth / Glen A. Mazis.
    p. cm.
    Includes bibliographical references and index.
    ISBN 1-879181-11-8
    1. Men—United States—Psychology. 2. Masculinity
(Psychology)—United States. 3. Men's movement—United
States. 4. Archetype (Psychology) I. Title: Trickster, magician,
and grieving man.
HQ1090.3.M37 1994
305.32—dc20   93-46768
                                                          CIP

Bear & Company, Inc.
Santa Fe, NM 87504-2860

Cover illustration: "Man, Lion and Bird"
by Niki Broyles © 1984
Cover & interior design: Marilyn Hager
Author photo: Catherine Wert
Editing: Brandt Morgan
Typography: Marilyn Hager

Printed in the United States of America by R. R. Donnelley
1 3 5 7 9 8 6 4 2

This book is dedicated to a brilliant young philosopher, Linda Singer, who died just as she was coming into her own. Her friendship and patience in showing me and many other males and females about the hidden, insidious dangers of current gender roles brought a new light into many lives.

It is also dedicated to another philosopher, Fred Elliston, whose life was taken by a drunk driver just as he, too, was finding his way. Fred had agonized over male gender issues for a long time and was still seeking new paradigms.

Contents

Acknowledgments

First and foremost, I must thank my mother, Charlotte Mazis, for her courage and loving-kindness in raising us at a time when being a single divorced mother was an uncommon and hard job in New York City. Her loving support and continued friendship have given me a strong foundation to see my potential and the potential of those around me. This book's advocacy of not allowing pain to obscure one's wonder at life was her lesson to me.

I also want to heartily thank Antoinette Vita Giardino (the "Incomparable Garden of Life") for her encouragement that I should write this book about what I knew so well and felt so deeply. She helped me believe in my calling, and her shining spirit was an inspiration.

Judith Johnson's encouragement throughout the peaks and valleys of the writing process helped me hold on to sanity. Also, Judith's ongoing comments on the manuscript as it emerged and on the many drafts often made me see where new work had to be done. The spiritual aid Judith also provided helped the writing stay faithful to a deeper source of inspiration than the daily cares.

Catherine Keller gave me my first opportunity to present these ideas in workshops and has encouraged me to this day to think about new ways to be creatively human. Her philosophical sisterhood has been, and continues to be, invaluable.

Friends are the staff of life. This book wouldn't have happened without the friendship of Tim Baker, Karen Malott, Bruce Wilshire, Donna Wilshire, Judith Johnson, Suren Lalvani, Eton Churchill, Pat Johnson, Peter Parisi, Troy Thomas, Linda Ross, Michael Barton, and Peter Madsen. Donna's insightful criticisms of the final draft were invaluable. The Humanities Department at Penn State Harrisburg and my chair, Bill Mahar, have been wonderful in their support. My teachers, Ed Casey and Mike Dillon, have always encouraged me in my wish to become more than the "ivory-towered" philosopher, and every semester my students are the people who show me the wonder once again.

I know it's not traditional, but I want to thank the "little Buddha," Phaedrus, my Burmese cat, for sixteen years of affection shared, which has also contributed to this book.

Finally, Barbara Hand Clow's enthusiasm for this project was the final spark I needed to ignite my writing process. Laura Karinch's copyediting has been a "goddess-send." The whole crew at Bear and Company are amazing in their support and openhearted way of dealing with authors. Barbara Drew has been an island of light and Gerry Clow a source of stimulation.

Foreword

Is this book too good to be true?

Some of us feminists have always suspected that men are capable of marvels. By this I do not mean that they can erect seven times seven Wonders of the World—this we know already, ad nauseam. Elite males have established their names and fames in monumental grandeur, much to the detriment of the majority populations of women, workers, children, people of color, and Earth creatures and elements exploited and denuded in the process. But this list of the despised of the Earth rarely includes that odd assortment of males not necessarily subject to servitude but nonetheless variously marginalized and repressed, persecuted or cruci-fied for their resistance to the war-and-monument-makers: the pacifists, the egalitarians, the artists, the defenders of women, the unorthodox mystics, the friends of the Earth. This species of alternative male seems to be proliferating just now, at the end of the millennium. Not perhaps at the rate we would like, nor ever with the political perfection we might prefer—but nonetheless appreciably. Let me suggest that this field of "newly flowering males" has grown up in direct response to the initiatives of feminism. And that inasmuch as they suffer and develop in accountability with women, we also owe them our support.

We—I—have tended to understand patriarchy as the original sin, out of which flows slavery, militarism, capital-ism, racism, dualism. . . . with some justification, I might add—but not if this means that sexism is the sole or worst oppression. And not if this means that men themselves, as such, are the demons. For instance, Afro-American feminists, who call themselves womanists, partly in order to distin-guish themselves from overly simplistic white feminist accounts of patriarchy, work for solidarity with their men while at the same time holding them accountable for sexism. Of course this works out differently when dealing with the great white male, who has proven, like Melville's erstwhile creature, peculiarly liable to demonization. White race solidarity is not what I as a white feminist want with "my" males. But something else, crucial to the further unfolding of "women's movement" (b. hooks's syntax) in the world, seems to me to be at stake in this matter of the worthy male. Let me call it a three-fold feminist honesty.

First, we sometimes speak of men as though they are hopelessly enmeshed in their sexism—whether in overt macho form or in subtler "sensitive" styles of parasitism. It has been important for women to "git man off our eyeball" (Alice Walker). And it has been important for men to hear the radicality of our critique. However, finally, the logic breaks down: for if men are irredeemable from their sexism, then of course there is no reason for them to struggle to outgrow it. Why on Earth sacrifice power if it makes no difference anyway? Well, of course, women rightly argue that we want men to change for their own sake—and this is exactly the kind of appeal Glen Mazis makes to his fellow fellows. He not only argues but textually embodies the sort of joyful play that becomes possible for men if and only if they stop denying their pain, their finitude, their relatedness. But if this sort of marvel is possible, then feminist honesty requires building it squarely into our talk and our action, our strategies and our attitudes.

Next, these men will mostly require some support of women if they are to sustain the griefwork needed, by Mazis's account, to get reconnected to body, Earth, connection itself. Now gratefully, Mazis does not himself for a moment appeal to women to help men out, to provide the traditional services of maternal succor, sisterly support, wifely devotion. Nor does he, à la Bly, counsel men to a new (old) man-to-man autonomy from women. Rather, he calls other males to take up their pain and walk—to stop leaving the relational work to women. But in so doing, of course they become open—and vulnerable—to relations with women and with men at a new depth of potentiality. This is the "e-motion" with which Glen challenges the men's movement—to move. Feminist affirmation of the insight and the energy of healing males—as they become good magicians, cooks, and grievers—may not be necessary to keep them from reverting. However, because they will still be treated by most men as traitors to the brotherhood, and because the whole point after all is the recognition of the web of relationships so badly rent by patriarchy, I would argue that honestly feminist women will choose to honor the efforts of "softening" men.

And thirdly: our lives as women are after all, *ipso facto,* "entertwined" with the lives of males. For better and—as we have made painfully conscious—often for worse, for lesbian as well as for straight, we have fathers, brothers, male friends, colleagues, possibly even lovers, life-partners and a son or two. Most of us feminists welcome and work within the ambiguity and hope of those relationships to men which we choose. Yet we may not know how to integrate these real-ities with our rhetoric. Or we may seek to minimize their presence. But even when we choose separatist paths, we deceive ourselves if we think we can divorce ourselves from the formative influences of males in our past and in our envi-ronment. Though some of us may have experienced too much of the "flying boys" and the "desert storms" (to borrow Mazis's imagery) to take much interest in the evolution of malekind, the attempt to purify ourselves of masculine con-tact implicates us in the worst patriarchal illusions of separa-tion. In fact, we will have to work through, over and again, the painful effects of the men in our lives, and in the process, own up to the hopes and possibilities wrapped in the suffer-ing. Most of us know this and practice this in our personal lives. But many of us have a hard time acknowledging the multiform depth of our involvement with males.

Healing may only be possible inasmuch as we recognize

that the system that warps male egos into warriors causes unjust male suffering as well—and that pretty much the same system (the "malestorm") disfigures female life at the same time. It is not a matter of equal blame. But it is a matter of equal responsibility to discern and to alter the system within and outside us. Glen Mazis offers us here a work for which there is none greater—for the purpose of calling men to their own self-healing responsibility to the web of life. In its fiery rebuttal of the regressive aspects of the men's movement, it opens up a space for the "newly flowering males" of the post-Vietnam generation. It also shows itself firmly (not soft here!) pro-feminist. But this is not the male feminism of one who leeches off of women's works and seeks legitimation by women. Rather this voice rises with humility and humor, with compassion and commitment, out of an unapologetically and self-critically male life-exploration. Because Mazis happens to be a philosopher by vocation, the intellectual depth resonating even in his lush texture of illustrations from popular culture makes good reading for anyone seeking to grasp our culture, anyone seeking some ground as we lurch apocalyptically toward a new millennium. But I also recommend this marvel of a work to women, who might recognize the strategic usefulness of a man-to-man deconstruction of the armor of masculinity. And who acknowledge that after all we as women will not come to terms with the complex genders of our own new creation without some fine "fellow" insight.

This book is too good not to be true.

Catherine Keller
Madison, New Jersey

C. *Keller, author of* From a Broken Web: Separation, Sexism and Self, *and presently finishing* Apocalypse Now and Then: A Feminist Approach to the End of the World, *teaches theology and religious studies at Drew University.*

Preface

Evolutionary Possibilities as a Generation Seizes Its Time: Flowering Males

I am forty years old. My formative, teenage years were during the sixties. My parents had been divorced when I was seven years old, and in the late fifties that seemed unheard of: I didn't know of another child whose parents were divorced. I was raised by my mother and my sister, who was five years older than I, and I have always been rather close to my mother and surrounded by women. Today, as a philosophy professor, I teach several types of philosophy, including "feminist philosophy." In other words, I am exactly the kind of male, the "female-identified" male, about whom Robert Bly and others are so concerned. Bly calls such men "the soft males" and says that although "they're not interested in harming the Earth or starting wars" and "have a gentle attitude toward life in their whole being and style of living," they are not "life-giving" and have "little vitality to offer." Bly assures us that he likes these men and that "they're lovely, valuable people," but still there is "something wrong" with them.[1]

Bly chooses his terms carefully, telling us, the "soft males," that he will take us deeper into realms "wet, dark, and low," which are the Taoist symbols for the feminine. Undoubtedly, he thinks we need to be assured that the way to true, hard maleness is through doorways that traditionally have been identified with the female. Bly also tells us that he is not trying to usher in a return to a prior style of masculine gender identification that was unreceptive, isolated, and brutal. Yet the response to his book—both feminist dismay and male war whooping—is intuitively correct, an appropriate reso-

TRICKSTER, MAGICIAN & GRIEVING MAN

nance to the images and the tone of Bly's words. The response is appropriate even to his title, "Iron John": another image of the impermeable, metallic, indestructible, primal male identity to be found outside societal networks, in a vision of nature as "other" to society, through warrior's behavior, heroic deeds, and finding transcendent causes.

There is more subtlety in Bly's book, but the tone is that of a male looking backward to an essence of masculinity rather than embracing the evolution of a new kind of male person. The effort to deconstruct some of these old images in order to understand the vitality of a newly emergent set of behaviors and understanding of life seems beyond Bly's ken.

I do not think someone of Bly's generation can speak for us, the newly flowering males of the world. I am tired of having Robert Bly's generation speak for me and tell me what I am about. I would like to speak for myself and hopefully for some of my peers who have had similar experiences and feelings. We are not wounded in the ways that Bly thinks we are, although I can find myself falling into the trancelike persuasion of his perspective. It would be easier to follow Bly's path and diagnosis than to really analyze what is unique to the experience of my generation that gives many males of my age certain abilities and opportunities not available to previous generations of males. Each moment in time and circumstance has its uniqueness, gifts that can be seized if recognized and then developed, and pitfalls that are specific to that constellation of events and forces.

It's interesting that the need to concentrate on my career and write academic philosophy forced me to keep this project on hold for many years, since the mid-1980s when I gave a series of lectures in Cincinnati about maleness. My notes remained in my drawer for the next seven years and I would wistfully look at them from time to time. It wasn't just reading Bly's book and knowing that I had to respond to it, nor was it just turning forty and finally feeling comfortable being the unique kind of male that I am and wanting to share and

support other males evolving in similar ways. The final cata-
lyst occurred when I reached the final pages of Bly's book
and read Bly's admission that although he had concentrated
on four of the seven male selves—the King, the Warrior, the
Lover, and the Wild Man—he recognized the importance of
three others—the Trickster, the Cook/Magician, and the
Grieving Man. I read that page, page 228 of *Iron John*, and felt
wonderfully affirmed. I ran to my desk and took out my out-
lines for the book about the male self that I had never written
and laughed to see in front of my eyes the proposed sketch of
the exploration of the three key images of maleness that I
thought were informing my own development: the Trickster,
the Cook/Magician, and the Grieving Man! Those had been
the archetypes I had discussed at Xavier University and the
Jung Society long ago, and now I knew I had to write about
them as my gift to the brothers of my generation.

A Prayer
for Women and Men,
Men and Women

Apparently, there may have been thousands of years when people, women and men, lived as children of the Goddess, of Mother, and as all children loved by this sweet planet, were equally cherished for their gifts. For at least four-and-a-half millennia, the peoples of a rationalized warrior mentality, worshipping the Absolute, which denies the sacredness of Earth, cycle, and the weaving of each being into a changing, flowing fabric with all others, have violated in the name of the male sword. Here is a prayer that we return to cherishing the Earth, feeling the flowing into each other of all beings, and that male and female will see the generative and caring possibilities of equal partnership with each other.

I pray that men will come to welcome women's anger as the chance to work through past violations into a new peace. I pray that men will learn to hear other voices and be transformed. There is, all around us, a wild magic that we waste and shut out of our lives. This prayer is an invitation to let that magical energy about us flow through us. It is especially an invitation to the males who have inflicted so much pain in their desperation to hide their own: may they come out of hiding and let be.

Introduction

Men Emerging from Isolating Circles of Pain

I was raised to believe that part of "being a man" was to be able to stand honestly before others and admit to having made mistakes. Yet it doesn't seem that we as a gender have been very good at taking responsibility for the damage we have wrought upon the planet, upon females, upon various groups we oppose, or even upon ourselves. This book is intended to be neither a "male-bashing" exercise nor a defensive retreat into a male enclave. Rather, I think it best for all of us—males, females, animals, and the Earth—if we both take responsibility for some of the shortcomings and behaviors of our past male identities and also look for the new growth and identities that are emerging within us. We may find that recent events are reminding us of ways to be male other than the sense of masculinity that has ruled since the warrior paradigm became ascendent. What we seek to achieve and to embody as males may have been distorted by a sense of heroism that was informed by a warrior's stance toward himself, others, and the Earth. We may find an older, and through it, a newer, way to be male than our traditional sense of masculinity has allowed.

As masculine beings, males have wrought a storm upon the Earth, a continuing maelstrom. A maelstrom is a turbulent storm that passes over and engulfs other things but is somehow self-enclosed. Its destructive power builds by feeding upon itself, having no outlet. When it interacts enough with its environment, it loses its separate and lethal identity. Until that point, however, it rages and uproots everything it lords over. It rains down upon other beings, and in its most

extreme forms washes away their identity in a flood of annihilation. The force of its release from self-enclosure becomes
the power that overwhelms that which it destroys. Thus have
men often passed over the Earth, its females, its animals, its
other men, raging and uprooting, invading and overwhelming—following the path of their own release at great cost to
others.

Whatever its political wisdom, the invasion of the Persian
Gulf in 1991 was a prime example of that maelstrom. Even its
vocabulary evoked a host of images reflective of a destructive
and outdated sense of masculinity. I believe certain men in
my generation are calling that masculine identity into question. We may not all have the words to express it; some of us
may even gladly serve in such wars, yet the traditional ideas
evoked by such a blatant and self-conscious appeal to the
"macho" may leave us feeling uncomfortable. Moreover, the
image of a "Desert Storm" intensifies the metaphor of the
maelstrom.

Like the maelstrom, "Desert Storm" invokes the concentration of male power over and against the opposing world
or others, but in even a more sterile, sullen, and stark display
of violation and self-enclosure. Flooding water, no matter
how destructive, still carries with it the moisture of "the
soft," the fluidity of the interactive, and the solvency of the
intermingling. However, a storm swirling in an already desiccated landscape, where the sands only shift in their indiffer-
ence to the rage above, leaves an even more stark sense of
self-enclosed rage, circling within itself with no apparent resolution other than an arbitrary halt. Such a halt is not a transformation, only a cessation of rage that can easily ignite
again.

The purpose of this book is twofold. First, it intends to
look at some of the self-defeating possibilities for males contained   in the images of the King, the Warrior, the Lover, and
the Wild Man, as explored by Robert Bly in his conjuring up
of "Iron John." This is understood by Bly and others as a

recovery of a *dimension of primal maleness*. These images of masculinity are presented as avenues to recovering a past that has been lost. The same quest is also contained in the images of Desert Storm, an attempt made by George Bush to revive similar images of lost male glory. How destructive these images of the masculine are for the well-being of men and those with whom they interact will be seen in exploring their deeper meanings. It will also be seen how this sense of masculinity, rather than being an essence of maleness or even an adequate rendering of male history, is rather the glorification of one strand of history and one interpretation of the heroic.

With this done, an even more important purpose of this book is to explore some of the emergent dimensions of the *transforming male self* embodied in the relatively unacknowledged images of the Trickster, the Cook/Magician, and the Grieving Man. I hope to show that the "soft male," rather than being a male who lacks vitality, embodies an abundant, fluid energy that has the potential to open up new directions for maleness, perhaps well beyond the understanding of the Bly-Bush generation of males. In seeing the value of these new experiences, I also hope to show that there are parts of our past and of other cultures that we can now appreciate as different possibilities for maleness.

Our sense of masculinity and heroism may have been distorted by a certain obscuring view of the past that claimed to see all of it. This view claimed to reveal our male "essence," when actually it may have been hiding part of our legacy to be more fully human. The masculine has been understood in terms of a particular sense of the hero, a cult of the hero, that may have been misrepresented to us from the time of the classical Greeks onward. We may find that the true hero is a different kind of male than we thought he was.

Part of the traditional male way of understanding is to assume that what is said is what is explicitly stated, what is clearly argued and presented, and not to pay much attention to the tone of what is said or to the metaphors and images invoked. However, I have found that much of what is conveyed to others comes through images, metaphors, tone, and emotion. It may be true that both Bly and Bush qualify what they say about maleness and war, but the images they invoke belie their limited understanding of the mature, complete male self and his relationship to the Earth. That is why it is important to speak with new images, even if they jar at first.

I choose to think of males "flowering" in new possibilities because it is time that men were identified with this beauty, this organic growth, this rootedness, this interconnectedness with the Earth. Flowers have been seen as either "effeminate" or "feminine" by previous generations of males. However, it is important to point out that flowers enliven the world. Furthermore, although a part of nature, flowers also enliven urban landscapes as well as wild ones. As such, they remind men that nature's enlivening power and beauty is everywhere. This power doesn't have to be sought on some grand quest or by retreating from mundane life and connection. Lastly, flowers are also bred in such a way that new hybrids emerge in a cooperation of natural fecundity and reflective intervention, as I hope new ways to be male can be bred.

Men have sometimes been referred to using the metaphor of a flower, as when one noted that the "flower of the generation" or "the flower of manhood" was cut off by being sent to war and slaughtered. Men have allowed themselves to be considered tenderly when they have sacrificed themselves for glory. However, there may be a way to flower and *continue* to blossom, rather than die the hero's death or lead a constricted life according to the heroic code. We must sound the depths of these old images and be critical, and then learn to speak our new potentials and truths in new terms.

I have been alluding to a distinction we should make clear at the outset: *masculinity is a social construction*. It is comprised of a loose set of role models, images, norms, and behaviors. It is a way of shaping our psyches and gaining identity. Becoming masculine is rewarded in many subtle ways within our American society. To violate its implicitly communicated boundaries is often to risk a loss of regard by others, outright disapproval, the loss of societal rewards, and, in the most extreme cases, vulnerability to violence. To be male does not mean one has to be masculine in the sense of assenting to these norms, behaving in this manner, and seeing the world according to this perspective. There are different ways to be a male and no one set way. To be human in all our dimensions is an ongoing process that changes in regard to the factors with which it is in relation. Being male is partly historical, cultural, biological, social, and so forth, without any single factor being the determining one. It is my belief that as humans we are always somewhat free to work with all parts of our being and to respond to others. We respond to our world—to nature, culture, and history—and we shape a future. What males might become is unknown. It is a challenge, a risk, and a hope for a more creative future.

THE
TRICKSTER,
MAGICIAN &
GRIEVING MAN

PART ONE

The
Raging
Desert Storm

CHAPTER ONE

Male Pride

The Masculine as Unacknowledged Archetype of Pain

Pain and Hurt

When we think of what makes a man "a man" in American society, many images and words come to mind, but I rather doubt that the word pain is among them. Rather, men like to think their identity is founded on such qualities as courage, persistence, determination, bravery or, at least, endurance. They have images of warriors, athletes, strong fathers, explorers, and providers in mind. We men, I believe, like to think of ourselves as masculine insofar as we are involved in directing, planning, leading, and achieving in the way that the character, Mrs. Ramsey, in Virginia Woolf's novel, *To the Lighthouse*, thinks about the nature of masculinity: "She let it uphold and sustain her, this admirable fabric of the masculine intelligence, which ran up and down, crossed this way and that, like iron girders, spanning the swaying fabric, upholding the world, so that she could trust herself to it utterly . . ."[1]

It is this heroic stance toward the world, even if only limited to facing the rather mundane obstacles of everyday life, that we men would like to hold onto as the heart of our iden-

3

tity, and it is this legacy of the hero that has been handed down to us in myth and everyday story as our model. Yet I would like to suggest that the hidden story of men is their enmeshment in a dimension of pain. The masculine identity is the embodiment of pain, a response to the pain of life that, instead of dealing creatively with it, hides it and disguises it. In keeping the pain locked inside the masculine psyche, we multiply the pain's power. The unacknowledged pain doesn't die, but rather is redirected and inflicted upon others and the world—sometimes unwittingly. Many aspects of male lives can be better understood once the fault lines of this encapsulated pain are detected.

The identity that males seek to achieve has been given to them in images of the archetypal life of the hero. A continual parallel is drawn between the stages of a hero's adventure and the stages of a man's life insofar as it is properly masculine. Whether viewed nightly on the television set or on the big screen of the movies or in the newspaper, males are always surrounded by the call to be heroic, to "be a man," and have been for thousands of years. It is also this myth that informs the perspective embodied in the current "men's movement"—where Bly's *Iron John* again provides a striking example. Joseph Campbell went so far as to call this "hero's adventure" the "monomyth" for the discovery of male identity.[2] This heroic model invariably involves a call to quest for some goal such as treasure, experience, or the sense of triumph, usually as a journey which involves the passing of hardships and tests, then a victory, and, finally, the return with a prize. This trajectory of masculine achievement also involves a set of character traits that make it possible. Remaining calm, courageous, rational, in control, and unswerving in the face of threat, pain, and loss are essential to the heroic identity. They dictate a certain way to construe pain and a certain way of dealing with both its feeling and import. The hero always surpasses his pain as an obstacle to his goals. However, what we will later have to question is whether this model of the hero is appropriate as a role model for male identity, and even more pointedly, whether this is the proper archetype of heroism, the One Myth ("monomyth"). Perhaps there is another sense of the hero that has been obscured by the warrior mentality that we must recover for ourselves, as we will attempt to do in the later chapters of this book.

It is hard to tell this story of male pain. Masculine identity asks us to tolerate pain in silence. As part of enforcing this norm, the masculinity dictates that to tell a tale of pain is to tell a sad, dreary tale—or even worse, a tale of self-pity—which is what often emerges when we finally break our long, self-imposed silences about how we hurt beneath our masks. The irony is that *not* giving voice to pain increases its intensity. Like the maelstrom, contained pain feeds on itself. Rather than avoiding pain by not voicing and sharing it, traditional masculinity ensures that it becomes an inwardly consuming force. The hero who is supposed to be impervious to pain becomes driven by its repressed force. The men who articulated classic Western philosophy and psychology have repeatedly told us that pain is to be avoided, that it is an evil to be eradicated, and that it must remain hidden and undiscussed. Thus they have made it the disguised center of our being.

I remember the anguish of a nurse who was ordered by a male doctor to give a heavy dose of tranquilizers to a woman who had just witnessed the death of her spouse of thirty years. The widow, the nurse, and I all knew she had a right to her pain, that experiencing the full pain of her loss was essential to her rediscovering the marrow and wonder of her life. We knew these darker tones would contribute to the new color of her life. However, the doctor was expressing the heroic attitude embodied in our medical practice and social norms that pain is evil, to be avoided, to be "tranquilized." We males have not only brought this attitude into the world, we've also taken it into the confines of our psyches. We can no longer afford this attitude. We can't move on to new identities until we take this pain skeleton out of our psychic closet and trace its origins in our heroic identity and see its effects on the world.

Pain is not in itself defeating or inimical to the joy of life. It is the other dimension of pain, the one created *in reaction* to the inevitable pain of life of aging, of death, of loss, of setback—that becomes searing in a different way. The hero wants to choose his pain. He can't accept life's power over him to dictate what pains he must undergo. When we try to avoid the normal and natural pain in life, we end up tearing apart our lives and the lives of others in an effort to tear out the pain. This effort can lead us to very dark places of violation. Over and over again, men have been guilty of manufacturing this "second dimension" of pain. The unacknowledged virulence created by the "masculine" reaction to the pain of life becomes the driving force for inflicting ever-increasing amounts of violation and pain upon other creatures, even on the planet itself. This whiplash reaction can create interlocking feedback cycles of pain and violation, which at various times and places threaten to set up "hell worlds" of sheer pain—like the countryside of Vietnam or Cambodia during the war, the cities of Europe during the Nazi occupation, and even many streets and households in contemporary America.

It is important to understand how we males have taken the inevitable pain of existence and incorporated it into our gender identity in a self-defeating way, and then see how this leads to self-perpetuating cycles of pain transferred toward people, creatures, and even the elements. It is not that we males are the source of all the world's pain, but we have poured incredible amounts of psychic distress into the emotional currents that circulate among us all. This is a fact that we can no longer afford to deny.

Each day, the news media report on events that are testimony to the existence of these cycles of violation. Males need to take to heart this existential reality. According to information gathered in 1992, every forty-three seconds in the United States, a female—usually a girl—is raped. These rapes could have been committed by females, but in fact they are committed by males. Although there is *no logical necessity* that we men be the cause of so much violation on the planet, we still cannot heal ourselves until we take responsibility for *the massive amount of violation we have perpetrated* and then look at our masculine identity in the mirror.

In looking at the masculine heroic response to pain, I'd like to keep the image of Siddhartha ("the Buddha") as a point of reference and contrast. Siddhartha is emblematic of a certain strength displayed by males in many cultural settings and epochs. Yet his path traces a direction away from the masculine response to pain. Siddhartha's response is particularly instructive, because initially it is heroic in the extreme. Only after much trial and self-examination does he turn it around.

By his father's design, Siddhartha lived his early years sheltered from the realities of life. He was kept preoccupied by palace life; however, his chance encounters with the great sources of pain in all human existence—aging, sickness, suffering, and death—drove him out of his father's palace on a quest for truth. Upon leaving the palace and riding out into the fields, he was at first overcome by the suffering of the men at work, the animals slaving under the plow, and even the worms that were cut up by the plow.[3] He saw that this inevitable suffering seemed to threaten the meaningfulness of life. His initial response was typical of the heroic quest for triumph over an all-powerful enemy: to challenge it, defeat it, and bend it to his incredible determination. If his body were to lead him to sickness, debilitation, and death, then he would overcome its hold on him, even if it required eating only a grain of rice a day for years. He saw his body as a mere vehicle that he would drive in a different direction. However, after many long and heroic battles of this sort—

different in content than those undertaken by most males, but similar in his impassioned, courageous, and stoically self-lacerating commitment—he discovered his great truth: this very pain could also become a release from suffering.

For Joseph Campbell, the Buddha remains a hero. He doesn't defeat pain, but he does find an answer to give to others. However, rather than bringing home a solution, an answer, to the question of how to face death, Siddhartha has abandoned the contest. He has discovered that death is not an evil. Pain is not an evil. To maintain control, as he sought to do, is not to defeat the vicissitudes of life but rather to create *needless suffering about pain and loss*. Siddhartha asks us to feel pain, to experience loss, and to acknowledge lack of control as part of the wonder of life, not as its defect. He has realized the warrior's idea of heroism and masculinity as maintaining control of the situation in the face of whatever setback is self-defeating. What Siddhartha understands by these ideas can only become comprehensible when we try to reenvision the world through humor, magic, and flow as discussed in the later parts of this book.

Pain is almost always discussed as though it were some "brute given" about which not much can be said other than tracing its causes and effects. I don't think this is true. In fact, pain can be described in detail. It has many aspects and characteristics that can be revealed in order to better understand its deeper meaning. Instead of assuming it is meaningless, as we often do, we need to analyze it more carefully. Once we see what the experience of pain is telling us and where it is taking us in our relations with ourselves and others, then we can better understand the ways in which we deal with it as males, and how and why we might begin to live to reenvision its place in our lives.

The pain of loss, of failing powers, and even of death itself, gets its virulence—its ability to eat away at our hearts, to destroy our sense of peace and aliveness—not from its own power or meaning but from the kind of resistance we give to it. It brings us back to the part of ourselves that is caught up in a web of interchange with the world we can't control. Since all of us have spun ourselves into these patterns of this extended web—which gets damaged by the tension of the many forces that comprise it—we feel rent, torn apart in the cloth of our making. Our extended being has been shredded in some way. Physical pain brings us back to the body as *impacted upon* by the environment. The body is only part of a larger ebb and flow across fluid boundaries. Even the parts our body—even its cells—are a *community* of beings which themselves interact and impact upon one another.

Physical pain is the visceral awareness of all the ways the body is continuous with its environment. Pain dissolves the boundaries of "within" and "without"; it is the announcement that we have been reached by other forces of which we are a part. Sometimes these impacts rupture our previous rhythm or structure, and sometimes they merely transform it. Since our sense of ourselves is in feeling the distinctive rhythm of who we are, where we are going, and our way of getting there, this disruption comes as a shock.

The breaking of our deeper rhythms is felt more keenly and is more significant than our current, predominantly materialistic worldview realizes. Siddhartha saw clearly how this bringing us back to the moment of feeling the impact of the constant interaction among beings in both our bodies and psyches is the heart of pain. Its rending quality, however, comes not only from registering the impact, but also feeling viscerally that it is pushing us into a transformation as a result of all these other beings. He saw how this takes us willy-nilly into experiencing our lack of control and the inevitability of constant change. This is the anguished streak that adds to the hurtful feeling of pain.

Siddhartha also realized that rather than fighting the tide and feeling drowned by it, he could let go into a larger flow. Furthermore, he experienced that he could even enjoy this flow of change. However, to achieve this he had to give up the need to control. He even had to give up the heroic sense of integrity, since "integrity" is actually the name for "remaining one, unchanging, unit." Siddhartha realized that being fully open to the world's impacts means we are constantly transforming, becoming beings of many selves. For Siddhartha, the hero's quest for the One True Self meant one would have to spend existence fighting pain's import. The fight is futile, and makes pain poisonous.

To be one, to be master, to demand of the Earth that our will be done—this stance toward existence has long been the masculine way to be strong. Whether or not this way hearkens back to the warrior clans that swept out of Asia four thousand years ago, it is deeply entrenched in modern America and it has profound consequences, both for us males and for those with whom we interact.

In thinking about these consequences, which men may not notice, it is interesting to recall that the word *pain* comes from the Greek word for *penalty*, in the sense of a "debt incurred." When we live on this Earth, our existence is made possible by the work of countless other beings, including those within our body and those without. Scientists are starting to see that organs, cells, and even the parts of cells were probably once independent organisms before they entered into interactive networks with other beings in order to make up the human "body."[4] Even the air we breathe or the food we eat is the product of the countless other beings. Similarly, countless persons have left us tools, languages, and cultures with which to make sense of our experience. Thus, each person has a great "debt incurred." When we ignore this debt, when we are oblivious to the interplay of energies, or when we try to "forge our own way" as if there were a "one," our wrenching pain announces the manyness of the self and its intertwining connections. The many beings we are and the many beings with which we are intertwined are all impacted by this willfulness, and we feel a tearing in the body—either in physical pain or in psychological-emotional pain.

The emotions are felt within our bodies because *our bodies are the waystations of the currents of our relations with the world*—our emotions. This is why I have not clearly distinguished physical pain from emotional pain: the meaning of the two is intermeshed. Only when the heroic model "splits off" from its body, as we will discuss, is there suddenly an opposition between psyche and soma—mind and body. Only then can the body be seen as an inert housing instead of a feelingful way of interconnecting.

Also, we must keep in mind that emotions are *movements* between us and the world. The meaning of *e-motion* in the literal significance of its root is a "movement out"—both from the person to the world and from the world to and through the person. Pain is the emotion that makes us feel the tensions in the interconnections of this flow. Pain undermines the attempt to take distance from the world. It is a bringing back to a sense that wells up viscerally from our being part of something we can't control. Pain is the feeling of the searing sense of our indebtedness and our incompleteness that floods through our bodies. In these moments we experience ourselves as no longer separate but part of a web of interconnecting forces that at times can gape open, strain, tear, and absorb shocks. This itself hurts.

The word *hurt* comes from a root that means "to be impacted, to be rammed." This is the sense in which life itself hurts, is painful. This is what the Buddha saw on the day he rode forth from his father's castle: that all beings are caught with and indebted to countless other beings, and yet all life impacts on all other life in such a way that we *rend* each other and eventually cause each other to pass away, no matter how respectful we are. This realization made Siddhartha cry tears of compassion for even the little insects damaged by the plow or by someone striding across the land.

This pain of existence, however, is different from the pain that is inflicted in violation of other beings. This latter pain can occur either unknowingly or not. If we deny our indebtedness because we see it involves us in a hurtful dimension of existence, then what feels like "merely defending ourselves" has more of an impact than that. If we steel ourselves in defense of entanglement, then we become like a blade that cuts these ties, even though we do not mean to hurt others. Of course, we may also resent being entwined with others and may actually knowingly strike out against these interconnections, feeling our attempt to get free is worth hurting others.

If our masculinity has required that our strength be displayed in being master—trying with all our might to carry out our wills no matter what others feel—then we are resisting this inevitable pain of being entwined with others. Unfortunately, most men today are in this category. Most of us are not able to acknowledge the pain of being human, of having been reached and momentarily overcome by aspects of the world not of our own making. However, in doing this we are denying the visceral and psychological sense of being the enmeshed, mortal creatures we are. Our own bodies and psyches become dangerous reminders of a fact of existence we want to avoid. But pain denied does not go away; it festers and multiplies. Nor should pain go away: We must all remain part of this web of beings and allow ourselves some feeling of being "impacted upon" or perish. Yet, this is not the darkest part of this denial, for being in control and projecting our will involves a need to become impermeable to this interplay of energies, and to create such barriers begins the rending of interconnectedness that is essential to all life. Furthermore, once we set up barriers, we've already taken the first step down a path toward a more violating assertion of identity at a cost to others within life's web.

Masculine pride is connected to many attributes: doing; achieving; standing erect; casting forth rules and principles;

withstanding resistance; overcoming obstacles; soaring above what holds down; grinning in the face of setback, violation, or fear; and cultivating reserves of strength in body and will. In many ways, these are admirable qualities when used at the appropriate times and when supplemented by other qualities; however, each of these attributes leaves a debt incurred—a residue of pain. To lift off from the ground and sever ties to Earth and loved ones or to absorb pain stoically and transform it into a will to persist, or to take the hurt and make it into a comradeship of mutually inflicted pain, or to dominate those with whom one is in conflict: all these actions are meant to keep males safeguarded from the pain of interconnectedness. The pain we cause in others by forging a direction that tears them from their connections is successfully blocked out. Yet the attempt to avoid feeling this pain only creates much greater pain: now there is a reservoir of pain from the interconnections that have been assaulted or severed, even though unacknowledged. By not working out with others the inevitable clashes—by instead ripping our way through them—the initial debt incurred of other beings becoming sacrificed for us is multiplied.

Both pain unacknowledged and pain inflicted on others become sources of further pain. If our own pain were acknowledged, we could seek out those with whom we were in conflict and share the hurt. Insofar as we men are closed off, however, these pains are not taken to heart in a way that could *reopen* us to the pain inflicted or the debt incurred. By doing this, we are deprived of coming back into contact and becoming reconnected to those with whom there was hurtful impact. This reconnection would be an opportunity to become transformed with others—to gain mutual growth from the original pain. Since the further pain was created in the blind building of a barrier, this pain manufactured for others and ourselves ultimately goes unregistered. The redeeming power of being hurt, which is to lead us back to others and see our pain as part of our debt to others, is lost.

Instead of taking these impacts to heart in order to allow a healing for all involved, there is a short circuit. We stay trapped within our pain, even though unknowingly. Thus, vicious cycles of violation are set into motion.

Some of this distance is necessary and healthy. There can't be a true sharing of emotion unless there is some separation which recognizes and respects the other apart from myself. Without proper boundaries established, there can't be a real meeting. We have to partially get beyond our feelings to experience the reality of the other person. If this distance is lacking, then everything we register emotionally becomes mere extensions of our own ego. Then, our feelings become self-absorbed concerns. It is just this kind of foisting onto others our own feelings that allows emotions as be seen as blinding rather than revealing. If we stay with our pain in this way, a self-indulgent depression can take the place of real grieving—which is a sensitivity to others. As we will discuss in the later parts of this book, this is a mistake made by some parts of the men's movement.

However, it hasn't generally been our masculine problem that we were too caught up in our feelings. In general, we have been all too proud in our ability to distance others. As Carol Gilligan pointed out in her groundbreaking book, *In a Different Voice*, comparing female and male development, whereas females generally start with a sense of connection with others, males generally start with the developmental task of becoming who they are by *separating* themselves from others—first from mother and then from others at large. This separation far exceeds the distance needed to respect the other's distinctiveness; in fact, it is the rupture of the natural interconnection between selves. It springs from the male sense that true identity is achieved only by becoming an *untouched* self, a discrete individual, a being of "integrity." At this remove, one's emotions become almost cryptic signs that one must "decipher," sent across a chasm to alien beings. The separated male is self-enclosed and generally uses his feelings only to see how these strange other beings fit into his plans for himself. Indeed, most of the classical Western philosophers—males—have analyzed emotions as potential "ego strengtheners" if kept in check by the will. They see emotion as telling us only whether or not someone or something is useful to the designs of our own egos. Registered in this way, pain becomes something locked in the chest. It is seen as a force that could weaken our will to walk our set path unless we absorb, block, deflect, or "handle" it in some way.

Rather than feeling pain, most males commonly strike out at someone else in order to lessen the impact. This cuts off the thread of interconnection with the other, yet hurt exists *between* us. By negating our interrelation, the place where we need to go together is blocked from access. As each person is forced to retreat to his or her side of the conflict, we lose that middle ground where we dangle together vulnerably, suspended by the caring thread that runs between us. Staying with the shared hurt in that open middle place would leave us free to change fluidly and spontaneously in response to the other. When we lash out at the other, rather than share our pain, we force this person back onto his or her solid ground, so that we may also retreat to our own solid ground.

This wounding of the other allows the male to take the pain he has kept locked in his chest and to heave it "out there," like garbage. This is a form of psychic pollution, both of the world and of others. It sets up a distanced competitive stance to see who can inflict more pain. The nuclear arms race was a worldly manifestation of this misuse of pain, this "debt incurred" among beings, using it in a distanced, disowning way to fuel a buildup of power to threaten and potentially hurt another nation. However, the *quality* of this hurting-from-a-distance is *different* from the quality of being hurt together, as the "arms race" also aptly symbolized.

When a hurt is shared and the conflict is used to bring

two or more people back to their interconnectedness, then there is an interchange, a process of mutual transformation. This interchange might remain painful as the parties absorb the impacts of their conflicting paths in life, but eventually they come to some new shared state of being that ends the hurt. When the pain is locked away and then projected onto another as a call to inflict still more pain, then there is no growing interrelatedness. The continued impacts become annihilating. They are unidirectional—building from the paralyzed pain in the chest that grows until it explodes. Then this pain is hurled in a further hurtful action that intends to "wipe out" the person. The irony is that originally the pain came from the depth of caring that bonded the two people. Now there is an attempt to do away with that other person. One ends up "stockpiling" weapons in order to hurt or destroy the other, no matter how senseless or insane it may become. The U.S. and the U.S.S.R. reached an ability to destroy all life on Earth thousands of times over with their nuclear arms. There was no possible embrace of pained, frightened human arms, only the distanced fist-shaking of hostile, unfeeling, prosthetic "arms."

A man feeling this kind of displaced, projected pain is like a blind Oedipus, the symbol for so much of our masculine gender history within the Western tradition. In Sophocles's telling of the myth, Tiresias points out to Oedipus that his obsession with finding out the "facts," with finding out who is "at fault" and who should be punished, has made him blind to whose house he lives in and who are his friends. Oedipus has become emotionally blind and numb to his relations with others. In his "blindness," he rages at others rather than taking to heart his painful web of interrelationships. When he finally blinds himself literally, stabbing out his eyes, he is only doing what he has done throughout the play: striking out at the externally distanced, projected sense of his inner pain, denying his sense of being intertwined with others in a fate he can't control.

That recognition would call for him to open vulnerably to these others—for example, to go inside and cry with Jocasta, his wife, mother, lover, and friend, and find a way to deal creatively and sensitively with those lives he has touched. Instead, he makes even his own eyes distant objects, blaming *them* for not "seeing" the facts of his situation sooner. The truth of his life then begins to dawn: without trying to dominate the situation—now no longer a king but only a blind beggar—Oedipus begins to "see" by acknowledging his interdependence with others and their emotional meaning for him.

As soon as Oedipus is physically blind, for the first time he sees the chorus as his friend and realizes that its members care for him when he hears the "tone" of their speech. Until now, Oedipus has not been able to feel Creon's love and loyalty or the kindness of Tiresias. He has even been insensitive to the love and despair of his wife and mother, Jocasta. He has no inkling what she is feeling, even when she withdraws into the palace and hangs herself—in spite of the fact that everyone else can feel her extreme pain and is openly concerned for her. Until now, Oedipus has looked to the sky god, Apollo, to give him reason and insight, to get "on top" of things, and to "get on" with the tasks of commanding.

If we read the play with compassion, we can feel Oedipus's chest bursting with pain at the recognition of the suffering he has caused others and to which he has been subjected by fate. This fate is the web of relationship into which he, *and all of us*, is born. It is beyond our control. Yet he is not yet ready to cry, to allow this pain to help him open to the impact of others, as he will do in his daughter-sister's arms twenty years later at Colonus when he's finally realized that love is most important. At this earlier moment, he can only strike out in violence, even against himself. This is an apt symbol, for our masculine striking out at others is eventually a self-lacerating way of dealing with the pain in our chests—

an action that only multiplies the pain that is locked away in there.

Before he becomes a beggar, Oedipus doesn't have the opportunity to "just be" with himself or with other people. He feels compelled to carry out his job, to stay on top, to stay in charge. Yet the nature of pain won't allow these strategies to go unchecked. Pain has two properties that are inimical to this masculine strategy of gaining identity. Pain has a different direction and rhythm than that of our attempt at remaining "above" and "on the go." If we let go and enter the feeling of pain, we find ourselves slowing down. Pain dwells in our bodies as a certain felt relationship to others that puts the brakes on our racing minds.

When we cling to our identities as doers and achievers, it is necessary for us to maintain a certain pace—speeding through the world—that can be justified in the cause of "efficiency." This can also be a way of not getting "caught" in relationships with others that require a feelingful response. When Oedipus makes a snap judgment of Creon—his uncle, brother, advisor, and friend—and decides to exile him, Creon warns him that such judgments are instantaneous, while the discovery of true friendship takes a long time. Emotional unfolding requires a certain "letting be" that allows us to dwell with others and with things, to tarry. To be emotionally sensitive and open, to allow ourselves to be vulnerable and moved, means to slow down. We have to stop reckoning with time, instead allowing time itself to linger—to do with us what it may. If we fail to enter these slower rhythms, we shut ourselves off from such emotional callings.

Of all emotions, pain has a great power to slow us down, if we let it be. As the sense in the core of our bodies of having been impacted upon by all these other beings, pain calls us to a very interwoven, complex enmeshment in many fine strands of interconnection. Or to use another metaphor, as a way of being called by our life, pain is the sounding of all the echoes of the people or forces in our lives that are impacting upon us at the moment. We must be rather still—and are drawn to become even more still—by allowing ourselves to reverberate with all these notes. A certain wrenching occurs in these impacts, a slowing down the momentum of life. This slowing may be overcome, but somewhere inside us we know there is a kind of halt to our rhythm as long as the pain is not yet worked through. We can feel the way this still place is connected to all the wrenching impacts. The gift of pain is in giving us this momentary pause to register these connections, before the natural pace of our lives reasserts itself.

Pain is a descent. Whether symbolized by a journey to the underworld, to the depths of one's soul, or just as a "down mood," pain dashes the dreams of the soaring male. From Plato's ascent to the sun to Icarus's winged attempt to fly to Perseus's soaring above his enemies to the modern film images of *Top Gun* or *Iron Eagles*, the male strategy of soaring above life has been much commented upon. We will return to this theme in discussing the appeal of the aerial war in our chapter on Desert Storm, but for now it is important to note that soaring above life is an attempt to deny pain its ability to return us to Earth and our shared fate with other mortal beings.

As Siddhartha is overcome with the pain of existence, he is moved to descend from his horse and even then to lower his gaze from the ploughman to the humble insects and worms upon the soil. Pain ensnares the momentum of our busy lives not only by slowing us down, but also by bringing us down to the depths of becoming caught up with other beings that can be passed over in taking charge *over* things and speeding beyond them. In soaring above—in doing, planning, and controlling—the pain of these hurtful impacts does not go away; rather, the strain grows all the greater as the distance from these enmeshments is stretched to a point of being terribly pulled but denied, unacknowledged, caught by something "down there." The whole "lower realm"— whether the Earth itself and its darkly fecund "rotting" source of nourishment and beauty, or of our own "lower regions"—becomes a site of phobic withdrawal.

Yes, the genital region is "front and center" in our society as a site to be dipped into—as on a bombing run from some flying machine—but the soaring male avoids really *living* in these "lower regions." The result is the flying male's fears of his own lower parts and thousands of years of seeing the female sex organs as a dirty, engulfing maw rather than as a beautiful spot to caress and experience as fully, slowly, and sensually as possible. The more "masculine" the male, the more he tends to fret about this strange region of his own being. Thus, we have the pitiful comedy of a society obsessed with "bombing runs" and "scores" in the genital region while widespread male impotence is seen as a problem with "plumbing" or "hardware." Yet, it is the detached approach to sexuality as a matter of sex "organs" that causes the problem of impotence—as a disconnection from the erotic flow between people. The masculine attitude leaves the pain of the lower world unexplored and then frets about fears of castration. Yet this flying above the richness of our male pain is the very knife that cuts us off, not only from our genitals but from all the fruits of the Earth. Pain offers a slow transformation, but the soaring male doesn't stay with it or wait for it. Only by staying low and moving slowly can we undercut the male ego, the doer, the soarer, the hero, *and* allow the process of the hurtful transformation to take us into new identities and a different joy.

When we men get to the point where we seem to no longer feel pain—even physical pain—then the face we present to the world is truly horrifying. Rather than the body being an openness to all other beings, it has been transformed into a blunt instrument of the will. It has become a hideaway for revenge on a distant hilltop. It is now the self-lacerating war machine. The male mass murderers, the male rapists, the male batterers—even the males who punish in more subtle, refined ways—no longer have eyes that make contact. Their eyes no longer reflect their pain as a way to find others, but instead they live at a terrible distance from this Earth of interconnecting energies. They can "look down" on their bodies and on the pitiful, weak way others are "slowed down" by feelings of empathy. Others are too weak to achieve their glorious, steel destinies. These men only feel "here" for the brief instant in which their victim cries out with the pain that was buried in their own chests. Their own pain is now so distant that they see it as a remnant of another lifetime before their "weakness" was overcome. We gentler males can look at these violent males and disown our fraternity with them, but each time we manipulate the women in our lives to feel our pain and cry for us, we are on the same path.

The Herculean Task of Denying Pain

The myth that speaks to most men of their lot in life and their attempt to deal with pain is that of Heracles, in the form he took in the classical Greek myths. [Since Heracles has entered popular culture known as "Hercules"—the later Roman form of his name—we will refer to him by that name.] This fertility god had been a consort to the Goddess. He was transformed by the Greek warrior ethos into the paradigm of the new masculine hero. His struggles to achieve glory and the burdens he had to bear speak deeply to most men. His need to inflict pain on others while distancing himself from sources of connection with others and from his own pain is the unacknowledged shadow side of his archetypal quest for glory. Since so much of the masculine ethos involves the denial of pain by becoming distant and inflicting it on others, while still carrying even more hurt inside, Hercules's story is instructive for understanding masculinity. Our attempt to soar with this great, hidden weight of the pain stored inside makes us feel burdened. We frequently shrug at this burden and say resignedly that it is our "Herculean" task in life. It is illuminating, therefore, to look at the details of Hercules's story for a moment as the story of male pain.

Hercules begins his life already caught up in one of those dramas of pain inflicted in such a way that it continues as a motive force for the infliction of more pain. We are all familiar with such stories ourselves. Sadly, most of us know of battering husbands who express the pain of childhood abuse from their fathers by now abusing their wives or children. The children then carry this pain into alcoholism or other behaviors that wound themselves and those who love them. Many of the myths of our Western tradition tell the tales of these linked stories of violation and pain—pain that has not been dealt with well but instead allowed to fester and become the motive force for further violation. Many of the myths that have been told to males to provide heroic images are of this type. Such myths allow males to glorify the crippling and violent way of dealing with pain that often marks the male hero, as is the case with Hercules.

In this story, Zeus, the leader of the Olympian gods, has wounded his mate, Hera, by consorting with Alcmena, Hercules's mortal mother. In hurt and anger, Hera sends two serpents to attack Hercules in the cradle. Hercules's first exploit is to strangle these serpents. This is a sad beginning to a sad but classically heroic life. The serpent is the old Goddess figure, the spirit of the Earth. The serpent shedding its skin had long been a symbol of the Earth's constant renewal—its transformation through endless cycles—in the preceding Goddess and nature-worshipping traditions. These are figures of *inspiration*, a breathing in of a certain spirit that goes through the pain of birth and rebirth. Instead of breathing in this spirit, Hercules *cuts the breath off* from these figures, drawing on the pain of rejection now encased within his chest to wrest the serpents' lives away.[5] He literally destroys their in-spiration, and with it the chance they represent for him to experience hurt, perish from it, and be reborn with a new skin.

The biological cycles here are symbolic of the emotional cycle we have to follow to be renewed in life. Thus, Hercules will live his life "going forward," achieving heroic deeds to prove his worth, never consciously allowing himself the cyclic return to Earth, never allowing himself to unravel—to die a psychic death and be reborn as a new self. Instead, he girds against psychic disorder until the final burst of his repressed unconsciousness. That burst is so violent that it becomes cataclysmic instead of naturally expressing itself as part of a cycle of alternating changes.

We have seen that the inevitable pain of life is that of mortality. Unlike Siddhartha, who finds release from suffering through embracing his pain and learning from it, Hercules undertakes great deeds in order to defeat the mortal condition and win immortality. This in itself seems to reflect much of the male dream: if we can accomplish enough and do it gloriously and heroically enough, somehow we believe we will stand above life and its defeats—especially its ultimate defeat, death. In this sense, Hercules is like most male mythic heroes; however, the symbolic meanings of several of his "twelve great labors" are also worth examining, for they have much to tell us about how men embody this unacknowledged, festering pain as part of their gender identity.

Hercules's first labor, to conquer the Nemean lion, is again met by strangling his foe, by taking away the lion's inspiration. So the noble creature is incorporated into the male glory by being destroyed by the hero. Yet the deed itself is rather pitiful. He strangles the animal in order to cut it off from the air and the spirit of nature. But Hercules doesn't just kill the lion, he also carries around its corpse, which is such a hideous sight that it inspires terror in everyone who sees him.

This quality of inspiring terror is seen to contribute to Hercules's heroic identity. This, too, is a sad image for boys to carry around, yet it is enacted daily in schoolyards and streets across America: boys gain increased masculine identity, self-esteem, and a sense of security through the increasing number of other little boys they are able to terrify. This coping strategy—whether of boys or of men—creates a vicious cycle. The male pain of being in situations out of immediate control is now intensified by these masculine chain reactions of further violence and is *seemingly relieved* by adding these additional levels of terror and brutalization perpetrated on other males. By being feared, we supposedly become less vulnerable. The sad truth is that we are trapped within that lion skin; we have cut off all potential for the nurturing ties that could have been made with all those boys (or later, men) that we terrorize. This makes the loss certain, the abrasive impacts inevitable, and only creates more unconscious pain.

In another of Hercules's heroic deeds, that of slaughtering the nine-headed hydra, he discovers that cutting off these female heads only redoubles his problem. So he resorts to burning them, then buries the middle, immortal head. In the pursuit of their masculinity, Western men have similarly attempted to burn and bury the power of women. We're finding, however, these "buried" histories, spiritual practices, and past societies are still present within women's deeper "Remembering," as Mary Daly puts it.[6] After millennia, they are even surfacing in more straightforward ways as feminist-inspired historians, archaeologists, and anthropologists dig up the buried past.[7]

In a way, burying the female hydra's immortal head is a key to my reinterpretation of many of the Greek and later myths that males have been told in the last few thousand years. I think it is time that the warrior tradition, along with the subjugation of women and the Earth, be brought into question. If many of the current feminist explorations into ancient Goddess cultures have any credence, we males can gain by admitting that these tales we've been told by heroic males are meant to bury these cultures' stress on cooperation, nurturance, and the interconnection between people and with nature. We feel great pride in our heroic masculinity.

Even apparently New Age men like Robert Bly tell us that
the nurturing male is "not exactly life-giving," betrays a "lack
of energy," and has "little vitality."[8] Such talk does not represent a "new age" for male identity; it is the old warrior mentality still holding on to its exploits and buried pain. We can
still admire some of the traditional male qualities, but must
have the courage to see that, overall, the stories in which they
are embedded promote a sick warrior mentality we no longer
need as a shield against pain.

Another of Hercules's tasks is to seek out the golden girdle of Hippolyta, who is one of the leaders of the Amazons, a
symbol of independent female power. Hippolyta finds Hercules attractive and offers him her girdle as a love gift.
Hercules, however, distrusts the Amazons and their queen,
and so slays her and takes the girdle. He kills her without
remorse, despite her offer of love, and then uses her own
weapons to kill off the other Amazon leaders and slaughter
their followers.[9]

Although each part of the Hercules myth has several different versions, the fact that the hero gains part of his identity
and glory at the expense of so much female violation deserves comment. It is an aspect of the myths that has been
ignored. Historically, part of our male avoidance of pain is
our denigration of the so-called "feminine" embrace of the
emotional interconnectedness of beings and our replacement
of the ancient Goddess myths with the more recent warrior-
oriented myths of the Greeks, Romans, and other Europeans.
Many feminists make a convincing case that much of this
rewriting of symbol and story first occurred at the time the
Greek myths were helping to accomplish the shift from
Goddess to patriarchal culture. As part of his "great labors,"
Hercules also captures the Ceryneian Hind, a Goddess symbol who is sacred to Artemis, one of the most powerful
Goddess figures within classical Greek mythology. In another
of his labors, he captures the Erythmanthian boar. Boars were
sacred symbols of the moon and were distinguished by their

crescent-shaped tusks, all symbols of the Goddess. Another task is to slaughter the Stymphalian birds, crane-sized birds resembling ibises, which were said by many to really be women. Then he has to master the four savage, man-eating mares of Diomedes. Finally, he captures the Cretan bull, which not only was sacred in the long Goddess tradition preceding classical Greek culture but also politically and socially was the centerpiece of the great Minoan culture centered on Crete, the last remaining Goddess-oriented culture before the Dorian-led Greek rise to dominance.

It is not incidental to Herculean strength that it violates the female and that male pain is disowned. By dominating and burying the Goddess symbol, Hercules banishes the idea of the triple Goddess. In her appearance, the Goddess was intended to mark the triune path of girl, mother, and crone. By calling these stages to attention and celebrating them, the Goddess way called for an acceptance of aging and facing death as part of a fruitful cycle. To the heroic masculine, this is a defeat to be challenged. The warrior doesn't acquiesce to pain or death. Violence against the Goddess way, now labeled "the feminine," becomes blurred, both in myth and in reality, with violence against women, as well as with violence against other men and the Earth.

Soaring above the Earth, fighting off enemies, distancing himself from all things mundane, it comes as an unthinkable challenge for Hercules to clean thirty years of excrement from the Augean stable. Certainly, the soaring hero is not going to allow himself to get caught in the "shit of life." Indeed, deciding that he must keep his distance from any excremental dimension, he changes the flow of the rivers Alpheus and Peneus to wash away the excrement. Thus, he manages to get rid of it all by "not soiling so much as his little finger."[10] Symbolically, he has forced a change in the flow of waters, the flow of feeling, in order to wash away all the "shit." Rather than get caught up in the waste that men have left behind them, rather than see the decay of life, he simply manipulates his environment to achieve a distance from it. Life is messy. All beings cause each other pain, and acknowledging it entails facing some "shit." Undoubtedly, Hercules presents us with a masculine trick that many of us are tempted to follow. However, even the myth demonstrates that denied pain only returns magnified later on. To see this, though, we must wait for the end of the story when Hercules's deeds are done.

All of Hercules's exploits have related themes. They are also related to the masculine response to pain. When Hercules steals the oxen of Geryon, he slays the giant and the two-headed dog and then raises the mountains as monuments to his triumph. He is always monumentalizing his ego. This, as Siddhartha demonstrates, is a way of denying the pain of all things "passing away" and denying the complications of interconnection, but it ultimately causes much greater and more pernicious pain.

This ego defense is also in evidence in Hercules's task of obtaining the golden apples of Atlas. When Hercules commands Atlas to get the golden apples from his daughters, the Hesperides, he is again taking riches from the female. Originally the apples were a gift from Mother Earth to Hera, but Hercules usurps these feminine riches under the guise of the male burden. He offers to hold up the world while Atlas gets the apples, and Atlas will do anything to be relieved of this duty for a moment. For his part, Hercules is teaching us males to take on the burden of upholding the world in order to get our way. Most of us suffer under this, expecting others to do our bidding. This suffering is a way of establishing our ego. This strain we've taken on can replace the pains of being open and vulnerable. Now we can be world supporters rather than mere mortals, and our groans under this burden can drown out the voices of our human pains.

Hercules also presents an image of how heroic men treat other men who are seen as being too "female-identified." In some tellings of the myth, Hercules slays Antaeus, who is the son of Mother Earth. As such, Antaeus is a walking reminder of our "debt incurred" to the innumerable beings of the Earth and to the spirit of the Goddess culture. Furthermore, Antaeus knows that he is invincible as long as he remains in contact with the Earth. Unlike most male heroes, he does not seek to soar above the Earth and he isn't threatened by his debt incurred. He is loyal to the nurturance that his mother had provided him and doesn't have to separate from this source in order to feel his own power. He can assume his own role as male while still acknowledging the mother who gave him his strength. There are few figures of masculine strength who can be so *inclusive*—who can take on male tasks and yet keep their indebtedness to the Mother. One exception may be Nietzsche's "Zarathustra" who proclaims it is the time of "going beyond 'man'" but to "remain faithful to the earth."[11]

Hercules, of course, uses his upward-looking Apollonian reason to conclude that if he suspends Antaeus in the air, he will destroy his contact with the Earth and halt his inspiration of strength gained from this connection. Now he is able to strangle him. This, too, is part of our male gender identity: to turn against those men who seem too feminine, or "female-identified," as if they had betrayed some sacred masculine code. Yet, this "either/or" logic—which pervades the heroic thinking of the Greek and European myths—is peculiar in its rigid exclusion. It is as though there were some impenetrable barrier between male and female that allowed no breach, as though there must be this gulf that separates masculine from feminine. There is no reason that a man cannot be as daring, as physically strong, or as courageous as Hercules and still be open to what are identified as "feminine" traits—gentleness, concern, and emotional vulnerability. It is only because the Herculean identity is a fortress against pain that it can tolerate no breach.

Of all his labors, it is probably Hercules's venture to the underworld that speaks best to his image for men in dealing with pain. The underworld represents the pain of life that has not been dealt with—the pain which, if taken to heart, would allow for a straightforward suffering and a return to spontaneity and vulnerability. As a mythical location in many traditions, the underworld is a place of remorse—a place where destinies become painfully intertwined, and where the resulting pain gives rise to further hurtful acts. It is a realm that demonstrates the inadequacy of the will to master all aspects of our destiny. As James Hillman has beautifully described, "It is that psychic space in which each of us is made to slow down; to unravel; to doubt the solid realities of our daily round of tasks; to feel the chill of death, disappointment, and despair; and to return to as to a place of painful rending over the tragedies of our lives and of life itself."[12]

Sometimes the male acknowledges this space within the psyche—that place of "going down," as Bly puts it[13]—so that the hero may rise up again from the ashes, burned clean. However, there is a great danger in seeing this region of pain as being justified only *in order to rid ourselves of this "heaviness,"* so that we can soar light again tomorrow. It may be that the trip to the underworld can have this effect, but not if it is entered into as a necessary evil leading to a beneficial result.[14] The underworld, the realm of pain, must be met as its own sovereign realm, as the face of life itself. It has as central a claim to the heart of existence as does joy. If we approach it as a necessary evil to be "handled," we do not meet it on its own terms. It is a nonrational dimension of the world, just as nonrational as the magic of joy.

When we really go to the underworld, it seems limitless, eternal, and all pervading. Pain becomes our experience of the world, and during this spell, the world becomes a place of pain. Paradoxically, only by so encountering this central pain of existence does it transform itself into the release that engenders joy, as Siddhartha and others have seen. Several of the Goddess-inspired myths emphasize the necessity and sovereignty of the underworld. Inanna, who is queen of heaven and Earth, accepts the equal power and dignity of this place and Persephone returns there for six months of every year.

Hercules's venture to the underworld is the last of his heroic exploits. He goes there to defeat the power of this place of darkness. He begins by using the power of "the Mysteries," the old Earth and Goddess ways left in Greece at this time, to wipe away his "blood guilt"—the pain that he has inflicted during his life. Although many of the male heroic myths include such moments of redemption, it is questionable whether one can be "cleansed" in this way. Such a cleansing assumes that the hero can swoop down and, with one deed, somehow "erase" the past and all its painful complications. At any rate, Hercules's main task in the underworld is to capture the three-headed dog, Cerberus, guardian of the underworld. When Hercules attacks Cerberus, the dog's three heads rise—each maned with serpents, the old Goddess symbol again. Hercules defeats Cerberus with the oft-repeated strategy of holding his opponents aloft and strangling them.

Besides removing Cerberus as guardian of the region of pain, Hercules also "rescues" Theseus, symbol of the masculine hero, from the underworld. This is what the heroic male does for his brothers: he helps them avoid being ensnared in their own pain. On the surface, this would seem to be a favor, yet it actually robs us men of the gift of returning to vulnerability and recognition of our debt incurred. To allow ourselves to return to this underworld in which pain, lack of control, and a dispersion of our sense of self permeates our sensibility, threatens our male gender identity's defenses and its denial of pain. It is significant that defeating the power of the underworld is Hercules's last labor. It sets a precedent implicit in all his labors for all males who strive to follow the Herculean path: avoid the dark reaches of pain that call for a halt to the defense of engaging in worldly activity.

The question remains, though, whether Hercules has

really defeated the power of the underworld or whether he has only symbolically buried his painful recognition of his lack of control over destiny—especially as it is bound up with others' destinies. For example, his unconscious is repeatedly getting the best of him. His first bout of madness occurs after he has slaughtered the Minyans (having first lopped off the hands, ears, and noses of their heralds), the second after vanquishing Pyraechmus and having his body torn in two by horses and exposed unburied to create terror. His madness is blamed on Hera, but one wonders whether all his horrific slaughter and violation of the most sacred taboos—such as respect for heralds and burying the dead—has not engendered within Hercules a monstrous debt incurred in his infliction of pain to avoid his own pain.

In his madness, Hercules slaughters six of his own children and flings their bodies into the fire. Killing one's own children is often part of the hero's plight. In fact, it is partly in restitution for this horrible act—as well as seeking immortality—that Hercules undertakes his twelve labors in the first place. It is also significant that his first act after completing his twelfth labor and bringing Cerberus to Eurystheus, is to kill three of his host's sons in his outrage over being offered only a slave's portion of the feast. One can only wonder at all the pent-up rage that results in Hercules slaughtering sons instead of nurturing them.

Unfortunately, many modern Herculean males have also aimed their pent-up rage at their sons or other men's sons. Chronos, the symbol for our Western sense of time, eats his children, just as, under the sway of this mentality, we see time and existence devouring our lives instead of enabling them. Thus, part of the Western masculine identity is to appear fearsome and be a threat to our sons, as well as to other living beings. Although Hercules desires immortality, in his madness, his unconsciousness seems to seek the opposite. He destroys one of the only forms of "immortality" available: nurturing our children so they can carry on our deeds and values within the cycles of time, the circle of birth and death.

After his labors, Hercules, abandons his wife, Megaera— whose children he had killed—and goes looking for a younger, more fortunate woman. His annihilation of those he loves, his mistreatment of women, his violation of Goddess symbols, and his antagonism toward aspects of life considered "feminine" are central to his identity. For this reason, it is fascinating to look at the myth of Hercules for unconscious feelings that express the repressed female within him. These stifled feelings, which may be seen to symbolically burst forth from within his Herculean unconscious later in his life, may lie within the heroic male unconscious in general.

After Hercules kills Iphitus, his guest, and is refused purification for the deed by the pythoness Xenoclea of the Delphic oracle, he again becomes insane for a time as the result of attacking the pythonness and desecrating the shrine. There are different versions of the story, but in Ovid's telling, Hercules enters a period in which he is brought to Asia and sold as a slave to Omphale, the queen of Lydia. For the next three years, he abandons his lion pelt and dresses in women's clothing, bedecking himself in jeweled necklaces, golden bracelets, and women's turbans. He also sits among the women teasing wool, spinning thread, and trembling when his mistress scolds him.

In another version of the tale, Hercules is a love slave to Omphale, and they go to a grotto and exchange clothes. Hercules stuffs himself into a network girdle for a small waist and splits Omphale's purple gown, even though he's unlaced it as much as possible. Pan, who follows them and falls in love with Omphale, mistakenly crawls tremblingly into bed with Hercules, since he is clad in her clothes. Hercules kicks Pan out of bed, and Pan henceforth distrusts clothes. Thus, aspects of homosexuality, of cross-dressing, and of delight in the so-called "feminine" that Hercules spurns in his heroic identity emerge floridly as longed-for dimensions during his period of "insanity." This sudden reversal is indicative of how masculinity in its opposition of anything that smacks of the "soft"—the "feminine"—betrays an unconscious fascination with it.

The masculine tendency to cast the female into the role of "the feminine" and to seek her as the Holy Grail of life— using her to sell cars, clothes, alcohol, or whatever—doesn't reveal a true desire for women as other human beings, but for the fetishized, disowned "feminine" that is actually part of the *male identity*. Hercules symbolizes our unconscious desperation to get back a dimension of ourselves that has been buried, annihilated, and spurned by our Herculean selves. On the one hand, Hercules glories in these violations of women, Goddess figures, children, guests, and all those aspects of life that have been labeled as "nurturing" and "feminine," but inside the Herculean psyche yawns a hunger for what has been pushed aside through fear of the vulnerability that embracing these traits would require.

Hercules would not have been Hercules, symbol of the masculine heroic stance toward life, if he had handled his fate's challenges in a different way. Had he been an Orpheus, he might have tried to enchant the serpents sent to his cradle with music or song—a very different sort of male. If he had befriended the serpents and gone back to Hera—not as antagonist to the mothering principle, forever to remain hostile, but to heal their emotional wounds together—a very different story would have unfolded. If he had lain in the shit for a while and tried to transform it (as a magician or alchemist might have done) rather than forcing rivers to flow according to his will and wash it away, he might have arrived at some different state of being. If he had loved Hippolyta and cherished the girdle as a gift—a response that would have opened new avenues of harmony between Amazonian and Herculean strength—he might have become a different man. If he had not reacted to the world with rage or the need to inspire terror, if he had not felt mortally wounded by insults and felt distrust for loving, gentle offers, Hercules might have achieved many of the same deeds, but in a different way—a symbolic expression of a more interactive male. This would have allowed him a different way to experience his pain. It would have been a heroic task of a different sort to use the painful events of his life to create new connections and growth. In addition to the pain of mortality, Hercules was born within a particular cycle of violation and pain between his parents, which troubles him and goads his behavior. If only that pain had been acknowledged, it could have opened opportunities for him to mend emotional connections with others.

I have emphasized those parts of Hercules's story that are glossed over in our intoxication with his heroic achievements. As men, we need to look at the *unnoticed* parts of masculine identity instead of clinging proudly to our achievements as a justification for our shortcomings. There are different ways of being heroic, courageous, assertive, expressive, strong, brave, and of including our full range of desires that also allow us to experience and work with our pain in a vulnerable, creative, and connected manner. However, we won't be able to articulate these possibilities until we see all the hidden penalties and pains of this Herculean denial of pain. The Herculean strokes that *seem* to cut men free from the sources of pain are actually a series of ruptures that all exact a high penalty. While denying its existence, the male identity is one built on pain.

CHAPTER TWO

It Hurts So Good

The Masculine Infliction of Pain as Self-Laceration

Puers and Flying above Pain

One morning in the early eighties, I was walking across campus with a colleague from the literature department. He was a gentle man, a man who enjoyed reading books and musing about things. Rather soft-spoken, he was from a Southern upbringing that emphasized a solicitous, respectful attitude toward others. Sometimes in class, he would go off into verbal reveries about the great men or the great ideas of American literature. He was always dressed with a certain distinctive care—not ostentatiously but in a way that expressed his desire to both show his respect and make others feel comfortable.

As we walked across the plaza, our conversation shifted to topics that were much more personal than we usually discussed. Suddenly, this gentle man stopped rather abruptly and exclaimed, "I miss it!" I looked at him quizzically. He met my eyes and said, "I miss killing. I miss the war. I never felt so alive!"

He told me how he had served in the Korean War, a fact about him that I had never realized. Here it was, more than thirty years later, and these feelings still fueled his soul on some deep level that was never obvious to me. I had known him, though not well, for some years, and found this a startling revelation. He told me how, in the war, he had felt real and fully present for the first and perhaps last time in his life. Unlike many others, this man had the courage to admit that there was something not only about the danger that thrilled him, but much more so, the actual being in combat: the release, the power, the license, and the freedom to destroy—after a life of being kept under wraps. His calm, gentlemanly demeanor was in many ways just a straitjacket. For once in his life—for a brief period during the war—he had been truly released.

I was shaken by this conversation, but I buried it somewhere deep inside until I started writing this book. Then my friend's image floated into my consciousness again. I saw him looking at me out of the corner of his eye, his gentle face suddenly betraying a suffused excitement, his eyes burning with a fire usually absent, flatly declaring that he missed his killing time.

In the first chapter, we examined the ways in which the heroic masculine retreats from the pain of life's uncontrollability by cutting ties to the web of all people and beings. We also saw how doing, taking up burdens, soaring above, responding to hurt by terrorizing and hurting others, building up speed, monumentalizing the ego, and seeking a triumph to symbolically defeat death are all part of a self-defeating attempt to overcome unacknowledged pain. In this chapter, we will look at how this approach to life alters our masculine sense of vitality—how violence goes beyond the projection of unacknowledged pain to the intoxicating experience of power gained by destroying other lives. Following this thread farther, we will see how even this release involves the unconscious thrill of knowing that ultimately we are destroying *our own life*. In other words, at its root, this intoxicating, sadistic, masculine violence is really *masochistic*.

Such violence has become a haunting presence within the masculine psyche, especially since it has infiltrated the unconsciousness as an inexplicable source of vitality. Violence is analogous to alcoholism: what starts as a strategy for keeping pain and vulnerability at bay soon becomes much more. It becomes a way of being, "laid on top of" the original life that led to violence but which now effectively blocks these origins with its own series of problems and demands. It is a creation which takes over the creator. The numbing of violence leaves the pain unreachable and creates a barrier for others in trying to address this person, other than dealing with his violence. The male who has retreated in this manner becomes gradually transmuted into a being who is addicted to a sense of vitality that comes from perpetrating violence.

This thrill is taken as a straightforward sense of pleasure or intoxication with power, but it is not. To feel no pity, disgust, or sympathetically shared pain with the one being violated takes a prior expenditure of emotional energy that prevents these natural feelings from arising. It is this creating of a barrier to naturally arising feelings that is the most direct payoff of violence. The perpetrator of violence has torn himself loose from the web of connection with others, and in so doing, has torn himself loose from his own feelings. This loss of feeling shared spontaneously with others and with oneself creates a hunger that violence now has to face. However, in this first step it seems to the hurting male that he has achieved relief from disconnecting. Thus, the apparently simple pleasure in hurting another, in violating their flesh or psyche, is actually very debilitating to the perpetrator.

In order to understand how this sense of vitality through violence works, we have to go farther into the phenomenon of *male absence* from the planet, even though we males seem ironically omnipresent in our domination of the globe. No matter how close we have come to remaking the planet "in our own image," the creations, the products, that fill the landscape do not give us a sense of being here. They are not really made in our truest image—reflective of the deepest reality of our human feeling. In fact, it is a cruel joke to discover the ways in which our collective identity actually *obliterates* our experience of being on the planet with others—even our own inner sense of ourselves—and the desperate measures we must undertake in order to try to get *back here*. Through our reaction to pain, we have in so many ways banished ourselves to what ironically is called "no man's land" that we have shut ourselves out of the very reality that we have so desperately constructed in our image.

It is ironic that when the Minoan civilization fell—and with it, the last truly Goddess-oriented way of life—the symbol of the winding labyrinth at Crete was soon replaced by the classical Greek attempt at straight, logical penetration to "truth about life." On an unconscious level, the new warrior-heroic male identity was itself an elaborate labyrinth—one that even today keeps us lost and wandering within ourselves, cut off from the lives we try to control. For the male who rapes or murders—and for all males who sometimes feel the thrill of inflicting pain on others—there is a complicated path these emotions travel that ultimately leads back through the labyrinth he's constructed. His feelings are no longer directly reachable and follow a twisted path. When they arrive at the interior place where a vulnerable self should be, instead there is only an emptiness. This is the path we must trace out in this chapter. To call ourselves back from the missing, back from the dead, may not only exact a painful price on others but on ourselves as well.

This question about how the emotions can become so distorted as to find joy in violence takes me back to the image of my former colleague. Here was a seemingly happy and gentle man who felt that only killing made him feel alive, allowed him to be fully himself, and somehow gave him a sense of being present in the world that he normally lacked. Where was he normally then? At the moment of his confession about missing killing, I realized that he was not there walking across campus in quite the way that I had always imagined. In some sense, he was telling me that he had *not been here* for all these years: in being discharged from war duty, he had been "dis-charged" of the electricity of really feeling alive, expressive, and fully present.

If we want to understand where this man was and where so many other males dwell, we need to return to the aspect of masculine identity represented as the "flying boy,"[1] the aviator, the one who climbs into the heavens, the one who embodies the spirit of the *puer*. Admittedly, there can be something noble and worthwhile about such aspirations to fly, but when flight becomes the only emotional avenue in which we feel at home, then problems emerge. This "boyish" flight can become a permanent place of residence. No one has described this spirit any better than James Hillman in his essay about the puer:

> The horizontal world, the space-time continuum which we call "reality," is not its world. . . . Death does not matter because the puer gives the feeling that it can come again another time, make another start. Mortality points to immortality, danger only heightens the unreality of "reality" and intensifies the vertical connection. Because of this vertical direct access to the spirit, this immediacy where vision of goal and goal itself are one, winged speed, haste—even the short cut—are imperative. The puer cannot do with indirection, with timing and patience. It knows little of the seasons and of waiting. And when it must rest or withdraw from the scene, then it seems to be stuck in a timeless state, innocent of passing years, out of tune with time. Its wandering is as the spirit wanders, without attachment and not as an odyssey of experience. It wanders to spend or to capture, and to ignite, to try its luck, but not with the aim of going home.[2]

This soaring above death toward a clear realm of spirit, buoyant and directly available, has informed much of Western thinking—and it is *boyish thinking*. Plato was very clear that men had to move vertically away from contamination with the body, emotions, and senses insofar as they represented an openness to the world of interconnection and change, for these things could imprison one in a world that blossoms and decays. He also made it clear that such ascendence was a masculine strength, while females, lacking proper self-control, tended to get caught up in their emotions and concerns with earthly affairs.[3]

If we remove the traditional masculine praise of this "place in the sky," we can see its properties as timeless, removed from process and nature, detached from emotion, and having no patience with indirectness. Then we realize it is an empty place. However, as a reflection of Western masculine identity, this empty place is not really in the sky as metaphysics or religion presents it. Rather it is found in the heart, the chest, of each male whose spirit soars off from openness and vulnerability.

As Nietzsche wrote: "Woe to him who hides wastelands within."[4] However, such emptiness cannot be confined only to the chest; it infects the entire world that surrounds the puer. It is as though this puer spirit surrounds the masculine with an etheric void or a zone of nonbeing. This disconnection means that the reality of the world is separated as if by some barrier. Unfortunately, this not only makes us men invulnerable to others but also it is impossible for us to reach out to others. Although we may now feel in control of our reality so that others cannot take us by surprise, we also discover that reality is no longer something that we can fully enter.

As Hillman implies, the natural world with its cycles and interplays, the timing and subtleties of personal relations, and the whole world of emotional nuance require a patient, open, fully present dwelling "down here." It is only this painstaking *staying with things in their subtlety* that allows us to undergo a creative "odyssey of experience." The puer spirit, however, doesn't see the uniqueness of each instant—how each indirect coming together of various beings and forces will never occur again and must be witnessed and worked with in its irreplaceable wonder. The puer spirit doesn't even see the currents and eddies that are all part of the painstaking process of working through everyday life *with others*. From the soaring heights, these concerns seem to be "trifling affairs," if they are visible at all.

For the soaring spirit, to flow and meander naturally, gradually winding and intertwining with others toward new happenings is to get "caught" in reality. He doesn't have the time or energy to discuss how he feels or stop to see how family members, friends, and colleagues are doing with their daily struggles and tasks. Sören Kierkegaard masterfully describes the place to which males retreat and how it transforms them. A master of control, the aesthete says of himself: "Carking care is my feudal castle. It is built like an eagle's nest upon the peak of a mountain lost in the clouds. No one can take it by storm. From this abode I dart down into the world of reality, to seize my prey; but I do not remain down there, I bear my quarry aloft to my stronghold. My booty is a picture I weave into the tapestries of my palace."[5] This "eagle's nest" is the aesthete's ability to detach from emotion, from vulnerable involvement with others, and stay locked away in his mind. It demands as much control of the situation as possible.[6] It is a soaring from which he darts into reality to seize what he wants. But what he wants is little more than images, memories, and packaged bits of experience that he can manipulate and enjoy as he sees fit.

As Hillman puts it, the puer spirit only dives into the world to capture, spend, or ignite—to in some way "try its luck" but not to dwell or inhabit. He doesn't want to take up residence in a place that is open to the unpredictable visitations of all kinds of people and forces that are part of this landscape. The soaring male *needs* to dart into the world in order to give his power an object upon which to have an impact—to experience for a moment *the evidence of his power* since he lives in a vacuum. He can choose how to aim this impact at others as a result of the advantage gained by being "above things." However, he is caught in the contradiction that he, more urgently than most others, is desperate to get something from this earthly reality that he dishonestly disdains—in order to nourish himself in his lonely place of isolation. Furthermore, he must keep it captive in some way in his hideout.

Kierkegaard goes on in the same poetic paragraph to describe how only an old man and a child inhabit this castle in the clouds. The child sits and listens to tales about the puer-aesthete's forays into reality and gazes at the images gained from his quests. These memories are evidence of heroic deeds and endless challenges met. Yet, this parable also expresses how the puer's path keeps him childlike—a Peter Pan. The puer spirit is often represented as a child. If we men would be quiet enough to listen seriously to the assessments of women, we would no doubt be hurt to discover that most women consider us to be children in some overwhelming and important sense. Insofar as we stay above life, we preserve a part of ourselves that is both charming and disturbing: the untested soul that is ignorant about the "experiential odyssey" of dealing with emotional pain and being transformed by it. Rather than a true childlikeness, it is more the *childishness* of not being sensitive enough to take on the pain of others and become involved in all the real dramas that age us and try our souls but also add the richness of maturity. These trials are not the Herculean challenges that monumentalize the ego, but instead are experiences that force us to set aside our egos.

There is in this soaring defense against pain an eternal youthfulness, but it is not the childlikeness of the Zen master who has experienced pain so deeply he has been released from the fight against it. This is why, at the heart of the defiant, male hero who disdains the "feminine" and the female, there is often an unconciousness need to be mothered. We males often have inklings of this need, yet instead of taking responsibility for it, we often blame it on the "clutching" or "smothering" quality of the female as Mother. Rather than discovering why masculinity supports a childish streak in us, we blame our mothers for having somehow "injected" or engendered it in us through their own weak dependency needs. Regardless of whether this might have been true in our youths, certainly as adults, we must assume responsibility for what we are now doing to keep some part of ourselves the "puer aeternitatis"—the "eternal boy."

Even more frightening is the other figure within the Kierkegaardian castle in the sky—the one telling the exploits. Kierkegaard describes this other male "self" as an "old man" who can only whisper and who lives "as one dead." This man is old not because he is aged chronologically but because he is somehow dead to life. As the character's diary unfolds, we see that this seducer (his prime preoccupation) is somehow paralyzed, empty, and in despair, even though he flies about town successfully seducing women and seeing himself as living life to the fullest.

Despite his bravado, there is a moment when the seducer admits his failure: "Vainly I seek to plunge myself into the boundless sea of joy; it cannot sustain me, or rather I cannot sustain myself. Once pleasure had but to beckon me, and I mounted, light of foot, sound and unafraid. When I rode slowly through the woods, it was as if I flew; now when the horse is ready to drop, it seems to me that I do not move."[7] This is the death at the heart of the flying boy's seemingly joyful life. Soaring above the painful dimension of life which becomes a kind of paralysis—a marriage to unrelenting pain in trying to avoid it.

This is the source of Hercules's unconscious desire to destroy his sons, as well as the source of his repressed longing to just sit on the ground and spin thread. Whether the male soars off into the heavens to seduce princesses, to find the Holy Grail, or in search of enemies to destroy, what he really seeks is to save himself from the threat of pain, mortality, and enmeshment in a world beyond his control. Having cut himself off from earthly support, he becomes his own god, but somewhere in his soul he is dead. For all his motion and outer achievement, his inner being remains essentially unchanged and starved for real encounters. His galloping steed gets him nowhere.

Absence and the Need for Violence

The dreaded truth of the soaring male is that in his attempt to get above the pain of life, he has locked himself into a living death. At this great distance, he has succeeded in not feeling—not even really experiencing—either the painful aspects of life or its real joys. The horror of this condition, however, can't really register, because he has short-circuited even the pain of being cut off. Thus, there is a vicious cycle, a "Catch-22,"[8] set up that the male can't escape.

There is real frustration that builds up in every male insofar as he follows the masculine identity down this road to a phantom existence. It is like finding oneself a part of "the day of the living dead" (an unconscious appeal of all these zombie horror movies) with the twist that he is in control of himself and the world and that others accept him as a "normal male." There is no great rescue coming, nor is there an enemy to destroy—except at the heart of his own being, in the spirit that has opted to fly off into the ether.

The greatest extreme of the flying boy is the serial killer—the man who has a need to be utterly and repeatedly violent. Such men have usually been brutally abused as boys and are so extremely distanced from their feelings and their sense of bodily connection to others and the world that they feel literally "not here" in time or space.[9] When this sense becomes so overwhelming that they feel utterly disconnected, they feel a need to torture and finally kill someone else as the only means of relocating themselves in time and space through the other's torment.

Of course, these are extreme cases—the masculine spirit

gone into an excess of crazed despair—but they are revealing of the masculine psyche. Two of the most popular films of 1991, *The Silence of the Lambs* and *Cape Fear*, both portray men who experience their bodies as machines and who look down upon the world from personal fortresses in the sky. In *Cape Fear*, before Robert de Niro's character inflicts prolonged agony on his victims, he holds a burning torch over his own flesh unfeelingly—almost a stock moment in such scenes—because he can't feel and because only extremes are able to kindle a flicker in him. Ultimately, even this extreme doesn't work, other than to demonstrate his horrifying distance from himself. He is too far from his openness to his own pain to feel it, so he has to force someone else to feel it for him. Then once his victims display their pain, he can read it from their expression and behavior as if looking at a distant sign. He has to settle for distant shows rather than living the life of feeling. The soaring spirit always runs the risk of becoming a vampire: he needs others to feel things for him in the day-to-day mundane life and he will try to feed off their experience. How many men confess laughingly that they let their women do the feeling for them—taking care of the emotional work with kids, family, friends, and colleagues—while they fly about doing their manly work or other tasks?

If we look at what men say about why they are drawn to war, its tie to the soaring strategy of denying pain and the flying boy's subsequent absence is rather obvious. In his article, "Why Men Love War," William Broyles offers a very brave account of why so many men feel like Broyles and Hiers, his buddy. Hiers declares "how much fun Vietnam was. I loved it. I loved it, and I can't tell anybody."[10] Broyles goes beyond all the socially acceptable reasons for liking service and for hating war. Says he bluntly, "I miss it because I loved it, loved it in strange and troubling ways" (p. 56).

One of these reasons is that it was an "experience of great intensity." Our masculine ethos does not normally allow feelings of great intensity to pervade our everyday experience, which is often flat and dull. War is—like other acts of transgression and violence—"an escape from the everyday into a special world where the bonds that hold us to our duties in daily life—the bonds of family, community, work—disappear" (p. 58). For the first time, some men feel alive.

This is the puer's joy—to be released—whereas the Zen master offers us another paradigm altogether: the male figure who can find this intensity in all of the most everyday activities, as well in the richness of all the bonds that tie us to others. Broyles also comments that in perpetrating these brutal, deadly acts, "you have explored regions in your soul that in most men will remain uncharted" (p. 58). Since most men maintain such a distance from themselves and their souls, it is understandable why this is appealing, but it is sad that we can't allow ourselves to do this exploring in vulnerable sharing with others during the course of our everyday lives. This also helps to explain why committing acts of violence with other men, especially in war, is appealing for its sense of comradeship (p. 58), since most men in their lonely castles are cut off from friendship of a deeper sort. Broyles goes so far as to call war "the only utopian experience most of us ever have," because it allows a "brotherly love" (p. 58).

However, what is most dangerous to men and to the world is how masculine detachment craves a new sense of heroic vitality, what Broyles calls "the love of destruction, the thrill of killing" (p. 61). As Ernest Hemingway, a modern spokesman for the heroic male, wrote, "Admit that you have liked to kill as all who are soldiers by choice have enjoyed it at some time whether they lie about it or not" (p. 61).

There is little sense in relating samples of the myriad stories of men's glee at killing, yet one image of Broyles's account stays with me. Again, it concerns a man who struck all those around him as an intellectual, a "sensitive" man who wrote in his journal daily. He was a lieutenant colonel put in charge of civil affairs, helping the Vietnamese improve the quality of their lives, since that seemed to reflect his supportive qualities. However, when left in a situation where the combat troops were gone and he had the opportunity to gun down many elite enemy troops in retreat by flare light, Broyles reports the following reaction: "That morning, as they were surveying what they had done and loading the dead NVA—all naked and covered with grease and mud so they could penetrate the barbed wire—on mechanical mules like so much garbage, there was a look of beatific contentment on the colonel's face that I had not seen except in charismatic churches. It was the look of a person transported into ecstasy" (p. 62).

This thrill is not fully explainable by the usual, more rational reasons. Yes, the thrill is partly the feeling of having great power, of possessing life's secret by taking it away, and partly the relief that one has triumphed and is still alive. However, these reasons don't get to the darkest region of male identity: the pure thrill of inflicting pain and destroying others, what Broyles calls the "intense beauty—divorced from all civilized values" (p. 62)—of killing someone.

Most men do not admit this, but somewhere deep inside us is a self that is screaming to be allowed to feel. Somewhere inside us is the desire to just be who we are, but we have had to leave it behind. We act this out symbolically in our pride and even gusto at how much pain we can take. Part of our thrill in football and other male sports is that we can absorb so much physical punishment and laugh about it, use it to feel motivated, to feel "vital." This is a *disguised admission* that we men need our pain—need to return to the painful Earth in order to rejoin ourselves and others as members of the community "here" on the planet.

In massacring others, we still have a connection to those others, however denied it may be. Humans are beings of sympathy. Our bodies open up to others and enter the emotional flow among people. This is a natural gift of interconnection. In destroying the other, we destroy ourselves, too. The Nazis used many techniques to combat this sympathy, including letting the troops who were machine-gunning the Jews get drunk enough to block off their emotions. To the extent that we as males have taken up this distanced, soaring position, we are living in a "no man's land." In order to experience emotionally, we have to be in contact with others. The e-"motions" provide *the motion of life* that gives us a sense of vitality. Emotion can be self-generated; however, then we are only "emoting," putting on a show for another. In order to achieve a sense of being caught up in the flow of life, we need to be open and vulnerable among others. In desperation, some men seek to inflict pain on others as a way of establishing this connection—and in war it is often done through a shared "hell world." Even hell is better than an empty void.

Actually, for the men who feel this thrill, the emotions don't register as those of a hell world. Broyles's testimony of these ecstasies amidst napalm or white phosphorus (his favorite, as all the destroyed beings went up in brilliant, cometlike bursts of light) focuses solely on the jolt of energy in intense feeling without connecting it to all the horror and suffering in the lives of those around them. Since an emotional deprivation has blunted these men's ability to savor the nuances of emotion, they simply experience their emotions as a "charge," a "jolt," a "kick." For extremely distanced men, just to experience this flow of strong voltage makes them feel alive, even though the meaning of the emotion is horrifying when taken sensitively to heart.

For the flying boy, however, it is not surprising that only a massive emotional charge could bridge this almost infinite gap. All that survives over this great distance is the brute power, not the subtlety, of the emotional experience. If a man has a reservoir of pain locked away in his being, then only a massive charge of pain can blast through and exacerbate his own pain and revive him for the moment. If there is some feeling allowed, then there is some feeling of life in an otherwise deadened being.

An image that captures this sentiment better than words is the final scene of Ingmar Bergman's 1978 film, *The Serpent's Egg*. I haven't seen the film in more than a decade, but this final image still haunts me. A German scientist has been subjecting various subjects to tortures, mainly of a psychological sort and unbeknownst to them. The subjects are being watched through mirrors in a building in which they think they are tenants. The German scientist is so detached, rational, and distanced that it is obvious as the film proceeds that he no longer feels anything. Finally, in a last attempt to experience something, to feel something, he watches *himself* in a mirror as he slowly slits his own throat. This is what men do. In violating others, we slit our own throats, knowing on some repressed level that we are hurting ourselves and others. But at least we have the thrill of finally *feeling*. We have returned from limbo to the planet, and that feels good.

When we see how Desert Storm, the war against Iraq, fulfills so many of the flying boy's dreams, its popularity is not so hard to understand. In this war, the realization of the deaths and horrors perpetrated upon other human beings— which should sadden us all, whether we supported the war or not—was particularly blunted. Even in "victory," there is usually some greater recognition and mourning over the fact that humans were led into a situation of such brutalization of other human beings. Yet in this war, such was generally not the case. One could say that this was due to the strikingly low number of casualties suffered by the U.S. and its allies, but I believe another reason is how perfectly the Gulf War fit the image of the flying boy's fantasy, the masculine dream.

I have already discussed in my introduction how the metaphor of "Desert Storm" in the Persian Gulf War seemed to capture the pent-up masculine rage that flies to great heights and rains its destruction down upon those under its influence. The desert setting only increases the barrenness and defenselessness of those below. Now let us look at why the war was presented to the public almost exclusively in terms of the "air war." There was obviously something both intoxicating and exculpating about the war being carried on primarily from the skies. To be able to dart down from the heavens and do our will without getting caught down there was the realization of a profound male fantasy.

If we go back to the first waves of the warrior culture sweeping down from the Asiatic and European northeast into Old Europe and then into the Mediterranean world during the fifth to third millennia B.C., we see evidence not only of the use of weapons, the idea of dominating others, but also the rootless "sky mentality" that was part of this new sense of reality. According to cultural researchers Marija Gimbutas and Riane Eisler, the shift in societies from "the generative, nurturing, and creative powers of nature" to a system of male dominance, violence and hierarchic social structure was also accompanied by a shift to "ever more effective technologies of destruction."[11] These new warrior groups, whom Gim-butas calls the Kurgans, were nomadic and valued speed and the skyward view. Their advances made in the "technology" of that time period were aimed at attempts to get higher, move more swiftly, and get beyond reach of the enemy. The "new living war machine, the armed man on a horse" was a frightful force, both in realizing this speedy soaring above others and the ability to escape unharmed.

The machinery and conduct of Desert Storm—at least on the level of the images it provided for both our conscious and unconscious viewing on our TV screens—was a culmination of this desired trajectory. We had achieved the ability to soar above the plane of destruction, dart down with incredible speed and control, and then fly away and not be caught in the mire of suffering. An amazing statistic that emerged from Desert Storm involved the increasing precision and control of our "air power." In World War II, it required an average of more than five hundred sorties, or individual bombing flights, to destroy a target. In the Vietnam War, it required more than five sorties to destroy a target. In Desert Storm, it required an average of only one or two sorties. The accuracy of bombs in World War II, gauged by the actual distance that fifty percent of them fell from the target, was in the thousands of feet. In the Vietnam War, this "circular error probable" had been reduced to hundreds of feet. In Desert Storm, the accuracy range was now "within feet."[12] A year later, the Pentagon was hailing this attack from the sky as the model for future conflicts.[13]

Thus the masculine sense of "soaring above" can be literally enacted to inflict mass violence on others. Even the names and descriptions of the machines that carry out such destruction are reflective of the masculine mythology. On January 17, 1991, between 2:00 and 2:30 a.m., there were about seven hundred aircraft soaring just outside Iraqi airspace ready to unleash Desert Storm. They were guided by several U.S. and Saudi AWACS planes—called "all-seeing" by CNN, the same phrase applied to many patriarchal gods—whose acronym stands for "Airborne Warning and Control System" aircraft. These are the suspended, all-seeing, all-knowing mechanical brains that are meant to control the action with their vantage from above. There was also guidance from Navy E2C "Hawkeye" radar planes.

The first "kill" in the air was made by flier Steve Tate at 3:15 a.m. at thirty thousand feet while leading four F-15C "Eagle" fighters. The plane destroyed was a "Mirage." Also instrumental in the fighting were the A-10 "Thunderbolts." We see here a series of names of flying and seeing creatures. There is also an allusion to the power of Zeus, the ultimate soaring masculine deity, who ruled from "on high" on Mount Olympus, changing shape to ravage women or avenge himself on enemies, throwing thunderbolts from the sky. The enemy plane destroyed conveniently has the name "Mirage"—which fits the unreality of this conflict when seen from above, as though it were not *real* men, women, and children being blown apart "down there" and in the sky.

As mentioned, when anger is pent up, it festers. It becomes a potentially furious, blinding, demonic, scorching force that may burst forth in such a darkly blasting way that it surprises even the perpetrator with its virulence, as when Hercules kills his own sons. Some of the names of the Desert Storm weapons reflect this—for example, the "Hellfire" missiles that knocked out the Iraqi radar system. The old prejudicial identification of Native Americans with this dark, furious, demonic force was also expressed in various names, including "Apache" helicopters and "Tomahawk" missiles.

What most delighted the masculine mind and captured the country's fancy was the specter of bombs that no longer fell from the sky but which themselves were models of controlled soaring ability—self-propelled and "internally guided" by laser, electro-optical, or infrared devices. Besides the "Hellfire" variety, there were also "HARM" missiles, a chilling acronym, and "Maverick" missiles, which probably better than any other name sums up the masculine warrior ethos of never fitting, always wandering, and able to wreak havoc at the slightest whim.

It has been frequently noted that the televised air war made the killing and destruction seem like a video game. It is not necessary to say more about this other than to note that in some sense *all* of life has this unreal aspect insofar as the masculine identity is concerned. The video game has a purely detached and manipulable "reality" that we can enter through a screen. It gives us a semblance of life while allowing us to remain at a distance from the very aspects of life that are "screened" for us. Both senses of this screening are important. First, we are shielded from unpleasant views. Second, we see only the part of the visual field we *want* to see—we screen what we *will*. When the B-52s dropped their bombs to "shape the battlefield"—in reference to the Iraqi Republican Guard—this was such a distanced video representation of slaughter that it didn't register as such. Even the term "shaping" is so distant from what it signifies, the slaughtering of enough of the enemy forces that they won't be a factor in the battle. This, too, represents human lives in terms of mere geometry; it is more video.

Similarly for the flying boy, so much of what hurts and violates in modern life is only noted on some detector screen through key operational terms—buzzwords—and doesn't really register, whether it's rape, psychological harassment, or assaults on others' dignity. This is a frightening trend. It may mean that the distance that led the deadened warrior male to have to inflict pain in order to feel something has become so perfected that perhaps even this destruction won't register with him. It may mean that even greater megadoses of violence at such distances will be needed for him to feel vital. One might hope he is so lost in the self-constructed labyrinth of numbness that he will have to come out in utter desperation; however, at the moment, he seems even more addicted to inflicting pain in order to bridge his deadening distance from the world.

Gilgamesh and the Heroic Quest for Vitality

One of the oldest tales of the male hero (dated around 2000 B.C.) is that of Gilgamesh, king of Uruk. Gilgamesh, like other male heroes, tends to be troubled by his mortality. He is also arrogant, antagonistic to images and divinities of nature and to the community.[14] He is a greatly powerful, beautiful, and courageous leader but plagues his own community by sleeping with all the virgins as they are about to wed and with all the warriors' daughters and wives, as well as by taking all their sons to destruction in his exploits.

In anguish, the citizens appeal to the gods for help, and the gods in turn appeal to Aruru, the goddess of creation. She tries to tame Gilgamesh by providing Enkidu, a challenger and comrade of equal strength, beauty, and courage. Enkidu comes to Uruk to prevent Gilgamesh from taking the virgins. The two fight and immediately become great friends. However, for Gilgamesh, a life of enjoying community, nature, and the friendship of Enkidu is not enough. Enkidu has lived at one with nature all his life, only "tamed" by the goddess to become Gilgamesh's friend. Even though Enkidu tries to share his love of nature and acceptance of death with him, Gilgamesh remains troubled.

When Gilgamesh dreams of his destiny—set by Enlil of the Mountain, father of the gods—Enkidu helps him to interpret what it means. He tells him that "everlasting life is not your destiny," but that he has been given great powers to bring light and dark to his people and that he must learn to deal justly with them. Gilgamesh wants none of this, concluding that his life is worthless unless he can achieve ultimate fame and reach "where no man's name is yet written" (p. 23). Gilgamesh is surprised that "the eyes of Enkidu were full of tears and his heart was sick" when he sees that his friend must have his glory in order to feel his life was well spent.

Gilgamesh persists and desires to slay the ferocious giant, Humbaba, as a way of securing glory for the both of them. Gilgamesh argues with the reluctant Enkidu as to why he must perform this deed: "Where is the man who can clamber to heaven? Only the gods live forever with glorious Shamash, but as for us men, our days are numbered, our occupations are a breath of wind" (p. 24). Unable to accept this earthly life and rankled that he is a part of a larger whole, Gilgamesh must tower above life and the final defeat of death. He explains that if he dies accomplishing this heroic deed, "Then if I fall I leave behind me a name that endures" (p. 24). When he compares such glory with the immortality of having children and being part of the ongoing human community, he finds this vertical ascent through fame that equals the gods' to be far superior.

Unable to convince Enkidu, Gilgamesh pleads his case with Shamash, the sun god, that skyward, blazing deity with whom the masculine hero in many cultures so often identifies. As the earliest myth of the time when the warrior mentality was beginning to dominate the planet, it is interesting to look at Gilgamesh's speech:

> O Shamash, hear me, hear me, Shamash, let my voice be heard. Here in the city man dies oppressed at heart, man perishes with despair in his heart. I have looked over the wall and I see bodies floating in the river, and that will be my lot also. Indeed, I know it is so, for whoever is tallest among men cannot reach the heavens, and the greatest cannot encompass the earth. Therefore I would enter that country: because I have not established my name stamped on brick as my destiny, I will go to the country where the cedar is cut. I will set up a name where the names of famous men are written; and where no man's name is written I will raise a monument to the gods. (p. 24)

One can palpably feel Gilgamesh's pain at the vision of these deaths, which announce his own death. It is the same anguish the Buddha was to feel at the same sight, yet Gilgamesh believes he can overcome this pain by soaring to the heights. He thinks he can outdistance and outlast pain and achieve the immortality of fame. In order to deal with the fundamentally painful "river of life," Gilgamesh only resorts to the creation of more pain. He plans to go to the land where the Tree of Life is cut in order to slay a giant— and in so doing, become a giant himself. Notice, too, how early the city as opposed to the mystical "Otherness" of far-away lands and nature is seen as a place of despair for the heroic male. For him, the city is the place where he is stuck with the mundane communal life.

Of course, the sky-dwelling sun god understands this anguish, and Gilgamesh and Enkidu (who goes along as a loyal friend) are allowed their adventure of slaying Humbaba. However, once this exploit is achieved, another familiar heroic motif enters the tale to plague the conquering heroes. Ishtar, the goddess of love and fertility, tries to woo Gilgamesh as her love. Of course, the masculine hero rebuffs the spirit of love and fertility, as he must in this role. The gods decide that it is not Gilgamesh who will die for turning his back on the spirit of life, but that it will be more painful for him to have his friend Enkidu die.

This *does* strike Gilgamesh's secret storehouse of pain: his inability to deal with loss and death. He rages at Enkidu's death. Finally, he has the greatest goldsmiths and stoneworkers erect a monumental statue of Enkidu to inspire others to honor his lost glory. Again, this is the model that has been set for us by the heroic male: to monumentalize ourselves and those we love before the inevitability of painful loss.

As might be expected, the loss of Enkidu makes Gilgamesh's repressed inability to accept mortality resurface in an even more harrowing way. Again, rather than allowing himself to be transformed, his impulse is to defeat his pain and the human condition.

In order to accomplish this, Gilgamesh goes on a quest for immortality. This time, fame will not do; he literally must get beyond death and the human condition. Fame did not save his great warrior friend, Enkidu. What was fame when the worms finally forced Gilgamesh to bury his friend after sitting with his corpse for seven days?

In a faraway land, Gilgamesh seeks out and finds Utnapishtim, the only mortal to be granted everlasting life by the gods. When he arrives, Utnapishtim doesn't see why the gods would assemble their powers for Gilgamesh's sake. Immortality was granted to Utnapishtim only because, long ago, during the worldwide floods, he had built an ark and rode out the floods that engulfed the Earth and thus preserved the chain of life. His gift was a reward for caretaking the continuity of life on the planet—the deepest sense of immortality in the pre-warrior mentality. However, Utnapishtim agrees to put Gilgamesh to the test. To earn immortality, he need only prevail against sleep for six days and seven nights.

As soon as Gilgamesh sits down, sleep starts to overcome

him. Utnapishtim remarks to his wife: "Look at him now, the strong man who would have everlasting life, even now the mists of sleep are drifting over him." After discussing the matter with his wife, Utnapishtim decides that Gilgamesh will probably not be able to believe that he has been defeated. So he tells her to bake a loaf of bread each day and put it by his head. When they wake Gilgamesh on the seventh day, he protests that he has hardly slept. They confront him with the loaves. He sees that the first loaf is hard, the second like leather, the third soggy, the fourth moldy, the fifth mildewed, the sixth fresh, and the seventh just removed from the embers. Then he knows that he has been asleep for a long time.

This is a wonderfully symbolic tale for the masculine hero. He is asked to combat the cycle of day and night, activity and rest, and he cannot. Even the hero can't stop the flow of time, its cycles and rhythms. Also, sleep issues from that underworld realm of hazy, deathlike, obscure phenomena—the very realm of life in which the masculine hero has no real defense or ability to cope.

As part of the cycle of day and night, sleep is essential to gaining vitality. As both rest and a relaxing of control, it symbolizes all the aspects of life that call for the attitude of *letting be* in order to be fruitful. Our one-sided emphasis on doing and taking charge becomes problematic for many of us males. The art of being, waiting, receiving, letting the power of even this world—let alone the underworld—seep into us is often lost.

However, there is also a sense in which this metaphor fits the heroic attitude all too well. There is a sense in which the soaring male hero is always asleep, not really here. The contrast with the Buddha is striking. In seeing the inevitable pain of mortality, Siddhartha surrenders to its flow—as a celebration of being transient and a part of the whole—and as a result becomes "fully awake." That is what the term *Buddha* means: "the one who woke up." In contrast, Gilgamesh, doesn't even notice that he has been asleep! Only by seeing the bread of life that has gone to waste does he realize how long he's been unconscious. It is the same for us: if we could see the loaves that have spoiled as we have soared about questing, we might realize to what extent we've been asleep.

The response of Gilgamesh is to despair at the passage of time and mortality: "What shall I do, O Utnapishtim, where shall I go? Already the thief in the night has hold of my limbs, death inhabits my room; wherever my foot rests, there I find death" (p. 29). At this point, Gilgamesh is worn out and can see life's passage only as a threat.

I have seen this same kind of despair in my friends and, in rare moments of honesty, in myself. It is a kind of hurt—a "male despair"—that women often find almost amusing. They are tired of hearing about it. It's not that our feelings are not genuine; it's just that we fail to see how going on the quest to overcome the limits of life inevitably makes life such a depressing trial. The very fact that we inflict this kind of suffering on ourselves sometimes prompts others to mock us for it. Yet we are the ones who impose this punishment on ourselves, refusing to break this cycle of pain, almost like cartoon characters that knowingly keep on running to their own undoing.

Utnapishtim plans only to refresh Gilgamesh with a bath and new clothes and send him home. But after his wife intervenes—she sees how worn out Gilgamesh is—Utnapishtim tells him "a secret thing, the mystery of the gods." He confides: "There is a plant which grows under the water, it has a prickle like a thorn, like a rose; it will wound your hands, but if you succeed in taking it, then your hands will hold that which restores his lost youth to a man" (pp. 29-30). When he hears this, Gilgamesh opens the sluices and is carried out to the deepest channel. There he ties rocks to his feet and dives down for the plant he sees in the depths. Although he hurts his hands, he gets the plant and sets out for Uruk with it. He plans to give it first to the old men, then eat some himself and recapture all his lost youth. He imagines Uruk now being called "The Old Men Are Young Again."

That night, Gilgamesh takes a bath in a pool in which a serpent is lying. Sensing the sweetness of the plant, the serpent rises out of the water and snatches it away. Gilgamesh sits down in despair and says to the ferryman: "O Urshanabi, was it for this that I toiled with my hands, is it for this I have wrung out my heart's blood? For myself I have gained nothing; not I, but the beast of the earth has joy of it now" (p. 30). Gilgamesh realizes that the serpent has carried the plant back to the depths of the waters and the Earth and that he has lost it. Gilgamesh and the ferryman leave the water and march back to Uruk. In the end, Gilgamesh has his city, which he proudly shows to the ferryman before he leaves him to return to the faraway land. He also has his tales of adventure. The tale ends, "He went on a long journey, was weary, worn out with labor, and returning engraved on a stone the whole story" (p. 31).

Of course, it is symbolically appropriate that the secret which restores lost youth is at the bottom of the deep waters. Water is the dynamic element of life that stands for the depths of the emotions or, in a Jungian sense, for the depths of the unconscious. It is the psychic element. The secret of youth in old age lies in the depths of the psyche. The flying boy, who is in pain but denies it, does not want to go to these depths of his psyche. He'd rather soar above his feelings. Gilgamesh has to tie weights onto his legs in order to descend to these depths. He only does this in the spirit of a heroic quest. To find the lasting vitality he seeks, however, he would have to take the weighty matters of mortality—for him, the painful loss of Enkidu, the painful frictions with the people of Uruk, and the pain of his own insecurity—*into his heart*. Only then would he be able to descend to the emotional depths and rediscover the vitality which has to be created ever anew.

The secret of this spirit of youth lies in a plant, a symbol of the Earth, of cycles of birth, decay, death, and nourishment. This should be a message to Gilgamesh. However, rather than becoming fully immersed in these cycles and finding the spirit of youth within the flow of life, he dreams of a magical transformation of himself and all his cronies into wonderboys. As John Barth states in his marvelous retelling of the Scheherazade myth, "The key to the treasure is the treasure."[15] Gilgamesh can't see that the secret of youth lies in eating his bread each day it is baked without worrying about the next day's bread or trying to find a loaf that will endure forever and never mold.

To grasp the plant causes pain because it is thorny. This, too, is appropriate: the secret of the authentic spirit of youth is in grasping the thorny richness of life, embracing situations which may be piercing, and finding a way to work through them. As we have seen, the heroic mentality soars away from the day-to-day pains of mortal life. Having projected his pain onto the world, the hero goes out to conquer the pain he sees in others, which is really his own. Thus, he dishonestly tries to deal with his own pain. Gilgamesh gladly experiences pain as part of a heroic adventure. He "takes the pain," as we males say, "with no problem." Yet such taking of pain to make his mark or to lash out against mortality, which so often comes down to lashing out against others, is just cutting his own hands; and even this pain isn't taken back to its sources at the bottom of the psychic waters. It is no wonder Gilgamesh loses his secret to the first serpent he encounters in the depths: it is a secret of the Earth—of the Goddess-inspired paths—which had found divinity within the mundane cycles of life, in the interconnection of all things, and the partnership of all people and creatures in a life process.

Gilgamesh realizes that he has lost the secret to a "beast of the Earth," but what he doesn't realize is that the secret is always there at the bottom of his own psyche, if he would but dive down and experience it. The only real joys Gilgamesh finds are in violating the town's virgins, in the great fight with Enkidu, in the slaughter of Humbaba, and in building monuments. No wonder he is weary at the end of his life! The pain that fuels the flying boy's forays into violence and adventure eventually festers into an abscess that drains away his vitality. Dead to the world, he goes on quests for the secret of life he will never find. So it must have been for my colleague walking across campus, distanced from feeling and deadened within the fortress of his mind, still longing for his killing time.

CHAPTER THREE

The Armored Tank and the Big Missile

*The Masculine Loss
of Authentic Embodiment
and Sexuality*

Caught within the Tank

One might think that, first struck by how physically fragile was his body, the warrior in his battle mentality came to adorn his body with more and more protection over the millennia. As such, the tank might be seen as the culmination of a long process of military evolution from tough skins to shields to vehicles to the fully enclosed missile-toting tanks of current warfare. However, I would like to suggest that it was the other way around: Originally, the masculine ideal of a body was a tank, and the mechanical tank was rendered in this image. Now, having created the externalized objects that can carry us through attacks our own bodies cannot endure, we try to mold our bodies to tanklike standards. We are in a feedback cycle with the machines we first created in our own image, but which we now attempt to emulate to complete our own self-image. I am not trying to make a particular historical or anthropological point here, but rather make us face how deeply some of our fascinations with our mechanisms of violence go into our own psyches, our own bodies, our own beings. We can justify tanks and missiles by their practical functions, but they also appeal to suppressed levels of our masculine consciousness.

It is difficult to explain how mechanical and alienating the masculine body ideal is, because we have so little idea about what a fully *human* body might be like. We have inherited centuries of Cartesian thinking that looks at the body as a machine—and before that, several thousand years of disdain for the open, sensitive, expressive, and revealing human body. Since the warrior mentality became the dominant paradigm some four thousand years ago, the body has been demeaned by the Greek, Roman, medieval Christian, and scientific ways of seeing the body as a receptacle, a mere housing for the mind or soul, a trap keeping us on the Earth and in the flow of earthly change that leads to death. Such a housing and tool of the mind—no matter what fancy terms are used to describe it—is essentially a mechanism. Simply put, all these traditions view the body as a machine. Before we can plumb the depths of this "body-as-tank" perception, we must somehow propose a different body perception with which to contrast it.

When we look at the simplest organisms, it is obvious that their "bodies," even if they are only blobs of protoplasm, are their means of being open to the environment, interacting with it, and becoming situated in relation to it—hopefully in ways maximally nourishing to them. As human beings, there is a quantum jump to a kind of life in which the body is wondrously inseparable from dimensions of thought, emotion, imagination, memory, communication, and expression. We have the kind of body for which each sensory input has woven into it meanings and interchanges with the world that go far beyond simple biological concerns. Although chemical and physical reactions take place within our bodies that might—if staged in a simple, isolating laboratory setup— appear to be merely mechanical, within the life of a whole person they are always enmeshed in the ways in which that person makes choices about the meaning of the environment. We are always seeking out, discovering through events and actions, who we are.

This way of seeking is always grounded in the way in which we position our bodies in relation to others and the world. Do we look deeply into the other's eyes and explore with our hearing the tone of their voice? Do we even really listen to what they are saying? Do we notice the frantic pace that has developed in our household in recent weeks or listen for the unusual silences that have set in between partners? Do we notice that this job makes our head ache and our body feel like lead, while the other job gives a bouncy, springy feeling to our step and a lilt or crackle to our voice? Do we notice that under an oppressive regime people walk stiffly with their eyes down? Do we notice that our father never looks into anyone's eyes while speaking? As the philosopher Merleau-Ponty put it, "Our body is our way *into* the world," not our way of being cut off from it.

Not only do we have these opportunities to plumb the meaning of our sensory experience, but we find ourselves caught up in certain ongoing perceptions that have already *made a pact* with our bodies to mean certain things. For example, Gilgamesh might have found himself standing more erect under an open sky, since it whispered to him of great, unlimited power—or found himself slumped and frowning when confronted with rivers, since for him they spoke of death and loss. For someone else, like Orpheus, the river might have sent a tingle through his body as his favorite spot of enchantment and connection with all creatures through the music of his lyre.

We find ourselves through what seems to "grab us" in the world: through what seems important in our own personal history and our shared familial and cultural history; through strong feelings we experience in certain situations; through the words we end up saying; through the ways that even the most simple aspects of our sensual life—red, cold, soft, sexy, or whatever—come to speak to us and assume a particular appearance for us. For example, if the experiences that cars excite me, that armed conflicts scare me, that I am embarrassed if someone shows a concern about me, that I always end up snapping defensively at those who work under my supervision, that the soft parts of someone's breast sicken me, or that green makes me nervous—all these perceptions have to do with the unique way the world speaks to my body. Sensory inputs are not mere inputs on detector screens about purely objective data.

In other words, we are not merely passive spectators encased *within* our bodies, peering out at what they experience. We worry about who we are and constantly add our sense of that identity through the people, things, ideas, and experiences with which we identify. If I am interested in discovering who I can become and what the world and others can become, there is an inexhaustible source of new meaning for me to try to discover, with and through others—they "reach" me, "touch" me, "fathom" me, "open" me, "add" to me, etc. These are not literal, physical things, but new nuances, new horizons, revelations of who I am and what life means.

The way to be so reached, we say, is to be vulnerable, to be receptive, to be open. But in what does such an openness consist? For example, to be "touched" by someone does not refer to the objective proximity of our physical substance to another's reaching zero, but rather about the "letting in" of an emotional, imaginative, and cognitive "flow" between two people. This can happen even if we are not physically touching, and it may fail to happen even if we *do* physically touch. As the word rightly indicates, touch *does* have to do with experiencing through our bodies—but in a richer way than we may be accustomed. This kind of sensitivity to others and the world is as real and palpable as the sensitivity of the retinal cones to light stimulation. It is part of the skill of coming back to our bodily presence and co-presence with others in a certain way. It is part of that expanded human sense of "taking in" the environment in such a way that we are suspended within it and moved by its currents.

This "open" sense of the body has been articulated in many ways. Peter Russell, in *The Global Brain*, calls it getting beyond the "skin-encapsulated ego," to seeing the body as having "leaky margins." Chaos theorists John Briggs and David Peat evoke a vision of an ongoing, nonlinear feedback process through the environment. Philosopher Maurice Merleau-Ponty sees the body as a strand of the "flesh of the world" that folds back on itself. Feminist theologian Mary Daly sees the body as a power of "biophilic bonding and bounding" that is everywhere within its environment. Buddhist teacher Tarthung Tulku describes the body as the site in which all time and all space bathes in a "knowing-ness" of shining forth. Novelist Margaret Atwood writes: "I am not an animal or a tree, I am the thing in which the trees and animals move and grow, I am a place."[1]

Perhaps D.H. Lawrence says it best in his poem, "Two Ways of Living and Dying," in which he contrasts an emotionally defended, mechanistic life with one that is emotionally vulnerable and sensitive. For him, the key to this shift is being fully open to the body and the richness of perceptual experience:

> While people live the life
> they are open to the restless skies, and
>   streams flow in and out
> darkly from the fecund cosmos, from the
>   angry red sun, from the moon
> up from the bounding earth, strange
>   pregnant streams, in and out of the flesh
> and man is an iridescent fountain, rising up to
>   flower[2]

The human body is always an environmental body, caught up in many strands of its situation. It is, to use the feminist metaphor, a web.[3] Our capacity to feel and express the energy and meaning of the web can be enlarged, diminished, or almost go unnoticed.

It is both our plight and our joy that all aspects of our being are our *responsibility*: that is, we must respond to them in some way, and the way in which we respond makes that aspect of our being *gradually more or less* during various periods of our lives or during our lifetime as a whole. Being emotional, rational, sensitive, imaginative, sensual, or whatever dimension of our being we wish to express is an ongoing task. We have to work with what we are given by nature, by culture, by history, and by our choices. This means we can do the opposite, too: if our emotions are denied and avoided for a long period, then after a while, we can't feel certain things. In the context of our current discussion, this means that if for thousands of years we men have denied that the body is an open avenue of emotional interchange, we do indeed create another sort of body which becomes our normal sense of being embodied. Repeated references to the body as a prison, a weapon, a temptation, or a machine can be seen not only as descriptions but also as *prescriptions*: if the metaphors are believed, men as a whole will live their lives in such a way as to make their bodies more machinelike and unfeeling.

A tank is an armored vehicle. It carries warriors through the landscape mechanically under the direction of the person who drives it. It is self-propelled and armed for combat, traditionally with cannons or machine guns but now with missiles and other sophisticated weaponry. Its treads are constructed to keep it moving forward through almost any sort of terrain or obstacle. If we look at these characteristics for a moment, their modeling after the ideal masculine body is obvious. Philosophically, the warrior mentality culminated in the Cartesian sense that the true person, the "mental substance," was merely housed within the mechanism of the body, which gave it a way to move through space and act upon objects. The body was directed by the mental substance, although through its mechanical interactions it had its own blind motive forces. In this philosophy, the mind has the same contained, external, and directive relationship to the body as the driver has to the tank.

However, the masculine ethos builds on this dualistic model. It maintains that the body is a separate entity from its world and other people, a self-contained base of operations. This detachment from the body is much like the separation between driver and tank and between tank and environment. The masculine body ideal strives to be firm, tough, and well armored so that painful obstacles do not stop it. For such an ideal, a body of steel like the tank would be the perfect achievement. Superman, as "man of steel," was undoubtedly an expression of this ideal. As men, we try to develop great force so that we can push aside or maneuver around objects in our way. Our muscles, fists, arms, and legs ideally should all be strong, tough, and quick enough to become potent weapons for defense and aggression. The tank is just an extrapolation of our masculine body ideal.

In most of our masculine sports, we discipline ourselves to become toughened to pain and menacing in our ability to ram through obstacles and "dish out" bodily pain to others. It is a discipline to become inured to the physical registration of pain, a complement to the psychological stance we've seen in the heroic mentality. Yet the more we become like tanks—armored, aggressive, self-contained—the more rigid and insensitive we become. Instead of cultivating the body as sensitively open to the most nuanced flows of energy in the environment, which would develop excellence in the body's perceptive abilities, this masculine ideal blockades against all such inputs and interweavings. Timm Rosenbach, for example, in explaining why he quit the National Football League in the early stages of his career at age twenty-six, despite being one of its most talented quarterbacks and making more than a million dollars a year, stated: "I felt programmed. I had become a machine. I became sick of it."[4]

The tank and the body as tank are equally marked by their ability to shut off potentially painful impacts from "getting inside" and hurting or causing damage. Insofar as this becomes our customary body style and identity, we develop an impermeability that fits well with the soaring masculine psyche. The problem with this way of experiencing the body is the same one we encountered with the masculine way of living the emotions. If we become impermeable to pain, we also stop the flow of reception to other sensations and emotions. We fail to take into account that the dammed flow had *more currents* than the merely targeted painful ones, and also that it was a *two-way flow*. Rosenbach gives a powerful description of this danger as he explores further his decision to quit football:

> I thought that I was turning into some sort of animal. You go through getting yourself psyched by hating the other team, the other players. You're so mean and hateful, you want to kill somebody. Football's so aggressive. Things get done by force. And then you come home, you're supposed to turn it off? "Oh, here's your lovin' daddy." It's not that easy. It was like I was an idiot.[5]

Rosenbach became alarmed that he couldn't register the loving feeling he had for his wife or for others, living in his tank-body, steeled in controlled aggression. He also realized he couldn't be emotionally expressive from within the tank-body.

This is beautifully seen in the ambiguity implied in the word *tank*. A tank is also a structure for *containing* something. It does not allow its contents—whether fluid, gas, or solid—to get outside its boundaries. The same is true of the body as tank: it is not just a defense; it is also a container that bottles up feelings, a prison that keeps us within walls of our own creation.

These unpliable, toughened bodies we come to inhabit are not very good for melting or folding into another person in the sensitivity of a hug or caress. They are not the best bodies for registering subtleties in our perceptual fields that let us know about vital emotional nuances. In extreme cases, they don't register much perceptual detail at all.

A wonderful moment occurs in the film, *The First Monday in October*, that eloquently makes this point. One of the Supreme Court judges returns home to find his wife packing to leave him. She complains that although he is not a bad man, he simply doesn't see her, doesn't feel her emotional needs. He is just blind to her and the emotional nuances of their relationship. He pleads for another chance. She finally pauses and asks him to close his eyes. She tells him that she will not divorce him if he can describe the wallpaper in their bedroom that they have occupied for twenty-five years. He can't, and she leaves.

Her point is the one I'm making here: behind the barrier of the tank-body is a man who is "on his mission," closed off to the sensory-emotional richness of his environment—which includes the feelings of others. Instead of being suspended "out there" in contact with others as a body *developed as an avenue of openness*, he is "in there" behind his armor, blind to the nuances of his situation. The price of his protection and direction is that he is unreachable, and she accordingly wants no more of it.

An equally frustrating problem of the tank armor is that its containment makes bodily expression so difficult. Instead of a sensitive, caressing, pliant, harmonizing hand or body with which to express emotion, men find themselves with hands that are hammers or weapons—too brutely forceful or tightly armored to register expressively all they would love to be able to demonstrate to others. The parody of the male hug, insofar as we have become overidentified with the masculine ideal, is the squeezing bear hug, which makes minimal contact and certainly is neither expressive nor receptive to all the emotional nuances that can flow between sensitive human bodies.

The forcefulness of such hugs or lovemaking or other embodied expressions of emotion is supposed to betoken strength of emotion for the armored body struggling to be expressive, but vehemence of emotion is not richness of feeling. This fact is often puzzling to the masculine hero and contrary to the Romantic movement's attempt to foster this idea. Quantity of affect does not betoken *depth of feeling*, which is more about the quality of resonating to the other. Achieving this emotional resonance requires staying with the unfolding process and rhythm of feeling. It requires an openness to complexity and a wide variety of gentle and fragile senses. It requires a light touch in order for two people to grow wider and more enmeshing under the spell of varied emotions. Emotional depth is more about letting go, allowing ourselves to be taken into certain tides and flows between or among people, than it is about bulldozing ahead or firing forcefully forward.

In its original inspiration, there is much about the male pursuit of sport that aims to express the beauty of the body in motion, to build community, and to affirm process. Tragically, however, much of contemporary sports is paradoxically "anti-embodiment." The masculine heroic attitude toward sports sees the athletic body as a tool to be used to achieve a purpose—to win. With this attitude, the body at play becomes just another tool for ego-building. Sports become a way of treating the body as a defense against vulnerability to others. The body as a tool is something that must be subordinate to the will, to the mind. Its potential announcements of feeling are to be ignored or, at most, monitored. So the body is "trained" to be tough, hard, bulky, fast, maneuverable, and powerful—in some brute way. In general, it is to become a "highly tuned machine." As Timm Rosenbach realized about life in the National Football League, both players and coaches "lose any feeling of being a human being," and within this world he felt his body had been reduced to the status of a useful tool and no more: "I feel they viewed me—us—as robots. A mechanism. And if you don't fit in the slot you're nothing to them."[6]

This does not mean that developing the body's amazing capacities necessarily has to be distancing or mechanizing—quite the opposite. If the body is our means of interchange with the world, enhancing bodily sharpness could bring us into greater touch with the world and others. The problem is our way of seeing the body as a mere instrument of the will and the particular hardened way it has become shaped for that purpose. We are being dishonest if we fail to recognize that part of the satisfaction of this training is the feeling of protection and power that we receive from remaking our bodies into impermeably defended and bludgeoning "tanks." When we consider how many boys are caught up in this athletic system, we must realize that it is a devastating blow to the newest generation's capacities to enjoy the sensitivity of their bodies.

For all its apparent emphasis on developing the body, the masculine heroic approach to sport can become paradoxically disembodying when it abandons the attuned responsive body for the self-willed tool. Such a body is now a machine. No longer enmeshed in its situation and sensitive to its surroundings, it is self-propelled. Sensitive human bodies are neither disengaged nor instruments of the will. As D.H. Lawrence cogently expresses it:

> But when people are only self-conscious
>   and self-willed
> they cannot die, their corpus still runs on,
> while nothing comes to them from the open
>   heaven, from earth, from the sun and moon
> to them, nothing, nothing;
> only the mechanical power of self-directed energy
> drives them on and on, like machines,
> on and on, with the triumphant sense of power,

like machines,
on and on, and their triumph in mere motion,
full of friction, full of grinding, full of danger to the
    gentle passengers
of growing life . . . [7]

A fully human body is one that is open to others and the world, a way of being in dialogue. The body as machine, on the other hand, is made to grind forth as a servant of will, power, and assertion. This can be seen clearly in a problem that plagues many of our young male athletes—that of taking steroids to make their bodies bulky, powerful, tough, and hyperfunctioning. These young men are using their bodies as mere tools, as vehicles for the will. They are forgetting that their bodies are also their avenues of openness to the world's larger meaning, and that they need to be responsive to their bodies' inner and outer biological balances or they will perish.

To make themselves less vulnerable to physical pain, such atheletes are creating for themselves more serious pain: yes, they can absorb a ferocious tackle, but their internal organs will tackle each other in disease. As Lyle Alzedo, a "man's man" on the football field, reminded us all during the last painful year of his life, these heroic men and boys will not lose the "first down" for their team, they will just lose years of their lives, as he did by abusing steroids in becoming one of the NFL's fiercest and toughest players. So obsessed can the hero become with victory that he will use his body as a tank, forgetting there are no replacement issues from the motor pool to give him a further ride.

Interestingly, the next lines of Lawrence's poem predict that those who make their bodies into machines are not only closed off and therefore dangerous to others, but also self-destructive:

but on and on, on and on, till the friction wears

them out
and the machine begins to wobble
and with hideous shrieks of steely rage and
    frustration
the worn-out machine at last breaks down:
it is finished, its race is over.[8]

Sports as playful activities can be a way to celebrate the body, but as the mark of being a "real man" and a hero, they can also degenerate into building that fortress and vehicle of "taking" and inflicting pain that transforms the play into another form of combat. The body as tank is not created through sporting or playful interaction with others; in its rigid self-assertion and obstacle smashing, it is a defensive violation of the whole idea of play. Sport is about displaying grace, prowess, and the excellence of the body in response to a larger interplay. Combat is about beating down other bodies.

The final irony about the body as tank is that, like other forms of traditional male "strength," it actually may be a form of weakness. Not only does it avoid vulnerability to pain—which admittedly is sometimes a practical necessity—but it also weakens the relationship between the body and the environment. The word *tank* comes from the Latin term, *tancare*, which means "to dam up" and "to weaken." This root gets at something profound. Retreating from contact with the environment creates the illusion of strength or sometimes gives momentary advantage, but in the long run, the greatest strength comes from an openness to other forces that allow transformation.

The tank succeeds by being so rigid, so impenetrable, that it can't be impacted. It is designed for combat, to withstand annihilating force—or at least to allow its occupants protection from a hostile environment. This is an obvious necessity in war. However, as a way to experience our bodies, it is a tragedy. We can't leave our body for another, as we can leave the tank behind. We *are* our bodies. If we've spent long years gradually steeling our bodies, senses, and emotions into armor, we are stuck in there. We bring our tank to the dinner table, to the desk at work, and to bed at night with our partner. The Latin root *tancare* points to damming a flow—which is a diminution, a weakening of the current of interchange. As tanks, we become fossilized. We lose our true human strengths of adaptability, responsiveness, and transformation.

How does the masculine heroic identity become desirous of embodying the tank? A brief allusion to Captain Ahab's story in Herman Melville's *Moby Dick* demonstrates the process. Ahab has sworn vengeance on the white whale that has taken his leg in a previous whaling voyage. Why? Because, as he says to his crew, "I'd strike the sun if it insulted me."[9] Here again we see the Herculean rage, as well as the puer philosophy of needing to soar to another realm and triumph: "All visible objects, man, are but as pasteboard masks. . . . If man will but strike, strike through the mask! How can the prisoner reach outside except by thrusting through the wall?" (p. 221).

For Ahab, this horizontal reality—the sensual world of mundane life—counts for nothing. He sees it as a "painted harlot"—again echoing the correlated devaluation of the female and the earthly. What he wants is the *vertical* reality, where the real action is that which he can't see, which the whale has come to symbolize for him: "I see in him outrageous strength. . . . That inscrutable thing is chiefly what I hate" (p. 221). So Ahab is off on the usual masculine, heroic quest, to defeat the source of vertical power in the cosmos and thus achieve a measure of immortality.

Ahab is also equipped with the hero's self-propelled, self-generating, unbending will: "The path to my fixed purpose is laid with iron rails" (p. 227). However, what is interesting is not only his blindness and numbness to the entire sensual

world, but his ideal of what his body should be. As he fanta-
sizes to the carpenter one day:

> I'll order a complete man after a desirable pattern.
> Imprimis, fifty feet high in his socks; then chest mod-
> elled after the Thames tunnel; then legs with roots to
> 'em, to stay in one place; then arms three feet through
> the wrist; no heart at all, brass forehead, and about a
> quarter of an acre of fine brains—and let me see—shall I
> order eyes to see outwards? No, but put a sky-light on
> top of his head to illuminate inwards. There, take that
> order, and away. (p. 599)

Ahab wants monumental size and strength. He wants the
armor of a brass forehead. He can do without feelings, so forget the heart. He doesn't need to see the sensual world at all.
All he needs are the powers of thought and internal illumination. The only part that doesn't seem to fit is his desire to be
rooted, but that is because he is mobile at sea and just wants
a stable footing in this unstable element. In fact, his puer
desire to soar in order to not "be stuck" is evidenced in his
next remark: "Cursed be that mortal-inter-indebtedness. . . I
would be as free as air" (p. 601). Ahab, who calls himself a
Greek god in this passage, combines the soaring, determined,
unconsciously pained quest for victory with the strategy of
becoming a self-propelled, invulnerable tank.

If only Ahab could have seen the M1A1 Abrams tanks—
the other stars of the Desert Storm encounters! These tanks
were so mobile, tough, and accurate in launching their missiles that of the 1,956 that engaged the Iraqi forces in battle
only four were disabled and four were damaged.[10] As in
Ahab's vision, the Abrams dispenses with direct visual contact with its environment and uses a laser beam that generates data about the target location. Then the M1A1's "quarter
of an acre of fine brains," its inboard computer, interprets the
beam and generates a "firing solution," which it continuously updates as the computer tracks the target. Finally, the

Abrams fires an antitank warhead with an aluminum casing that falls off in flight, leaving a uranium penetrator rod to smash at high velocity through the enemy tank's armor.

In three-and-a-half days of fighting, three thousand Iraqi tanks were destroyed or captured. It was the largest tank battle ever. One Abrams tank took two direct hits from an Iraqi tank in the turret, its most vulnerable spot. Although the crew was shaken, the tank commander slewed his turret around, and the gunner "lased," fired, and "killed" the Iraqi tank that had hit them. In moments like this, the Abrams created images to send back to the United States that satisfied the most heartfelt Ahabian heroic longings.

In keeping with a portion of our masculine fantasy, the tank as a container keeps the enemy from "spilling their guts" so that we can watch these tank "kills" and be shielded from the suffering going on "inside," locked away within the armor. Again, this is not to criticize the use of tanks in war—this book is not about how to conduct a war—but just to point out how deeply these images and machines are connected to psychological and metaphysical urgings. The masculine tank body has found a wonderful externalized equivalent and paradigm for its dreams.

A final irony is provided by our current slang usage of a verb form of tank. In current usage, to "tank" an athletic contest is to withdraw one's full presence from the match—to simply "go through the motions" and not give it a good try. This suggests something about the fearless male warrior on his steed, flying in the air, behind his shield, or within his tank. It's a distanced, detached, safe, disengaged way to encounter challenges. If it becomes our only approach, then despite all our apparent energy and activity, it may have become a way of "tanking" life itself!

The Lethal Sexuality of the Megaton

What is true of the tank is also true of the missile. Neither are modern inventions, even though in their present technologically advanced form they may seem to be. In the deepest sense, they are the ancient legacy of the last four-and-a-half millennia of the warrior mentality. The missile is a symbol for a way of coming into contact with others and acting upon them. We even have a slang phrase that betrays this: "to nuke" someone or something. Becoming like a missile has its own distinctive qualities, which may or may not be appropriate to the situation.

If we wish to understand the deeper levels of our masculine love of missiles and our identification with their powers in various aspects of our lives, we will have to look closely at its particular qualities. In this section, I would like to look carefully at all the metaphors, all the unnoticed aspects of missiles and their flight, so that we can gradually feel all the hidden emotional and symbolic dimensions of this masculine image of sexuality. Since the missile mentality dictates how many males perceive sexuality—as "scoring the target"—and sex then becomes a metaphor for other desires, missile images have wider references that can be better understood by thoroughly exploring this root metaphor.

To the extent that we men soar above the reach of others, there is a need for us to find a way to bridge the great gap that separates us from the vital flow of life. Thus, we must "send out" some messenger in order to make some connection with others. Although we might feel vital within our fortress of armor high above the world, we also know that somehow we must bridge the gap we've created in order to make an impact. The flying boy must make some contact in order to sustain himself, yet being so far removed, he has no direct way of doing so. Thus, he must become a *master of distances*.

This has been part of the gift of the masculine perspective: finding ways of monitoring and crossing great distances, ranging over the skies in such a way that we have come to feel at home there. Our masculine games delight in these abilities: to throw a projectile far yet accurately, to be able to glide along connected to the sky and the long trajectory of various balls so that our bodies can come effortlessly to meet them. We seem to have embedded in our bodies an uncanny "aerial sense," almost as if a part of our being were "out there, above" and delighted in drifting on the winds. As I reach seamlessly for the touchdown pass entering my hands, I am returning to myself running from a shared flight in the sky that is fluid, natural, and almost a projected equivalent of how a bird would play about the skies, swooping on the air currents. Our masculine body is extended in the sky, and its space opens up as a center for our manipulations.

I do not mean to denigrate such male abilities. I, myself, love them and remember with a vivid thrill moments such as when a football glided featheringly down into my outstretched hands, or the time when I hurled a basketball the length of the court and swished a bucket just as the game ended. The problem enters with our aerial bodies when, as flying boys, we can *only* deal with certain situations "from above," because that has become the only way we can deal with the world's challenges. It is here that the destructive side of the missile becomes evident.

The missile is the invention that allows us to touch someone, have an impact, or make our presence felt when it is too dangerous for us to be actually present. First, it is important to note that the projectile thrown over this great distance targeted at a certain spot is not just an indifferent object. The missile is a carrier of our intention. If, as in its military use, the missile is destructive, a weapon for killing or hurting others, it expresses our intention to hurt or kill someone—and yet we wish to do it in such a way that we are not physically present and vulnerable to counterattack. Whatever country fires a missile at another country's people, it is those distant people in the country of origin who have performed this act—the missile was just a means, an intermediary. If we intend to communicate but it is too dangerous or impractical to send people in the void of space, we send a missile to put a satellite into space. Yet, we are the doers of the deed, not the missile itself. There is a real magic achieved here: we do something in such a way that we are literally absent from the scene and not open to the immediate response or repercussions set off by the action.

Nor is it a reciprocally shared situation: when we send a missile, we will in some sense profoundly alter a situation or a place in which we are not directly involved. In that sense, it is not "taking a stand," since this implies a reciprocally shared situation in which we try to make others see the power or the wisdom of what we assert, and we in turn are open to seeing the power of their position. The missile is a way of implementing the puer's idea of the action of gods: to impact the world while escaping the hold of events set into motion within that world.

This absence and the nonreciprocity of this situation becomes highly problematical: it creates a power imbalance that makes taking responsibility gratuitous—like "the gods." Yes, they are the authors of various actions, but they merely *deign* to identify with their acts and to enter into dialogue about the repercussions of what they have wrought. They must be *supplicated* in order to grant this boon, since there is not the necessity for them to be responsible as they literally are not there. Only by the graciousness of their will do they sometimes take on this responsibility from "on high."

It is not coincidental that the implementation of the shift from what Riane Eisler calls the "cooperator" model of society to the "dominator" model spread by early invading warriors was catalyzed by raining blows down upon others from the height and mobility of the horse's back. This was probably the first truly devastating form of the missile. Thus, the missile is a refinement and extension of the flying boy strategy: instead of actually "darting down" into reality with its ever-present danger that one might get "caught" down there, launching a missile from "on high" or from afar allows our will to be done with no one there at all to be held responsible within reciprocal relationship.

The inherent imbalance in power created by the missile means that its use is justified only for survival in the face of overwhelming danger. The cost entailed is that the idea of true dialogue is abandoned from the outset. With this in mind, it is important for us to consider whether the danger that the masculine vision sees in various situations or "launch sites" is real. If the missile is really a paradigm for many of our actions, in which items are "sent out" toward others or the world on certain manipulated trajectories to create an explosive impact (such as in masculine models of sexuality, "bombardments" of products, ideas, and feelings), then we must really consider what sorts of dangers are being avoided and what sorts of power imbalances are being created in each instance. If the masculine identity resorts to the use of the missile in many situations that should involve an openness to pain in order to achieve a really meaningful and direct interaction, then we might be needlessly damaging many of our possible relations with others and our environment from a "first strike" panic.

Let us return for a moment to the tale of Ahab and the white whale, *Moby Dick*. Ahab, who is "safe" within his tank of a body, remains untouched both by the beautiful sea world around him and the nobility of the crew members such as Queequeg, the spiritual harpooner. By contrast, these same experiences have transformed the sailor Ishmael who came on board a depressed loner. Now, through the experiences of the voyage, he has become someone who feels connected to both humanity and even to his brother and sister whales and their natural world.

From Ahab's vantage point, where he feels akin to the power of the sun, he seeks obsessively to rain his lethal power down upon the whale. It is finally a harpoon—a form of missile—that he will throw out from his being into the heart of the whale to shatter its life. He has had his own blood welded into the steel of his harpoon in order to make it clear that this missile symbolizes his destructive power over the whale. The words that he shouts in his final show-down with the whale are telling for understanding the dream of missile power within the heroic mentality: "I turn my body from the sun. . . . Oh, lonely death on lonely life! Oh, now I feel my topmost greatness lies in my topmost grief. Ho, ho! from all your furthest bounds, pour ye now in, ye bold billows of my whole foregone life, and top this one piled comber of my death! . . . To the last I grapple with thee; from hell's heart I stab at thee . . . *thus*, I give up the spear!" (p. 721).

Ahab's accumulated pain, festering, locked inside the tank, kept at indefinite remove from healing interaction with others in the sunlike heights of his heroic pride, has in some way made him "madness maddened," as he recognizes in a rare moment of lucid self-awareness. This madness, stoked by hurt imprisoned and projected as the overwhelming hurt-fulness of the whale, fashions the hell's heart Ahab melds into his warhead to aim at the whale. It is his grief ungrieved, unacknowledged, unexperienced openly, that is that "top-most greatness," that high altitude megatonnage of explosive violence, aimed now at the whale. From his remove, Ahab is a lonely being who can only make an impact by creating the death he has lived within for years, locked away in a living death despite his bluster.

Ahab's story captures the hurtful side of the male hero: the distrust of the sensual, emotional world; the attempt to distance, control, and wreak revenge on the uncontrollable aspects of human destiny; the determination to be victorious at all costs; the unacknowledged pain, redoubled by ascend-ing to a great altitude and making the body an armored tank; and the use of great talents to attempt a monumen-tal feat at the cost of meaningful human relations and self-development.

Ahab's belief in the missile is also significant: it demonstrates power; a way to reach back into that horizontal spacetime world he's abandoned; a way to return pain into the world instead of being stuck with it at the lonely heights; a way to expel and deal out the hell of death to others from a distance; and a sense that this is a despairing act, the singular sense of the clichéd hero who "dies with his boots on"—the sense of having been backed into a corner where there is no hope of further life, just glory in death, that heroic *burst* of vitality. The burst might actually succeed in destroying the enemy and allowing the hero to live "to fight another day," but it has this quality of responding to the need of one "final flaring forth with one's all": a quality singularly captured by the missile's bursting forth in incendiary glory and finding its mark in the same fashion.

Many of the characteristics of the missile are necessities given by the position of the flying boy in relation to others. Living in isolated and great remove from others, how else can the masculine ego "send out" its expressions in order to have an impact on others? From his great remove, acts of subtlety, of gentle sensitivity, will be lost in their contours: only the most dazzling light can be seen, and only acts of great force will carry over such distances—distances in which the flying boy must reckon with the diminishing effects of his acts as they traverse this span. Since he has resorted to the use of the missile in order to stay at a safe remove, he is limited to dealing with others through something that will never have full presence, despite his efforts to have it stand for his intentions. The missile doesn't stay within the personal sphere of the sender to become indelibly marked by the sender's unique identity. The taking of the other's hand or some other caress, for example, is an expression of the hand which *can be* very much enmeshed in the spiritual and psychological sphere of that person. The particular rhythm, manner, and expressiveness of that taking of the hand or caress, if given as an extension and flowing out from the person's emotional state, seems to come right "from the heart" in a way unique to that person and this situation.

By contrast, the missile by design works mechanically and is not directly expressive of the sender. The only way in which it can be intrinsically expressive of any sense of its sender is perhaps in the power of its impact on the other. This quantity of impact, given the distance to be traversed and the paucity of other means of distinguishing the sender's feelings, has often been an obsessive concern of the masculine style. Whatever is "sent out" toward the other or the world has to have great force, make a great impact, and forcefulness is taken as a measure of feeling. However, to "make a big splash" is not necessarily to convey much emotional meaning. The flow of feeling between two people needs currents of subtlety to really give the feelings their fullest sense.

The recipient of the missile can only feel one thing: the impact of something of force coming from out of the sky. The missile is almost by definition going to be explosive on impact. We have augmented our military missiles with "warheads," but even an empty missile arrives with a concussive impact. Again, there may be certain situations in which this is an advantage, but insofar as flying boys habitually resort to missiles, this might not be the most meaningful kind of contact. Flying boys may convince themselves and even others, especially the women they woo, that to be "hit hard" or "knocked for a loop" is thrilling, is a sign of love, but most men would be surprised to find out to what extent they are being humored or tolerated in the apparently appreciative reactions to their bombardments.

In fact, flying boys are often experienced by women as rather abusive in their explosiveness and forcefulness. Also, the nature of this impact means that the missile itself will probably explode on contact, which means it is a short-lived kind of expression unless followed up by launch after launch, as during Fourth of July fireworks displays. This limits the meaning that can be expressed. The message can only be iterative, spectacular, impactful, or perhaps splashy, but it will lack the ongoing subtlety and deepening of a slowly unfolding continuous manner of contact. It also makes for a certain kind of discontinuous rhythm, which itself can be expressive of a discontinuity in emotional flow between people, in which the masculine hero gets to "duck behind" the tank or fortress wall between launches.

The nature of the missile shot involves other characteristic related qualities. Given the distance to be traversed and the external relation of the missile to the sender, the launcher must always be concerned about whether the missile is going to stay "on the course." This gives rise to increasing concerns about developing better "guidance and self-propulsion systems" to be embedded within the missile. This gives rise to the pathetic industry of "erection aids" for men, who think the trick to making love is just that—a trick—and a matter of a drug or penis implant that will keep their missile on target. Men are now having injections and implants to make their penises wider as well as longer. Woody Allen's film, *Everything You Always Wanted to Know about Sex, But Were Afraid to Ask*, contains a segment that places the viewer within the consciousness of a male as he has sex with a partner. The viewer is presented with a "control room," which represents the man's consciousness as he worries whether he can have an erection and maintain it. He has to distract himself by thinking of baseball scores from the excitement of the encounter so he won't explode in premature ejaculation. He calculates whether his forcefulness is sufficient to impress her, while not too much to "go off" too soon. In the meantime, he has no real contact with the subtleties of emotional flow between them. Most of Allen's films are unusually honest in demonstrating how, for the male partner, sex is not communion—not "making love"—but rather is a tracking of the penile missile's performance.

We have already commented on the technological break-throughs that have been made in the actual guided missile systems. As a metaphor for how we men often send our messages out to the world, this means that our focus must often be absorbed in the performance of the missile. If this is our focus, then we cannot be sensitive to the ongoing, ever-changing, multi-nuanced interaction with those with whom we are communicating. The missile launcher may even have a strong interest in "fixing" recipients in their motions of mood and response to give as stationary a target as possible. To keep up with an ever-changing partner and the myriad possible changing directions of experience and emotion may make for a very complex "launching situation"; hence the masculine heroic pattern may be to get a fix on the other and hold the target there. It is interesting that when discussing gender differences in my classes, males most often complain of women's constantly changing in their feelings, ideas, and behaviors as the most frustrating aspect for them of caring about women. Rather than an opportunity for growth and vitality, this openness to the flow of life is seen as undermining their ability to hold their partner in a constant place where they can handle her.

The missile must also build up a certain momentum in order to fly. As part of its force, it must have a certain speed. The flight of the missile is usually a fleet, blinding display or a rapid traversing of distance. It is not a slow, meandering path, open to many differing changes and directions. The missile as it shoots forward is perhaps taken as one of the clearest symbols of that aspect of life of moving forward in a linear fashion—making progress, penetrating through things. It is a wondrous progress because, in its lack of impediment, it doesn't traverse paths that are populated with others with whom it must deal, rather it makes its own way through open skies. The only thing that might be able to block its path is some other equally missile-like projectile. The fact that it arrives "from above" adds to its luster of being almost as if it were the doing of a "higher power"—something more noble, less tarnished, more godlike.

The area of personal emotional life in which the symbolism of the missile is almost overwhelming is in the masculine, heroic representation of sexuality and the status of the phallus. The penis as the center of masculine concern with sex takes its cue from the missile in every possibly analogous quality. The boy starts out thinking about sexual matters by worrying about the size of his penis. Does he have a six- or an eight-"incher"? Or, in other words, do his loins house a ten- or twenty- or thirty-megaton warhead? The first tales that surround the adolescent male mythology about sexuality in this American culture are stories about and yearnings for "scoring the target." The target, the female vagina, is just that: a place to aim at and "hit on" with the least possible enmeshment of "getting caught" down there on the raid. This is both in terms of the possible emotional involvement, but also literal terms, as if the girl's sexual organs were not an opening to lingeringly caress her being, but just a dangerous and distasteful target to "score on" and leave. The male aim is to "get off" with ejaculation and after explosiveness to depart.

The masculine insistence on intercourse as only "really counting" as sexual sharing can be seen to be part of the "missile syndrome." Instead, the lingering, caressing, and openly playing with all parts of the body to evoke, prolong, and further articulate the feeling flow between two persons—continuously stroking, caressing, exploring, and enfolding each other's bodies without the "big launch"—would be to abandon the safe distance of the firing pad.

The missile mentality explains why masculine myths portray that forcefulness in lovemaking equals passion, oblivious to how often this force can be a bruising violation and disconnection between partners. The missile evokes concerns about guidance, and the masculine concern about the performance of the penis is the concern for a tool being aimed across a heroic emotional distance to accomplish an erotic feat. This concern is self-defeating, a cruel joke that males perpetrate upon themselves. If, instead of the self-propelled, self-guided missile, we could start to experience the penis as inseparable from our whole being—not powered by internal mechanics "turned on" by the sight of a captivating target, but rather as part of a larger current of communication—such worries would cease. As part of a flow through the shared being of partners, our penises are to be empowered or "com-pelled," which means to pick up the energy of propulsion *with and through the other*.

If we males could see that full sexual expression is not a matter of the "blast off" power of our penises, but rather the act of allowing our male bodies to come into one shared field of expression and current of feeling with a partner, then, magically, flaccid penises would suddenly become quite stimulated—by the look in the other's eyes, by the tone of the words shared as caresses, and by a hundred different nuanced, fleeting aspects of expression within the shared situation. In our obsessive concern with the workings of our "big boy" rockets, these are the aspects of lovemaking that many of us do not even experience, any more than the judge experienced the color and pattern of the wallpaper in *The First Monday in October*. These are aspects that just don't register on the "target screens."

It is almost as if there is an exhaustive "control-room" countdown and "systems check" going on in our minds as we prepare for "launch"—which is exactly the image that Woody Allen used in his film. We are thrilled or concerned with the mechanics of "scoring" the target. Then the excitement that could have been directly transferred to us as open and expressively resonating bodies is lost in the workings of a series of parts that make up the mechanical body. In our masculine guise, we are part tank and part sky fortress, armed with its missile.

The word *magically* used above in describing the potential shared excitement between partners is not meant in any
sarcastic sense; there is a magic that can be created between
people as irrational distances disappear and the exact opposite movement of the flying boy takes place—a bringing
together that makes separation feel unreal.

Here again, the avoidance of vulnerability to pain creates
"hell worlds" of much greater pain. Our withdrawal into
the masculine missile model of sexuality means that the
debt incurred—past hurts of love—experienced through the
body which could be touched intimately and healed, instead
becomes a target of "scoring"—and, therefore, of further hurts. All people have experienced pain through sexuality; however, they can't be healed by a missile display. This
can only deepen the hurt, even if it is unconscious. Missile sexuality is a hostile interaction, even if both partners
have been taught that the ballistic display is a great thrill and
provides a "kick;" however, for his partner the masculine
launch also gives a "kick" in the sense of a blow dealt out.

In a culture that on the surface is obsessed with sexuality,
there is much pain involved in our sexual interactions that
goes publicly unacknowledged. Instead, such distanced
interactions are glamorized. For males, the price of the flying
boy identity is a loss of any truly intimately emotional sexual
sharing and being, despite the ever-growing arsenals and the
ability to "make a kill." This is a self-defeating path for us
males and a dangerous trajectory for our target-partners. This
way of experiencing sexuality leads to a confusion of sex and
violence.

In his discussion of why men love war, the connection
between sexuality and violence is palpable for Broyles. Each
man he knew discovered an "incredible intensity that war
brings to sex." If sexuality were not about the missile mentality, this would not be so. However, Broyles's description of
the meaning of sex shows a direct linkage between the two
for the masculine heroic mentality: "Sex is the weapon of life,

the shooting sperm sent like an army of guerrillas to penetrate the egg's defenses—the only victory that matters."[11]
Here, the sensibility of "scoring on the enemy" has been carried beyond the interpersonal to the biological sphere.

From the frustration and pain that must result from this
model of sexuality emerges a masculine resignation about
ever *reaching* the other through sex. If we are sincere in wanting to communicate deeper feelings through sexuality but are
caught in the masculine missile model of sexuality, we will
feel how this is a self-defeating gesture. Masculinity, in turn,
can recycle this pain and frustration into an ever more cava-
lier attitude about the sexual bombing run—the attitude that
"they're all just bimbos anyway." What can happen then is
frightening, and does happen every forty-three seconds in
this country: the male can literally use his penis as a missile
to violate the target, to rape the "enemy." Each severing of
the threads that tie the rapist to others does not lessen his
pain, however; it only leaves the pain more isolated within
him, drives him further into the distant sky, and makes him
more apt to find new targets. It is a vicious self-defeating
cycle and obviously one that is annihilating to others.

We will never truly deal with the sources of all the sexual
crimes in this country, from sexual abuse of children, the
elderly, rape of women, to the nightly millions of alienating
interactions between "lovers," until we deal with how we
men can regain fully human (that is to say, open and sensitive) bodies, abandoning our tank-bodies and disarming our
missile stockpiles. Changing attitudes is not sufficient. We
will have to alter our sense of our bodies.

At its deepest level, the symbolic appeal of the missile
involves the thrill of stoically accepting the return fire. Both
are intermixed: despairing of real contact, the masculine perpetrator enjoys the other's violation and also thrills to his
own, since it justifies the attack mode. We can think back on
the decades of cold war between the United States and the
USSR at its most ludicrous moments with our crazily escalat-

ing stockpile of missiles. Our countries seemed surreally locked into one of those schoolyard duels about "whose is longer." The ensuing threatened extinction of the planet with which we had to live was the surreality of distance: only when we are so distanced from what we lord over with our missiles can we seriously consider the insanity of destroying the globe without feeling. At that moment, we almost invite destruction as the ultimate jolt of affect that justifies our hostility.

The end of Ahab's tale gives us the feel of this insanity. Finally confronting the white whale, Ahab's harpoon does find its target. As the whale lurches forward in stricken panic, the line from the harpoon goes whizzing past Ahab, who clears its path but is somehow, in a "flying turn" of line, caught by the neck. He is dragged to his doom by the very whale he has harpooned. This is symbolic of the masculine hero's attack from on high: he doesn't see the lingering connections to the beings he has targeted. He doesn't realize the way in which his own neck is also "on the line" with those people he "scores on."

Desert Storm was a showcase of missile power and pride, at least as it was presented by the president and the military through the media. The attack on Iraq began during the night of January 16-17, 1991, as U.S. Navy specialists huddled over computer screens in several warships and entered targeting codes into the computers that fed the complex geographical data into Tomahawk Cruise missiles. In the opening salvo that night, nine warships fired fifty-two Tomahawk missiles and all but one hit their targets.[12] The total of Tomahawks fired against Iraq reached two hundred and sixteen after three days of the war. The Tomahawk runs on its own engine after its booster burns out, uses altitude-sensing radar for guidance, and finds its target by means of the on-board computer comparing the terrain with maps programmed in its memory (p. 166). These missiles achieved what the hero has always sought: a way to extend his will with accuracy over incredible stretches of distance and make an explosive impact on his target.

The spellbinding effect of this technological mastery met a deep psychological need in the American public, as did all the so-called "smart bombs" such as the Paveway, guided by the laser beams of the F-111F fighters and their own on-board computers. Seven percent of the bombs dropped on Iraq were of this self-guiding missile type—6,520 tons of the 88,500 tons dropped (p. 147)—but clearly these most fascinated the public. Perhaps most captivating were the SLAM missiles launched from the A-7E Corsair II planes from fifty miles away. Not only were they guided by their own computer navigational system, but they also sent a video image back to the pilot for guiding the missile even further toward its target (p. 146).

Here is the symbol perfected: the flying boy aloft at an immense distance, still seeing through his missile extension and in control until it actually impacts. These video images when they were broadcast on TV to the American public were spellbinding to many viewers. The emotional impact that many victims were being slaughtered seemed eerily lost in the dream of distance and control that the missile symbolizes. This intoxication only seemed to deepen when our Patriot missiles succeeded in shooting down many of Iraq's SCUD missiles. Now we could *really* dwell in the sky.

The military has transformed the dreams of the masculine warrior hero into material reality. This is dangerous because it feeds on fears that have been kept alive at the depths of the masculine soul for thousands of years. The mix of actual threat with dreaded fantasy makes it impossible at times to separate the practical exigencies of a situation from the repressed, disguised, self-destructive, and violent impulses long harbored within the male psyche. It also means that the boundaries of sexuality, warfare, violence, and a distanced way of controlling daily affairs become blurred.

For example, a politician may thrill at launching a

"sound bite" that is as distanced and manipulated as a missile and as explosive. Part of the thrill is sexual and violent, while part is the intoxication of control. New products are also "launched" into the market with their specific "target populations." They are constructed in such a way that their appeal will "take off" and "hit the mark" in ways that have nothing to do with their intrinsic value, but are only intended to make an impact on people. We have so many ways of "sending out"—which is the Latin root meaning of the "missile"—to make an impact. The symbolic boundaries of our personal and public lives are not as clear as we pretend, and the dreams of missile power of the flying boy often become the nightmares of those who live below him.

CHAPTER FOUR

The Briefing

The Masculine Fear of Words of Feeling

Declarations of Truth

All forms of language are also central to masculine defenses and hidden pain. The male identifies himself with the word: he is the keeper of the word, while females and the world are mute. This is the story we tell ourselves as men and that is told in the myths and fables of our tradition, yet we men are perhaps the least articulate creatures when it comes to speaking our hearts and putting into language what is at the core of life.

The male poets have put into language essential rhythms and insights into what it means to be a part of life as mortal, feeling, interdependent creatures. But the poets are those men who are "different," who don't fit the traditional male-gender identity. The usual use of language practiced by males is yet another example of a "power" that is a cover, a way to defend and avoid the heart of existence with both its pain and wonder.

At the great height to which the flying boy aspires lives the light. "The word" that the flying boy brings down from the mountain—that he strains to hear and write down for others listening to the eternal harmony of the spheres—is the message that has emerged from that light. The masculine mythic realm takes it as self-evident that this light is the light of reason, logic, and truth. The word, when it is enlightened by such truth, is our way of ordering, reflecting, and communicating within this world that higher light of the vertical realm.

This world down here can seem confusing, depending on what we focus on and how we speak about it—or at least that's how it seems from the distance of the flying boy. But with the power of the enlightened word, the masculine hero can draw validation from higher powers of truth to create a realm that is objective, lawlike, and well controlled. Plato made it clear, for example, that for all telling words there were corresponding "higher forms" that embodied the truth in the form of universal laws about everything. These pure forms were like the power of the sun above the visible world: there was a higher, purely rational truth of pure mind and spirit that illuminated this world, and the male was best able to capture some of its truth by climbing aloft through pure reason and logic. The images are all Plato's, and they have stuck, including the moralistic repetition of the term purity. Whether it is Jungian archetypal psychology or Freudian analysis, the masculine spirit is symbolized as the logos, the keeper of the law, the highest truth through the power of articulation, reason, and language.

The word in this scheme becomes a tool for securely passing along data about the world. For the masculine purpose of control, the word is not intrinsically magical: that ancient power of perhaps evoking the presence of wonder, of mystery, and of a sense of resonating intimacy with a befriending world is lost in the cry for a language that is easily definable, linear, and logical. Again, the same schematic applies: man, the speaker, makes his pronouncements from on high, bestowing names upon things as if they are greatly honored by being included in his sphere of influence. They can thereby pass from dumb, brute, inert material to the intelligibility and meaningfulness that emanates from man, the light-bringer. The world is down there for us flying boys to use, and our words themselves are like missiles sent out to impact on the world and blast into its brutely resistant nature so we can mold it to our bidding.

An alternative to this model of man the speaker confronting the dumb world is humans listening to the murmurings and the rustlings of the world, hearkening to its rhythms in such a way that we speak *with* the elements of the natural world that surround us. Many other cultures have felt they were in a dialogue with the natural world, including Native American peoples. This would challenge the masculine ego's belief that we are the self-creators of meaning, the propulsive force in the progress of our understanding. This enlightenment we bring to the world is supposed to proceed in a straight line onward and upward in puer trajectory. By contrast with this vision, the Taoist sense of the word is to use language to make evident its inability to fully capture the experience of the world. This approach invites us to hearken more closely to nonhuman communications and let go of the illusion that we can grasp reality through language. This is called the practice of *wu-yen*, of achieving "no-words." It suggests to people to watch and be silent and let the poetry of the world return to language to speak with us. Of course, the *Tao Te Ching* was written during one of the greatest outbreaks of warrior conquests and gratuitous massacres in the history of the world, and its verses were meant to be a challenge to this warrior way of being. It was meant to show a path of "letting go" and "letting be" and entering the "flow" of existence, its repeated metaphor. It is the Taoist who says upon climbing the mountain that he or she has "befriended" the mountain, not conquered it. It is also symbolically important that the *Tao* counsels its male leaders to descend to the "spirit of the valley," *ku-shen*, which is identified with a humble openness, rather than aspire for the proud heights as does the masculine hero.

Before we continue describing how the male gender identity deals with language, another story may give us an image to picture these concerns. One of the central tales of the cultural line from Plato to modern Europe-America is the myth of Oedipus. It is a story often told as a tale supposed to warn us not to fight some abstract notion of "fate"—in which most of us don't believe—and so is taken as a mere curiosity. Sometimes it is taken as a tale about the man who put up a good, tragic fight against these "higher powers," and in that sense Oedipus is also taken at least partly as a good masculine hero who got a bad deal. However, the myth is much more about a certain masculine conception of what words mean, how to speak to others, how to listen to them, how emotional relations are to be valued in comparison to objective concerns, and the role of reason in relation to emotion.

Prior to the famous portrayal of Oedipus in Sophocles's play, Oedipus becomes king of Thebes by defeating the Sphinx. A ferocious half-woman, half-lion creature, the Sphinx had challenged the population of Thebes to answer her riddle or die. The riddle was "What walks on four legs in the morning, two legs in the afternoon, and three in the evening?" The answer, of course, is "man," who crawls, walks, and uses a cane at different stages of life. The Sphinx had destroyed many of the young Theban men, who couldn't answer her riddle, but Oedipus had answered correctly and thereby defeated the Sphinx.

The king of Thebes had been Laos. Oedipus was his son, but had been abandoned by his father to die, because Laos had been frightened by the prophecy that he would be killed by his own son. This is how Oedipus came to be raised in Corinth and not know his true father. Unknowingly, Oedipus did indeed kill his father on the highway in a chivalric face-off with his father's rude drivers. When Laos did not return, Creon, his brother, ruled in his place. However, when his own son died after failing to defeat the Sphinx, Creon offered the throne as reward for anyone who could defeat her. Since

Jocasta, the former queen, was also offered as a reward, Oedipus fulfilled the other part of the prophecy by marrying and hence "lying" with his mother.

All of this, however, is background to where Sophocles begins relating the myth. As the play begins, there is a plague in Thebes, because the gods are displeased that Laos's killer has not been discovered or brought to justice. Oedipus is identified with Apollo, the sun god, the light bringer, and the source of truth. In fact, Oedipus sees himself as the one who will get rid of the Theban plague by solving the mystery of who is responsible for Laos's death. On one level, there is an obvious irony about Oedipus's factual ignorance, pursuing *himself* as the murderer, but the symbolic deeper ignorance as the tale unfolds of who he is and what his life is about is frightening—or at least should be—for most of the masculine ethos. Oedipus sees himself as a hero, one who can bring light: "Then once more I must bring what is dark to light."[1] He feels that he can uncover what is hidden, sort out the confused or mysterious, and keep working until the problem is solved. He feels confident in this ability because of his defeat of the Sphinx through guessing her riddle.

Now we come to the heart of the matter. If we look at how Oedipus lives his life as the hero, *we might wonder whether he did solve the riddle.* Certainly, he "solved" it as a verbal exercise: he gave the right answer. However, did he really understand what the answer meant? The possibility of two kinds of understanding—a merely verbal one, one that is merely "correct," or another that is a deeper taking to heart, a seeing in the nuances of one's situation, a putting to the test with others, a seeing of the emotional implications, and an ability to keep finding greater depths of meaning within the words spoken—is very much at issue with the masculine sense of language and truth.

To really solve the Sphinx's riddle requires more than just saying the word *man*. This riddle is life's primary one. To solve it in a deeper sense entails learning about the cycles of life and what they should mean to us. We would have to take to heart the waxing and waning of human powers and the subsequent need to accept the workings of larger forces in our lives. We would have to see the need to join others in community, since we are not self-sufficient except perhaps briefly at "noon." We would have to come to accept that no security is final. These meanings, contained in the fuller sense of the riddle, have not even been considered by Oedipus yet—supposedly many years after he has "solved the riddle." Yes, he mouthed the answer, but that is not the same as a deeper understanding of all the riddle has to say. Yes, Oedipus can manipulate words well and sort through facts, but this is not to fully use all that language has to offer. Besides, some riddles are not to be solved; they are to be kept for further feeling, wondering, musing—kept close to the heart—rather than going on the quest for the answer or seeking to merely win a contest. It is worth quoting Barth again: "The key to the treasure is the treasure."

Now Oedipus has a new riddle to solve: Who killed the king? He is already anticipating that he will again gain glory from a successful quest. In his search for the facts needed "to bring the light to the dark," he proceeds on a series of dialogues. The first is with Tiresias, the old, blind seer, who has often helped the city. Tiresias is able *to see by listening well*— by listening to the rustlings of the birds and hearing the nature of things. Oedipus becomes enraged when Tiresias tells him, "How dreadful knowledge of the truth can be,/ When there's no help in the truth" (p. 16). Tiresias is, of course, referring both to the facts of the case—he knows the king will be crushed if he discovers the truth—and also to his deeper understanding that truth, as the correct solution, as words that point only to an objective situation, is not always helpful in itself.

Oedipus can't bear this idea, nor does he really understand it. He responds by deciding that Tiresias is cold, unfeeling, and arrogant to not join in the hunt for the facts. Tiresias replies, "You call me unfeeling. If only you could see the nature of your own feelings . . ." (p. 17). Tiresias is right on many levels: Oedipus is not only factually ignorant, but he is also a stranger to himself and to his feelings. Tiresias tells Oedipus, "Bear your fate, and I'll bear mine. It is better so: trust what I say" (p. 16). However, Oedipus, like the line of heroes from Gilgamesh onward, is determined always to master whatever fate he has in the world. He calls Tiresias "ungracious" and "unhelpful" for saying this. He has no ability to sense the underlying concern and care that motivate Tiresias's words.

Weighing the objective facts and seeing only that Tiresias has not divulged the information he has, Oedipus increasingly condemns him, calling him worthless, witless, senseless, and mad. Tiresias keeps addressing his rage, but Oedipus can only answer, "Rage? Why not!" At one point, Tiresias actually does tell him that he—Oedipus—is the sought-after murderer, but he cannot even process the facts of the case because he is so emotionally addled. Instead, he taunts Tiresias: "You child of endless night! You cannot hurt me or any other man who sees the sun" (p. 20). This faith in seeing things, in grasping the truth of the sun, in aspiring toward control of the world that is supposed to be gained by knowing the world as a set of facts, is central to Oedipus's sense of self. Given his quest, Oedipus can only see Tiresias as a traitor, even though he has been true to Oedipus and a helper of the city throughout his long life.

It is interesting to look at the kind of understanding that Tiresias represents as compared to Oedipus. Tiresias presents a challenge to Oedipus that comes from outside the masculine rules. He is well suited to do this symbolically, since he is the only mortal to have been both a male and a female. Tiresias was out walking in the forest and saw two snakes copulating. Upon seeing this sight, he was transformed into a female and for seven years lived as a woman. Seven years later, while walking in the woods, he again saw snakes copulating and was transformed back into a male. He has become blind because one night Zeus and Hera were arguing about who had it better during sexual intercourse—a man or a woman. Since Tiresias was the only one who could give a firsthand comparison, he was called upon to settle the dispute. Hera was trying to show the tough lot of women and was infuriated when Tiresias stated that certainly women have the better of it in sexual intercourse. In her anger at his response, she blinded him.

However, although denied the literal light, the vision of objects, Tiresias has a deeper understanding and a deeper use of words than Oedipus, who deals only in literal, verbal truths. After he has been thoroughly abused by the king, Tiresias finally declares to Oedipus, "Listen to me. You mock my blindness, do you?/ But I say that you, with both your eyes, are blind:/ You cannot see the wretchedness of your life,/ Nor in whose house you live, no, nor with whom" (p. 21). As Sophocles's audience, we can listen to these words literally and smile knowingly that Oedipus isn't aware of all the objective facts of his history. However, there is a deeper level to what Tiresias is saying that addresses the threat that Sophocles presents about the emerging heroic masculine mentality.

If we think back to that scene in the movie, *The First Monday in October*, this is what the departing wife is trying to tell her unseeing and unfeeling husband, the Supreme Court justice. Despite all his power of reasoned discrimination in matters of the law, sensually, emotionally, and relationally he is just "not at home," not really "there." The distanced male doesn't really know his wife, his children, his friends, or his co-workers except as they fit into his scheme for meeting his own needs. He can say some objective things about them, but *who they really are* is something of which he is totally ignorant. Also, how things "really stand" in his house is probably as unknown to him as to the judge who is utterly amazed that his wife has been living in emotional isolation for the past quarter of a century. Finally, as we have seen throughout, the masculine identity is designed at its core to hide from "the wretchedness" of his own life rather than deal with the pain. The rest of the tale as told by Sophocles gives horrifying testimony to this level of Oedipus's ignorance or blindness.

Although to the audience it is obvious that Oedipus is angry, he believes his reaction to Tiresias's words is an objective judgment: Tiresias can only be a scoundrel and a traitor, and Creon, who sent for Tiresias, must also be a scoundrel and a traitor. Oedipus has judged the facts—namely that Tiresias didn't divulge information—and he doesn't want to see what motivates him or in what feeling relation they stand. Oedipus exclaims, "Am I to bear this from him? Damnation take you! Out of this place! Out of my sight!" (p. 22). Rather than stay in painful emotional confrontation, Tiresias is ordered out of sight (the ultimate threat).

As he is leaving, Tiresias tells Oedipus that being "a great man once at solving riddles" is the very cause of his problem: "It brought about your ruin" (p. 23). Those who watch or read this scene in Sophocles's representation of the myth know this is true on a factual level, but it is also true on the level that Oedipus has come to overestimate his power of rationality to grasp and conquer situations. This egoistic identification as solver-of-riddles has—as Tiresias rightly adds—made Oedipus "a blind man who has eyes now." His is the blindness of those who are out of contact, who are so distanced they are "out of touch," who are so barricaded within their tank bodies they don't feel and experience emotional nuances.

This blindness is most striking when Creon returns to find himself facing Oedipus's rage and judgment that he is a traitor. Yet Creon is not only Oedipus's uncle, unbeknownst to him, but also the man who awarded him the kingdom, helped him tirelessly for years, and never desired any honors other than the satisfaction of helping the kingdom. Creon is shocked by Oedipus's accusation that he suddenly desires to usurp the kingship and declares to him: "You do wrong when you take good for bad, bad men for good. A true friend thrown aside—why life itself is not more precious! In time you will know this well: For time, and time alone, will show the just man, though scoundrels are discovered in a day" (p. 30). This is a speech that Oedipus cannot hear, neither in how it is spoken nor in what it says.

The chorus hears Creon's words and, impressed with his concern, warns Oedipus against making "judgments too quickly." However, Oedipus can only think of how to "be quick to parry him" in verbal combat. Creon speaks as a friend and loyal advisor, but Oedipus only sees that he might "let this man win everything." Creon has tried to tell him how friends are only known through a long process of involvement and open exchange that takes place slowly over time. He warns Oedipus that without this ability he mistakes the deeper nature of men, seeing their actions only at face value, as if they were facts that could be tallied and computed. The chorus again tries to help Oedipus hear this warning by reminding him: "A friend so sworn should not be baited so, in blind malice, and without final proof" (p. 33). Oedipus is too out of touch with himself and others to even see his own malice toward Tiresias or Creon.

Oedipus uses language as a tool to get his job done, to measure the words of others as objective testimonies, and has no real idea who is his friend, who cares for him and who doesn't. Such understanding only comes from an open heart, from making connection with others and hearing the feeling tone of their words. This inability of Oedipus, and its importance for his eventual transformation from the distanced "light king" to a loving and virtuous man, becomes more striking as the tale proceeds. We will return to this after looking at the symbolic weight of this split between the verbal level and the level of experience Oedipus has imposed on his kingdom. Oedipus's problem with language is symbolic of the masculine problem with language.

A significant problem with the claim of the hero—whether he be political leader, warrior-king, scientific pioneer, philosopher-king, ship's captain, or whatever sort of ascending trailblazer—is his declaration that others must see that his words capture correctly some Holy Grail of truth. Joseph Campbell defines the hero as the one who gains access to a higher realm that has the answer to life's riddles. Despite Campbell's enthusiasm, there is a problem in the hero creating a split between the mundane world and his distanced realm from which his words supposedly originate. A situation ensues in which a hero leader can declare that loyal citizens like Tiresias and Creon are traitors or that death squads are "peacekeepers" or that a male sexual harasser is a "victim" while the victim is a "destroying witch." It is common that abusing fathers who beat their children, then sexually molest them, declare that they are loving fathers and that what they do is "not dirty."

The masculine scheme of claiming *the* truth—and a "higher one" at that—fits the flying boy's personal defenses seamlessly. If we are not ourselves reachable and our own relation to reality is itself distanced, having to be deciphered from afar, then a dangerous split opens up between the world of experience and the world that the flying boy *declares* to be the real world. Without the flying boy's distance and disconnection, claiming to cross a gap between reality and the words used to describe it would not be such a problem, because we could just look around together and check it out.

However, no one is going to be able to sit an Ahab down for a heart-to-heart talk about the pain of losing a leg, of disappointing a new, much younger bride (about whose satisfaction he is probably anxious), or even help him see the nature of the whales, people, and whaling voyages that are all around him. For Ahab, even though the waters are a few feet from the deck where he paces, even though one day he sees mother whales sporting lovingly and playfully with their calves as they surround the ship, even though there are examples of human goodness occurring in front of him on the *Pequod* (such as the day when Queequeg selflessly saves another crewman), these are distant sights with which he has no vital connection. No floods of feeling come over him from what he sees. Rather, it is like being inside an M1A1 Abrams tank or the command center of the destroyer firing a Tomahawk missile or the cockpit of an F-111 fighter facing computer screens that generate only blips representing the surrounding world in terms of potential targets labeled "enemy" or "non-enemy." What appears to these blockaded observers gets labeled in a limited language that is then self-enclosing.

Once pronounced, the terms of engagement are set. Certain words are admissible and certain ones are not, no matter what their potential relationship to the real world might be. So we can't really enter a dialogue with this hero/truth teller. This leaves a stunned public watching televised hearings and seeing the leaders of this country fight merely verbal battles with little connection to a shared reality. Instead, these masculine leaders parry one another, as if the only reality were in their words, which now have to be manipulated most craftily and skillfully. In the realm they've constructed, language use determines the constructed reality of the issues at hand. Reality itself is not accessible in this web of words.[2] They create a "world of words" with its own logic and possibilities. An industry has emerged of creating "spin" through hired "spin doctors": whatever actually happens can be "languaged forth" in such a way that the leaders in question were "right" in their assessment of the situation, even if the situation is discovered to be the opposite case in another ten minutes and calls for a totally new spin, a new verbal cloak.

The astonishing thing is the trick of the hero to make it seem apparently *obvious* that he has access to this higher light. He asserts that it is just a matter of facts that anyone can see. This, however, is not just masculine naivete—it's a lie. The hero knows on some level that he is making a leap across a gap to the mundane world. His belief in himself not only keeps his momentum going, but he feels he can power others into the same flight path. For his power to be complete, though, it must be absolute, so he denies he is being manipulative.

For example, in Ahab's encounter with Moby Dick, it is a pretty straightforward matter that he lost his leg by being mangled by the white whale. However, the emotional, spiritual, and psychological meaning of that event is not as obvious as Ahab claims. Is it true that the whale clipped Ahab's leg with malicious intent? Perhaps the whale didn't even know what it was doing. Perhaps it was just terrified. Perhaps it was trying to escape. Even if it were a malicious action, does this show that the whale somehow is connected to a larger maliciousness? Even if this is so, is it occasion for revenge? Or perhaps remorse? Or wonder? Or seeking human love?

Such questions are even more woven into the fabric of human relationships when we discuss social issues such as the meaning of the police beating of Rodney King in Los Angeles in 1991. Was the significance of the beating an act of anger, terror, intoxication with power, racially inspired hatred, or frustration with overwork? Or another question which riveted the country in the same year was the nature of the interaction between Anita Hill and Clarence Thomas. Harassment? Egoism? Insensitivity? Good humor? These are the kinds of questions millions of children and wives face every day in their own lives when they question the meaning of their father's abusive actions toward his family. If the masculine ego as leader declares, like Oedipus, that truth is obvious, just a matter of seeing the facts illuminated by words, isn't he trying to create a realm in which we are all trapped using words to "parry" each other? Isn't this a world in which the speaker is safe from really being open to the painful complexity of what is going on that could potentially deeply involve him? Doesn't this open a split between those seeking to give us the answers, and our richer, more complex shared experience? We end up with a frustrating juxtaposition of the words from on high and the mundane world to which they refer. The only real cement between them then seems to be the use of power. Oedipus is king, and declares Creon and Tiresias traitors, so they are traitors, since Oedipus has the power as king. This leaves Oedipus unreachable and others the targets of his use of words to impact upon them as he sees fit.

Empty Words

Words can be a way of moving into closer interconnection with others. However, then they are words spoken with an invitation to be further enunciated by and with others. This involves the speakers in probing, stumbling, listening, feeling, meditating, questioning, and spontaneous responding. Rather than announce slogans to one another, we would have to be open to incomplete utterings, open-ended suggestions, surprising exclamations, holding silent, and tuning in to the tone of the dialogue. This kind of communicating requires extending beyond the thought-out reactions, diving into depths, slowing down to really listen, being sensitive to rhythms, paying attention to the body's gestures, using imagination freely, risking sounding foolish, and, in general, opening to the feeling side of words. Yet we are almost never invited to do this, and we are almost never listened to in this way, for the masculine mentality of speech preparation— being pointed, forceful, organized, aggressive or at least assertive, well defended, planned for our objectives, linear, contained, controlled, clear, conducive to closure, and polished, if possible—is discouraging of engaging speech.

To be truly engaged with another in speech, throwing aside our particular trajectory in order to allow the other to move us in new directions distinctive to our interacting, is to find an avenue in which we can almost magically throw aside the boundaries of isolated existence and find a common place from which to experience the world. Whether there are boundaries of history, culture, experience, point of view, or differing purposes, if we really engage in using words to articulate fully the "private feelings" of each person, in an open-ended way in which translating terms will slowly be arrived at, then these feelings suddenly can be recognizable, palpable, and understandable by others. This is the special wonder of being human: words have an enchantment—what Mary Daly calls "the radiant power of words"[3] to "carry us beyond" the literal meaning of "meta-phor"—beyond fixed boundaries to a greater sense of "be-ing" as we participate in the dynamic unfolding of the world and others.

By carrying us beyond isolation, words can have the property of *helping increase the fluidity of the world*. When words are fluid, rigid boundaries dissolve, there is a give and take and distances are connected as part of the same tide, the same current: each being becomes just a moment or an eddy in a movement that circulates among all beings. This is in contrast to the masculine model we've described: at home in the heights, in an inaccessible control tower up high, darting down into reality, which is made up of beings who are objectified and made as fixed and defined as possible in order to be good targets. The word as a tool for keeping things in place, as a definer of boundaries, as a way of keeping track of things and of taking stock, keeps the long-distance, manipulative game of flying boys going. Words sketch out secure flight paths for efficient sorties. Words just provide further data for updating the target screens, while the interlocutors are safely screened behind their consoles in their cockpits.

In fairy tales, it is often the case that word formulas are given special properties to transform reality. The greatest magic is the power of the incantation to make someone appear or disappear. The magician or sorceress says "abracadabra" and whoosh! the sought-after spirit or person appears, becomes manifest, can now be spoken to and engaged. This is a telling symbol: words can be magical incantations to make people or spirits appear. The person who was a distant presence—not even really that, just an object, a nameless someone encountered several times at work or on the street or through friends—suddenly one night enters into a meaningful conversation and "pours their heart out," as we say. Suddenly, this other person appears before us as a real presence, takes shape, gains identity, can be felt, and experienced in his or her uniqueness. This person will never quite slip back into oblivion for us, the other person, nor will the connection that was opened between us ever be fully eradicated, although it needs to be renewed through further talks for the "spell" to keep working. The same is true for conjuring emotional realities. We can speak "from the heart" to others, and suddenly all can feel a certain emotion that has been conjured by the magic power of words. Language has this incantatory power in our everyday lives, without any fantastical happenings occurring.

It is just this kind of magic that is lost by using words for mere "briefings"—by sticking to the facts, informing others objectively, talking always about the world of getting tasks accomplished, and sticking to a planned program. Since this is the kind of talk that the masculine heroic promotes, such language use complements the denial of pain, the assumption of aerial height, the impermeability of the tank body, the logistics of "darting down" into the world to help insure the unreachability of the male so defended. In some sense, sticking with this minimal language use means the male may not even exist, may not be present in some very vital sense, when he is sought out. Instead, there is only an . . . "abracadabra". . . poof! where a person could be!

The masculine use of words is often a very pointed attempt to become absent. Just as I was writing this chapter, two friends of mine split up their marriage after trying to keep it going for almost a decade. They have a two-year-old daughter. The night after he helped his wife move out, I went out to dinner with the husband. He was in agony, but he proceeded in a calm, cheerful manner to discuss with the other male at dinner football, soccer, baseball, the major leagues, the minor leagues, and his own high school career for approximately three hours without a moment's break. It was a virtuoso performance of using words as a shield from the pain of reality.

Certainly, there is a place for such defenses. Unfortunately for this man—and for millions of others in this country—this is an addictive, unrelenting posture, and his wife has left him for the very reason that she can't find him. Emotionally, he is in the desert beyond any calls to come home. Whether he is discussing cars, sports, computers, the stock market, plumbing, or whatever, the masculine ego has a stock of words as shields to pull out in order to provide an endless, circling path above and beyond in conversation—a path that keeps him safely out of reach.

All these factors have to do with an issue that has raged recently as a result of the men's movement, and particularly in response to Robert Bly's *Iron John* and his workshops: the "absent father." Bly would have us blame the post-Industrial Revolution environment that has taken the father out of the home and away to either factory or office for creating an absence in the lives of children. Bly asserts that as this trend continued, men were also engaged in tasks that could not be shared with children. Father would return home spent and with little to share with his children, instead of working with his sons and showing them skills that they could engage in together. This shared work, he adds, was once a vehicle of initiation into the sphere of the father.

I think this tale, although very appealing to males, is only another example of the male gender strategy that we have seen: the avoidance of connection, rather than being acknowledged as our own doing, is projected onto external forces or persons as the objects of hostility. We can blame History, Factory, and Office. It is not history or the office or economic conditions that are the source of this painful disconnection between fathers and sons, nor between fathers and the rest of their families and friends; *it is we males ourselves who are to blame.* This is not a new problem as Bly and others in the men's movement would have us believe. It is at the very core of a tradition we have been following for several thousand years with the rise of the warrior-hero and his impact as a model for the male psyche. He is "absent." He is "not here." We cannot live at an emotional distance above and beyond and still be here for our sons, daughters, mates, families, or friends.

The Industrial Revolution did not take away the son's father: he was never there from the beginning—from the historical beginning of the warrior-hero mentality and from the first instant of each son's life. Bly and those who lament the lost age of father and son's laboring together are romanticizing a rather arduous past that did not miraculously allow men as fathers to be emotionally open. During that time, they were under even greater stress than today, with greater economic and social duress. The shared laboring that went on was not necessarily a labor of love—at least not love expressed in any open and nourishing way. Certainly there were loving fathers and fathers who were very open and emotionally vulnerable, just as there are today. However, the general model for being a man was not more nourishing toward sons and other human beings.

The father's absence is not a matter of physical absence; it is a matter of *emotional* absence, an inaccessibility beyond barriers and at a distance. The infant can feel at the beginning of its life whether its father has slipped into a fear of open vulnerability. To be absent is at the heart of the male legacy.

In some sense, this has not been all bad for sons and daughters: children, as all human beings, need presence, loving support, and some room in which to grow, some absence. Most social systems during the rule of this masculine gender identity have unequally given to the mother all the presence and to the father the absence. However, even if there is some compensation in the overall system, assigning to males and females unbalanced roles is damaging to all involved. Each gets to act out only incomplete parts of being human.

The father's absence is felt, yet it is contradicted by the words he uses. He gives us words that betoken love, yet they seem like empty promises. We expect to be held, caressed, and nurtured, but these things are short-circuited whenever males retreat into their armor. The real masculine hero has never been very good with words, and maybe this is fortunate. The words he does speak set up an opposition between the hunger for love from fathers that Bly discusses—a hunger that hurts inside the body—and the words that are used as a way of avoiding contact. When we are disappointed that the words lead to no real contact, it leaves us distrusting that words can be magical ways of finding others. Or it can lead to believing that words are never any more than an unfair game to be used to manipulate. Mostly, we expect the father to be silent when words are needed as emotional openings.

To see a little more deeply into the ties between the masculine attitude toward emotions, the use of language, ways of understanding ourselves and others, and the lack of male presence, let's return to Sophocles's presentation of the myth of Oedipus at the point at which we left him. Oedipus has banished Creon rather than having him killed for being a traitor, but as Creon says of Oedipus: "Ugly in yielding, as you were ugly in rage! Natures like yours chiefly torment themselves" (p. 34). Oedipus's fleeing from contact from others has made him a violent, raging man, but this is only self-laceration in the end.

Now Oedipus begins to suspect that he is the murderer of Laos. However, a messenger arrives from Corinth to tell him that his supposed father, Polybus, has died. The factual irony, of course, is that the king and queen of Corinth were not his real parents. But what is most telling about this scene is Oedipus's emotional reaction. Jocasta, his wife and mother,

tells him that he no longer need fear the prophecy that he
would kill his father, since his father has died a natural death,
but Oedipus's reaction is revealing:

> Jocasta: From now on never think of those things
>   again.
> Oedipus: And yet—must I not fear my mother's
>   bed?
> Jocasta: Why should anyone in this world be
>   afraid, since Fate rules us and nothing can be
>   foreseen? A man should live only for the
>   present day. Have no more fear of sleeping
>   with your mother: How many men, in dreams,
>   have lain with their mothers! No reasonable
>   man is troubled by such things.
> Oedipus: That is true; only—if only my mother
>   were not still alive! But she is alive. I cannot
>   help my dread. (p. 49)

Again, there is the irony on a factual level that Oedipus is
doing exactly what he fears, sleeping with his mother, without knowing it. However, this passage also expresses an attitude toward emotions that Oedipus, at this stage in his life,
can't fathom. Jocasta is trying to make him see that emotions,
fantasies, impulses, and the so-called irrational side of life are
not fearsome. Just because one feels certain things, one
doesn't necessarily have to act on them; they can just be felt.
For Oedipus, however, they are blind forces, these feelings,
these passions which can just sweep over a person, against
which there is no defense other than avoiding the situations
in which they can be felt. Somehow, Oedipus fears he has so
little control over his passions that he would be swept up and
carry his mother off to bed if such an urge occurred.

Oedipus conceives of emotions as forces in need of control, forces that might compel us to action we might find
objectionable if we were not under their spell. This dread of
feeling maintains Oedipus as the king of control, which

means he is distanced from all people, including himself. This fear of emotion is indicative of heroic isolation. Freud, in reading these lines of *Oedipus Rex*, saw in them the validation for his theory of seething, repressed, unconscious drives. However, the play actually implies the distrust of even those emotions that are consciously known—as if all emotions were unruly forces for the masculine ego to contend with. The possibility that there are unconscious emotions only adds to the masculine fear of the emotional life. Our need for control would only feed the reservoir of emotion that is pushed out of consciousness and add to that pathology that interests Freud—a vicious cycle. This may happen to us, rather than dealing completely with conscious emotion. Many of us men do become more like the Freudian model of human psychology because we become so unknown to ourselves. Unable to face our emotional life, we relegate much of our being to the unconscious.

As the play's events proceed, the facts start to be revealed and Jocasta realizes what actually is the case. She asks Oedipus to stop the quest for the objective truth of the situation, realizing it will not help anyone and will be hurtful to all involved: "For God's love, let us have no more questioning! Is your life nothing to you? My own is pain enough to bear" (p. 55). However, Oedipus is unable to hear Jocasta. He assumes that she is worried about the fact that it might be discovered in the inquiry that he is not a "blue-blood," and that she is afraid her status will be tarnished: "You need not worry. Suppose my mother a slave, and born of slaves: no baseness can touch you" (p. 56).

Oedipus persists in being tone-deaf to Jocasta's sense of despair and concern for both of them and the family. His declaration could well stand as a motto for his life: "I will not listen: the truth must be made known." He is not really capable of listening to emotions and must stay on his quest for the solution to the riddle.

When Jocasta tells him that "everything that I say is for

your own good," he persists in not hearing her true concern
for him. The most chilling moment in the entire myth occurs
in the next instant, when Jocasta, Oedipus's mother, wife,
mate, partner, friend—how much closer could one be with
another human being?—falls into despair. But Oedipus
declares, "Go one of you, and bring the shepherd here. Let us
leave this woman to brag of her royal name" (p. 55). He
doesn't feel her emotions at all. He discounts her as caught in
petty concerns, making a stock judgment from stereotypes
about women. Jocasta sees this and departs with the words,
"Ah, miserable! That is the only word I have for you now.
That is the only word that I can ever have" (p. 56).

The chorus, who represent what one would think the
average human is capable of thinking, feeling, and interpret-
ing, is very concerned about Jocasta and upset at her mood:
"Why has she left us, Oedipus? Why has she gone in such a
passion of sorrow? I fear this silence: Something dreadful
may come of it" (p. 56). Yet Oedipus, who should be so close
to this woman, still has not the slightest emotional inkling of
what Jocasta is feeling—it's just not available within the limits of his target-screen mentality. His last comment is truly
horrific: "Let it come! However base my birth, I must know
about it. The Queen, like a woman, is perhaps ashamed to
think of my low origin. But I am a child of Luck; I cannot be
dishonored" (p. 56). With his emotional barriers, his detached
judgments made according to his practical concerns, he has
been emotionally blind to Jocasta—and she has gone into the
palace accompanied by his mockery! Emotionally abandoned
by him, she hangs herself.

Yes, Oedipus, was "fated" to kill his father and sleep with
his mother, but he had choices about how to live out that life.
There are factors beyond our control for all of us—symbolically represented by "fate"—but how do we enter into relationship with them? The masculine ethos concentrates
on results, not on the quality of the process, not on the "how"
one lives. For Oedipus, a large part of how he could have

lived a better life was in how he communicated with others. He did not have to be cruel, callous, rageful, and hurtful in what he said to Creon, Tiresias, and Jocasta. For example, Oedipus and Jocasta could have gone into the palace together and painfully explored all their feelings together and devised some emotionally creative way to deal with these events. But this is beyond the ken of the masculine hero, riding his steed alone, emotionally blocked off, and intent on winning the day.

Oedipus's last action in this heroic mode is the punishment he inflicts upon himself. After the facts are revealed that he has killed Laos and that Jocasta was his mother as well as his wife, he discovers that Jocasta has hung herself. Oedipus takes the brooches from her gown and pounds out his eyes, blaming his own eyes for his previous blindness. Again, he makes a rageful and vengeful judgment that masks something deeper. He inflicts terrible pain on himself, but the source of the problem is a deeper pain, and one he will face slowly over the next twenty years. It is an emotional blindness that plagues him. As yet, he has no words to explore or express emotions. Without the words, it's difficult to know what we feel.

The masculine defense against emotional blindness is to retreat further into blindness. For the hero whose lack of hearkening to feeling tones, whose censoring of emotional expression has created pain, the response is to communicate even less. Oedipus has both impulses immediately: "If I could have stifled my hearing at its source, I would have done it and made all this body a tight cell of misery, blank to light and sound: So I should have been safe in a dark agony beyond all recollection" (p. 71). To do this would only be to make more extreme the usual masculine condition, which masks its "dark agony." Striking out his eyes is to rage against something objective rather than to take the deeper, fuller emotional responsibility for his way of approaching life.

However, in the last moments of this play, we see an inkling of what Oedipus will start to achieve on his long path to Colonus. Now stripped of kingship and citizenship, he wanders as a blind beggar rather than as the hero. Even before he has left Thebes, we see his first small but significant act of emotional apprehension by *listening to the tone of the words used* by the chorus as they address him. He can feel their concern and expresses his appreciation:

> Ah dear friend
> Are you faithful even yet, you alone?
> Are you still standing near me, will you stay
>   here,
> Patient, to care for the blind?
>   The blind man!
> Yet even blind I know who it is attends me,
> By the voices tone—
> Though my new darkness hide the comforter (p. 69).

It has taken his world being smashed, his becoming an outcast, and his being put in a physically dependent position, but suddenly—stripped of his usual masculine heroic roles and capabilities—Oedipus notices the emotional tone of those around him, listens for friends, and starts to appreciate what caring means. The other picture that Sophocles gives of Oedipus twenty years later, in *Oedipus at Colonus*, is instructive as we move into the next section of the book to see where men can turn to find resources for blossoming emotionally— within some aspects of male gender identities that have been ignored or misinterpreted. Oedipus's distrust of emotion and his subsequent flight to a rationally controlled distance from others allow us to see the motivating source for his tone-deaf objective use of language and its obsession with speaking only about the "facts."

It is important to understand that this aspect of masculine defenses, this deployment of words, also played into the enormous hidden appeal of Desert Storm as presented to us by the media, the military, and our government. The Gulf War was unique both in how much of it was transmitted directly for immediate viewing to the public and for its briefing system set up by the Pentagon and General Schwarzkopf to guarantee military control of the news. In the Gulf War, the briefings were given and questions fielded by general officers directly involved in the direction of the war. The Pentagon briefings were usually opened by Louis A. Williams, U.S. Assistant Secretary of Defense for Public Affairs, who had worked in radio and television before going to Washington. The remainder of the daily briefing was usually conducted by Army Lieutenant General Thomas Kelly, director of operations for the Joint Chiefs of Staff, along with Rear Admiral Michael McConnell, head of intelligence for the joint staff. In Riyadh, Saudi Arabia, there were also regular briefings, at first by a number of officers but then later by Marine Brigadier General Richard (Butch) Neal.[4]

The briefings presented the war as a set of statistics, facts, and logistical problems. It was portrayed as an objective situation to be articulated to the public with clarity, little speculation, no emotion, and without discussion of its larger meaning. Even its scope was presented as if the world were viewed only within the strict confines set up by targeting screens. Everything else was neither seen nor discussed. There was a "screened" (with both senses of that word intended) presentation that gave the impression of being an open coverage of the war, while actually it was a strict censorship of reporting. The reporters were pooled, and the movement of journalists and photographers was restricted and required a military escort. Although the television screens displayed images of smart bombs making direct hits on targets, no misses were shown, even though requested by the press. Also, for more than two months after the end of the war, Army censors would not release the thousands of battlefield photos (pp. 159-60).

The masculine gender identity's sense of speech as

focused on a certain task, objective in nature, adequately conveyed by facts and statistics, and not to be broached by questions of emotion, was maintained with a precision rivaling the performance of the smart bombs—precision bombing and precision wording. Actually, one could make a case that the use of language and its control during Desert Storm was another fabulously effective "air war," not only controlling the airwaves but also successfully targeting a constant barrage of words used as missiles to knock out any resistance to the heroic quest.

The briefing is a use of language that emphasizes a controlled, packaged, noninteractive, nonexploratory sending of messages about performance and facts sent out into the world that says little about people's felt relation with those events, nor does it open the world to wonder or people to transformation. The briefing may be necessary at times, but as an ongoing way to use language, it violates possibilities of deeper communication.

As Creon says to Oedipus, the kind of communication that deepens relatedness to others or to the natural world takes a long time. It takes a long time because it is gradual, has to be enacted in myriad ways, indirectly accumulates, moves at a pace that allows for saturation, transforms the people involved in the dialogue, speaks through the unfolding of emotional patterns, and calls for a working with language to find ways to express what is unique in the relationship. The briefing is just that: a cutting off of all those slowly elongated strands of communication and relation, a cutting short the time needed for real communing through language, a cutting off of give and take to give priority to a bombardment with words.

These comments on language should be applied to this book, a work of language. The idea of this book is not to bombard the masculine with words, to see our gender identity from a distance as some objective fact to be condemned. Part of the problem with the masculine language use is that it makes any dialogue difficult—even the dialogue with our-selves that is necessary to make contact with ourselves in an intimate way that makes transformation possible. I was shocked by one of the therapists I saw in my twenties who told me at the end of our year together that, despite being thoughtful, despite being a philosopher who always dis-cussed issues, until this point in my life I had not been an introspective person at all.

A key use of language that the masculine heroic identity has blocked is that of articulating our responsibility. With that in mind, I fear that these chapters could be taken as "male bashing" if read by men in a certain masculine frame of mind. If words are only missiles, and if they are only good for targeting enemies, then to turn them critically upon our-selves will be seen as just self-destructive and as violating as Oedipus's gouging out his eyes. Perhaps this is part of the reason why the masculine heroic ego has been so loathe to talk about itself, to undertake introspective self-critique, and why it feels so attacked by others wanting to enter into a crit-ical dialogue about the "male inner workings."

However, if taking responsibility is a way of gaining the ability to respond, then in this case, for us males to own up to the shortcomings of our identities and deeds would be a way of responding to ourselves. Rather than being locked in cer-tain patterns of behavior, certain ways of seeing ourselves, we could be free to respond to our own feelings in new ways: to play with our identity instead of having to defend, defend, defend. Then words could be rejoined with feelings as a means of exploring ourselves and expanding our presence in the world. Then those who do use words with feeling would no longer have to be targeted as threats, which calls for retal-iatory strikes with our missile words.

PART TWO

Some Forgotten
Male Oases

CHAPTER FIVE

Letting Be, Finding Other Worlds, and Celebrating Interconnection

Mastering Our Fate versus Letting Be

It is difficult to see how we males can find our way back to Earth from the inner psychic heights to which we've soared, protected by armor, aiming our missiles at the world, and issuing briefings. However, it is the contention of the rest of this book that there are many other images of maleness in history, in other cultures, and even within our current society that are trailmarkers of this path back. These images, stories, and alternative notions to masculinity are often forgotten or go unnoticed. Sometimes they are fragmentary and need to be gathered together and given a coherent context.

It is interesting that the myth of Oedipus, to which many of us were exposed in high school, is usually presented as the hero's tragedy—as if that were the whole tale. We read *Oedipus Rex* or are told the part of the myth up to Oedipus's downfall. The lesson seems to be that we must accept the hero's life even while knowing that it may lead us to tragedy. Part of the hero's legacy, after all, is that sometimes he must fight against impossible odds but that this does not make him less a hero. It is the strong, bold, and unflinching way he fights his challenge that renders him a hero. However, in our retelling of the myth in this book, we have seen how the heroic stance as embodied by Oedipus is actually self-defeating and can only lead to self-destruction and hurting others. Whether we see Oedipus as a hero who is flawed in some way or as part of a heroic tradition that is itself flawed, we have not yet explored the whole idea of the hero and whether other notions could take its place. So let us see what the rest of this hero's story tells us and then see whether it helps us find another kind of model for heroes.

There is another part of the myth of Oedipus—about his last days—that Sophocles actually wrote first. In it, Oedipus ends his life in a far different way than the heroic way he began it. The older Oedipus in *Oedipus at Colonus* presents many different values than those espoused by the younger heroic Oedipus. These other values and ways of behaving are important indicators of where we men must go in order to leave our addiction to heights, distance, tanklike barriers, and screening words.

It is also important to examine the conflict between the first and second part of the Oedipus myth, because in them we may also see that the issues raised are still being played out on our equivalent of the Athens stage—in our current Hollywood box office hits. Like the Athenian plays, our movies articulate the tensions within our society. We are in the midst of a time that is questioning masculinity and its heroic values, and the messages we are receiving from our culture are quite conflicting. I hope we can see this as a conflict we already recognize from a long history—and one with a creative resolution that we seem to have forgotten.

In the play about the end of his life, Oedipus comes to the grove at Colonus after twenty years of wandering as a beggar with his daughter, Antigone. He has been exiled from the kingdom after his downfall. As the murderer of his father, husband of his mother, and a self-inflicted blind man, he has been summarily dismissed from his city with only his one loyal daughter to accompany him. The fact that, after twenty years of wandering and living hand to mouth, they come to a grove of Dionysus is significant. Dionysus symbolizes the emotions, the joining with others, the giving up of control—all the opposites of the heroic Apollo, the god with whom the young heroic Oedipus was identified. Coming to this spot marks Oedipus's psychic movement away from Apollo's sense of the hero as the individualistic, rational, light-bringing leader.

At the beginning of Sophocles's play, Oedipus immediately announces a rather startling revelation: rather than being miserable as a blind beggar, he declares: "Suffering and time, vast time, have been instructors in contentment, which kingliness teaches too" (p. 82). Oedipus has learned to learn from pain rather than avoid it. Suffering has not embittered him, nor has it weakened or dispirited him; neither has the passage of time, which has robbed his youth and rendered him a rather physically feeble older man. Quite to the contrary, now Oedipus claims that his pain has taught him contentment. He never before had been contented, since he saw life's pains as challenges to be overcome by his heroism. Here, at Colonus, he sees that there is no reason that kingliness or even being a hero could not have taught him the same lesson, if he could have been open and vulnerable in that position. However, Oedipus had clung rigidly to the attributes of kingliness and heroism as a way of hiding from these painful lessons—as is the case for those of us who cling to the masculine ego. It took cataclysmic losses for Oedipus to be transformed. How pain, how "suffering and time," can teach contentment has to be interpreted from the play by looking at how Oedipus now understands his identity, how it leads him to behave, and what it causes him to value. These images can start us looking in another direction for a more responsive and happier male identity. We may also find they are issues with which we are currently grappling.

One of Oedipus's first statements in this play is to suggest to his daughter that they pause and wait "and take our cue from what we hear." To listen to others—to be open and responsive—instead of blazing the path according to his own opinion has become part of Oedipus's new stance toward finding his way. He is told that he should have had more respect for this grove as the home of the Furies, the three left-over figures from the older Goddess tradition. These figures are not comely creatures. They, like Oedipus, are of foreboding appearance. They are intended to call to mind past suffering, just as Oedipus himself has become such a figure for others.

The Furies are tall, dark, relentless women whose heads are ringed with serpents. They are obviously remnants of the older tradition of the Triple Goddess—the virgin, mother, and crone—who for thousands of years symbolized the natural cycles of the Earth. Now that the warrior paradigm of excellence has usurped the message of the Goddess, the Furies have been incorporated into the newer Olympian spiritual scheme as avenging spirits of the older tradition. These female demons plague persons who have not made expiation for past transgressions, especially against family and mother. Oedipus prays to these goddesses for guidance. In addressing them as "goddesses," he is implicitly recognizing an older sense of values he had forgotten as the newer masculine hero—the values of belonging, of cherishing those with whom we are bonded, and of the divinity of Mother Earth. Earlier in his obsession with defeating heroic challenges, he had no sensitivity to his mother and lover, friend and uncle, elders and community. He had betrayed an unassailable distance from these summons.

Throughout this play, however, Oedipus seeks the advice and wisdom of others. This is perhaps best summed up in his statement to Antigone: "Lead me on, then, child, to where we may speak or listen respectfully;/ Let us not fight necessity" (p. 91). This is quite a change from the man of the heroic mold determined to beat necessity and heed only his own insights.

In the twenty years that have passed, now it is Polyneices and Eteocles (the two sons of Oedipus) and Creon who have taken over the heroic masculine roles and are obsessed with glory and power. They are fighting for leadership of Thebes. Each has become defensive, aggressive, and unyielding. They have led their people into civil war. Polyneices and Creon want Oedipus as a good-luck charm for their side of the battle against Eteocles, because they have heard that Oedipus in his transformed state is now honored by the gods. However, typical of the distanced hero-warrior, they merely see Oedipus as a tool for their designs. They have no real understanding of the ways in which he has changed and why he is to be honored. Any real communication with them is futile.

Now it is Oedipus who provides a contrast to these arrogant hero-warriors. As often as he refused to listen to others when he was a young hero-in-charge, Oedipus now constantly seeks to confer with others. When he inadvertently offends the rites, he asks of the chorus, "Dear friend! I'll do whatever you advise," and then asks further, "In what way should I do so? Tell me, friends?" (p. 105). This concern for the feelings and ideas of others is echoed in the manner of Theseus, who demonstrates that a strong leader can also be humble and open.

The key moment for this transformed Oedipus occurs when Polyneices wants to speak with him, which Oedipus knows will actually be only an abusive attempt to coerce him to fit Polyneices's greedy plans. Oedipus doesn't want to see him, yet he listens to Antigone and Theseus. They confront him about his attitude toward emotions in a way that echoes Jocasta's speech to him twenty years earlier:

> Oedipus: Nothing could be more painful than to listen
>   to him.
> Theseus: But why? Is it not possible to listen
>   Without doing anything you need not do?
>   Why should it distress you so to hear him?
> Oedipus: My lord, even his voice is hateful.

Don't overrule me; don't make me yield in this!
Theseus: But now consider if you are not obliged
   To do so by his supplication here:
   Perhaps you have a duty to the god.
Antigone: Father: listen to me, even if I am young.
   Allow this man to satisfy his conscience
   And give the gods whatever he thinks their due.
   And let our brother come here, for my sake.
   Don't be afraid: he will not throw you off
   In your resolve, nor speak offensively.
   What is the harm in hearing what he says?
   . . . Other men have bad sons,
   And other men are swift to anger: yet
   They will accept advice, they will be swayed
   By their friends pleading, even against
      their nature.
   . . . Ah, yield to us! If our request is just,
   We need not, surely, be importunate;
   And you, to whom I have not been hard,
   Should not be obdurate with me!
Oedipus: Child, your talk wins you a pleasure
   That will be a pain for me. If you have set
   Your heart on it, so be it. (pp. 144-5)

Not only does Oedipus change his mind about something that he initially felt he could not even bear to discuss, but he has to confront his underlying attitude about emotion. Again, he is afraid that his anger will be an uncontrollable force that will sweep him into actions he will regret. Antigone, like Jocasta before her, explains how all people feel these irrational urges and emotional pains, but how if they stay in touch with the larger context of their lives—those who care about them and their commitments in the world—these other forces will help guide them to deal with their emotions more responsibly and creatively.

     We do not have to stand guard over ourselves and fight our own feelings if we are not fortresses. Only if we stay in our fortress defended against emotional vulnerability do these emotions paradoxically take on a force that becomes uncontrollable. Traditional masculinity involves a self-defeating prophecy: in fear of the power of emotion, the heroic ego steels itself and avoids the threat, which is exactly what gives the emotions this increased power to overwhelm.

This time Oedipus chooses to stay open and in dialogue. He sees his son, who indeed is arrogant, callous, hurtful, and altogether infuriating. However, Oedipus doesn't shy away from the pain his son inflicts and deals as well with this hurtfulness as anyone could. He is able to respond both emotionally and rationally to express the error of his son's ways— without losing his focus on who he has become and how he wants to conduct himself. It is evident that he is empowered and able to do this as part of a community of friends and loved ones, from whom he draws strength, direction, and courage.

Oedipus insists throughout the play that he has found contentment. How this is possible is made clear in the last scene of his life. As he is about to die, he shares a tearful farewell with his two daughters, saying: "You shall no longer bear the burden of taking care of me—I know it was hard, my children./And yet one word frees us from all the weight and pain of life:/That word is love. Never shall you have more than you have had from me" (pp. 161-2). Oedipus has come to value human connection above all else, and that has allowed him to become another sort of person. It is the quality of his relationship with his daughters that has made his beggar's life more rewarding than a king's. He and his daughters have come to communicate openly, to work together, and to use their relationship to encounter others together creatively. This is the kind of vision Oedipus lacked as king. It is the kind of vision all masculine heroes lack, insofar as they think the victory over obstacles is the essence of life. We may improve the empty lives of those we love with more things obtained but at the same time leave them miserable, not knowing us or sharing in our feelings.

With this new vision, although literally blind, Oedipus

leads all the others to the spot where the gods give him the honor of being directly whisked into "the beyond." There is a lesson here, too, for the masculine spirit: it is only when Oedipus gives up his pretensions to soar like the gods, to earn glory, that he indeed in some way achieves glory. Perhaps the puer spirit must learn that the transcendence it seeks cannot be produced directly or deliberately as a product of will and determination, but only comes about indirectly as a result of other commitments to the mundane life here on Earth with others.

Of course, this is the theme—accepting hurtful events that are beyond our control—for which Oedipus is most known. However, the image usually conjured is of the young Oedipus *forced* to angrily and despairingly accept fate. In the context of heroic masculinity, coming to accept "fate" is to abandon the hero's challenge. The hero fights the inevitable, whether it's Gilgamesh being unable to accept the death of Enkidu, the protagonist of *Fitzcaraldo* who will bring opera to the jungles of South America even if the supply boat has to be carried over mountains, or Hercules going down to fight the power of death in the underworld. Conversely, in his setbacks, Oedipus gradually finds the ways to allow his new experiences to transform him.

Sophocles was writing at a time in which the warrior mentality, the masculine desire to ascend to the heavens—to turn away from vulnerable embodiment and emotion—was still in tension with a Goddess-nature tradition that stressed connection, cycle, and openness to the Earth spirit. He exemplifys well the dangers of going too far with the new rational, distanced, and intended control of the Earth, others, and oneself.

Oedipus has haunted the deeper reaches of the male psyche for thousands of years. Freud thought this power to haunt males was generated by a conflicted love of the mother and hostility toward the father—postulating the specters before which the young masculine consciousness and uncon-

sciousness must shudder: the engulfing mother and the cas-
trating father. This again is a heroically masculine reading of
the meaning of the myth. It assumes that the task of maturing
is to separate from the mother, from the Earth, and from too
much intimacy with others—as if a man might otherwise be
"engulfed" by connectedness. It posits a competitive relationship between father and son, which is easy enough to create
through the dictates of masculinity, but is not the only possible relationship between fathers and sons.

I would like to propose another reading of why Oedipus
has so ominously and mysteriously plagued the masculine
psyche. I believe Oedipus represents the ultimate threat to all
of us males insofar as we become too caught up in the hero-
warrior-leader mentality—the danger that we will *lacerate*
ourselves, not by gouging out our eyes, but rather *by cutting
ourselves off from life*. Here is another displacement of fear and
responsibility: we males know who cuts off our life, our true
flowering maleness. It is not the Father wielding a blade
threatening to cut off our penises, as Freud put it—but it is
we, ourselves, insofar as we leave our lives behind to enter
some unreachable place.

The older Oedipus has given us images of general directions to move away from our heroic mode and back toward
the Earth, toward the fullness of life in interaction. Before we
move on to more specific images of how we can turn away
from the masculine mode, it is important to see how these
issues are very much alive in our world of today. As Athens
had its yearly competition to crown the creators of the best
plays, so we too have our Academy Awards for our best
films of the year.

In 1993, in the midst of public questioning whether traditional masculinity is the proper paradigm for males, the "Best
Picture" and "Best Director" awards were given to *The Unforgiven* and Clint Eastwood. This 1992 film and its director were widely publicized and commented upon as having
seriously questioned the heroic ethos epitomized by "the

Western." Of course, Clint Eastwood is a symbol for the popular culture of masculinity itself. During a lifetime playing roles as cowboys, hard-bitten detectives, and macho heroes of all sorts, he has become the "John Wayne"—the tough-as-nails champion—for a new generation. His famous *Dirty Harry* line, "Make my day"—a dare to enemies to challenge him and be killed—has even been quoted by presidents.

The Unforgiven has been seen by commentators and critics as part of the phenomenon of 1992-93 in which the macho President Bush was replaced by the "softer male," Bill Clinton. The film was seen as part of popular culture's entertaining the sight of the new president and vice-president warmly embracing on the stages at their rallies—of men giving up the old, hard, distant masculine persona.

The film begins with the mutilation of a prostitute, in response to the oldest of masculine affronts: the customer's penis length has been found humorously small. The woman receives no justice; only the owner of the brothel is to have his "investment" reimbursed by the offenders forfeiting to him some of their ponies, since the mutilated whore will no longer generate profits. The town sheriff, the saloon owner, and the town itself are all complicit in the further degradation of the whores. Despite the opposition, the whores try to gain justice by hiring killers to punish the offenders, but they are initially thwarted by the brutal sheriff and the saloon owner.

These plot twists are intended to demonstrate the questioning of traditional masculinist and sexist values: the exploitation of the whores is openly portrayed as such, the collusion of the authorities to further oppress the women is obvious, and the women are shown as active enough to go beyond these constraints. However, the dimension of the film that really caps this questioning of the Western in its masculine mentality is its portrayal of the protagonist William Munny (played by Eastwood) as an ex-gunslinger and outlaw, who now regrets his former drinking, killing, and cruel-

ty. He has been "reformed" by his wife during the past decade, but she has tragically died three years before the events
of the film. In the film's beginning, Munny is seen minding
his children, mourning his dead wife, and vowing to keep to
his reformed ways, when he is tempted back into the killing
business for the good cause of defending the whores and
earning five hundred dollars for his two children's future.

That *The Unforgiven* has been seen as a critique of cowboy
heroism, a questioning of the value of masculinity, and an
exposé of sexism in the Western genre is deeply disturbing. It
is disturbing in the same way that I am appalled that the
"men's movement" or Robert Bly's *Iron John* is seen to question masculinity. This interpretation only demonstrates the
opposite: how deeply entrenched are these attitudes, such
that we are blind to their glorification and can't see what is
entailed in genuinely questioning them. What seems to happen is that we are captured by a few catch phrases or by the
surface of what we're presented with and fail to see that these
issues go much deeper. If we don't look at the deeper contexts and use our senses and emotions to fullest capacity, we
will keep being manipulated and fall back into the same out-
moded way of being male.

We can learn from *The Unforgiven* why the macho protagonist can't be authentically changed within the context of the
film, for unwittingly the film does demonstrate why so many
supposed attempts at transformation become another case of
a "wolf in sheep's clothing." The film supposedly debunks
the myths of the gunslinging heroes. Little Bill, the sheriff,
brutally beats the first gunslinger, English Bob, who arrives
seeking employment by the whores to kill the offenders.
English Bob has been the subject of a biography, *The Duke of
Death*, which glorifies all his heroic exploits. Since Little Bill
wins over the respect and attention of Bob's biographer, he
recounts to him how all of Bob's great exploits were fabrica-
tions, as were most of the gunslinging stories of the Wild
West. As Little Bill correctly recounts, rather than gunfighters

blasting away other men at lightning speed and great distances, most shootouts were actually drunken, pathetic
encounters in which the men involved could barely aim their
guns, shooting each other in the back or at close range, when
the adversary was in the toilet, or in some other equally in-
glorious manner.

Also, the Scofield Kid, who first rousts out Munny for the
killing, is gradually revealed as a nearsighted, immature
young man who can't even see his targets. Rather than gun-
ning down five men, as he claims, he has never killed a man.
Furthermore, the killings of the two men assailants are both
portrayed as rather cruel and pathetic attempts at glory. The
first is killed clumsily as he crawls around begging for his life
and a drink of water, and the second is shot as he sits in the
outhouse. Given these portrayals and the repeated protesta-
tions of Munny and his friend, Ned Roundtree, that they
know killing is wrong and is gruesome work, the film claims
to have undermined the masculine heroic portrayal of the
Western.

The fact is that everything about the film only *reinforces
all the heroic masculine stereotypes*, not only on the level of the
action but even more importantly in its tone, emotional message, and omission of all that is vital to a critique of such
masculinity. First of all, the film ends with Munny doing the
utterly impossible—outdrawing and outshooting an entire
room full of men (while others flee in terror). So despite all
the debunking, the impossible heroic feat is brought back to
amaze the viewers. The scene is presented as thrilling, as
wondrous, and as a victory for Munny over the "bad guys"—
in this case the brutal sheriff, whom our hero brutally kills
while he is lying there helpless, telling him no one deserves
what they get in life. Meanwhile, according to the film's logic,
Munny has killed both his targets, avenged his fallen comrade, gained the money for his children, taught the Scofield
Kid a lesson, and "liberated" the whores and the town from
the powers of corruption. The Scofield Kid wasn't good

enough to cut the hero grade, and the town really needed Munny. In the guise of the reluctant hero, the depressed hero—a time-honored tradition—Munny is presented as
the all-conquering hero. This is the thrill and reversal with
which the film is designed to leave us. We can "have our cake
and eat it too"—both criticize the old macho hero and watch
him achieve all that he ever did. Only his contradictory verbal remorse and apparent self-awareness make it appear different.

Of course, this is another example of the "doublethink"
we've discussed before. Labeling something differently
doesn't change its reality at a deeper emotional level, the
level felt in the body when all the senses are alive, the level
that looks at the quality of the relationships involved in the
situation. From the opening of the film, we see and feel in
hundreds of small ways that Munny never represents an
alternative to the macho hero. In his portrayed relationship
with his children, there is not a moment of tenderness, of real
emotional contact, or even genuine concern for their welfare.
If he had really cared for them, he would have stayed with
them, been truly emotionally present. He would have seen
that the quality of his emotional interaction was more important to their upbringing and welfare than earning money for
them by killing people. Now, that would be an interesting
anti-Western: Eastwood picking flowers with his son, laughing and singing with his daughter, hugging his kids in front
of the fire at night, talking to them about the moral and psychological questions they have to face growing up, organizing a better community to deal with problems like the
oppression of the whores, etc.

Munny keeps touting how the children's mother is the
one who made him see that killing, drinking, and being cruel
was wrong. He sits by her grave several times affirming this
fact. The irony is that he is correct in a way he doesn't intend.
He hasn't changed except for pretending to himself to take
on someone else's values which he still doesn't embody. As in

the masculine tradition, it is the woman who somehow embodies this other reality, which he monumentalizes but doesn't really live. Throughout the film, he is stern, cold, unexpressive, withdrawn, bitter, and depressed. This is not an alternative to the masculine heroic; it is the flying boy who has merely crashed. He may be in pieces, but they add up to the same old boy.

Both Munny and his buddy, Ned, keep saying they've changed. Yet Munny doesn't even embrace his children when he leaves them alone to fend for themselves on the isolated prairie, and neither he nor Ned have a word for Ned's wife, Alice Two-Trees, as they leave her. They are emotionally inaccessible, proud of how tough they are. Neither can talk about their pain, and they distance themselves from the horror of what they're doing by labeling it in defensible ways (although Ned less so than Munny). A man who had really come back to Earth—to his senses and to his sensitive feelings—would be shattered by the carnage at the end of the film. Like the SS officers who had to keep drinking themselves into a stupor in order to stomach machine-gunning the Jews into their mass graves, the gunslingers in the film numb themselves with their whiskey. It is Munny's distance, locked into his masculinity, that allows him to face his children. If he had become an openly feeling man, he wouldn't be able to cold-bloodedly kill eight people and then return home and embrace his children.

The Unforgiven ends with a panning shot of Munny's silhouette in front of a Western sunset. Next to him is the silhouette of his wife's tombstone. The shot has the same "Marlboro Man" sensibility and emotional overtone with which we grew up: glorifying rugged masculinity. The only difference is the memorial to the dead woman. However, once we think about it, the hero was always accompanied by the dead woman: she was the keeper of the civilizing values, excluded and safely buried.

The parallel between this movie and Bly's *Iron John* is

striking. Both speak about remorse over the isolated, inaccessible, and cruel aspects of heroic masculinity. Yet both use images of iron, hardness, toughness, quests, contests, unshakable will, comradeship, separateness, and the primal Self. As paradigms for male transformation, they are disastrous. If we are ever to abandon the high-altitude, armored, distant, and isolated stance of heroic masculinity, we must enter into emotional expressiveness, vulnerability, connection with others, and the rich sensitivity of our bodies. We must learn to use mortality and lack of control over parts of our world and others as avenues for creativity, not challenges to be mastered. There is a good reason why William Munny couldn't really become someone truly different, and it is important to examine why this is the case.

Finding Other Worlds

Was it coincidental that Oedipus had to wander for twenty years as a beggar before he saw himself and the world in a new way? (Actually, he was in the *process* of coming to see himself and the world in a different way throughout those twenty years.) Could Oedipus have experienced the same transformation in Thebes, reigning as king, living in a palace? How important was it to his process of change to be living under the stars, on the dusty roads, wandering, not knowing where his next meal would come from, always being helped and accompanied by his daughter? Conversely, how important was it to William Munny's lack of true change that he stayed in the same world and came back to the same situation?

To be masculine in the way we've described means that we males think that we carry our heroic qualities—our weapons to face life's challenges—with us no matter where we go. We claim that our real world is our inner self—the hero's heart, the heart of a lion. We claim that to be dependent upon a certain setting or upon the presence and actions of others in order to display our masculine qualities would mean that somehow we were lacking the hero's self-sufficiency. Of course, this idea has never really been put to the test, since for thousands of years the warrior male has set up a certain world of social relations that has supported his masculine outlook and way of behaving—it has just not been obvious that this was the case, since it has been the unquestioned norm. The masculine role has been rewarded in numerous ways, and those who have questioned it have been punished or excluded.

This has allowed the myth to be passed down that to be a hero is to single-handedly "do it all." It all comes from us and not our world, we are told. The reason why the hero is supposedly able to do it all flows from his strength of self. This strength, which allows for heroic self-sufficiency, is portrayed as intrinsically good. It is not questioned whether it is the outcome of creating a world and a way of life that allows this psychological stance in us. Since we have been raised in such a setting, not only does it seem as though "self" is something separate from its world, but we can't even see how self and the world are connected.

As American men, we have inherited the Herculean task of holding up the world and the world of those we love. Our support for holding up the world is our strength as male selves. For decades, television has presented a succession of males starting with Ralph Cramden, Ward Cleaver, Archie Bunker, and others who come home at night weary with the weight of responsibility of *Father Knows Best*. This burden must fall on the male's solitary shoulders, since his psyche dwells at a distance from its world and others. Distant and walled off from others, a part of the Herculean ethos or the warrior mentality is that the male is the leader.

A man also knows that the second part of this wisdom is that "what I don't do won't happen." What seems like male "common sense" stems from the male isolation from others and becomes a self-fulfilling prophecy. The hero is so self-enclosed, he is left alone in his struggle. Even with his supportive family all around him and wanting to help, they can't "get in." Virginia Woolf expresses this very poignantly in *To the Lighthouse* when she describes the overall condition of the strong father and husband figure of the novel, Mr. Ramsey: "It was his fate, his peculiarity, whether he wished it or not, to come out thus on a spit of land which the sea is slowly eating away, and there to stand, like a desolate sea-bird, alone."[1] Mr. Ramsey is pictured as feeling the need to lead his family, his wife, and even humanity toward the light while he is left "to stand on his little ledge facing the dark of human ignorance." This condition has led to a very peculiar notion of self and the hero that to us may seem commonsensical but that in fact may be at odds with perceptions of self and hero in other times and cultures.

Another film of the early 1990s, *The Doctor*, demonstrates how this notion of the heroic self rules the lives of many males and then may come to be challenged. William Hurt plays a doctor/father/husband who is always "in charge" and "on top of things"—that is until the day when he suddenly becomes the patient. Diagnosed as cancer, his illness makes his chronic condition obvious: he is really suffering from walled-in isolation. His medical practice has been a way to face people only as "cases" to be dealt with. His patients have been deductive puzzles whose solution awaited his mastery and skill as surgeon. He has never needed to encounter them as human beings. He has become so methodical and efficient in his ability to encapsulate others (seeing their flesh-and-blood reality as mere annoyances that block his clearer view of their cases) that he has come to deal with everything in this manner.

Now, suddenly, his pain becomes overwhelming as he faces a mortal threat to his life and he realizes his longstanding isolation. The pains that he never had time for get his attention as he notices how he feels for the first time in many years. His family, friends, and colleagues can't reach through his barriers and cross the distance to help him with his distress. As is true of any good hero, he alone must "handle it."

The hero-male, if he does come to feel the pain of his situation and the impetus of that pain to somehow change to adapt to it, usually looks either to change the world or to change himself. He has been trained to "solve" the problem. Given his stance in opposition to the world, the problem is either with the world or with him. His first assumption is that there must be something he can do to right the situation. However, as the character in *The Doctor* discovers, the world may not yield to his efforts to change it. For this character, the medical establishment, which he himself has never questioned, may not be open to change, and his cancer may or may not change its course. The issues his illness have raised are not going to be solved quickly by just "fixing" something "out there."

The doctor, therefore, is forced for the first time to see his own emotional inadequacies. For the first time, he sees the ways in which his defended existence has always been causing pain for his wife, his family, his friends, and himself. However, what the male hero discovers at this point, much to his chagrin, is that he can't just change himself like he can change the parts in his car. Something else has to happen.

At this moment, we men find that not only has our culture given us a masculine identity that has warped the self, but that the only ways for us to undergo transformation have been blocked by that very notion of the isolated self. However painful this is for each of us individually, we as a group have an analogous problem in facing our shortcomings. Given the corner we're backed into, our culture has reached a similar point of frustration—particularly for white males. We realize something is wrong. We realize we can't keep acting the same way, or even the planet may die. We can't keep shutting out females, other cultures that have become global neighbors, or members of other cultures who are a vital part of our own increasingly diverse society. We are also realizing the emotional poverty of the masculinity we've maintained in order to keep our distance. We can't keep excluding and hurting other groups by depriving them of their fair share, and we can't keep hurting ourselves by distorting our psyches. Yet we can't simply just change these "inner selves" that would make us more open to others.

The 1993 film, *Falling Down*, portrays this dilemma powerfully in the plight of its protagonist, "D-Fens," an unemployed defense-worker who has a vanity license plate with this inscription. The film is the story of his rampage across Los Angeles. Caught in a traffic jam one morning, full of frustration at things that he can't control—that he's been laid off, that he's isolated, that Los Angeles is changing, and that he has alienated his wife and son without understanding how he has done so—he sets off walking "home." He is so out of touch emotionally, he doesn't even realize he no longer has a home. As a result of his emotionally controlling and overbearing behavior, his wife and child have only fear of him and will never take him back. As he encounters the disenfranchised—whether Chicano youths, Vietnam veterans, or unemployed street people—he can't read the nature of their suffering and feels only self-pity that no one cares about his isolation. His anger bursts forth in a trail of violence against all "the others." He can't deal with the complexity of the world or with being challenged by new relationships.

A very parallel moment occurred in George Bush's failed attempt at re-election when, in a Richmond question-and-answer exchange, Bush stood dumbfounded when an Afro-American woman asked him if he knew what it felt like to be out of work. Did he know what it was like to be part of another world where times were tough? It was obvious to the audience that he had not the slightest inkling. He could mouth words about others' plight, but he couldn't really connect with their experience. The gap was obvious.

Only by going in another direction—one that doesn't fit the binary logic of "me or it"—can we males begin to see the promise of the Trickster, Magician, and Grieving Man. This other direction leads to *new worlds*. Instead of just one factual world, set in its ways and patterns, there has to appear to us myriad possible new worlds to enter. Traditional hero-males may think this means there are new worlds to voyage off to or conquer. However, the male who recognizes his pain doesn't have to go anywhere to find new worlds—they were right there all the time.

Let's return to *The Doctor*. The protagonist is forced to see, in his own hospital, the world of patients—the world of suffering, fear, courage, frustration, and facing death to which he has been oblivious. He has noticed these other worlds, but always from afar and with no real understanding, without ever daring to enter them, feel them, and see how things look from there. However, now the other patients, his new feelings about the threat of his cancer, and his new patterns of activity allow him to see his profession, the nature of relationships, the meaning of his own life, and even the natural world in a new way. In a climactic scene in which he travels to the desert with another cancer patient, he experiences the reality of the landscape and the ability to sense and feel in a new way. Not even the power of the natural world had really penetrated his senses or moved him emotionally for quite some time, up in his control tower. Now, he has seen the landscape through the eyes of his new and dying friend. He has been forced to enter a series of new worlds when he walks into his own hospital, his own house, the natural landscape, and eventually when he finally returns to his own office. It is this "web of relationships" that allows him to change—indirectly, gradually, and in response to others.

The point is made clearer if we contrast the 1991 film, *Regarding Henry*, with *The Unforgiven*, which was released six months later. *Regarding Henry* was dismissed by most critics and the public as having less to say about transforming masculinity, when actually it had far *more* to say. It was dismissed as implausible, yet the nature of that perceived implausibility is perhaps the key issue for men to face in finding a new identity. In the film, the protagonist, Henry Turner, is a very successful, aggressive, and driven lawyer. He is shot in the head and chest during a robbery. He emerges from a coma and then undergoes a long rehabilitation as a different sort of male.

The film was said to be unrealistic—that a shot in the head and a period of anoxia would not produce such a profound change in personality and values. However, to attribute a simple cause-and-effect relationship between Henry's injuries and his subsequent transformation in personality and values is a very limited reading of the film—although understandable, since it is an interpretation that follows from the heroic sense of self we're discussing. What is not being seen is that Henry doesn't change, rather he is changed by the new people, environments, and relationships he must encounter on his odyssey.

Henry Turner starts out as a winner. He is the leader of a large and prestigious law firm. He is shown in the opening scene convincing the jury to disallow their emotions and show no sympathy for the victim of medical malpractice at East Shore Hospital. He knows that the patient, Mr. Matthews, did tell the hospital staff that he was a diabetic and that his tragic mistreatment and disablement could have been prevented if this information had been heeded. However, since there is no public record of this exchange, Henry suppresses the evidence that would reveal it, and uses Mr. Matthews's alcoholic past to cast disbelief on his testimony. When Henry wins the case for the hospital, compounding Matthews's tragedy, he feels only elation at his victory for the firm and happily accepts his partners' toasts. As we find out later in the film, both Henry and his wife were having affairs with other law partners, had no real communication between them, and his daughter lives in fear of his controlling, distant attitude. Before Henry is shot, he is the masculine hero.

What was overlooked in the critics' reaction to the film was the radical shift in the worlds in which Henry finds himself after his injury. When he awakens from his coma, he has no memory, and no motor or cognitive skills. He must relearn his life, and he is sent off to a rehabilitation center to do so. What the film makes clear in side comments—although unnoticed by its commentators—is that Henry was raised by a father and within a familial setting where he was taught the values of being aggressive, unreachable, controlling, and dominating. He was expected to keep up the tradition of being the leader of the law firm. However, his second "upbringing" is far different.

For the next six months, Henry is cared for and constantly accompanied by Bradley, his rehabilitation therapist. Bradley is an Afro-American who is spontaneous, emotionally expressive, embodied, fully present, humorous, sexual, honest, and interested in people. He is also caring and affirming of the process of life rather than a proponent of achieving goals. In fact, Bradley himself has gone through a trauma to arrive at his present value system and way of being with others. As a football player, he had seriously injured his knees, but his rehabilitation therapist was an admirable person who helped him see that goals and glory are not what life is all about.

Like Oedipus, both Bradley and Henry (with Bradley's help) come to use a blow of fate and their subsequent suffering to open themselves more fully to life and the richness of community. Pain can bring one back into more intimate connection with others. This is very unlike Munny, who seems to have sunk even further into his isolation with the pain of his wife's death. Rather than going to others and processing his hurt, Munny only increases his walls, bitterness, and repressed hostility. It may be true that Henry had also been so defended that it took a cataclysm like being shot to open him to new possibilities, but he does not find them by himself; he finds them by being immersed in a completely different world and in completely different relationships. Bradley's world is one that Henry would have never seen before—or if he had, he would have scoffed at it.

However, this isn't the only new world Henry enters. When he returns from the hospital, he has to spend a lot of time at home accompanied by his daughter, Rachel. She teaches him to see things in a new way, and they enter into an intimate, supportive, and fun relationship for the first time. We see them spending time on her bed playing games and reading together—which she reteaches him to do—or playing with the puppy Henry brings home. The playfulness Bradley has helped Henry develop is deepened with Rachel. Equally significant is the amount of time that Henry now spends with Sarah, his wife. The old Henry worked almost every moment he was awake and had no experience of what was important to Sarah. Now they can spend time sharing experiences like walking in Central Park. Henry finds himself doing things like holding hands and kissing Sarah in public, but these changes occur because they now fit in with the new context of his life. In a different situation, with the beckoning of different relationships, different parts of Henry can come to the fore.

As Henry starts to regain all his faculties, he returns to his old world at the law firm. At first, he doesn't have the mental abilities to resume his work. However, as he starts to recover, the fact that he has experienced other worlds leaves him feeling repulsed by his old environment, his old values, and the people he has considered friends. In one scene, his former coworkers lament Henry's change, saying, "He was the best"—meaning that everyone was terrified of the old Henry.

As Henry regains his cognitive abilities, he looks at how he handled Mr. Matthews's case and declares to his partners, "What we did was wrong." Of course, his colleagues, in their desire to win at all costs, think he has become a fool. Henry sees that "I don't fit in anymore." Now that he has discovered his wife and daughter in intimacy, play, and affection and Bradley encourages him to find something to do that will mesh with these values, he sees who he is becoming. He realizes suddenly, "I don't like who I was." However, what the film demonstrates is that even with all the transformation away from his former masculine heroic identity, Henry will have to keep building a different kind of world—a world with different opportunities for relationships and embodying different values—if he wants to continue becoming a different sort of male.

When Henry quits his profession as a lawyer, and when he takes the suppressed evidence to a startled Mrs. Matthews, he is carrying through on building a new world. As he hands Mrs. Matthews the evidence that will change her and her husband's lives, she asks him why he is doing this. Henry answers, "I've changed." That is true, but what is also true is that in acting on a new set of values, Henry is creating and solidifying a new world with different sorts of relationships that will help him change even more. It is a feedback cycle that will allow others to help Henry help himself *be* in a new way. Henry makes other important moves, too. He asks that they withdraw Rachel from the prestigious boarding school she's just entered, that they abandon their old plans of having her "climb the ladder of success." Henry tells the startled schoolmistress, who is in the midst of exhorting her charges on the need to succeed, "I missed her first eleven years. I don't want to miss any more." For Henry, the most important thing now is "to be a family, as long as we can"—knowing that he can't control everything but that relationships are the foundation of his new world.

The sense that the self doesn't exist apart from a world, and that we have to enter new worlds in order to find new selves, also adds to the point we've made previously that to change we must "let be." We males need to enter other worlds and let them affect and effect us. We have to "let them be," for only by becoming enmeshed with them do we become different. This means that change occurs not through will power, but rather through openness to others. We *allow others to impact on us*, which is sometimes a painful experience and sometimes movingly joyous. It is an indirect process, by being with them in their world, caught up together. The hero, of course, wants to be "in charge." He wants the change to be direct. He wants it clean and not messily involving. Change takes allowance, time, and involvement.

The changes in Henry can be seen as implausible. They may seem implausible for one reason: the masculine sense of self is so well defended that it is difficult to see how the suffering male inside can be touched—can be affected enough—to be able to change. Maybe it would take something equivalent to being shot in the head to reach most of us. That is not a weakness of the film, however, but a statement of how successful we've been in constructing our armor and creating distance. It is also a statement about the world we maintain to help us avoid change. Even being shot in the head wouldn't have been enough to transform Henry. It was the work of Bradley, Sarah, and Rachel, that allowed Henry to see and experience other worlds—the worlds of an Afro-American male, a female, and a child.

It is really more implausible that we men should continue to choose living in ways that starve ourselves emotionally—that hurt ourselves and others crazily and needlessly—than to choose more fulfilling lives. If some alien beings were to observe us doing this to ourselves, they would undoubtedly think it preposterous that we could exist in such a way. This implausible scenario of life only appears plausible because we have constructed a painful world that supports it—a violent and inhumane world. *Regarding Henry* shows the emotional, psychological, behavioral, and value shifts needed to create new worlds where new kinds of males could live—and where male lives of rewarding playfulness, concern, and intimacy would become quite plausible.

Another film that was immensely popular in 1991, *Dances with Wolves*, also portrays a male protagonist who undergoes a transformation by opening himself to a new world—the world of the Lakota Indians of the nineteenth century.

However, in order to consider this film's import to our finding a better sense of self, we need to turn to one more key
question: whether our distorted sense of the masculine
hero has hidden within it other creative possibilities for
being male.

The Truest Hero

It was the Greeks who developed the cult of the hero as
we've come to know it. For them, the hero was semi-divine.
Being a *daimon*—between mortals and gods—the hero was to
be honored and celebrated. Above other mortals, he was on
his way to being like the Olympian figures of the new war-
rior-inspired religion. Most of us were taught in school that
"our civilization" began with classical Greece—particularly
with fifth century B.C. Athens. Our background to that civilization was presented through Greek myths like those of
Hercules or Oedipus. These were the myths that gave us
males our model for a kind of masculinity based on the warrior. It was a time when the thousands of years of devotion to
Mother Earth, the Great Goddess—the spirit within all nature
and all its movements and creatures—was being replaced
with the devotion to a set of ruling powers governed by a
warrior ethic of hierarchy, domination, and getting beyond
the Earth and body to a "higher and purer" realm. This shift
in ideas was paralleled by the demotion not only of the
Goddess, but of women themselves to subservient and politically disenfranchised positions, as well as by the notion that
all non-Greeks were "barbarians." Like many of our other
notions, the idea of the masculine hero seems to stem from
this period and this shift in consciousness.

However, before this there had been heroes of a different
sort. Men and women had a different sense of their place in
the whole and their relationships to one another. For many
thousands of years, in Southeastern Europe and the Mediterranean areas—as well as in Crete, Sumer, Babylon, Asia
Minor and Southeast Asia,[2] —there had been what Marija

Gimbutas has called "the civilization of the Goddess." The main theme that the Goddess symbolized for these cultures was "the cyclic mystery of birth, death, and the renewal of life, involving not only human life but all life on Earth. Symbols and images cluster around the parthenogenic (self-generating) Goddess who is the single source of all life. Her energy is manifest in springs and wells, in the Moon, Sun, and Earth, and in all animals and plants."[3] The planet itself and all its creatures were seen as divine, as having spirit within them, as being "spirit-ed". The sense that we were all children of the Mother—of the Goddess—as the divinity within all nature and existence, meant everything had a place here on Earth and in her cycles. As such, the Goddess gave life and death as equally intertwined, not one as boon and one as curse, and she herself rose and fell with the rising and dying of the plants (p. 399).

Similarly, there was not the great emphasis on individuality as a means to become distinguished and somehow symbolically defeat the sting of death, but rather a sense of fitting into the whole regenerating process. This was true for all of Mother Earth's children, both males and females. For the Goddess, the male part in this cycle was harmonious with the rest of her offspring: "Male gods also exist, not as creators but as guardians of wild nature, or as metaphors of life energy and the spirits of seasonal vegetation" (p. 399). The divinity in the male and female was to be found in the guardianship of the Earth's wondrous cascade of life and beauty.

If the deeper sense of human identity for both sexes is part of a larger cycle, then it is natural that both males and females should be seen as reciprocal rather than opposed. In such a scheme, sexuality is not about competition, seduction, or domination; rather, it is the physical expression and symbol of interdependence and communion. Male gods were not "heroes" in the sense that we now think of the hero (p. 249).

In envisioning the symbolic relationship between goddesses and gods at this time, Gimbutas writes:

> I see male gods as partners, consorts, and brothers of
> the goddesses. Although man is not the true life-giving
> force and fatherhood was unknown in early times,
> man's sexual and physical power was esteemed as mag-
> ically enhancing female life-giving powers. Female and
> male sexes were not dichotomized in the Neolithic; on
> the contrary, it was believed their fusing created potency
> necessary to charge nature with life powers. Goddesses
> of regeneration were sometimes portrayed with male
> genitals or with phallic necks. (p. 249)

So, if we think of the span of time of the Neolithic—from
before 7000 B.C. to after 3000 B.C.—there existed rather
advanced and sophisticated societies in which male and
female were not opposed but were partners in augmenting
each other's energies. The male paradigm was that of adding
to the life-birthing energies magically, through intimacy. Each
sex could flow into the other's identity as a child of the Earth,
even symbolized in their mixed embodiment. The "sacred
marriage"—the ceremonial coming together of goddess and
god or goddess and consort—was part of the rituals of many
of these societies. It was not seen as one sex coming to claim
or dominate the other but as the fusing of Earth's creative
powers.

Such a sensibility survived beyond the Neolithic age into
the Sumerian, Cretan, Babylonian, and even Minoan civiliza-
tions before becoming obliterated by the waves of invading,
horse-mounted warrior peoples. The cyclic view of time as
regenerating life and nature as a whole came to be challenged
by the warrior peoples' belief that time is linear and death is
final. For them, the only way to survive death was through
achieving personal distinction, an afterlife, and glory through
power. The warrior Indo-Europeans were oriented to the sky,
light, and speed. They "worshipped the swiftness of the arrow and the sharpness of the blade. The touch of the axe
awakened powers" (p. 399). The power was of wielding

death and achieving the glory of the fallen hero. The communal graves of the Goddess cultures were superceded with the hero's aspiration to have an individual tomb to mark his glory.

One of the oldest myths of which we have written record is the Sumerian myth of Inanna, which shows, even at the time of the first coming of the warriors, that there was still a harmony of goddesses and gods—of female and male—as children of Mother Earth.[4] The entire tale of Inanna's being joined with her partner, Dumuzi, is sweetly erotic, with equality and reciprocity between the partners. As they enter the sacred marriage together, their own joining is inseparable from the fertility and powers of nature. As they come to each other, they are in a garden—a garden that is inseparable from their lush lovemaking itself:

> Before my brother coming in song,
> Who rose to me out of the poplar leaves,
> Who came to me in the midday heat,
> Before my lord Dumuzi,
> I poured plants out of my womb,
> I placed plants before him,
> I poured out plants before him,
> I placed grain before him,
> I poured out grain before him,
> I poured out grain from my womb.

The joining of these lovers is joyous, caring, sweet, and very sensual. They are not cast out of the garden for their frank sensuality and sexuality—as in the tradition we know better—but rather these delights only weave them into its fabric more tightly. Dumuzi is called at different times boy, lord, bridegroom, honey-man, brother, father, shepherd, priest, and king; and Inanna is called girl, sister, bride, daughter, mother, lady of the evening, priestess, and queen. The two continually address one another in a variety of such names. The roles they play change and spiral back and forth between them from moment to moment. Each cry for the bed of kingship is counterbalanced by the cry for the bed of queenship.

Even in their lovemaking, both flow in and out of roles, counterbalancing each other: "He shaped my loins with his fair hands,/The shepherd Dumuzi filled my lap with cream and milk,/He stroked my pubic hair,/He watered my womb," which she responds to with "Now I will caress my high priest on the bed,/I will caress the faithful shepherd Dumuzi,/I will caress his loins,/the shepherdship of the land . . ." (p. 43). There are few narratives written that can match this holy story's frank embracing of sensuality and sexuality as inseparable from love and spirituality, in which male and female, human and nature, are all woven together with joy and affirmation.

The male and female are enormously hungry in their lovemaking, yet this passion leads to: "He put his hand in her hand./He put his hand to her heart./Sweet is the sleep of hand-to-hand./Sweeter still the sleep of heart-to-heart" (p. 43). What results from their passion is not the satiation of individuals seeking security from one another but the augmentation of elemental powers that are inseparable from the whole—whose flow has been opened more fully and sweetly in their joining. Human love and care—the polarity of the sexes—is merely a channel for the creative energy of the whole to find an expressive shape.

In this context, the sense of "the hero" is quite different. Rather than the individual who must separate from those he loves and from his community to go on a quest—to display bravery, determination, endurance, and to bring back a prize that will insure fame in order to ward off the threat of mortality—the hero has a different role. The hero in the context of the Goddess is one whose power is part of the fertility of the whole, whose sexuality adds to the life force expressed in the coming together of all realms of nature, whose journey in life is to the heart of the community where he can shepherd others into ways of interacting lovingly, and whose strength lies in his capacity to be a guardian against any powers that might rupture the vital interconnections among the members of the planetary community.

In this sense, the hero's path leads into the heart of the labyrinth in its original sense: not a maze through which the hero has to make his way, but one path winding in an inevitable return to the center, to the power of the Great Mother as womb, in order to be reborn.[5] When this image is transformed by the warrior model of the hero, the journey is *out* of the labyrinth, away from the power of the bull and the double-axe (which were the labyrinth's symbols and also ancient Goddess symbols) and away from entanglements with the Earth. The greatest of the new warrior-heroes, Theseus, escapes from and destroys the labyrinth at Crete, the last remaining great symbol of the Goddess.

We find that both the history of the term *hero* and the history of its exemplars betray a different sense of the hero, a sense that has since been lost. In the Greek, the root for *hero* is the same root as for *Hera*. For thousands of years before she became the wife of Zeus in the Greek recasting of older myths, Hera was a name and symbol of the Goddess. Both Hera and hero are from the root that means "protector."[6] Each is a protector of the Earth's fertility and sacredness. Both come together in the sacred marriage to protect the whole.

Another sense that was attached to the root of *hero* in the Greek was as spirits or ghosts that were dedicated to the Goddess—to Hera.[7] The hero was not opposed to the Earth and its cycles—nor to the female and Mother—but was its consort, son, and harmonious power.

Hercules also had a long history as a fertility god and consort of Hera, as a power of the Earth and celebrant of the Goddess. Even the symbols that he acquires later as a warrior hero seem derived from earlier Goddess, Earth–centered symbols. His club was originally the bough of a tree, connected to the Goddess symbol of the Tree of Life, the organic growth up out of the Earth—and in the crook of his arm was a cornucopia[8]—the "horn of plenty" which came from the Goddess taking form as a cow giving forth her fruits through the hollow horn.[9]

When Hercules becomes the warrior-hero, these symbols of fertility and the generous overflow of Mother Earth become either weapons for inflicting violence and death or tokens of his victories over fallen enemies. It makes sense that even his lion skin originally was not a warrior's trophy and symbol to inspire terror in his enemies but rather a way of indicating that "Hercules was Hera's mate, lover, and partner in Creation," in which their relationship "was based on what they had in common—beginning with a mutual capacity for ecstasy and power to generate life—not who had power over the other."[10] The lion had long been symbol for Hera and for the Goddess, and may have been symbol of their partnership.[11] So even our archetype of the masculine hero, whose labors we feel are ours as males, probably was a very different sort of hero initially.

So much of the warrior model of masculinity stresses opposition to the female, both in the sense that "feminine" traits are to be avoided as defects in character and in the needed separation from the spell of the Mother. Since the Mother is symbol of the Earth, much of masculinity separates us from the Earth. Perhaps this was part of the rejection of a prior, competing way of life that is foolish for us to still carry as part of who we want to be as "real men." From this perspective, we can see that the strange lapse into being with females and wearing feminine dress that overtook Hercules later in his life might not only be the emergence of the repressed female side, but may also be a reminder that in earlier times, male and female were partners with so much in common that the roles swung back and forth.

This would seem to help explain why priests in the Hercules cults were traditionally dressed in women's clothing.[12] It also explains why the twelve labors of Hercules had origi-

nally been interpreted as the twelve labors of moving the sun
through its zodiacal houses as subject to the goddess
Omphale, who was the center of the Earth, the hub of a cosmic wheel.[13] The original sense of the hero seems to be as
partner with the female and the Goddess in the cosmic flowering of the Earth. This partnership was not a sign of weakness, but rather the spirit that shepherds, cares, brings into
connection, puts itself at the service of birthing new lives,
and returns always to the heart of things.

If this is the truest hero—the partner, the consort, the one
who enters reciprocal relationships and allows cycles to catch
him in their sway—then we males might be able to become
heroes in a different way than the traditional masculine-war-
rior model we've been given. The person who is true is trustworthy. In our masculine guise, we males have not always
been trustworthy in the deepest sense: allowing others to
share our fate, caring about the whole, and having faith that
our worth comes from being part of the web of life. We have
led many to death and destruction on our quests, rather than
leading them back to the heart of things. This also explains
the further tragedy of myths like those of Hercules: in
unremitting violence and violation of the Goddess tradition,
there is not only a symbolic dishonoring and hurting of
females, of the Earth, and of an important part of our species'
past, but we are destroying a paradigm that gave us a fulfilling and proud place to bring out our male excellence while at
the same time benefiting all.

The disillusion with the warrior-hero is what the protagonist of *Dances with Wolves* realizes at the opening of the film.
John Dunbar has seen the pointlessness of the mass slaughters of the Civil War and is in despair that his wounded foot
may be removed. He decides to kill himself by leading a
hopeless and suicidal charge across a field, which has been
the site of a hopeless and meaningless standoff for days
between Union and Confederate troops. However, as Dunbar
relates, "In trying to produce my own death, I was elevated

to the status of a living hero." His reward is to keep his foot—thanks to the attention of the commanding officer's personal surgeon—and be assigned wherever he chooses.

Dunbar chooses to leave war and glory behind and to see the frontier—the only unspoiled nature left—"before it's gone." His lesson about the wisdom of leaders is reinforced when his new commanding officer at Fort Hays grants him an even more remote posting in the wilderness—Fort Sedgewick—a tiny outpost consisting of one cabin—and then toasts him, boasts that he's peed in his pants and no one can do anything about it, and then blows his head off with his revolver. It is with this disillusion with where the heroic has led us that Dunbar is opened to the wonder of the prairie landscape and to the ways of the Lakota tribe he encounters.

The Lakota allow Dunbar to see a way of life that seeks to fit in with the environment and help all to be fruitful together. Through Lakota eyes, he sees the arrogance that has led the white man to feel masculine by shooting buffalo for the mere sport and glory of the kill. Dunbar and the entire tribe are sickened by the sight of a prairie meadow filled with slaughtered carcasses rotting, senselessly killed for sport and left by the whites. For the Lakota, the heroic stance is to be grateful to the buffalo as brothers to humans, to accept the successful outcome of the hunt as a gift from the Earth for nourishing other creatures and to use every part of the gift. When Dunbar is captured by his own troops later in the film, they torture him brutally with taunts that he is no longer a man. They are right about his transformation—he's not their type of hero or masculine male anymore.

It is Henry in *Regarding Henry* who shows most clearly what another sense of hero could be like for our contemporary culture once we have seen the sad, self-defeating dimension of the hero-warrior. Henry no longer wants to win at any price, to have status as his goal in life. Instead, he prefers to become "unmanly," stay at home with his daughter and wife, and be playful and intimate. His posture, his tone of voice, and even the way he looks at others have become soft, warm, and engaging—quite a contrast to the Harrison Ford in the beginning of the film who looks through others and beyond them to his goals, stands erect and unyielding, and speaks with the hard edge of one-way announcements to the world. The transformed Henry *embraces* the females in his life, both literally and in the sense of helping them connect with each other and himself. To nourish their natural flourishing and intimacy become his priorities in life. He sees that he can help this process, rather than be "out there" bagging trophies and leaving the rest of life to them. Henry has become a new type of male who hearkens back to the *original* sense of the hero. For our macho culture, this is hard to see. Most would agree with Henry's friends that he has "gone soft"—both in the head and the heart. No doubt this is what Bradley's friends also thought, when he left football to help people in emotional turmoil, gently caring for their broken bodies, helping rekindle their joy in life.

Whatever President Clinton may or may not achieve as president, he too represents a return to the leader who fits in with the larger whole and joins with the female to work together. His insistence on a partnership with Hillary—in which she is part of the team, with equal abilities and credentials and maintaining her own identity as Hillary Rodham—has disconcerted many in 1993. Yet what else does the Hera-Hercules, goddess-god paradigm of partnership mean in our modern life? It means that the male will no longer be the isolated one needing to make it on his own. He will be enmeshed in relationships, in communicating and deciding with others, and in trusting others to carry their share as a way of trusting himself as part of a whole.

To move to this new sense of the ancient male hero as consort, son, father, friend, lover, boy, and honey-man will take some shift on our culture's part. However, it will give us a sense of maleness of which we can feel proud, because in nourishing others, we nourish ourselves. The traditional hero, the macho-masculine warrior-leader, has purchased his glory too often with the blood—or at least inflicted pain—of others. This makes us feel pain in being male—a pain we must deny, or if not, deny who we are. Now we can love ourselves as loving others. Henry is left smiling warmly, excited by working out the day-to-day details of life with Sarah and Rachel, while William Munny is indeed left unforgiven—by others and by himself—feeling empty and bitter, sitting beside a grave and feeling none of the wonder of that splendid Marlboro-man sunset.

The new heroic strength is in allowing connection. This occurs by letting fate be and working with it, and by allowing others to be who they are and finding emerging possibilities for meeting on that basis. This new ancient hero finds others by entering their worlds and letting that be, too. Paradoxically, the most interesting new person this type of hero will find in this new world is himself—a new self called forth by the power of alternative worlds. These worlds can only work this magic, however, if like the earliest Hercules, he is there as a force of fertility to let the whole blossom forth and to join his energies with that blossoming.

CHAPTER SIX

We're Kidding

The Trickster, Getting Wet, and Becoming Ensnared

Foolish Tricksters
versus Productive Heroes

One of the reasons that his former coworkers consider Henry brain-damaged at the end of the film *Regarding Henry* is the fact that he laughs—he laughs a lot. He has recovered from the aftereffects of his coma by the end of the film, but from the perspective of his new world he finds many things funny. No longer can he take seriously the driven and unscrupulous need to defeat the competition and become as rich and powerful as possible. Instead, Henry prefers to pull jokes, to play in the park, and to share pleasantries with others. The former Henry Turner found all of life deadly serious: each occurrence in his life, no matter how trivial, reflected on his ego and his progress toward greater power and control.

This is the humorless plight of the heroically masculine way of the warrior-male. The line between work and play, duty and fun, seriousness and foolishness, propriety and silliness, and being in control and being duped is very clear, as is the priority of all the "productive" characteristics listed first in each pair. To all of Henry's former friends—serious men, masculine men, productive heroes—he has become a fool. For them, he is "no longer the man he was." They think this is a plight to which he is condemned. They can't see that this is Henry's choice and that for him it is a happy choice. The joke is on them. If they were open enough to see Henry's new power—a much different power than Henry's former macho forcefulness—they would see that he has become a trickster.

From the perspective of the masculine hero, the type of trickster Henry has become looks like a mere fool—someone who can't cope well with life, who has given up on the quest, and who chooses to lose self-respect by laughing at himself and allowing others to laugh at him. From the perspective of the warrior-hero, the fool has neither the desire nor the ability to take charge of life and others and wrest what he wants from them. Rather than pursuing those serious objects of attention that lead to power or wealth or glory or success, the fool gets caught up in "unimportant things."

One of the most famous fools in European culture is the fool in Shakespeare's *King Lear*. The other characters in the play all think that his occupation is frivolous and that he has no grasp over what is important in life—that is, ambition, gaining power, and manipulating others. With none of the attributes of the hero-warrior, the fool is scarcely even a man in the others' eyes. From their perspective, it is part of Lear's downfall that he is reduced to the company of the fool. However, it is with the fool on the heath, exposed to nature and to "the wind and the rain," that Lear learns to hear the messages of the Earth, of interconnection with others, and sees through the false values of status, wealth, and power. The fool tricks Lear—just as several other foolish characters in the play trick others—into returning to the elemental sense of life. The fool undermines Lear's ego and in tricking him out of his old roles helps to set him free. This is always the trickster's ultimate gift: to help others free themselves from the alienation of taking themselves too seriously. At the moment of revelation, Lear utters the famous line, "Take physic, pomp."[1] He is purged of the false values of competition, acquisition, and status.

The warrior-hero tradition has not been able to see this liberating dimension of the trickster. Given our heroic masculine priorities of success, victory, and power over others, we males tend to see the trickster as someone who must want these same things in life but who is somehow too "weak" to achieve them straightforwardly, so he resorts to becoming a manipulator. The nature of the trick is equally misunderstood. The trick, too, we think, must be an underhanded, sneaky, and desperate way to succeed. So we think about "the trick" as a driven but slick act of weakness, as in the case of "Tricky Dick" Nixon. Watergate is a perfect example of the sort of trick that seeks to unfairly defeat another. Nixon didn't have the confidence that he could defeat his opponents in a fair contest, so he resorted to "dirty tricks."

Even among those who have been trying to help us re-examine our identities, there is a misunderstanding and mistrust of the trickster. Robert Moore and Douglas Gillette in their recent book, *The Magician Within: Accessing the Shamanic in the Male Psyche*, characterize the trickster as the male "who recognizes his manipulative skills and revels in them."[2] They see the trickster as seeking to gain power, just as other archetypal masculine figures do, but in an even more cold-bloodedly manipulative way. The trickster makes fools of others, which from the male heroic standpoint is quite a defeat to undergo. The recipient of the trick is seen as a victim robbed of self-control and status. The one tricked has been led to unknowingly do something that has been set up to backfire and make him or her the object of laughter. This is the antithesis of being victorious and the object of respect and fear, as the masculine hero desires. This judgment about the power of the trickster leads to the masculine assessment of the trickster as a male who is "detached from the common concern for the welfare of others."[3] This makes the trickster look like other masculine roles—distant, trying to control others, but doing so dishonestly and ignobly. However, it may only *appear* that this is the case because the heroic masculine may not be able to receive a true trick for what it is—a gift offered.

Given our heroic blinders, what the trickster figure really represents as a potential of the male psyche is not well understood. Although we presently have trickster figures in our culture, and have them in our own past myths and images, it is hard for us to see them for what they are. This is why it is helpful to look to other cultures that provide the context—the world—in which such figures make more sense. This is a task that males are going to have to pursue, especially white males: listening to other groups and other cultures to find new ways to be. Within the dominant cultural setting of the United States, even when other notions for men are voiced as a challenge to the heroically masculine, it is hard to see them, to take them seriously, and to really understand their full import, since they are unsupported by the larger context.

It is no accident that the psuedo-critique of the macho hero in *The Unforgiven* got all the attention, since it appealed to all our well-ingrained heroic impulses, while *Regarding Henry* was seen as implausible and "not serious." Given our cultural context, it would be difficult for it to appear otherwise. Although we need to find the opportunities within our culture to challenge ourselves, sometimes it is helpful to see new images in very different worlds first. Then suddenly we can see aspects of our world that were not obvious before. Since men have been so powerful in constructing the dominant cultural mechanisms, this will be even more true of seeing alternatives to our current idea of male identity in its masculinity. Really the two tasks are inseparable: listening to other voices (whether female, non-human, historical, or culturally diverse) that we dominant males have shut out and also finding within our most taken-for-granted contexts differences in identity that have remained invisible or devalued.

When the new Henry returns to his former world, he finds the seriousness of his former colleagues to succeed comical and also morally objectionable. In doing so, he is fulfilling the role the trickster has always fulfilled: seeing and revealing the absurdity of societal norms. The trickster was and still is a part of many Native American cultures. He often appears in stories that are not at first recognizable to outsiders as trickster stories, since, in addition to appearing in human form, he might appear as a raven, hare, crow, or some other animal. Although more obvious in the Native American societies, the trickster spirit and trickster figures seem to appear in all cultures. He is at first most recognizable by an overriding message that is a direct challenge to the warrior version of the hero who insists that to push toward the goal or victory is most important. The trickster celebrates that aspect of all people—and even of animals and the material world—that doesn't stay focused on achieving goals, but instead wants to go awry, to break down, to goof off—to just "fool around." There is something in people and in the world itself that flourishes with a certain amount of order, direction, and purpose. Yet the opposite tendency is also vital— the erratic movement toward disorder, wandering, and the sheer affirmation of just *being* without achieving anything in particular.

When the Native American trickster figures were becoming better known to Europeans and Americans—in part because of Paul Radin's work, *The Trickster: A Study in American Indian Mythology*—both the universality of the trickster spirit and the loss of appreciating this spirit in modern society struck Carl Jung. In his response to the power of the Native American trickster tales, he applied his genius at appreciating the myths of all cultures, and seeing their connections and the powers of their symbols on our collective psyche. He saw in the trickster a numinous quality important to all cultures, but he also sadly realized that "the so-called civilized man has forgotten the trickster."[4]

We modern males have forgotten the trickster because it doesn't fit our current identity. Just like Lear's fool, just like the transformed Henry, there is something about the trickster and his spirit that is elemental, that could touch a chord in all of us, and that in spite of ourselves could bring a smile to our faces. However, the trickster figure to us seems almost embarrassing, something that we men in our need for control, to stay serious, and to remain true to our heroic responsibilities to succeed must leave behind.

Karl Kerenyi, one of the foremost experts on Greek mythology, commented on these Native American tales. He wrote: "There is much trickery at large in the world, all sorts of sly and cunning tricks among human beings, animals and even plants, which could no more remain hidden from the storyteller whose inner life was as much bound up with the world as his outer one. . ."5 He sees the trickster spirit all around and within us, and he can see parallels within the traditions that are more familiar to European and American culture—say, in the sly Hermes figure of Greek myths. Yet Kerenyi also points to our inability to see the deeper, repressed side of the trickster. Even though on the surface Hercules seems his exact opposite—"Hercules, the *trickless* hero with the club," as he was called—he may have that spirit deep inside him. This kind of hero, who after his heroic exploits winds up spinning wool with the women and dressed as one of them, may not *want* to see his trickster side. If we males are to keep looking straight ahead and chase the Grail, we will avoid the trickster. All that embodies his spirit in life we categorize at best as foolishness—and at worst as an obstacle to be overcome. Yet if we persist in doing this, we are out of balance. The hero as conqueror takes one aspect of life and chokes out the greater richness of life.

In other words, there is a dimension of life in which beings end up in places they never intended to be, in which things that seem to be one thing turn out to be another, in which we head in a direction and end up in the opposite place, in which our very intention of achieving something becomes the means of failing at that task. For us males as heroes, this is unfortunate, something to be avoided, even cut out of our lives if possible. Yet as Kerenyi states, one who is bound up with the texture of the outer reality as the key to inner realities may take these trickster aspects of life to heart and learn to celebrate them. Success and failure may not be in such grim opposition. There may be a humorous dimension to life that will never touch the masculine hero.

We males under the Herculean burden of our roles may even admit this, but we will add that it is of no real consequence. For the serious masculine achiever, humor is not essential to life. However, this may be a lethal statement, not only to our spiritual well-being but to the well-being of the lives of all other creatures on the planet. For Henry's colleagues, the games and tricks he plays with his daughter and with the puppy, and even the smiles he'd like to elicit from them, are a "waste of time"—an aside from the serious business of life. Yet not only does this impoverish their lives, it changes who they are and how they treat others.

For the trickster and for those who are gladdened by his spirit and who may even see him as divine, the detours of life are not negative or to be overcome but rather delightful and part of the wonder of being alive. The fact that we failed because the world was not the way we thought it was is not a cause for rage, despair, or frustration, but for mirth, laughter, and a bit of wonder. In its anti-heroic ethos, this may at first seem perplexing to most males. It is the challenge of humor to seriousness, of the charm of going in circles to the appeal of linear progress.

The Native American trickster tales—especially the cycle of tales Radin collected from the Winnebago tribe—push these aspects of reality in our face. The trickster figure of these tales, called Wakdjunkaga by the Winnebago people, forces us males to confront aspects of life and of ourselves that we would rather avoid. The trickster tales are almost exact opposites of the heroic tales we've grown up with as paradigms of "real manhood." Rather than a great heroic quest, the trickster in these tales finds himself embroiled in the most down-to-earth challenges possible—in spite of his starting out as a great chief.

My favorite trickster challenge to the heroic ethos is the tale of Wakdjunkaga's encounter with a talking bulb. Like heroic tales, this one involves a challenge—not one from a great warrior or champion but from a bit of the vegetable world. Furthermore, the challenge is all about excrement and bowel control. Here, we go back to the most elemental level of life. The heroic tale never lingers on the details of elimination—that is a matter for toddlers, not for heroic males! That is part of the reason why we males should listen to the trickster and let him lead us back to the earthy details of being alive and embodied.

In this anti-heroic world of the trickster, the challenge is issued to Wakdjunkaga by the talking bulb, whom he overhears declaring, "He who chews me will defecate; he will defecate!" The main danger Trickster will face is not an army of warrior foes but rather the piles of excrement streaming out of Trickster himself—up and over the treetops to which he comes to escape in order to avoid being buried by his prodigious defecation. It is just the sort of challenge that Hercules washed away from the Augean stables by diverting a river, thereby keeping his hands clean. The world into which Trickster takes us is one in which there is a deep humor, a special kind of delight—even in piles of shit that engulf trees and Trickster himself. It is also a world in which Trickster is tricked as much as he tricks; he is not just the hero-agent but is caught in a reciprocal play with the world and others. Unlike the hero of the warrior tradition, Trickster does not seek to stay above others or beyond their reach but enters into relationship with those he encounters in his trickster's play.

The trickster also has a different sense of ego. As we have seen, it was during the shift to the warrior culture from the preceding Goddess and nature culture that suddenly the hero's burial with his weapons and spoils that distinguish

him from others and mark him with a glory th⟨
death's power became important. Status, glory, an⟨
guished ego become the warrior-hero's way and o⟨
as masculine males. The trickster, by contrast, has ⟨
concerns and is often found in humble positions that would
be humiliating for the masculine hero. It's not that he doesn't
play with the glory-gaining quests of the hero—but for the
trickster these are not serious, just a way to trick others and
himself into humorous adventures.

A contemporary trickster-like figure is the character
Perry, played by Robin Williams in the 1991 film, *The Fisher
King*. He is a homeless person who wears ragtag clothes, lives
in a boiler room, makes sculptures out of colorful and out-
landish collections of garbage, and hasn't taken a bath in
quite some time. He is a humble figure who weaves various
tricks that help others find parts of themselves. The trickster—unlike the hero who works from above, gains and uses
power over others, and seeks greatness—shows the transforming power of the humble, of the lower regions, and the
attainment of mirth.

The trickster's way of proceeding is often a mockery of
the heroic ethos: rather than an epic clash or an impossible
quest, he returns to the modest level of the most basic human
needs. At the beginning of the tale of his wild defecation,
Trickster learns humility. After first eating the bulb, Trickster
states:

> "Well, where is the bulb gone that talked so much? Why
> indeed should I defecate? When I feel like defecating,
> then I shall defecate, no sooner. How could such an
> object make me defecate!" Thus spoke Trickster. Even
> as he spoke, however, he began to break wind. "Well
> this, I suppose, is what he meant. Yet the bulb said I
> would defecate, and I am merely expelling gas. In any
> case I am a great man even if I do expel a little gas!"
> Thus he spoke. As he was talking he broke wind again.
> This time it was really quite strong. "Well, what a fool-
> ish one I am. This is why I am called Foolish One,

Trickster." Now he began to break wind again and again." So this is why the bulb spoke as it did, I suppose". (p. 25)

Trickster realizes that he is foolish, that his puffed-up heroics can't even stand up to this power from the vegetable world. As the inevitable process continues, Trickster soon calls the bulb a "great thing" and is in wonder at its power. Before long, he not only defecates above the treetops but ends up falling into the dung and disappearing within it. His own pretensions to having a heroic will are seen as silly by those hearing the tale and even by Trickster himself. This is a far cry from Hercules, who cannot tolerate having his will thwarted at all without going into a blind rage.

In another moment of the tale that could be a wonderful parody of Oedipus, Trickster walks blindly about the forest. He is blind because he is covered with a thick, dry coating of excrement, after he has fallen into his prodigious defecation. He keeps asking the trees the way to the water. After each tree responds, he keeps going until he knocks into another tree, which tells him the way to go to renew his direction. Only when he finally knocks into the trunk of the basswood, which identifies itself as such, does he know he is saved, for that tree stands by the water's edge. It is said that Trickster almost died from being coated in the dried excrement and "if the trees had not spoken to him, he certainly would have died" (p. 28). Oedipus and so many of the long line of heroes would not even listen to their wives or friends, let alone the trees! It is obvious that with the image of the trickster, a symbol of other parts of the self, we are moving into a different realm from the masculine heroic.

For the Winnebago people, Wakdjunkaga was a savior figure, although certainly not in the mode of the warrior-hero who rides into town like Bill Munny and slaughters everyone in sight. Nor is he like Achilles, Hercules, Aeneas, Caesar, Charlemagne, Lancelot, Daniel Boone, or Patton, or any other leader-warrior-heroes. Nor is he a paragon of any sort, rising above life and its foibles, as the legions of Western heroes symbolized wearing white hats and striding off into the sunset.

Radin quotes a Winnebago man who appreciated what Trickster brought to life. Even though he first admits that Trickster committed bad acts—which some would call sins, the man admits—he insists they are not sins. The reason he gives for his conclusion is the exact opposite of the one we have used to measure our masculine heroes—that they were good men because of their inner psychic attributes and qualities, despite the fact that they brought mass slaughter, pain, and suffering to others. The man says of Trickster: "He never committed any sin at all" because ". . . one thing he never did: he never went on the warpath, he never waged war. Wakdjunkaga roamed about this world and loved all things. He called them brothers and yet they abused him. Never could he get the better of anyone. Everyone played tricks on him" (p. 147).

The adventures of Trickster involve many human weaknesses—both his and of the many he encounters—yet they do not include the attempt to annihilate others. Trickster's world, like the rest of the natural world, can be cruel, as when one creature eats another out of hunger; however, there are no scenes like Achilles or Aeneas cutting down one enemy after another with their flashing, and glorified, swords. As Radin puts it, explaining the Winnebago's comments, Trickster was a "positive force, a builder, not a destroyer" (p. 148).

It is the rare hero in our masculine tradition who doesn't go off to war. Rather than the detachment of the hero who moves through the world with a set purpose, the trickster is caught up in all the smallest details of the world, with all its creatures, and can make adventures of seemingly insignificant events. His trickery is not detached or defended; it has that childlike quality of being open and vulnerable. Therefore, one trick leads to another, so the joke always ends up going around the circle of all those involved.

It is necessary to look more closely at the ideas of humor, deception, and trickery, in order to see what deeper meanings they have, for in our idea of the heroic mode, they have been swept aside as part of the more superficial dimension of life. They are "kid's stuff" that we serious, responsible men outgrow. However, their meaning may be more profound from another perspective. The masculine heroic mode has been very serious in the deepest sense of that word: that our intention is in earnest, that our purpose is unquestionable, or that the object of our quest has a great value in itself that would reflect on the one who achieves it, like the paradigmatic Holy Grail.

We have seen how this attitude is part of a detachment, a splitting off from the world and of the beings within the world. Its best symbol is that of a "desert storm," because in addition to its violent side, it is a desiccating way to be: there is an aridity, a rigidity, and a need to fend off the dissolving with others in order to stay safe and impermeable. Humor is the challenge to this dry life. The humors were fluids—bodily fluids. In fact, the root meaning of word *humor* means "to be wet." Allowing ourselves to enter into a humorous world is allowing ourselves to become wet. With humor, the dryness of life is overcome, and the rigidity of boundaries that comes with greater aridity is suddenly dissolved. Seriousness is washed away.

To become wet is to enter another element that doesn't glance indifferently off our body—it saturates. In truly entering the wetness of the deeply humorous, we enter other tides, other flows of energy. A stock joke in any comic's repertoire or of any comic play is to suddenly have a bucket of water drop on someone and make them absolutely wet. Becoming wet is symbolic of becoming saturated by the power of water—as ebb and flow, the rhythm of life, the psychic sphere, and as the world streaming with change. There is a call answered in immersing ourselves in this wetness—this water-spirit. We answer an ancient call. We go back to something at the source of our lives, our common source. In encountering the element of water, we often enter it bodily—or at least enter its spell, even while watching it. It is not something that is indifferently traversed—even the ship that plows across its surface picks up its rhythm, its motion. It is this elemental sense of entering ancient tides that comes with becoming wet and entering the water world.

As Radin says of the trickster spirit: "He does not belong to the world of men but to a much older world" (p. 148). There is a sense of return, of joining with flows and rhythms that have pulsed commonly throughout human existence. This is the power of humor to melt those caught in a face-off in which they have lost sight of their common humanity with those standing in opposition to them: a good laugh with those others "brings them down a notch," makes palpable some simpler flow of being human together.

Another recent trickster figure, Chauncey Gardener, played by Peter Sellers, appears in the 1979 film, *Being There*. Chauncey is able to inspire laughter in the serious-minded Washington crowd in which he suddenly finds himself. After he is hit, but not really injured, by a senator's chauffeur, he is kept at the senator's house. Chauncey is a simple-minded gardener who has been kept sheltered his entire adult life by his employer, who has just died. While the senator's private doctors observe Chauncey for a few days to make sure he is not injured, the senator, his wife, and all the serious men around him suddenly start to become more alive, warmer, and able to connect with others as Chauncey unwittingly both inspires laughter and tricks them out of their usual behaviors. The same is true of Perry in *The Fisher King*. When he enters the life of Jack Lucas, a jaded radio star and a man in crisis, Perry calls Jack back to a simpler world of watching clouds and feeling sensitive to others' day-to-day cares, pulling him away from his absorption in big network deals, big-time biographies, and the sophisticated New York jet-set life.

The trickster tricks and is tricked. The word *trick* comes from roots that point back to "deceive," which in turn points back to the root meaning to "ensnare." There is an interplay in the trick and its kind of humor that involves us with others or the natural world in which we are "caught up in the web" of the actions, reactions, and emotions of others in their own "wetness." We get tangled up with them, move with their timing, wait for their further moves, and are drawn almost irresistibly to "play a trick back" on them and keep the enmeshment alive. Insofar as we trick one another, we are both on a string together.

This kind of interplay seems to be closer to the *originally intended* sense of the word *revenge*, rather than the sort of deadly serious, non-reciprocal actions that pass for "revenge" today. Again, the warrior mentality seems to have wiped away earlier meanings. In its original sense, *revenge* involved the entering of a relationship, a contest of sorts. "To revenge" was not merely to annihilate or do away with someone else, as if they were merely an unpleasant object, but instead actually meant "to free someone from servitude by claiming the other as free." By throwing down the challenge and taking one's actions to heart, I am declaring the other as a responsible agent. I want to respond to this person and take him or her as able to respond to me. This person is not a drone, but someone who has taken a free action that I dispute. It is this sort of recognition that the trickster brings. In its original spirit, to trick and to trick back was *this sort of revenge*. Whatever my position in a larger social context, if I am presented with a trick, then at least within the bounds of my relationship with the trickster, it is implied that I have a choice. I have freedom in my response, or there simply is no trick. If the other beings whom we would like to trick are not acknowledged as free, then they are merely being conducted or directed like water or air through a conduit, but they are not being tricked.

The trick is an attempt *to influence the other's choice*, so that they end up choosing some action that is at odds with their avowed intention. For the trick to succeed, the other must at some point (that is too late) recognize that they *did* make a choice that in some way ensnared them in something that was at odds with the interest they had thought they were pursuing. That is the humor of the trick. Thus, Jack Lucas can't believe that Perry has manipulated him into spending time with some of the homeless characters of Perry's world, but he must laugh at himself as he starts to realize that he likes them: he's been tricked into affections he would never have entered willingly or self-consciously. Fortunately for Jack, Perry has disrupted his reality, as all good tricksters do. Humor can be deep, too. To reveal and transform the most profound levels of existence is not the monopoly of serious-ness, as we seem to believe.

There is a second dimension to the trick that also is a dec-laration of freedom for all involved in the ensuing series of jokes, tricks, and games. The trickster departs from being serious in "trumping" the set rules. He is the spirit of disor-der, chaos, and rules breaking down, and this breakdown of the expected catches us in his tricks. Insofar as we trick back, we also have entered the realm of "dis-ordering" the usual. The trickster's spell is infectious: in playing his jokes and tricks, he liberates us all from the rules that usually make us servants of the serious world. We become free to respond in unusual and creative ways: if we lack this creativity, there won't be much of a trick.

When the trickster enters into a relationship with us in which we are declared free and equal, he opens himself to our own chaos-making powers impacting upon his own exis-tence. This is not the revenge of the hero like Hercules, who crushingly holds his enemies away from their own sources of inspiration and wants merely to destroy them; nor is it the modern masculine revenge, which is a humorless violation. Given the heroic mentality, it may seem that one either strikes back or is passive in the face of being hurt by others; one either "dishes it out" or "takes it." However, the trickster path is somewhere in between these opposite stances: we don't just have to absorb a hurt without response; instead, the lighthearted or humorously aggressive trick creates a space for playing out the consequences equally and for all to process what it means together: we laugh together and recognize our foolishness together. Even if the other "got the best of me" this time, our having a laugh together implies some mutual recognition and an open-endedness to the process that I might "get him back" next time. This differs from the masculine, willful grinding-into-oblivion inflicted upon others by the hero above the fray exacting his revenge. This flying boy's revenge almost invariably becomes unmitigated and annihilating as the seductive sense of being invulnerable draws him into excess. The humorous or tricky kind of revenge, whose roots refer to an innocence and a kind of happiness, may even be silly. It can occur even in a struggle if there is humor and wetness allowed. Even though the situation may have started out with very highly charged emotions—perhaps even hurt or anger—humor and silliness can transform these feelings into a more playful give-and-take.

It is almost impossible to draw warrior-enemies back from their unmitigated violence by being trickster-like, since there is not the mutual openness the trickster usually needs for his mirth, but Perry—in *The Fisher King*—manages to break into Jack Lucas's life by performing just such a feat. Lucas, who originally became a cult radio figure by dishing out cynical, hostile, and insulting responses to his call-in audience, has hit bottom a year after egging on a caller with an anti-yuppie tirade. Lucas managed to insult the caller, expose his insecurities, and aggravate his hostilities to such a degree that the caller, Edwin Malnick, goes into a New York yuppie hangout and opens fire, killing seven. Overcome with the aftershocks of his own repressed hostility, Lucas has hit bottom and the bottle the night Perry saves him. Dead drunk and depressed, Lucas is viciously attacked by two middle-class males who get their fun by beating and burning society's derelicts. Perry thwarts the attack as he and a bunch of his homeless cohorts appear in ludicrous, scrap-heap jousting costumes, joking and finally breaking into a comically sung rendition of Gershwin's homage to New York. The attackers are disconcerted, confused, frightened, and tricked into fleeing by the absurdly behaving group, which is led by Perry.

Elemental, Open Sensuality and Sexuality

In the world of the trickster it's difficult to believe our senses. On the other hand, it is because we are absorbed by our senses that the trick can be brought off. Both in the Native American trickster tales and in other versions of such stories, the trickster opens up a new world of sensation, emotion, and being called by the body. His tricks restore our bodily intensity. However, *he is equally ensnared by his own enlivened senses.*

This is not a distanced, cerebral world. In the Winnebago tales, the hungers and sensations of the body are primary, whether it's Trickster's need to defecate, whether it's the competitive hunger for food whetted by aromas, whether Trickster fashions a vulva from an elk's liver and satisfies the fox's and jaybird's sexual longing, whether all are enthralled by a baby's need to see a piece of white cloud, or whether Trickster is distracted from dinner by hearing squeaks that lure him into becoming caught in the cracks of trees.

The focus of these tricks on the body and sensuality reminds us that the oldest sense of the word *joke* is centered on the body. However, the sense revived is not that of the body as tank—as defended, inaccessible, and rigid—but the open, vulnerable and expressive body. When the body is experienced in this immediacy, then every movement is telling and full of emotional charge. We laugh at the trickster because we feel in our bodies the tensions, hungers, and feelings in which he, too, is ensnared. Even our modern comics know that laughter and jokes start out from the basis of the body.

The word *joke* originally meant "gesture," or how the body moves in communicating sense, in making meaning. The word *gest* as the root of gesture also refers to *gist*, or that which "to depend on." In the trickster's world, there is a return to something elemental, that level of meaning that quivers in our root feelings in the body. Despite all other senses of identity that are built upon our immediate sense of our bodies, and despite all the other concerns which flow from it and return to enrich it, there is the foundational sense that *we are bodies*: we are breathing, eating, sensing animals. This is the ground level of existing upon which "to depend" for a sense of our aliveness and reality.

As Jung says, the trickster takes us back to a world we have lost in our "progress." Its characteristics—wetness, embodiment, free response, creativity, and chaos—are like signs on a path to follow toward the trickster's world. To return to this world is to return to a more elemental sense of life.

As we discussed previously, the traditional masculine relationship to the body is a distanced and organized one: we *use* our body for various tasks and train it to be a better (tougher, stronger, more maneuverable, etc.) instrument for achieving the bidding of our will. The body is seen as a vehicle, an object whose parts can be measured in terms of objectives and that hopefully will perform with the uniform functioning of a well-oiled machine. Given this paradigm, we consider the task of maturing as the "integration" of the body into a well-functioning unit and a barrier of defense.

The embodiment of the trickster is in stark contrast to this paradigm. Not only is he always aware of his body's sensations and urges, but his body itself seems to be a *community* rather than a continuously functioning unit. Periodically, it disintegrates, swept into an anarchy of claims made by the various body sensations. His dialogue is not only with others, with parts of nature, and with his thinking process, but continually returns to exchanges with parts of his body, negotiating their needs, hearing their claims, and often being drawn into painfully discovering what they can contribute to his well-being.

In one of the first stories in the Winnebago cycle, Trickster is about to eat a buffalo that he stabbed and killed with his right hand, but soon the left hand also grabs for buffalo meat. There is an ongoing struggle that leads to a fight between his two arms: "In this manner did Trickster make both his arms quarrel. That quarrel soon turned into a vicious fight, and the left arm was badly cut up. 'Oh, oh! Why did I do this? Why have I done this? I have made myself suffer!' The left arm was bleeding profusely" (p. 8). Going with these claims of parts of the body in conflict causes Trickster to suffer, and this is why he is sometimes called a fool.

At another time, when Trickster leaves his anus in charge of watching over the roasting ducks, the anus fails to scare off the foxes with its exhalations of gas. Trickster is upset by this and burns his anus in punishment. Furthermore, in doing this, his intestines have contracted and fallen off piece by piece, which the Trickster has picked up on his path and started to eat. He finds them delicious, but when he realizes they are his own intestines, he ties them together inside his body. He realizes this is why he is called *the Foolish One* (p. 18).

To be absorbed in the life of the hand or the ear or the bottoms of the feet on the surface of the ground may seem foolish to the modern masculine male, but it is particularly this acuity that can make men creatures who are fully here with others—with sensitive, attuned, and expressive bodies. Whether it is the Gestalt therapist or the Zen master, many other paths of wisdom have realized that to come back to our senses, feeling our bodies as fully concentrated, fully aware, and fully present begins to transform us from self-propelled violating egos into beings who are caught in the sensitive web of life with others. The trickster's bodily anarchy appears foolish, but it is a wise foolishness that we males desperately need.

The fool is the one who doesn't know where he is going. His ardor leads him to impractical outcomes, like being a "fool for love." He is "too open" to others and is "fooled" by them. He lacks forethought and just acts spontaneously. Trickster is taken in by the voices of his body in his continued hunger for life, and foolishly so. As heroically masculine males, we have been trained to be more in control of our bodies, senses, and feelings. Unlike Trickster, we don't normally get "taken in" if our nose tells us of the deliciousness of our neighbor's dinner, or our ears hear the intolerance in a man's voice, or our stomach is in a knot going into this job, or our breathing is shallow and rapid talking to this woman, or our eye is lost in the lush green of that canvas we were told is too "primitive," or our whole nervous system feels like it's racing on the steroids the coach gave to us to perform better. In our masculine functioning, most of us keep these feelings off our detector screens in deference to staying with the designated protocols of our daily missions: not bothering neighbors, not getting involved with strangers, doing the status job, keeping our passions ordered, maintaining our standards of taste, and doing whatever it takes to win.

Whatever appeals are made to the masculine senses are for the most part "put through proper channels." However, to become more tricksterlike, we could at times return to the world of the senses, of various parts of the body, and find new sources of becoming enlivened and involved with the world. Plans may go awry. We might suffer some. Yet suddenly we might stop the meeting because of that bunch of incredibly vibrant yellow flowers outside the window waving playfully or stop the lecture to our co-worker when we feel the thickening in our throat in response to sadness he is feeling that his marriage is breaking up. We could just follow these strange paths for a moment. We could be foolish.

"No," says the leader, the organizer, the male hero within us, "the world will cease if we wander from the designated path." Yet this is the most frequent occurrence in the Trickster myths; he suddenly has the urge "to wander," just wander. Part of his wandering ability (for to wander well is an art) is that the parts of his body are alive to their own sensual realities and the feelings they engender, as well as being part of a more unified, organized body.

There are other spiritual paths that listen for the voices of each part of the body in their anti-heroic attempt to be fully spontaneous to whatever beckons. For most achievers, especially the male on the Herculean path, it would seem like the height of foolishness to devote part of the day to sitting on cushions and becoming utterly at one with our breathing process. Not one other thing is thought about or achieved— "nothing gets done"—except finely tuning our awareness of the breath slowly going in and out of our body, or "being breathed" by the world. This practice of *shikan taza* of Zen Buddhists is said to utterly transform the rest of our life by returning us to the body, to the senses—not as carriers of the ego's plans but as a means of really "being here" on Earth. So the Zen Master (whom we will consider in a moment as another form of Trickster) claims as his highest wisdom: "When I eat, I eat; when I walk, I walk; when I sleep, I sleep." He fully experiences each sensation of his body open to the world. Trickster eats his own intestines, being nourished by the body's sweetness first, remembering its biological function second.

This is similar to the story of the Buddha who is chased over a cliff by two hungry tigers. He grabs onto a vine as he is falling. Below him are two more hungry tigers. Two mice are gnawing away at the vine onto which he is holding, suspended. However, noticing a ripe strawberry on the vine in front of him, he plucks it and eats it. His face breaks into a radiant smile as he utterly enjoys the sweet taste of the berry. This is the same foolishness of Trickster.

Also, as the anus story symbolizes, Trickster trusts parts of his body to do his bidding for him. Sometimes he is hurt and disappointed, for trusting in the spontaneity of the body in touch with its environment is not infallible, it just means that we are "really there," going where the flow moves at the moment. The hero attempts to insure against failure from the beginning and to stay in control over himself and others. Trickster is tossed here and there and is able to laugh at himself, even when in pain.

Trickster is always hungry for food, for life, for adventure, for fun, for interacting with others, and for sexual sharing. This hunger is an openness to be "taken in" by whatever enmeshment others offer to him. Unlike the distant hero, emptied out by his expenditures of energy across the distance of the void between himself and the world and who seeks replenishment of life energy through a sexual "score," Trickster's sexuality seems an overflowing of his playing, enjoying, and wanting to engage others. His sexuality is not defined by specific functionings of determined organs, nor is his identity threatened by deviations in performance or bolstered by achieving goals. His sexuality doesn't fit into any set categories, anymore than any other aspect of his existence. He breaks all boundaries and defies all rules.

At the beginning of the Winnebago Trickster cycle, Trickster announces that he is going on the warpath, and the people have a feast with him as a part of his preparation. However, toward the end of the banquet, he disappears and is later found in bed with a woman instead. Trickster does this another two times, each time being found making love to a woman instead of making war. The second time he offers the remark: "Why, what else is there to be done?" (p. 5). The story must go this way, as much as Hercules must spurn Hippolyte. What makes a hero like Hercules a hero is that making war and winning the day are his priorities, not responding to Hippolyte's unexpected warmth. What makes a trickster like Wadjunkaga a trickster is that he will never actually make war on anyone and will instead wander off into sexual delight or a feast or into humor or into whatever escapade somehow brings him into attunement with the flow of the world.

The fourth time Wadjunkaga fails to make war, he has to perform various outrageous actions in order to discourage the others from staying with him on the warpath, but finally: "From there on he continued alone. He ambled along calling all the objects in the world younger brothers when speaking to them. He and all objects in the world understood one another, understood, indeed, one another's language" (p. 7). Trickster is in communication with all animate beings and even with inanimate ones. The deepest source of erotic energy is that of perception itself: the entire sensual realm and all its objects are through their communion in perception in some sort of energizing intercourse. Trickster has this sense of the world. In contrast, our masculinity says this is foolishness: things must be kept at their proper distance to be manipulated and controlled. Given his distance and his focus on the genital "target," it is even difficult for the hero to feel overtaken by the sheer sensual delight of toes and necks and backs and hidden spots of soft skin on the women with whom he is having sex, let alone finding rock, bark, cloud, and grass speaking in erotic whispers to his body!

This contrast can be seen in the interaction of Perry and Jack Lucas in *The Fisher King*. Perry is able to go on effusively about the joy of one of those "great, mystical bowel movements," to walk into Grand Central station and suddenly see the entire jostling rush-hour crowd as a wonderful, rhythmic, syncopated waltz number (which the camera allows us to see through his eyes), or to lie for hours marveling at the cloud shapes and playing with them in his game of "cloud busting" (in which, if you concentrate hard enough, you can break up the clouds). These are tricks of feeling more intensely alive, more intensely here, and of bringing ourselves into a sensitivity of contact with others, the world, and our own bodies. Perry also feels that electric, erotic, and pantheistic trickster sexuality. He rips off his clothes in Central Park late at night in order to "free up the little guy." He dances around naked and implores Jack to feel the joy of "letting the little guy flap around in the breeze." Perry can feel the eroticism of breeze and grass and moonlight playing upon his penis without having to "score" on a woman.

It has been pointed out how, in fear of vulnerability to pain, our masculine gender identity has dictated that we distance ourselves from others. Even though we may be in the closest physical proximity possible with a woman, where our bodies are literally within and surrounding each other, we males may not "be there" in any *felt proximity*, may not have entered any relationship of "closeness" either emotionally or spiritually. The trickster embodies and symbolizes the magical potential of emotion that has the exact opposite logic: even though physically distant, we can be in touch with distant beings in our emotional flow and our spiritual identification.

In the Winnebago stories, Trickster's penis is at first so enormous that when erect it keeps removing his blanket, so he carries it about on his back in a box. This overwhelming size refers to his enormous hunger for erotic interplay with all the world. Trickster sends his penis across the waters of a lake, where it lodges itself squarely in the chief's daughter's vagina. Unlike the masculine hero, he is not afraid of "getting caught in there" (even though in this particular case, one might better understand such a fear). In fact, he doesn't want the intercourse to end, but the old wise woman who is brought to bring an end to it sings to Trickster to pull out, and he does. However, he laments the end of such pleasure for them both, and implies that even though he was literally across the lake, emotionally he was very caught up in this intercourse.

That is the magic power of emotion and the body. Those who painted animals on the walls of caves were not trying to manipulate the animals as the scientific, masculine, warrior interpretation has it; they wanted to feel kinship and identity with the creatures in the forest whom they had to hunt as part of the cycle of life. For sexuality to be a real joining or communing rather than "scoring on a target," there must be this magic of emotion that collapses the distance among beings. The masculine gender identity erects boundaries. Sexuality, when entered into with a magic available to anyone who is emotionally vulnerable, makes boundaries collapse.

Our masculine common sense has been that sexuality is a blind drive that must be controlled. The trickster shows that the strength of sexuality that comes from deep bodily attunement and contact with others and nature is powerful but not blind. It is the result of the masculine hero's distance from others that his sexuality becomes so driven that he will rape and ravage the other (as incidentally portrayed in so many of the traditional warrior epics and tales) or at least construct a society obsessed with the images of empty sexuality with women as prey. This is the psuedo-sexuality of the warrior who never really makes love with a woman—never opens himself to the union of bodies as a union of spirit and emotion, no matter how many women he penetrates with his penis. The violence of masculinity's sex drive, its vehemence, is the cry of the distant man starving in the desert. We see Jack with three partners in *The Fisher King*, but when he is at his most powerful, wearing expensive suits, being driven in limousines, and getting back his "star-power," he has exchanged Ann—who loves him deeply—for a woman he describes as perfect in the plastic, poster-model way. It is obvious he feels no closeness with the poster woman, but he has consumed her like all his other status symbols. This kind of consumerist hunger will never fill the void of our masculinity's distance from its own existence.

By contrast, Perry has the sexual hunger of the trickster—deep, moving and spontaneous—but this does not mean he goes around being sexually violating. He kiddingly expresses the intensity of his appreciation of Ann's sexual attractiveness (which Jack has been ignoring in his self-absorption), outrageously starting to rip off his clothes and sing her praises. However, we see in the film that his spontaneity actually makes his sexuality, although powerful, very sensitive to the situation and the feelings of the other. When he finally has an opportunity to sleep with Lydia, the woman of his dreams, he wants to wait until their sexual sharing can follow their intimacy and emotional readiness. Perry will delay until that time arrives—despite, as he says, "having an erection the size of Florida." In the meantime, he is careful that they appreciate the power of their first kiss, emotionally and erotically. This is much more than Jack or any macho man would feel for a string of beauties they might bed.

Another notable aspect of Trickster's sexuality is that it isn't confined to specific roles. Not only is Trickster not contained by gender roles, neither is his sexuality determined by biology. Trickster is in some way heterosexual, as his slipping off from the warpath banquets to cohabit with women attests, but even more so by his comment at one point in the Winnebago saga that "It is about time that I went back to the woman to whom I am really married" (p. 24). However, this declaration of loyalty to his wife is being made in comparison to his relationship with his husband! Trickster has married this man and borne his children after making a vulva from an elk's liver and breasts from elk kidneys. He is said to have made a "very handsome woman," and Trickster is referred to within this part of the tale as "she."

However, his remark betrays that for him this marriage and transformation are not as real for him as his mating with a woman, his wife. This suggests that he does uphold some sort of societal order, but not as an exclusive principle or norm, nor does he feel bound to any one form of sexual or familial expression. Symbolically, there is a blurring of male-female boundaries, just as in the case of Tiresias, that suggests some sort of more playful attitude toward gender distinctions, toward the power of biology to determine human affairs, and toward embracing aspects of male and female within each person in a more open and expressive manner. In our contemporary example, we also find Perry not as afraid of sharing affection with another male and unconcerned about how others will label this affection. He declares about Jack, "I love this guy. I'm loopy about this guy." As he shouts this out, he is hugging Jack, who at this stage in the film is obviously uncomfortable showing affection toward another male.

The trickster in the Winnebago tales isn't any less male by also being able to be female too. Here is a male who can both send his penis across a lake and have babies! The differing sexualities only add to his sexual being, to his erotic hunger and pansexuality with the world. Yet the traditional masculine ego upholds a bizarre piece of thinking that any female being that is sensed within a male somehow subtracts from his "real manhood." At first blush, this seems hard to understand. Playing football in addition to baseball doesn't make us less able to hit the ball, but rather cultivates our overall athleticism. Playing the violin as well as playing the piano only augments our musical sensitivity. It would seem obvious that to be able to be male in many ways and to be female in many ways, to play at many roles as defined by our culture and history, only augments our abilities as social human beings and gives us wider sensitivities to bring to whatever male activities we pursue. By having more to offer, it certainly would not mean we were any less able to be male.

The same would seem to be true for woman and for all variations of human sensibility: the more roles and activities we can play, the richer we will be in each. However, the masculine panic that any "female" behaviors and feelings will somehow compromise "maleness" can only stem from a rather tenuous sense of being able to be a male—as if this were some possession of ours we might easily lose. Trickster has no such doubts about himself: he does fully whatever he does in his male functioning, whether having intercourse with women in the middle of war parties or sending his penis across the lake. He also can be fully female when he wants to be.

However, the flying boy, the masculine ego, is so far removed from the sphere of the immediate flow of shared sexual feelings and energies that he is very threatened about who he is and how he will function. Since he makes love from afar, "scoring on a target," he doesn't have the palpable sense of his own identity as based on the fullness of his feeling and the richness of his enmeshment in his body as expressive and sensitive. Nor does he have a real feeling for his partner's experience. He has only a shaky sense of both lovers' identities. This has to be reinforced by making the woman into the image of the sought-after goal or target, and he aspires to the image of "sexual top gun." His security comes not from felt connection but from repeatedly hitting the target. This image-identity—substituted for the reality of the overflowing immediacy of the emotionally magical, vulnerable interchange—is always going to be in doubt and in need of heated defense.

This insecurity about our own identity is so painful, it is projected onto others as sources of pain. Others can always doubt our masculinity; therefore, these others become objects of hostility. Masculine heroes must assert their shaky sense of "maleness" by attacking others who can be labeled as "deficient" in their level of "maleness," because they are also capable of aspects of "femaleness." The trickster stands opposed to this panic. He gets to play all parts, feel all feelings, and have it add to his adventure of life.

Boundary Crossings, Shapeshifting, and Wonder

The last aspect of Trickster's sexuality in the Winnebago tales introduces another element of male identity that goes beyond sexuality. Trickster has sex with women as a man, with a man as a woman, and with the fox, the jaybird, and the nit. However, not only does he change into animals, into different guises as human, but whatever identity he assumes is apt to change. When the raccoons return home to find their dead children, "Soon Trickster came over to them again. He had changed himself into another person . . ." (pp. 30-31).

Trickster is a "shapeshifter." Although he is recognizable through his peculiar accent in the sense of the unique spirit embodied in his actions, he can always assume new forms. This is symbolic for a way to live that is always open to new perspectives, new roles, and trying out new selves. Our identity does not have to be forged, defended, and maintained at a distance from impacts that might transform it, but we can let all the selves summoned by the variety of situations in our life find their places in a rhythm that still will be unique to our particular pitch.

To limit this discussion to a multiplicity of selves, as if we contained an inner community of beings, is not quite right. As we discussed previously, our masculinist vision is skewed toward the "insides" of the armored tank—as if character were an "inner" thing, a subjective phenomenon, as if there were some thing called "a self" that stands apart from the world. Rather, in keeping with the vision we developed in the last chapter, we might now say that as a correlate to this "shapeshifting" is the fact that Trickster moves among many worlds. Mythologically, this is represented by the trickster passing easily among realms: from this surface world to the heavens or down to underworlds. As Gary Snyder wrote in "Through the Smoke Hole," a poem in praise of tricksters:

There is another world above this one, or outside

of this one;
the way to it is thru the smoke of this one and the
    hole that smoke goes through.
The ladder is the way to the smoke hole;
the ladder holds up, some say, the world above; it
might have been a tree or a pole;
I think that it is merely a way.

Fire is at the foot of the ladder.
The fire is in the center.
The walls are round.
There is also another world below or
    inside this one.
The way down there is thru smoke.
It is not necessary to think of a series.

Raven and Magpie do not need the ladder.
They fly thru the smoke holes shrieking and
    stealing.
Coyote falls thru;
    we recognize him only as a clumsy relative, a
    father in old clothes we don't wish to see with
    our friends . . .[6]

In other words, there are different realms—different worlds
—and they can be experienced when we abandon the serious
business of always focusing on getting the job done, walking
with blinders through this varied world. Others try to ascend
or descend to these worlds on pilgrimages, but the trickster
spirits just fly or fall through, often with no particular glory.
For the hero, such passages are often seen as quests; yet they
happen easily for the trickster, sometimes even by mistake or
out of clumsiness. The boundaries are just not there for the
trickster, because he doesn't believe in them.

Jung identifies Hermes as another trickster figure: he flits
among the worlds envisioned by the Greeks, delivering messages from the divine Olympian realm to the human realm.
He is also able to go to the underworld and back. We all can

soar among such spiritual realms—and do, as long as we allow ourselves to see them. We can "soar to the light" *right here*—seeing suddenly this illumination is *here*—shining in and through all beings. This way the Trickster is "here" and "above." We can be plunged into the gloom of underworlds and see the death-dripping darkness, coldness, and ghostliness of all beings, and so be "here" and "below." We can soar and plunge within short time spans. When the doctors in *The Fisher King* label Perry's condition "catatonia," they can't see he has gone "below" to face all his demons.

The masculine gender identity scoffs at such "instability" as just a matter of "feelings" and holds onto this world as solid and occupying one space and one time: the so-called real world it mistakenly feels it can keep under control. This control is justified as being logical, rational, and keeping in mind the more important things in life. So at first, Jack Lucas decides to leave Perry's crazy world behind and take control of his life. He returns to his rational, aggressive, detached and acquisitive life. Soon he is again riding around in limousines and making big deals. However, he finds the heights toward which he's aspiring empty. Perry's emotional, imaginative, and metaphysical world of spirit and mystery, where the priority is true friendship among people, calls him back. The heights Perry seeks are not above others, but the tricksterlike flights Snyder describes, in which we casually fly shrieking with fire in our heart, finding wonder in the world. The tricksters only see a hodgepodge of worlds and resonating selves and seek to be enlivened while alive.

For Jack Lucas, the world is measured in dollars and cents, in beautiful women, and in how far his career could go in fame and power. Perry introduces him to realms that he scoffs at. Perry's sense of the Little People (spiritual beings who talk with him) or of the Red Knight (who we come to understand is a vision of the senseless spirit of the warrior's violence and cruelty run amok) or of the Holy Grail (symbolizing the magic of the world that is always at our fingertips) are aspects of Perry's life that Jack finds utterly crazy at first. Jack has to learn that although these realms aren't objectively measurable doesn't mean that the world isn't inspirited.

There are zones one can enter that hold emotional and spiritual realities opened by the trickster's games. Some of these zones are dark and dangerous, such as the one of hurt and degrading rejection that Edwin Malnick entered into before he shot down seven innocent people—one of whom was Perry's wife. He was lost in the hurt from the violence he had experienced and ends up passing it on to others. We have to be given a context and a way to trust the experience of the power of emotion. Then others can help us. However, by not seeing these emotional worlds, we certainly are not prepared to use creatively their messages to us.

These zones open for the shapeshifter, as he uses different identities to enter new realms. In a charming part of the Winnebago cycle of tales, Trickster takes up with the fox, jay-bird, and nit, after each declares that in a difficult world they are looking for a pleasant place to live. Trickster says, "I have always wanted to have a companion, so let us live together." They search and find a spot by the river they all feel is "a lovely piece of land with red oaks growing upon it. It was indeed a beautiful place."[7] So it is the spirit of the trickster that brings these creatures together, because he can live in many worlds. Throughout the saga, the Winnebago trickster moves through identities and worlds, taking up with people as leader, son, bride, father, mother, and with all sorts of creatures—all in rapidly shifting identities.

The hero, by contrast, although often meeting many varied people or creatures, keeps to his course and does not give up his identity. He perseveres toward his goal, his purpose, which is intended only to monumentalize, solidify, and even glorify his identity or his essence. For the masculine hero, this constant change of identity and world would amount to "getting lost." Thus, for most of us males, there is a strong pressure to know "who we are" and not be compromised by others. Given our distance, our tanklike barriers, and the nonreciprocity of our bombing runs, there really is not much chance to shapeshift with those we encounter in their varied worlds.

A radical break with this tradition is portrayed in *Dances with Wolves*, when we see John Dunbar shift his shape from loyal cavalry officer to a member of the Lakota tribe. He does this by entering the Lakota world instead of heroically maintaining his outpost. Once he enters their world, he begins to feel the *feelings* of the Lakota. He sees the violence of the white world and the respect for nature of the Lakota. However, he is reviled, hated, and violated by his fellow soldiers who discover his transformation. The masculine ego's inability to empathize with those who really are different and live in different worlds stems from this inability to shapeshift. One can't just see into the sense of another's world from behind barriers and at a distance. For a moment, one really has to become a being like the other and be surrounded for that instant by their world, or else there is no real empathetic understanding. The masculine ego strictly separates the worlds that go with these identities. The world of the "respectable" white European has nothing to do with the world of the Lakota, and a cavalry officer has an essence incompatible with that of Native Americans—"those savages" as the masculine soldiers refer to the far-less-savage Lakota.

The trickster's ability to shapeshift, to enter other worlds, and to bring others together should be a strong message to American males. The movement of this Native American wisdom could lead men away from the desert storm of masculine captivity. It has long been a myth of masculinity that there is some male essence. When males are hurt and confused, this masculine myth tells them to band together in a "man's world" and get back to being "real men." The way out of a hurtful situation, says this masculine wisdom, is to go back to some "primal maleness." This is the logic of the current men's movement: to get back to the "wild man" with his pure, primal maleness—to separate from others and to bond in male solidarity. These are the actions our warrior masculinity has always dictated, with the isolating and violent results we've examined.

The trickster gives an image of a vital male being who can always become someone new and who always has at his disposal a multiplicity of ways to be. This is in stark contrast to the presupposition that there is some "primal essence" of masculinity to be retrieved from the bottom of a lake or in the company of other "wild men." The trickster is always *in process*, as symbolized by his wandering and his continual ensnarement with others. The changes that are constantly occurring for the Trickster are *with and through* others. We males don't need to separate; we need to connect with others, finally, in order to allow others to have a growing impact upon us. The wandering male, who is truly open to the impact of his experiences, from Odysseus onward, doesn't return home the same person. He has shape-shifted, become different persons along the way, and returns as a richer community of selves in response to the community of others he has encountered. Only the male who is barricaded behind his armor and who remains at a distance, returns home the same rocklike and stagnant being who set out. In some sense he never set out, but instead "stayed in" behind barriers. The solidity and mythification of an "Iron John" is the petrification of what could be a truly vital, dynamically unfolding process of being for males.

In *The Fisher King*, Jack Lucas is utterly obsessed with himself before he goes on his odyssey. In the beginning of the film, he surveys his penthouse and his rocketing career and declares, "Thank God I'm me." This changes after Malnick, as the newspaper puts it, "called the radio looking for friendship," but thanks to Jack's response, ends up "finding only pain." Malnick's killing seven people makes Jack see how he has passed his own hurt on to others through a disguised hostility for which he is richly rewarded in this masculine world. Ann—who sees clearly and speaks her mind—tells Jack, "You hate people." After being saved by Perry's trickery, Jack wants to leave Perry's world behind, but Perry tells him the myth of the Fisher King.

The King, after spending the night alone, has a vision of the Holy Grail—Christ's cup from the last supper—in the flames, but when he reaches into the fire, he is only wounded as the cup disappears. As Perry tells the tale to Jack, the elderly dying King (whose wound has gone deeper after a life of unsuccessfully seeking the Grail) is "sick with experience." A fool comes to his bed and hears the King complain of thirst. The fool gives him a drink from a cup beside the King. The cup is the Grail. The amazed King asks the fool how he found the Grail. The fool answers, "I don't know. I only know you were thirsty." Perry ends the story by telling Jack that now he, Jack, is the one to get the Grail, which Perry has spied in the background of a picture in *Architecture* magazine. It's in the house of a millionaire on the upper East Side, a man named Langdon Carmichael. Jack thinks Perry is crazy, but comes to want to help him. This is how Perry tricks him into finding himself. Up to this point, Jack has only cared for an empty image of himself—the reflection of the masculine success story.

The point of Perry's telling of the Fisher King story is that the quest for the Grail as something wonderful that will save our life is futile. Moreover, it is this longing that causes the pain of life to become deeply wounding. Only a fool—a trickster—can see the obvious. Life itself becomes a vicious trick on men through the masculine ethos. Life becomes an impossible quest—a never-ending trial in the desert. The fool only knows the King is thirsty. Through compassion, and responding to his need, the magic is there beside him, as it was all the time. The King—the masculine male—can't see this in his straining for life's solution, for the answer to the riddle, the great victory.

Perry follows the tale by telling Jack, "You're a real human being—you're a friend." Jack's scornful response is to say, "I'm scum. I'm shit." His self-hatred is just the flip side of his egoism and hostility. With the props of success, he mistakenly feels above others, and without them he's nothing. Neither is true—either for Jack or for any masculine male. Jack also says, "There's no magic. You know none of this is true." This is why Jack is bereft. If he won't believe in the wonder and magic of life, then his own proper self-worth as part of that wonder and magic can't shine through.

Jack's first steps toward finding himself occur when he decides to trick Lydia into going down to Ann's video store, and then to trick both Lydia and Perry into going on a date together. In tricking them, Jack himself is tricked into starting to become someone else. For the first time, he shows some kindness and concern for others. For the first time, Ann tells him he's done something she's proud of him for doing. In laughing with Perry and Lydia, Ann and Jack have their first real moments of closeness. However, after this, Jack is scared of becoming vulnerable and returns to his jet-set life, leaving Perry, Lydia, and Ann to their world. When Jack does return—to Perry, who has slipped back into catatonia—he is fighting the emptiness of his high-flying life and grudgingly realizes that only by entering other people's lives can he really change.

As Jack struggles with himself, he tells Perry he won't seek the Grail for him. He says, "Everything's been going great. I'm not responsible. I'm not going to risk my great life." Jack is not going to risk his success "to get some cup for a vegetable." Yet in another moment, he admits he has nothing, despite the beautiful women, money, and power. He is right: he is not responsible (as blameworthy) for Perry's wife's death, but he is responsible (response-able) as Perry's friend. Jack declares to the catatonic Perry, "If I do this, it's because I want to do this for you, not because I'm guilty or cursed."

That's precisely what Perry needs in order to succeed as a trickster—not to manipulate Jack for some task that has no meaning in itself, but to get Jack to *choose* to become involved, to be ensnared in love and friendship. Then all his actions take on great meaning—whether the Grail is supernatural or just a silly souvenir from some organizational function of a few decades ago, as it is in this case. Jack thinks he's getting a cup, but what he's risking his life for is to get himself back as a person who can love and care about others. The joke, happily, is on him. When he's done this, Perry awakens, since he's just been waiting for a world in which there is some sense of kindness and friendship. This restores his joy of life. The last moment of the film has Jack leading a chorus of Perry's fellow psychiatric patients in a rendition of "I love New York."

We must take seriously the fact that our society has no full-blooded trickster figures. The images I've mentioned are always to be found at the margins of society—in psychiatric settings, after great traumas, in the simple-minded, in the disenfranchised, and in other outcast regions. We do not leave a central space for the trickster as divine, as talented, as voluntarily cultivated, or as essential to the functioning of our society.

In *Daughters of Copper Woman*, Anne Cameron describes the Nootka society as one that always placed great honor and importance on having a few clowns in each town. The clown would go around making fun of leaders, of powerful people, and of other citizens, to help them take themselves and their opinions and feelings less seriously. The clowns were given complete license and respect. The chief might be ridiculed, as much as anyone. Our masculine way of taking ourselves so seriously has not been conducive to this deep humor of seeing ourselves as fools, as we all are at times. We won't allow our president to be a fool at times—if he is, then how can he be a "real man," a "real leader"? Nor do we allow ourselves to be deeply foolish about our own lives—to become tricked, ensnared, and dissolved by humor.

The trickster also has lessons for us about the issue of "male initiation." The men's movement has decried our society's lack of male initiation. We men feel we need to get started on the road to proper masculinity by other men. Yet, as the trickster takes up with different people or different animals, he learns new tricks, takes on new shapes, finds new ways to have pleasure and new tasks to undertake. This is what it means to be "taken into" a world—initiated—not only tricked but truly encountering others and being given a new start through them and being accepted into their society. We don't really have the same pressing need to be initiated into traditional masculine ways that have already molded our lives, as we do to be initiated into new worlds and to be able to take on new shapes.

In initiations, one is accepted into a certain community and introduced to the skills and values of that community. Certainly, there can only be value for young males being "initiated" by older males. It is also true that there can only be value by being initiated into any community that shows concern among its members. It would be most valuable then, if young males can be "initiated" into communities of all sorts, with women's groups, with differing cultural, ethnic, and religious perspectives, and other kinds of understanding. The more "belonging" we can manage, the better. The exclusive focus on missing male initiation is misguided.

It may be that there was some historical need for an "iron" sense of masculinity, an impermeable, unyielding, unchanging, unflinching, and dense sense of self. However, there is no need to claim this as a buried essence that we must uncover to be real men again, and that men can become men only by sticking to the same imprinting done by others. The trick is to see that in our current "having wandered" through our evolutionary process and arriving at the 1990s can allow us a sense of self that could result from *many* groups working together to initiate males, as well as others. We could gain from the historical liberations of women and of formerly oppressed ethnic and national groups, as well as from the information revolution which teaches us about a pluralism of ways to be human. We could appreciate the dawning awareness that we don't have to master other species and the natural world in order to survive, but rather the opposite: that we can learn from the different spirits of other innumerable creatures and even inanimate beings. Males need these others for true initiation, a start on new ways to be.

In *The Once and Future King*, T. H. White, who was disgusted with the masculine ethos and the continual warfare that it spawned, imagined a different kind of initiation for the young Arthur. His education before he became the famous King is left to the magician, Merlin. Merlin undertook Arthur's education and his initiation into manhood by turning him into every sort of animal. Each time, Arthur is given the opportunity to communicate with members of the species and to experience their activities. This allows him to begin life by learning the ways of all the Earth's creatures. Arthur turns out to be a very atypical male—one who, although a hero, is not masculine in several ways: not being possessive about his woman, open to vulnerable friendships, trying to end wars, and preventing might from having sway over compassion.

To be initiated means to be given a start, not to be held back by ideas that belonged to outdated worlds in which being a male (particularly a white male) means asserting oneself at the expense of women, of Afro-Americans, of Native Americans, of immigrant groups, and of much of the natural world. If we are going to give all younger males a sense of belonging, of being wanted and celebrated, and also of being given a start in all the opportunities that our age affords, we males don't want to go back to the Iron Age, but ahead into new gestures of community. Males don't need yet another excuse for male separatism—we've had too many "men's clubs"—rather, it's time to be initiated into a larger communal life of plurality, equality, and reciprocity with other groups of people, and to be initiated into the larger life of the planet's beings, both organic and inorganic.

Tricksters also show us that there is something wrong with the usual masculine way of being initiated. It is too serious. When we are initiated in a masculine way, we expect to fight to the death for this new group and way of life. This is not the trick that initiation should play. It should open us to new options, lightly and humorously. The trickster is taken into communities but never utterly so. We know that someday someone will suddenly discover that he is different, that he doesn't have the same solid essence of those others in the group and will be seen as a shapeshifter. When the Winnebago trickster becomes a woman and has three sons as the chief's son's wife, she (Trickster) lives in the community for some time until one day when the women are running around the fire pit in play, "something rotten" is dropped by Trickster. All suddenly realize, despite her apparent female identity, it is the shapeshifting Trickster, and his place in the community is lost.

One can be initiated into a group or a community in a perfectly seamless way in which there is a complete identification. For the trickster, this is never possible. He never can become that totally one identity: something is always "rotten" in the eyes of "the true believers." This is a healthy attribute the trickster teaches us: to belong but never totally, utterly, where one can no longer change shape, question, or leave the group. We see around the globe right now, whether in religious fundamentalism or ethnic chauvinism, the great tragedy of males who identify utterly with the group into which they have been initiated. They are insulated in a group armor, intolerant and capable of great violence toward others. By contrast with this and the hero, the trickster is "in between" the opposite dangers: seamless initiation verging on fanaticism and walking our path in solitary isolation. He can join communities but always keeps a foot outside the circle for another path. He will join the group only in humor, with a fluidity that keeps the group evolving, and he can always open to other tides.

We males need to have the same humor about our masculine heritage. We must see the ways in which it's a joke, a tricky gesture that can help dissolve boundaries among us, but that also must be opened up to include all living and nonliving beings with whom we are ensnared on this planet. It is not a matter of recapturing the "inner male" in some serious and solemn way but more a matter of being able to laugh at ourselves and at older males. If we could all laugh at ourselves together, then we could (together and with other groups) really initiate in the sense of welcoming and being welcomed to begin on a new path.

Many critiques of the masculine gender identity read like lectures to the boys to just be "good boys." As such, they can be dismissed by the masculine ethos as just "too idealistic," as just unrealistically dealing only with the "good news" of life. The trickster is not so easy to dismiss. He is not a "good boy"—he encompasses many of the "darker" aspects of the male heroic mentality (i.e. competitiveness, acquisitiveness, aggression, vengefulness, and deceptiveness). However, he does so in a way that is spontaneous, mutual, lighthearted, and interactive, and he thereby short-circuits the annihilating paths these traits might otherwise take.

It is the traditional masculine male's insularity, seriousness, self-righteousness, hierarchical and non-reciprocal nature that leads these traits to be expressed in ways in which there is no real dialogue with others and in which they gather force like a desert storm. The spirituality of the trickster is openhearted and irreverent, unlike the fundamentalists who can broach no opposition nor look at themselves and their faith with humor.

One of Jung's prime examples of the trickster spirit in the

European tradition was the annual "ass festivals" of medieval Christianity, in which donkeys were brought into the church for the mass and the priest and the congregation brayed at the end of the mass.[9] Jung thought this showed a strength of belief in Christianity and a living sense of its wonder, since its practitioners could laugh at themselves and still believe. We could add to this image that of the laughing Zen master who "spits on the Buddha." In the midst of following a path assiduously, this jokester spirit is open to self-mockery instead of the grim seriousness of much masculinist religion that leads to religious crusades and violating oppressions of all sorts.

One can have dark sides and even express them as long as they remain accessible, open to becoming tempered by self-doubts or doubts suggested by others. The trickster attitude toward others is engaging rather than withdrawing. This allows for mutual transformation instead of the closure of a learning process that occurs when one side is silenced by being violated. The trickster allows himself to feel the pain of confrontation with others, but it is a pain that mixes with humor. Instead of remaining self-enclosed and festering into dangerous violence, it enters a larger flow of interaction where its course is influenced and changed. In general, the trickster points in the direction that "dis-orders" seriousness and tends toward play.

CHAPTER SEVEN

We're Playing

Supportive Agon and Shining Forth in Sheer Being

Shaking Seriousness through Play

Perhaps we wouldn't be so much in need of the trickster if the masculine ethos were not so serious. With the Herculean task of holding up the world, the hero has no time to play. Furthermore, being serious and getting things done are seen as strictly opposed to play. Even when we males do take time out to play, we tend to do so in such a serious manner that there is not much playful spirit in our play. We tend to think of children as those who play in the true spirit of the word.

When we are serious, our tasks can become "a matter of life and death." But what that really means is that we are dead already if we feel this way. Seriousness is deadly; it kills the childlike part of us. The masculine hero's ultimate warning about his hostility and determination to win at all costs is to announce to others that he is *"deadly* serious." To be serious means that achieving the goal is all important. It also means that the value of the goal is beyond question.

To wonder whether the goal is really worth the kind of restricted life it might take to achieve it is already not to be serious—the truly heroic are not plagued with such doubts. When we are so captured by the goal as to become utterly serious, then the process of achieving the task becomes irrelevant. When the process becomes something we have to "get through," then we are *gone*—we're not really here with others. That's when the trickster tries to ensnare us, to involve us with life's process. When he gets Jack to go after the Holy Grail, Perry is really tricking Jack into deciding that his serious goals—the big career, money, and power—are not as important as just doing something that has no real goal but expresses a truly felt connection to someone else. Jack wouldn't have to be tricked if he could learn to let go and spend part of every day singing "I love New York" with people or lying naked at midnight in Central Park "busting clouds" with Perry, as he does at the film's end. With such time to play, different kinds of connections with others and with our work begin to emerge.

If the masculine defense is to keep the distance of control intact, however, the choice to play seems like an all-or-nothing choice. If there is a chink in the armor or a period of landing back on the Earth, the masculine fear is that we will be stuck down there or corrupted from the path of seriousness. Either we are devoted unflinchingly to the goals at hand or we've "lost it."

We see this masculine attitude being stressed in the conflict at the heart of the 1989 film, *Dead Poet's Society*. Here, too, Robin Williams plays a character, John Keating, who seeks to disrupt the masculine ethos—in this case, of a boy's preparatory school called Welton Academy. He walks into his first literature class whistling the "1812 Overture" and leads the boys into the school foyer, where the pictures of former students who died during the war are on display. He tells them the pictures are whispering a message to them and then rasps under his breath, "*Carpe diem*"—"Seize the day."

He tells them to make their lives extraordinary, and he tries to make each class period so. Whether it is standing on the teacher's desk to get a different perspective, having them tear out of their readers the stuffy introduction on how to rate each poem, or striding around campus until they find their own gait, Keating fills each class with the spirit of play instead of with the deadly serious business of "being educated." Of course, the other faculty and administrators decide Keating is not sufficiently serious and fire him. The purpose of education, when conceived in a serious manner, is to impart a certain knowledge. For Keating, its purpose is to make his students fall in love with language, to feel the great passions, "what we stay alive for," and to realize "that the powerful play goes on, and you may contribute a verse." He wants his students to be alive, engaged, spontaneous, creative, and having fun—the hallmarks of the finest kind of play—and to be freed from the seriousness that will kill the childlikeness in them that alone can make them come alive with wonder.

"Come on out and play!" How many of us heard that cry when we were boys. It might seem an accident that this call to play was usually joined with an invitation to "come out"—"to venture out"—from where we were before play. It could be attributed to the meaningless coincidence that little boys who play live in the confines of their parents' houses. However, I'd like to claim that even when we are living in our own house or no house, the call to play is always a conjoined invitation to "come outside." Play can only happen when people leave boundaries behind, when the usual frameworks for measuring what is necessary and useful to get things done are overstepped and we let go into a special shared energy flow. For the masculine gender identity, this means coming back from the distance, descending to Earth, coming out from behind the tanklike defenses, and leaving the ego confines behind. The type of energy flow and feeling sense of play are distinctive and inseparable.

The verb *play* comes from roots that signify "to leap for joy, to dance, to celebrate, and to be glad." If in our normal identity we hide behind the masks of what we are seeking to achieve and the past tokens of what we have achieved, then in play we must come out from behind all that. These barriers that serve as shields from the pain of life are also enclosures that block our access to this spontaneous celebration—this sudden flashing forth of joy. To play is to do something for the sheer joy both in being able to do and the doing. It is a celebrating that we are alive, sentient, interactive, expressive, and able in so many ways.

In *Dead Poet's Society*, the other faculty and administrators are very proud of all the accomplished leaders that Welton Academy has produced. They justify their constricted, control-oriented, and distanced relationship to the boys and also their lifeless classes by pointing to their success in molding the boys into leaders. They are inaccessible to the joy of discovery, of camaraderie with the boys, and of the spontaneous fun that can occur in the class. They are not able to make learning play—it must be serious or else. Unfortunately, the leaders they produce will be dead at heart—part of the toll who seem to be here but who are lost and distanced from others on this planet.

People who are so absent *don't realize how lethal they are* to those who are sensitive to human interaction, who need joy and creativity as part of life and wish to share it. Neil Perry is Keating's student who best understands the injunction of *carpe diem*. He is emotionally expressive and filled with the joy of life. His father keeps trying to stifle his spirit and make him a sober, goal-oriented achiever. Neil's father's work is carried forth by the lifeless men who run Welton Academy. They all collude to kill Neil Perry's spirit. His father is blind to Neil's life, only seeing it in terms of achieving a powerful and rich position. Neil is so hurt by their insensitivity, so despairing about ever being able to celebrate life and his talents in a world run by controlling, joyless men—that he shoots himself in his father's study. They had just succeeded in barring him from the frivolous activity of acting—to turn to a serious profession like being a doctor. Neil could recognize a death sentence. Unfortunately, he was too young to know that their jurisdiction is not absolute.

In discouraging the spontaneous, celebratory act of getting caught up in the *process* of doing things with others—
which is always apt to break out into play or have fun as its
only goal—the masculine ethos distances us from full embodiment. Although stressing the body as armored defense
or vehicle, its distance from vulnerable interaction is at the
same time a distance from the body as emotionally sensitive
and sensually perceptive. As in the realm of the Trickster,
play is frequently, though not always, *a return to the body*: that
ongoing, unacknowledged miracle that we are part of a web
with the world such that our motions, senses, emotions,
imaginations, memories, and ideas are meshed into the fabric
of the world. Each mirrors, complements, and extends into
the other.

In the sphere of play that highlights the body, there is celebration and joy in the fact that we can run, skip, jump,
swing, throw, dive, pump, pirouette, see, hear, judge distance, coordinate, strain, relax, endure, and a thousand other
amazing actions of the body—and all with grace, with a particularly touching beauty that is viscerally thrilling. This
gracefulness of the body that spills out in play has to do with
experiencing how the body can fit in with its environment,
meshing with those around it and within their web of
motion, and with being able to fit into the body's own flow as
a community of members, hand with eye, leg with arm. It is a
celebration of matching rhythms among people, of people
with objects in the world—like balls—and of parts of the
body in their own expressively generated sense of rhythm.

This joy in embodiment is about the body spilling over its
sense of boundedness, about allowing the creation of shared
rhythms, and about cultivating a finely tuned, open responsiveness to all around us in the play space. This is the opposite of the masculine identity's sense of the body used in a
defensive stance toward the world. The flying boy watches
and connects with his targets from behind a target screen,
within his fortified ego. The tank embodiment is not porous,

rhythmic, dancing, skipping, pirouetting, and meshing with its environment.

However, even in play that doesn't focus on the body as much, such as in playing with words, there is the same joy in just doing—perhaps in just being creatures of language, so the players dare to be silly and string together words in a salad of jostling meanings, just enjoying their sounds resounding and the new, unexpected meanings that suddenly emerge. This sheer celebration of doing is another kind of return: a childlike sense of being engaged with the world and others. We adults can be exasperated with children for their lack of seriousness at times when we want them to get something done, but children just get caught up in the fun of the doing itself. For many adults, especially for heroically burdened males, the doing is only the means to an end.

The possibility of rediscovering this childlike attitude of play versus the "seriousness" that he saw around him was the focus of Nietzsche's critique of society—although his work has been terribly misunderstood and misrepresented. However, to look at what he said for a moment is important here, since one of his chief concerns was that the idea of "man"—indicating a certain kind of identity—had outlived its usefulness. Nietzsche's advocacy of "going beyond" man was not to create a "superman," as he has been mistranslated and misunderstood to have said, but rather to journey to the "highest stage" of development: "the child." He looked at men and saw that most of us spend our lives as "camels," bearing burdens we have taken on our backs and trying mightily to achieve our goals despite all obstacles. He did acknowledge that some men went beyond this to become "lions," blazing their own paths and fighting their own battles. However, he saw that the obsession with achieving goals, of whatever sort, is a negative approach to life. It is an attempt to defeat the pain of death and take on the world. He saw this was a defense against "going under": an inability to take pain, disappointment, and our overall sense that life is beyond our control (what he would call *finitude*) to heart, and be shattered for a time.

For Nietzsche, we could only really affirm being human if we became childlike: "Why must the preying lion still become a child? The child is innocence and forgetting, a new beginning, a game, a self-propelled wheel, a first movement, a sacred 'Yes.' For the game of creation, my brothers, a sacred 'Yes' is needed."[1] The childlike attitude toward life can turn even the most serious actions into play. Even if our lives depend on achieving the goals, the opportunity that life provides us is to enjoy the process in working toward those goals. Life itself is an invitation to play. It is the resistance involved in the working toward goals that gives life its activity, which makes up its substance. We can either resent our work, life's activity and substance, or we can enter our struggles as part of an opportunity to play. If one has this attitude then all endeavors are part of a game—a saying "yes" to the very fact of human doing. To play is to celebrate—to take joy.

Nietzsche described this transformation from a serious attitude toward life into a playful one as the turn from "life for the sake of goals" into "goals for the sake of life." If we play with life, *then our goals are just the means of getting us fully immersed in the process.* For example, scoring touchdowns is just a tool for spurring us on to give our full effort so we can immerse ourselves in the intoxication of pumping our legs, the tranquillity of gliding down the field, the welcome caress of the sun on our face, and the pungent harmony of our gracefulness in leaping up into the air and having the ball come together with outstretched hands without breaking stride. In the "serious" attitude, life's experiences are just to be "gotten through" on the way to the goal, which is then just replaced with another goal, and all life is lived waiting for a future and never being fully alive and celebratory in the moment.

When I teach Nietzsche to my students, I ask how many of them would be able to celebrate their education if at the end of their four years they were told they were not going to receive a diploma, but that they had been allowed for four years to experience the joy of learning. Very few students can deal with that thought: most say they are just "putting in the time" for the goal of obtaining a diploma. A few say they love the process of coming to school and being part of a community of learners. Those few students have a more playful attitude toward their activity, which is what sheer play isolates for our celebration. This is the childlike embrace of the moment and of being fully present to its shining quality. If we can do this, then it is not a light from above that informs life, but each action, each object, and each person encountered in our play becomes an incandescent force.

Yet the picture of life given from the traditional masculine perspective is serious. Zarathustra is the figure in Nietzsche's mythic parable of a male who seeks to find a way to become more childlike but keeps falling back into seriousness. Nietzsche's description of the pitfalls of seriousness etches a haunting picture of how masculinity lives under the burden of the specter of Herculean labors. Suffering under this weight destroys the spirit of play and exacerbates an inner despair:

> Not long ago I walked gloomily through the deadly pallor of dusk—gloomy and hard, with lips pressed together. Not only one sun had set for me. A path that ascended defiantly through stones, malicious, lonely, not cheered by herb or shrub—a mountain path crunched under the defiance of my foot. Striding silently over the mocking clatter of pebbles, crushing the rock that made it slip, my foot forced its way upward. Upward—defying that spirit of gravity, my devil and archenemy. Upward—although he sat on me, half dwarf, half mole, lame, making lame, dripping lead into my ear, leaden thoughts into my brain. "O Zarathustra," he whispered mockingly, syllable by syllable; "you philosopher's stone! You threw yourself high, but every stone that is thrown must fall.

Sentenced to yourself and your own stoning—O,
Zarathustra, far indeed have you thrown the stone, but
it will fall back on yourself."[2]

This is the image of the male and the vision of life that
has informed the masculine identity and brought with it this
crushing weight of seriousness. The hero walks alone, up a
path, a forbidding path, following a way that is defiantly cut
out of unyielding stones. He walks stoically, in a spirit of
defiance and unyielding determination. Life is a mountain to
surmount and conquer. The spirit of gravity pulls down,
because it tells the heroic male that whatever is thrown up
must come down; that no matter what he achieves it will not
ultimately defeat life's finitude; that friends like Enkidu will
die; and that even the monuments Gilgamesh erects will
eventually wear away. Whether Hercules, Gilgamesh, Ahab,
or the man next door, the one who chooses to be a hero seeks
this higher, upward path—whether to greater glory and status or higher on "the ladder of success"—but this very seeking in the face of impossible odds makes him feel pulled
downward all the time. This is "male despair."

Despite our masculine reveries, we know we can't just
soar off into the pure light and still be human. We know this,
and it hurts. This hurt makes us even more defiant. The
"spirit of gravity" is a wonderful image—the inner male
voice that makes us want to ascend, to get on top of life—yet
in so urging, it is responsible for the pull downward, for it
also is "grave"—that is, both serious and the spirit of death
rather than a celebration of life. According to Nietzsche, this
attitude of wanting to achieve goals to justify our life is a
response to the setbacks, the hurts of life, and particularly to
time's threat of eventually ending our life. In the face of this
pain, we have wanted to get revenge on life's process and on
time itself. However, since this dynamic passage is what life
itself is really about, Nietzsche says that this spirit of revenge
means we are sick of life.

For Nietzsche, to play is to celebrate the very thing that is so depressing for us: that there is no ultimate mountain to climb, no final heroic victory of any sort that will defeat life's flux and death's threat. He contends that for us the intuition that the heroic quest is futile leaves us sick. His image for this sickness is that a snake has crawled into our throat and bit fast, leaving us with an incredible nausea for life. The snake is the old Goddess symbol that was chosen for its reference to cyclic time. The snake sheds its skin and renews itself in the midst of life.

The snake is sometimes portrayed biting its own tail, forming a circle of time in which there is nowhere to go, no sky for the flying boy to soar off into after the Great Prize, but instead a coming back always to the same place, the place one has on this Earth, doing over and over again the simple earthly tasks. If, as Nietzsche says, we could bite into this snake and instead celebrate that there is nowhere to go, no ultimate achievement to accomplish in order to save the day, then we could be radiant, laughing, childlike beings affirming the process of life for its own sake.

In *Thus Spoke Zarathustra*, the shepherd—certainly a symbol for the masculine impulse to lead others and watch over them—is writhing on the ground, overcome by nausea, the snake hanging out of his throat. Zarathustra screams with every passion in him for the shepherd to bite into the snake. When the shepherd bites "with a good bite" into the snake and spews the head away, he jumps up, "one changed, radiant, laughing! Never yet on earth has a human being laughed as he laughed!" (p. 272) This is the laugh of play. If we could find humor in not going anywhere, the joke would be on us—not in a malicious sense, but life "would be our gesture," our vehicle for just being active and shining forth in that activity. So, in *Dead Poet's Society*, when students raise their hands and volunteer answers that are incorrect, Keating imitates a buzzer or bell going off and thanks them for playing—a parody of the game show. Instead of feeling bad, they laugh. Yet, isn't that a way we can look at all so-called failures? "Thanks for playing!" is what life is saying to us if heard in this receptive, humorous way of being.

It is this sense of life as play that the Zen master tries to teach others through his own life. There is a story of a Zen master who, when about to die, gathers his students about him and asks one to take down his last words. The master says: "All my life I've been sitting on the banks of a great river and selling water." Then he adds, "Ho, ho, ho!" and dies happily. This is the spirit of play. Ultimately, it doesn't matter whether we achieve any goal, but only whether we are fully present and enthralled with what we are doing—as a child caught up in its play.

The masculine spirit would object to this in the name of responsibility and obligation: "There are important goals that must be achieved for the good of many, and I am obligated to them, whether to my people or my family, to carry out this mission with seriousness." However, the Zen master's response would be to say, as did Nietzsche, that to lose the love of life doesn't accomplish these goals or obligations. We can enjoy the process and still achieve goals.

Actually, to be able to play may mean that the goals are achieved even more adequately as the indirect blossom of a fully affirmed process rather than as a product of will, determination, and masculine heroism. In *Zen and the Art of Archery*, Eugen Herrigal struggles for seven years to learn Japanese archery and hit a bull's-eye. One night, the master shows him that when he has let go of his desperation—or even any specific intention—to hit the target, and instead fully enters into the joy of the ritual dance preparing the bow and the shot, then he may learn to hit the bull's-eye even in a pitch-dark firing hall!

To make sure Herrigal gets the point, the master dances the ritual preparation and fires twice into the pitch dark. He asks Herrigal to retrieve the target from the darkened end of the hall. To his amazement, Herrigal finds both arrows in the center of the bull's-eye—and that the second arrow has split the first in half! Herrigal himself discovers that when he no longer focuses on hitting the target but instead enters the spirit of play and just enjoys the ritual—the embodied sense and rhythm of stretching and shooting the bow and arrow— he suddenly can hit the target! When we are open to the wonder of life, as if life were playing with us, we may still be successes.

However, the heroic mentality tells us, no, we must close ourselves off from entering this ongoing joyfulness as the price of winning the day. Given the prevalence of this attitude, it should not be surprising that in our society even those who do win and are celebrated as victorious heroes, after spending their lives engaged in "games" or "contests" are unable to play. We still call them "players," but we know they are lacking the childlike spirit of play that has that special glow whose warmth we miss. Instead of seeing in these figures men who have been able to keep alive their childlike spirit, we are disappointed.

Robert Altman's 1991 film, *The Player*, is a dark comment on this masculine inability to play. The irony of the title and the film is that the main character is not a player in any sense of the word that we have been discussing; rather, he is a traditional, serious, Herculean male. He can't affirm the process of his life and occupation at all because he is so caught up in achieving success. He can only "work." He is not the only one. Equally obsessed with "scoring" are all the players of the film who are engaged in the "Hollywood game." Paradoxically, a player in this context means someone who "gets results," who "wins big," no matter how it is done. Of course, this is just the opposite of the spirit of true play.

How could it be otherwise when even those "players" who would seem to have the best chance at preserving the spirit of play by making their "living" at sports—whose very life activity is that of a game and a contest—do not play? Sports are not a "living" for them in the sense of a playful way of being but only in the sense of accumulating money, which they mistakenly take to be the essence of life. Instead of finding people who are full of the play spirit, increasingly our sports heroes are a new kind of businessman—serious men out for worldly success—and we lament the days of sports when there were men who played ball just for the sheer joy of the game, just to be doing it, and didn't care much about salaries or other "payoffs." Now we can recognize the childlikeness these men brought with their love of the game, since it seems to be gone in the new "players." However, this brings home the lesson that it is not the content of the activity itself that determines whether it's play or not, since games can become serious business when they lack the play spirit. Rather, play is a way to *be*, a becoming playful, that can enliven any of life's activities with a different glow, a different sense, and a different relationship among people.

In his poem, "Lapis Lazuli," W. B. Yeats evokes images which suggest that the most serious business can be done by those who have kept the spirit of the child and the spirit of play alive:

> Yet they, should the last scene be there,
> The great stage curtain about to drop,
> If worthy their prominent part in the play,
> Do not break up their lines to weep.
> They know that Lear and Hamlet are gay;
> Gaiety transfiguring all that dread.
> All men have aimed at, found and lost . . .[3]

Yeats evokes images of immigrants, leaders, artists—of all who try to achieve something notable or difficult with their lives. If they are to be worthy of becoming prominent in the human drama, he says, they must have that inextinguishable spark of playfulness in their souls: "All things fall and are built again,/And those that build them are gay." Yeats suggests that the insistence on seriousness as a criterion for productivity threatens our sense of aliveness and meaning in life, and that it ultimately threatens the vitality that is the mainspring of life. *Vitality does not come from sources of heroic assertion* but from the letting go that the child knew and men may have to relearn.

Yeats's final portrayal of this kind of wisdom is a carving made of lapis lazuli of two old Chinese men sitting on a mountainside looking on "all the tragic scene." The men are able to feel the mournfulness of human failures, of the passing away of loved ones, and the accomplishments in the flow of time, and yet "Their eyes mid many wrinkles, their eyes,/ Their ancient, glittering eyes, are gay." Yeats suggests that even the farthest reaches of human endeavor can become a way of being playful, a return to childlikeness that is an ancient wisdom rather than the youth-worshipping defiance of self-assertion that has been the masculine model for vitality. The seeming vitality of the young knight tilting with enemies may be a grim, serious, worn-out sense of vitality that has not yet shed its snakeskin to be reborn into a different sort of joy as part of a process in which there is no ultimate victory.

Playful, Supportive Conflict

The play aspect of male existence in modern America could be augmented if it were transformed. The boyhood common language of sport could cut across many class, ethnic, and economic lines if it could be kept from becoming too serious. We men have betrayed ourselves by turning sport into an organized commercial establishment. Partly, our masculine interest in sport is the same old walled-off defense system: sports are used to distract ourselves and as a way to avoid dealing with areas of life that call for vulnerability. Partly, too, interest in sports is manufactured by big business for profit. Also, there is a certain amount of *childish* competitiveness and emotional immaturity that takes us to the playground or to the basement or to the streets to join in a game as an attempt to bolster our insecure egos. Finally, as we mentioned in the chapter on language as a barrier, we can use talk and obsession with sports as another kind of plating for our tank armor and to distance ourselves from painful aspects of our lives. Instead of taking personal relations to heart, we males can become riveted to what happens on professional playing fields across the country—hence, a nation of "football widows."

It would be an important start if we men could embrace the appeal of play in sport to find a healthy ability to be childlike at times. In the childlike embrace of life as play, of a quickened pulse and of the gracefulness of our bodies engaged with others, we can enter into the competition that *binds* hearts and builds moments of excellence. As Keating says to his soccer players in *Dead Poet's Society*, "Sports are a chance for other human beings to push us to excel." As he says this, he has each player recite a famous line of poetry that expresses an instant of exaltation as each steps up to kick the ball. Masculinity calls for the seriousness of the heroic stance toward life, shouldering burdens, worrying about threats, and finding solutions; yet when play calls out, the same harried, stoic being breaks into a lope or cracks a smile and dismisses the "serious business" of life for the game, whether as participant or spectator. If we could at least start to be playful here, maybe we could carry it over to other dimensions of life.

If we men were really to celebrate our playfulness, to transform this aspect of our masculine role, then we might discover that direct participation in sport and game is a way to bring the body and senses into union with the Earth and others in a rhythm of grace and motion. Most play occurs in some sort of game or contest, but not if the contest is another way to feel pressured to succeed and to dominate others—a perversion of its original sense.

The initial Greek concept of *agon* is that of a contest—a sport, a playful competition—in which those who play against each other play *for* each other by becoming the counterbalance of each other. It is a way of building a special sort of community. If men could achieve the playfulness of true *agon*, then as each would look into the eyes of his competitors, each would grow larger or leaner or more graceful or faster as he was caught up in the spell of the game and brought to new heights of sheer doing. With *agon*, the idea of sport or game or play is to "show off" for one another—not in the sense of an explicit goal, which undermines the game, as in "hot dogging", but as the joyfulness of being caught up in play and achieving a certain gracefulness that is witnessed by the others who are playing. This is why sports naturally give rise to the allure of becoming a spectator, which expands the original witnessing of these instants of "glad grace" to a much wider circle. Souls come together in the fire of the game to be transformed and linked in the magic of the moment.

We have not used this power of play to link people and restore both their gracefulness and self-esteem in the gentle way that play can inspire. A wonderful evocation of these powers of play is expressed by John Harrison, who both wrote and directed the 1990 film, *Beautiful Dreamers*. This film is a particularly compelling image of the power of play because it is based on an incident that actually occurred in 1880 in London, Ontario, and involves the American male who perhaps most exemplifies the power of play—Walt Whitman.

The main character, Dr. Morris Bucke, has just been appointed superintendent of the London Asylum for the Insane. Bucke is initially skeptical of the use of restraints, chemical therapy, psychosurgery, removal of "hysteric's" ovaries, and other invasive procedures. However, only after walking out of a professional conference in Philadelphia where he vainly criticizies his colleagues for their cruel manipulations of patients in order to achieve the behavior that the doctors desire and deem appropriate, does he meet up with Whitman. As he storms out of the meeting, Whitman chases after him to voice his support for Bucke's contentions. These contentions include the idea that "feeling precedes thinking." Bucke believes that reaching patients emotionally will help their thinking problems.

Taking Whitman back to London for consultation and support, Bucke starts to change the asylum procedures. He orders that restraints and drugs be halted. Instead, the female patients are to be played music, encouraged to sing, and engaged in dancing with the staff, while the males should be taken outside and involved in playing various team sports. Bucke announces—to the shock of his staff—that the new policy toward patients is to be summed up as "exercise, playing games, and having fun."

Of course, the patients are not concerned about winning at cricket or their smart appearance at dancing. Instead, they laugh, feel their bodies move in new ways, and get caught up in the various moments of the game or dance. As they play, they start to emerge from their isolation and interact with others. They start to find their own unique ways of expressing themselves. They start to wake up to life and to themselves.

To really enter the spirit of play would call for an end to our masculine concern with having power, with being leaders, and with being in control. We men sometimes seem surprised that we are often seen as wanting to be above others; however, not only has history given evidence of this desire, but the distanced, defended, masculine stance has tended always to move in this direction. In the film *Falling Down*, the Michael Douglas character, "D-Fens," is continually surprised that others see him as the aggressor or the oppressor, but his defended way of being leaves others no opening for reciprocal relationship, and his repressed hostility is continually bubbling to the surface. Given the prevalence of the masculine ethos, men need to understand that others might be wary that there could be a truly playful sort of competition with males. Living in a society in which a woman is raped every forty-three seconds and in which men control most of the powerful institutions can make it very difficult for women to see males as able to be playfully competitive.

However, if we males were limited to picking just one aspect of our being that could be transformed into a way to open to others, I would start with men at play. Yes, we have all seen boys and even grown men go home in tears when they were devalued or abused by other males who had a serious "win-at-all-costs" attitude toward the game. However, more often than in almost any other area of society, on playing fields we find men helping other men learn skills, supporting each other's moods, having affectionate body contact, showing a wide range of emotions, being aware of each other's weaknesses, working together, appreciating differences in style, not judging each other's "manliness," and entering a shared joy at just being alive and active together. On these playing fields, one is most likely to see white and Afro-American; straight and gay; Catholic, Protestant, and Jew; Irish, Puerto Rican, and Indian; hippy and conservative; old and young; and all sorts of men just being easily and openly together. On playing fields, for once, we males step out of our tanks, from behind our targeting screens, come down from the skies, and just laugh and hug together—as long as the masculine imperative can be kept from distorting the game and breaking its fragile spell.

In order to really allow play to become a transformative force for our stifling masculinity, we need to recapture a more childlike attitude toward the world. As we noted before, on our targeting screens, what shows up is seen only under the label "friend" or "enemy." Yet the play spirit challenges this seriously held opposition, as well as others. If the world is divided only into those who are "for me" or "against me," or between those who are "for us" or "against us," then the openness to becoming enmeshed with others—that we've identified as emotional vulnerability—cannot occur. Another opposition that follows from this dualistic way of thinking is the way of categorizing emotional states between "taking care" of those on our side and "taking on" those who are to be distrusted as potential enemies—as if emotionally there existed either support or confrontation, affirmation or challenge, blind loyalty or treacherous questioning, and ultimately, either love or hate. Vital relationships with others are more complex, and so are the sensitive feelings that engender and accompany them. Already in what we've said about the nature of *agon*, it is apparent that play makes us feel the need to be opposed to the other person in order to become fully ourselves. However, this opposition is in the spirit of play; it is opposition as connection and comradeship rather than opposition as annihilation in the way of Hercules and other heroes.

Both of these aspects of play—to overcome absolute differences and to use conflict to help all parties excel—motivate Bucke to invite the townspeople up to the asylum grounds for a day of picnicking and playing together—the "lunatics" included. What happens is that in the play spirit of the gathering, the townspeople realize that the lunatics are not as different as they had supposed. This is not an intellectual realization, though—in their playing there is an immediate, felt enchantment that brings all the people together. For example, as the musicians play, both the inmates and the townspeople are equally amused and held in the music's spell. The music and other activities create an immediate experience of connection between both groups. The asylum inmates start to experience the townspeople as not as frightening as they had seemed.

It is a contest that really transforms the standoff. The person most opposed to liberalizing the policies of the asylum is Bucke's wife's uncle, Randolph Haines. He is a buddy of the other members of the "old guard" of the town, who all feel threatened by these changes. He tells the mayor that in the face of Bucke's new treatment of the patients, "We're relics, you and I." His insecurities and hostility are so deeply felt that he adds, "There's a new blade in the guillotine, and it's very, very sharp." However, Randolph is also an avid cricket player and the captain of the town's crack cricket team. Reluctantly, he agrees to play a game against the asylum inmates.

One of the most abused patients is Leonard, who, besides being withdrawn and confused, has trouble speaking, and his hands and face are contorted. Because he used to masturbate regularly, he was kept in restraints with his hands in heavy gloves and chained to posts above his bed. He has responded well to Bucke's obvious concern and affection, and Bucke sees what a gentle and kind man Leonard is beneath his contorted and confused exterior. Whitman has started the staff working with Leonard to get back some use of his hands by throwing him the ball and having him try to catch it.

When Randolph comes to bat, he hits the cricket ball in a very high fly ball. Leonard gathers himself under it, and despite his crippled hands, makes the catch. He screams out in sheer delight, and no one at the picnic can resist being swept up into the magic of the moment. The contest, which turns out to be more playful than it might have been, given the prior hostilities, pushes Leonard, Randolph, and the other participants and spectators beyond themselves to new levels of security and acceptance.

In some way, I and the person who opposes me in a playful contest—or we who indulge in sheer play—seem not to be "me" nor to really be "them." Rather, it is the "me" that is being "played at," the role that I've been given in the game. The way the other opposes me is also not from the heart of their self-interest but from the "player's position" they've taken up in the game. Yet the "me" that I've played at is not simply "not me" either. In the spell of play, the solidity of who I am and who the other players are can loosen up and become more complex, more rich.

Play enters a realm that seems partly fantasy or imagination or "make-believe." However, what happens in play is not to be neatly divided from "reality." Play can significantly *alter* my reality. Also, as we said, the most serious doings in "reality" may be taken up in a way that make them more like play. The line between so-called fantasy and reality is more blurred than we might like to think—and certainly more blurred than the masculine identity has asserted from Oedipus onward in its attempt to keep an unquestionable grasp on facts and identities. Play shakes these supposedly secure foundations and oppositions. In having this power, play can extend its spell into other aspects of life—aspects that seem difficult to masculine identity. The schoolboys who join the Dead Poet's Society, meeting at night in a cave after sneaking away from campus, play at being poets, Bohemians, spiritual adventurers, and free thinkers. It is fun. They laugh and are caught in the spell of these moments. What happens, however, is that these moments of play *do* change their lives. They start to become something else—souls alive to the wonder of life who dare to seize the day, as Keating hoped they would.

The masculine ethos has problems with the kind of conflict that is at the heart of forging a long-term, loving relationship. To love takes the courage to continually challenge the other and allow oneself to be challenged. However profound these challenges are, however, they can't be undertaken in a spirit of deadly seriousness, as if the other person must change. This must be a *playful* challenge. It must also be a challenge to go further into the possibilities of play—to play with one's life—but in this instance, together. It requires that one be able to hold up Hamlet's mirror to others and confront them with the possibility that they are many; that they have the potentialities of many selves and can always grow beyond current definitions; that perhaps unknown even to themselves, they play roles and can play even more. Yet, this is a confrontation intended to open the other's being, to add to who they are. Hamlet's act of confronting his mother, Gertrude, and his uncle, Claudius, in order to reveal to them other selves took great courage. "You go not till I set you up in a glass,/ Where you may see the inmost part of yourself." Care requires this mirroring back to the person other dimensions of oneself.

We realize that the power of the contest in play has an aggressive dimension, but we misplace its deeper meaning. It is not the winning or losing that is the heart of the struggle in a contest. The aggression of the contest is the challenge given to the other person to become something else, something beyond his or her present being. The identity of the other person is to be transformed within the spell of play, to be seen, felt, and experienced as an added dimension of that person. The prefix *con* signifies that it is a test with the other, taken on together. Hamlet's mirror not only reveals the shortcomings not noticed before, but it is also the place where new possibilities are played out in the eyes of others who will recognize our changes and possibilities. So, if I can be transformed, perhaps just for a moment at first, in the clear regard of the other, I can also become other to myself.

However, in our "serious" approach to others, categorizing them in order to dispose of them in some way, the regard we cast toward the other is often confining, and sometimes even crushing. Often, these glances are attempts to dismiss, use, or dominate the other. This type of gaze is the so-called Sartrean "look," in which we seek to overcome the subjectivity of the other by either reducing this person to a mere object or by dominating or seducing his or her "look"—so the other looks at us in the way we seek to be seen—in order to bolster our own insecure sense of being. We males often look at one another in this way, and are addicted to regarding women as possible prey—as objects to be controlled or conquered.

To genuinely play with another, however, is to look at the other in the sheer fascination of watching this person possibly become a being to be cheered or celebrated. When caught up in the spirit of the game, we seek for ourselves and others to reach beyond to become something else. In the spell of the

agon, it doesn't matter what daily struggles preceded or
awaits; we hope for that moment of shining play in which we
become beautiful for the moment of that play, even though it
is a flashing instant to be lost when the game ends. To com-
pete with strength and vigor on this "agonistic" field gives
the other the resistance needed as a springboard to go beyond oneself.

To play is to set aside the daily concerns of life and the
more typical male antagonism of aggression toward others
that comes from our pained, contained, frustrated sense of
ourselves and to "let down our guard" in order to "take time
out" to play. In the spirit of play, we can let go of a definite
boundary, a definite identity, and let others shine forth, and
we do so in a reciprocal witnessing and supportiveness with
others. This is a vital way of entering relationships that, if
experienced in its joy and liberation from defensiveness, can
carry us beyond the realm of sheer play. If we males can't become playful in this way, as our masculine seriousness has
often made difficult, then we can't love fully. We have to play
with the other in love to find that impossible middle line that
includes both challenging and supporting the other. It can't
be drawn rationally, it can only be cast forth in the playful spell.

This is what Whitman is able to do with Bucke in *Beautiful Dreamers*. Whitman has him "come outside" and play,
and Bucke plays beyond his old boundaries. When Whitman
met him, Bucke was a cautious, self-doubting, and withdrawn man. Whitman saw in him other possibilities—other
selves waiting for a chance to be exercised. From the moment
Whitman takes him home to Camden and rolls on the floor
with his mentally retarded brother, he starts to draw Bucke
into a play-filled existence. They wander the fields together,
singing operas, pitch cricket balls for hours, play piano and
sing accompaniment (even as they're transporting it on a
wagon through the countryside to the asylum), fly kites, and
spend hours wading in the river, rubbing mud all over each

other and swimming. All the while, Whitman is encouraging Bucke to "scatter all that you've achieved" and allowing him to feel this increased self-esteem and vitality in their play. The new boldness found in this play is able to be acted on the stage of reality at the hospital when Bucke changes the rules. His actions there are still infused with the play spirit that gradually infects others. Even Dr. Let, Bucke's psycho-surgery-obsessed colleague, gradually succumbs to the spell of the inmates singing, dancing, and playing cricket, and puts down his scalpel.

Playing New Selves into Existence

To fully enter the realm of play is a way to open up the emotional tides that have become inaccessible or seemingly "dried up." However, emotions do not dry up: they are inex-haustible, and they are not of our own making. Emotions come from our relations with the world, but the masculine ego in its distance from the world can lose its connection to this source of emotion. Only when we think of emotions as "inner realities" versus "outer realities," as we have seen in the dualistic masculine mentality, can we fear we have "lost" our emotions as men. Emotions as that wet circulation of cur-rents of life with the world will be restored as soon as our openness to the world is restored. Yet as long as we are cir-cling above, stuck in the confines of our tanks and cockpits, it is a frightening prospect to rejoin these flows of earthly life. That is why it may be important to call men to "come outside and play." By doing so, we are calling men out to an area of life that is less threatening, since it is a time-out from "real life" and its hurtful problems. Yet play has a power that sneaks up on us—it is a trick of sorts—and that is the key to its magic to infuse life with celebration.

In his classic study of the nature of play, *Homo Ludens*, Johan Huizinga emphasizes the characteristics that set play aside from the rest of life while also showing how it is at the root of so many creative possibilities. He calls play "a stepping out of 'real' life into a temporary sphere of activity with a disposition all of its own."[4] When we play, we carve out a niche in space and time—as, for example, when suddenly the lawn is now "bocce court," and it's "bocce time" until the last point is scored. Play also requires that we give ourselves up to its call and that we join with others who are playing in a linkage that creates a special "play-community" within the duration of the game.

When play happens, then "play casts a spell over us; it is 'enchanting,' 'captivating'" (p. 10). Huizinga agrees there is no purpose to the game other than getting us involved in the process, and this special time, place, community, and spell facilitate this, since its goal is not to achieve something, even winning. Play sets up a dimension in which a spell can catch us just to be involved in that particular "play-purpose." In doing this, there is a transformation, a becoming something for the very significance of becoming it. If we play at being aliens visiting the planet or at ghosts, it is just to become an alien or a ghost for the time of the play spell. Even sports are an attempt to feel ourselves in new ways, such as supple-body-straining-dancing-in-the-air, perhaps.

However, at the heart of these transformations is something potentially deeper. Huizinga sees that without play, love is not possible, and also that it allows ceremony and a way to connect with the sacred in which "play may rise to heights of beauty and sublimity that leave seriousness far behind" (p. 8). Here, too, another opposition collapses: between the lighthearted and the profound, between the limited in scope and that which goes to the widest horizons of significance. Play seems to capture both. It does so by trading on a certain power of emotion. We enter emotional tides in what seems like a small space and yet find something greater.

Emotion itself has this double sense of seeming more confined and yet also wider ranging. At first, what holds us emotionally seems confined to a smaller realm than we can absorb through our far-ranging rational thought. Yet emotion *resonates* further: it doesn't range over and dominate the landscape of our life, but at times it works out from a moment and place in our life to infiltrate everything with a new tide, a new sense of things. Emotion seems to take us into its own drama in time and place—as, for example, when we feel anger toward our partner for something done to hurt us. For that moment of flaring anger, our other qualities of character, our long history together, and our other shared significances are swept aside. That person may have done something trivial; we may have had a complex and rich relationship for decades; and the world may be collapsing with some catastrophe; but at that moment of anger, all we feel is the flaming toward that person-who-was-utterly-rude-and-insensitive-to-my-dear-friends and nothing else.

However, this small niche of the "world of feeling" can invade our larger world. For example, your being rude to my friends was a small happening in the context of twenty years of events between us, but somehow the anger you touched off that night has now switched my gestalt, my overall take, on you as a partner. This one act has suddenly linked up with thousands of other acts over the years that have formed a new pattern, a new sense about your possibilities. Suddenly I feel that I won't go on with you. This is the startling, unpredictable power that masculinity avoids when we flee from openness to emotion. However, emotion is invaluable for making manifest what was hidden in the world, dispersed, and unexperienceable in such a palpable way. Suddenly, through emotion we see a whole new world or have an entirely new sense about others or ourselves. Emotion is the power to suddenly be in a new way, to come to be there fully—immersed in one's life.

Play opens us to this emotional realm. I play at being things that I have dreamed about or sensed as possibilities, and suddenly there I am, shining forth in the light of the play space displaying this new characteristic or ability. The celebration of sheer doing is, at a deeper level, a celebration of just sheer being. We celebrate who we can be in various new aspects or even old aspects that we hadn't really expressed fully. This is why the Zen master claims that in his playful attitude he not only really walks, talks, and eats, or *does*, but also *is*—is as "really and fully here." In his lighthearted but total absorption, he is really in contact with us.

This play that allows us to shine forth is utterly infectious. Once, at a gathering with Zen Master Eido Roshi at a posh Yale reception with a few hundred other people present, I shone forth in a way that I still can't believe decades later. The Master was asked about the nature of the Bodhisattva and responded by asking if anyone knew how to sing "The Impossible Dream" from the musical, *Man of La Mancha*, since this song would demonstrate the Bodhisattva spirit. I sprang up and volunteered, a man with no musical voice who had never before and has never since sung in front of a group, and sang out, "To dream the impossible dream, to fight the unbeatable foe . . ." and so forth, in front of this crowd at Yale! I was not in the slightest bit self-conscious. I was just swept up in the Eido's laughing, playful spirit, and I shone forth in a new way whose moment of shining will always be part of who I am.

Yet the masculine perspective objects that the lawn is the lawn, it doesn't really change into something different as "bocce court," nor am I different as the singer of Don Quixote's refrain. It is true that these differences are not ones that will show up on the target screens: they don't fit in with the masculine, rationalizing view of the world as a collection of objects that are totally independent of each other. Huizinga speaks of a ritual dance in which the dancer not only represents a kangaroo but within the spell of the dance, in this sacred kind of play, *is* the kangaroo (p. 25). Of course, the dancer is not changed into the anatomy and physiology of a kangaroo. Huizinga says that one "half-believes" that one has become the kangaroo in the ritual for that moment when one is "seized upon" by the play spirit. He says the key is that we fall into the mood and take up the emotion appropriate to that transformation. Logic tells us that we are ourselves and not a kangaroo, but logic doesn't cover all the richness of reality; it leaves out realms of meaning—the very realms of meaning we will need to supplement the straitjacket of masculinity.

We "half-believe" while we are playing because the transformation is "empty" (*sunyata*) in the Buddhist sense: we are not *really* the kangaroo as a chunk of hard being at the fever pitch of the kangaroo dance. But the whole point is that we are not *anything* in that sense. Seeing the world in terms of sheer physicality comes closest to this notion of reality, but that blocks off our human reality. We are "Glen" or "Mary" or "John" in an open and creative way as "half-believing" in the play of those identities. We realize that we can add to the vibrancy, luster, and fullness of presence of those identities in the same way that we can add to "kangaroo being" by really letting go into playing at being what we are. If we can enter this deeper level of play, we can gain *more life*; not in the sense that Gilgamesh went on the quest to add more years to his life span, but as being more in the present with others. Playing at one's identity can add new dimensions and depth to one's identity through the interplay with others. In play we get to "half-believe," which is neither believing nor disbelieving, but a way of taking on more presence into our identity. We play ourselves into transformations of self.

For example, in *Beautiful Dreamers*, Bucke's wife, Jesse, watches with increasing resentment as Whitman and her husband frolic all around town. She has been brought up in a very proper, strict background and is scandalized by small social transgressions, such as Whitman and Bucke grabbing their asparagus by the end, slopping butter sauce on it, and dangling it down their throats. Having them wandering around town singing, consorting with lunatics, flying kites, and being the subject of disapproving gossip is more than she can tolerate. She wants Whitman to leave. However, all along, it is obvious that there is a part of Jesse that would love to come out from behind her walls and play, too. When Bucke refuses to throw Whitman out, Jesse retreats to bed and reads *Leaves of Grass*. She's still resistant but intrigued. Only when she finds Whitman and Bucke naked in the mud of the river one hot summer day does she decide to enter the play spell, too. She slowly strips off all her clothes, chiding them into letting her join the play—a rather daring move for 1880. They all frolic in the water and enjoy the afternoon. A chord has been reached in Jesse that probably could not have been reached except through the power of the play spirit. She will never be the same woman—reserved, bitter, distant, and so worried about social propriety. She has dared to play at being a new daring and spontaneous Jesse and in so doing becomes transformed into that woman.

Play in all its levels moves in the opposite direction of the fear of death and the rage at mortality that fired the heroic souls of Gilgamesh, Hercules, and Ahab. Play can be seen in all aspects of existence, even on the metaphysical or cosmic level. In the Hindu mythic tradition, the sense of play, called *lila*, not only indicates the way that saviors come to Earth—as when Krishna, caught up in wild dancing, happens to stamp out the Earth's demons—but also how things themselves dance in and out of existence. The masculine ethos, in its seriousness, believes that its own conduct should be grave, and also believes the flux of existing is an assault upon the cosmic gravity of some masculine Supreme Being who orders and controls and whose example we follow.

Play has the power to release us into a deeper flow in which we are challenged by the game to shine forth in the sheer effulgence of our being. Yet this being is just that: a showing with others, an engaged playing that will change, that has to be rekindled and will pass away. Yet to enter this flow of the game of existence without defenses and without attempting to "get above" this fray, is to gain for the moment the only real being with others that we have on Earth. Shake-

speare, a master of the play and of the idea of what it means
to act with others—to play our part—painted perhaps the
best picture of existence itself as this flow (in what perhaps
was his farewell and best piece of wisdom):

> You do look, my son, in a moved sort,
> As if you were dismayed; be cheerful sir.
> Our revels are now ended. These our actors,
> As I foretold you, were all spirits and
> Are melted into air, into thin air;
> And like the baseless fabric of this vision,
> The cloud-capped towers, the gorgeous
>   palaces,
> The solemn temples, the great globe itself,
> Yea, all we inherit, shall dissolve,
> And like this insubstantial pageant faded,
> Leave not a rack behind. We are such stuff
> As dreams are made on, and our little life
> Is rounded with a sleep.[5]

We are players who are taken up in a felt relation with
other moving visions and woven into a fabric that is base-
less—foundationless—although deep in its meaning within
each gesture, each sensual entranceway into further plays.
This realm of becoming is made palpable, taken into our bodies by emotion and celebrated by play. It takes vulnerability,
letting go of distance and the dream of being a monument. It
is sad that the masculine identity has resisted this letting go
to become part of the flowing pageant, because all the creatures of the Earth need us men to play our part on the global
stage.

CHAPTER EIGHT

A Good Cook
Is Hard to Find

*Magicians and Cooks
Bring Forth the
Nourishment of the World*

Magic as Connecting
through Time and Space

The masculine view of the world characterizes magic in two mistaken ways that rob life of much of its meaning. For one, magic is mistakenly seen as a matter of power. The second is that magic is seen as supernatural. To see magic as supernatural power obviously fits the masculine images and fantasies we've explored. First, to make magic a matter of power means to further the fantasies of control over people or things. Secondly, to be so removed from the web of life that we could act "super-naturally"—that is, from a place above or beyond nature—fits the flying boy's desires of soaring above life. To see magic this way, given the masculine psyche is quite understandable, but it renders us incapable of seeing how the real magic of existence occurs throughout our lives.

In *Beautiful Dreamers*, Leonard, flailing his crippled arms about and gurgling with joy, catches the cricket ball, and the entire town watching is moved to tears. That is an utterly magical moment. If we are looking for magic in another place, we might not see it happening right in front of us —in fact, we may break the spell of what it is capable of achieving.

Magic is not supernatural; it is mundane. Actually, it is the *fabric* of mundane life. This is not to necessarily deny that supernatural magic exists, too, but that is not the concern of this book. What is of concern here is that by exclusively conceiving of magic in terms of power and the supernatural, we are left with no way to speak of the ongoing magic of life that sustains us and without which we would surely die. Magic sustains us as much as food, water, or air. On some level that masculinity teaches us to deny, we emotionally understand there is magic in each smile, in each laugh, and in each heartfelt emotion.

As we retreat in the heroic mode to our barricaded aerial view, we conceive of the world below as a collection of things to be manipulated and controlled. This projected vision is further imagined as one in which by the male's presence— and so in his mind—all human presence can be removed, as if it never had been there. What is imagined is an utterly desiccated, lifeless world of indifferent objects in which beauty and all emotional qualities don't *really* exist. Human reactions—especially "feminine" reactions—are just "add on's" to reality. They are merely *subjective*. In the masculine view, reality just stands there and challenges us, like the enemy to the warrior hero. Instead of seeing our gifts and functions as emerging only within a concert with other beings, we claim our abilities as self-contained and self-generated—our *property*. So what we see in the world is this collection of inert, mute, passive objects, juxtaposed and interacting in a mechanical way, like billiard balls slamming into each other in chains of cause and effect—the world as machine. Of course, it is up to the hero to organize and run this world of objects. It is also up to the hero to create beauty and joy from the raw materials of the planet—not to receive them graceful-ly as gifts.

Certainly, in this world view, there is no magic infiltrat-ing the Earth itself. Since the world is seen as a collection of objects to be manipulated and controlled, the only way to look at magic is to see it as some sort of supernatural manip-ulation and control over things. This is yet another painful form of self-denial. If there is a wild and wonderful magic all around us and we set up a world where we can't experience it, then masculinity has again left us to increase our pain and be left as the isolated Hercules holding up the world. This way of referring to magic's power is a parody. However, it is a parody that keeps us distant from a truer magic, unable to embrace its meaning and to tap into its ongoing flow among all beings.

In the patriarchal world, magic is thus defined as control-ling events without going through the logical or verifiable steps in space and time—those links of "cause and effect" that classical science focuses on and that technology manipu-lates. It is "acting at a distance." However, once we begin to look at our lives, instead of using the "common sense" of our society, we notice that many things work outside the links of cause and effect. Even if, in part, certain events are caused, that doesn't exhaust all they're about. There are choice, trans-formation, creation, jumping, skipping, and spontaneous forms of interconnection forged among all beings in many ways. Even "hard science," in sticking to physical phenome-na, has realized that although some aspects of the world are almost mechanical in their interaction, much of it works in leaps, patterns, and spontaneous interactive changes.

Scientists have realized that even particles "know" each other—that they are not just mechanically, externally related but somehow mirror each other in their being as if they were "aware."[1] Certainly among humans, there is no cause-and-effect relationship about why love can be born and sustained, why friendships die, why religions shed light on the value of things, why a vision for a political order suddenly seems out-moded one day and on another day catches fire, why that person's smile is so mysterious and pregnant with hopeful possibilities, or why certain people have a sparkle that makes others in their presence suddenly more energetic and capable of doing what they wish.

Not long ago, our masculine-informed science looked at native peoples (they were actually more apt to be called "sav-ages") and declared that their magical practices were super-stitious, primitive, and ineffectual. These anthropologists, historians, scientists, and other "experts" assumed that such peoples were concerned with the same things they were: how to dominate, manipulate, and master their environments from a vantage point outside any real interrelation with it. However, the magic practiced by native peoples the world over, both historically and currently, is almost always suc-cessful. Although magic may well be "action at a distance," it is not the kind of manipulative action that the heroic mentali-ty focuses on. The magic of rituals and ceremonies *does* defy the laws of cause and effect because it focuses on other dimensions of existence. These dimensions may not even be visible to the masculine vision, which stays distant and is armored from the flow of emotion, of energy, and of connect-edness as experienced by those who stay part of the web of Earth—not an exclusively human group, I might add.

The patriarchal interpreters of other cultures always saw these practices as some heroic effort to master events against great odds. With this paradigm, we can't understand the magic of ritual. The hunters who used magic were not seek-ing to somehow influence supernaturally the course of events or to manipulate their prey within range of their arrows or lances. Rain dancers aren't necessarily trying to supernatural-ly cause the accumulation of moisture in order for rain to fall. Healing ceremonies of the Native Americans aren't necessari-ly trying to intervene supernaturally in the proliferation of cancer cells in the body or the spread of antigens in the body.

What magic is about is the *expansion of relatedness* and the facilitation of the truest sort of action that can be taken by human beings within life: the forging, shaping, and retuning of the nature of connection and relationship with other people and other beings. Magic *is* "acting at a distance," but the nature of the acting is an emotional, identified *connecting* such that the distance is both there and not there. Supposed boundaries open and energy flows are established in magic.

We males will never see much of what happens on Earth if we maintain our masculine vision that all action is about achieving goals. In *Dances with Wolves*, John Dunbar spends days refurbishing his outpost—repairing, cleaning, and organizing it. That is one kind of action—tangible, practical, and largely material. He also spends much time observing and communing with the land, sky, wind, light, and creatures around his outpost. He makes expressive drawings, writes poetic diary entries, and muses about the meaning of his life and existence in general. He even enters a relationship of sorts with a wolf that lives nearby. On one wonderful day, when he is trying to shoo the wolf away, they start to play, chasing each other back and forth. On another night, under the open sky and with black prairie all around, Dunbar dances a wonderful, celebratory dance around a blazing fire. He also has his first talks with a few of the Lakota braves, who begin to see common ground with him. All these are acts of a different sort—finding resonances, experiencing different qualities of energy, opening avenues of kinship, seeing beauty, finding shared horizons, and deepening those horizons. Such actions don't show up on ledger sheets, scientific reports, or other objective accountings, but that doesn't mean they are any less real. In fact, they may even change lives and help to make them worth living.

While one type of action is about manipulating things, the other is about such things as dimensions of meaning, emotional colorings, sources of vitality, experiences of kinship, senses of value, and the kindling of desire. One is visi-

ble to the distanced vision of the masculine perspective, and
one is invisible to it. This is evidenced dramatically when the
soldiers who take over Dunbar's outpost register no sense of
wonder about his diary and its drawings but instead use its
pages for toilet paper. Insofar as this type of human action
remains invisible to the masculine vision, then magic as
"action at a distance" will also never appear. Even our masculine heroes have been plagued with this rather one-sided
vision of the facts—not seeing the other realms of human
activity—as Oedipus so hauntingly reminds us.

Certainly, the Native American hunter wished to have a
bountiful hunt, but it was more important to his people to
establish some sort of harmony with the animals with whom
they shared a fate and a respectful relationship. The dance or
the painting was meant to give the people a felt sense of what
it was what like in the realm of the buffalo or the deer. These
animals were brothers and sisters who felt cold, desperation,
and joy, and other kindred stirrings to which the people
sought connection. Thus, the people entered a cycle, a circle
of life, in which they joined an attunement existing among all
beings. Certainly, some of these people may have been more
concerned about the fullness of their stomachs, but the world
in which magic occurred was a *relational* world, in which a
connection to all beings out of compassion and respect was a
priority for the well-being of all.

For one of the first times in the context of popular culture, this is well expressed in a scene in *Dances with Wolves*.
The Lakota tribe is sickened when they see how the white
men have shot the buffalo as a display of power in their
weaponry and of their marksmanship. The buffalo have been
killed for fun—for sport—and are left rotting in the sun. This
makes the buffalo an object, a thing to be manipulated, domi-
nated, and even wantonly destroyed. The buffalo are being
used to bolster the white men's masculine egos. By contrast,
the Lakota hunt the buffalo as brothers, as both related in the

larger circle of life and as partners in a relationship of concern and respect.

This same attitude toward the hunted is expressed by the Lakota medicine man, Archie Fire Lame Deer, in *Gift of Power*: "Before Grandpa took the life of an animal—and also after he had killed it—he prayed and gave thanks to the four-leggeds who gave their flesh so that the two-leggeds can survive. He always told an animal he had killed, 'Forgive me, Brother, but the people have to live.' He taught me never to kill for pleasure. . . ."[2] Only through understanding the connectedness among beings and the fact that there is more to life's circle than mere material survival can magic make sense.

This kind of understanding also appears in Tony Hillerman's popular novels, when he speaks of the world of the Navajo people. It is a different way of seeing the world—*a different world*—that gives a different meaning to the purpose of magic in the healing ceremonies of Native Americans. So, to give another example of how magic could be understood in its own context and terms, and not through the masculine-scientific trivialization of magic, let's turn to a passage of Hillerman's that expresses the heart of this difference. In an aside in *Coyote Waits*, one of the characters exemplifies the very different understanding of such ceremonies:

> Chee lingered over the section in which Ashie Pinto had described the ceremonial curing. . . . It stirred the memory of a curing he'd attended as a child. The cure had been conducted by a *hataalii* who had been very tall and had seemed then to be incredibly ancient. The patient had been Chee's paternal grandmother, a woman he had loved with an intensity of a lonely child and the event had formed one of his earliest really vivid memories. The cold wind, the starlight, the perfume of the piñon and juniper burning in the great fires that illuminated the dance ground. Even now, he could see it all, and the remembered aroma overpowered the mustiness

of this office. Most of all, he remembered the *hataalii* standing gray and thin and tall over his grandmother, holding a tortoiseshell rattle and a prayer plume of eagle feathers, chanting the poetry from the emergence story, making Old Lady Many Mules one with White Shell Girl, restoring her to beauty and harmony. And restore her it had. Chee remembered staying at the old woman's place, playing with his cousins and their sheepdogs, seeing his grandmother happy again, hearing her laughter. She had died, of course. The disease was lung cancer, or perhaps tuberculosis, and people with such diseases died—as all people do. But it had been the cure that had caused him to think that he would learn the great curing ways, the songs and the sand paintings, and become a *hataalii* for his people.[3]

Chee was so impressed with the magical power of this curing ceremony that he can still smell it, feel the wind, see the starlight, decades later. This grandmother had meant so much to him that it was obvious how significant it was to him that the curing ceremony had been successful. It had so swept him away with its power to be successful and change people's lives that he has spent his adult life in the difficult pursuit of trying to become such a healer while also pursuing his career in law enforcement. The magic worked—*and*, of course, his grandmother still died. She was cured.

Anthropologists, scientists, and others in our masculine world who want to get things done by manipulating them and changing the course of events don't understand that the patient can die and the magic is successful and the patient is cured. Chee tells us that the old woman was restored to harmony with things, that she regained her power of play, her ability to laugh, her ability to delight in children and to frisk with the dogs. She regained a sense of joy and beauty that comes from the emotional richness of experiencing the interconnection of all beings. In the ceremony, she became White Shell Girl, finding her emotional attunement with the world by taking up the spirit of White Shell Girl. No, of course, she didn't literally change the atoms of her flesh; rather, hers was a more important change—a transformation in her way of being in relation to the world, which restored an avenue of feeling. Chee and the Navajos accept that people die, but they also know that we can help ourselves and others to continually be reborn into wonder and deep emotional relation.

Magic leads us back to our responsibility to the world. Masculine beliefs tell us that to be detoured into magic and emotion is an irresponsible path while *real* men, like Hercules and Atlas, hold up the world of "real affairs." The magician counters this assertion by saying that the wondrous aspect of existence—that light from within things that makes them sparkle with an energy that is nourishing to our vitality—is lost if we fail to be responsible for the world as beings of "response-ability." However, the magician also understands that Hercules or Oedipus or anyone under sway of the masculine perspective can't really see the magic of those "in whose house he lives." The traditional male hero really doesn't experience the magic strands that make distances collapse and beings interpenetrate in their essence even though they are physically distinct.

To see magic, we have to believe. We tell our children this wisdom as if it were a story to comfort them from the harsh reality of life, rather than realizing that it is at the heart of human reality that only children and people who have kept their childlike wonder alive can understand.

Before this power of belief is misunderstood as being aimed at the supernatural, let's look at how necessary belief is in order for us to be able to function in almost any way. Philosopher Maurice Merleau-Ponty's work on the nature of perception demonstrated that human perception is not a blank, mechanical registering of meaning. As passively taking in sensation, perception is meaningless. Only because we actively believe we can find meaning in phenomena we confront do the senses keep resolving the perceptual input until it crystalizes with a certain form and significance.[4] For example, the sentences you are reading can only make sense to you because you believe they will make sense; therefore, you are open to their unfolding in such a way that they can take on meaning. You hold on to the meaning of the first part of the sentence in the belief that all the words that follow will gradually complete a coherent thought, and it is this holding onto partial meanings in the expectation of further meaning that makes the overall meaning possible.

This is true of all areas of life. John Cage's most famous piece, 4:53, in which the pianist enters the concert hall and sits at the piano, seemingly in readiness to play but never breaking the silence, highlights the listener's contribution to the existence of the music. If the audience were not ready to hear "music," there would be no music. We must believe in music, or there will only be noise. The *belief* in music is not sufficient in itself to create music, but it is essential. Similarly, in order to experience death, we must believe in death. Before we acquire this belief as young children we may see lifeless creatures, but the phenomenon of death is hidden and experienced as the creature "sleeping" or "pretending" in some way.

Belief can open a way of access to certain parts of existence: we have to believe in love in order to be able to experience it, yet the belief doesn't create it; it *allows* loving actions to be seen, felt, and recognized as such rather than just experienced as manipulations or self-serving actions of the other. The fact that distance rather than always separating can be a medium of interconnection (which is the magical at work) can only be experienced if we believe in it. The fact that distinctness among beings is not an unbreachable barrier but an opportunity to experience the identification through emotional attunement—in which boundaries blur—can only be experienced if we believe in this magic.

For the masculine ethos, belief is problematical. To distrust is the first rule of the warrior mentality. To live behind armor or at a distance means that we fashion our lives in the projection of possible violation. To believe that all life is inter-connected undermines the view upon which the warrior bases his life: us versus them. It makes no sense to destroy others if they are a part of us and we are a part of them. Then we are just hurting ourselves in striking out at them. If belief in magic requires an even further step of seeing that all beings potentially reach all the core of all other beings then we must heed not only other people and other creatures, but all beings—including rocks, water, and soil—and listen for their messages of whatever sort. This kind of belief requires an open, spontaneous, and caring presence to all beings—not a distant, defended, and hostile stance. For men to experience magic, we must let go—not only come out from behind our defenses but also jump off trustingly into the tide of the world's interconnected beings.

John Fowles's novel, *The Magus*, addresses our masculine inability to discover new aspects of ourselves and the world through belief—through trusting the beckoning invitations of other people or even of nature to take us down uncharted paths—and how this robs so many men of experiencing the magic of existence. The protagonist of the novel, Nicolas Urfe, distrusts everyone, since for him all others are poten-tially liable to exploit or even humiliate him. He can't believe that Alison loves him—at least not in the sense of really accepting all of who he is—although she does. Nicolas is always dreaming of the ideal woman, the ideal place, the ideal experience, as a way of never having to take completely to heart that he *is* with *this* woman or in *this* place or having *this* experience. In other words, Nicolas uses the flying-boy tactics of being distant from his immediate situation in light of some perfect situation "up there." Ultimately, he doesn't believe in his life, in himself, or in others. In some sense, he can't believe "any of this is happening" about his day-to-day life, since he is caught in masculine distance and doesn't *con-nect* with his life. Nicolas is everyman, caught in the mascu-line trap.

Nicolas is drawn into the summer tricks of the Magus, the Magician Maurice Conchis, a very rich man who engages a group of people every summer to explore the reaches of the human psyche. Conchis, like all magicians, uses various tricks to ensnare Nicolas and invites him to let go and play in some very elaborate games. These games include acted out scenarios of myths, a World War Two incident, romantic encounters, meeting a schizophrenic patient, being put on trial—situations of all kinds—but Nicolas is never allowed to know which of them are just enactments by the hired cast and which are real. Conchis is trying to show Nicolas that his disbelief, his distancing skepticism about "real" events and other people's feelings, is the same issue he has always had with life. Conchis is trying to show him that he must let go of his masculine distance and distrust or he won't be able to experience the magic of this beautiful Greek summer with the cast of talented, interesting people (including the twins—Julie and June—whom he won't trust with his love) nor will he experience the magic of his life. Nicolas doesn't know whether Julie loves him or whether she's just "acting," but he has the same problem in "real life." He's not even sure if he knows which twin is Julie or which is June at various times. However, this, too, is just like his life, and the masculine life in general—in which one woman seems just like the next, since the flying boy is really not in contact with his partner.

In an attempt to help Nicolas, Conchis provides him with the following brief tale about how important it is to believe in life *despite* its just being a play, a flow of energies that can't be pinned down or controlled. Only then does magic exist. The tale, called *The Prince and the Magician*, points to the direction we must follow in order to abandon our masculine absence and enter the realm of magic:

> Once upon a time, there was a young prince who believed in all things but three. He did not believe in princesses, he did not believe in islands, he did not believe in God. His father, the king, told him that such

things did not exist. As there were no princesses or islands in his father's domains, and no sign of God, the young prince believed his father.

But then, one day, the prince ran away from his palace. He came to the next land. There, to his astonishment, from every coast he saw islands, and on these islands, strange and troubling creatures whom he dared not name. As he was searching for a boat, a man in full evening dress approached him along the shore.

"Are those real islands?" asked the young prince.

"Of course they are real islands," said the man in evening dress.

"And those strange and troubling creatures?"

"They are all genuine and authentic princesses."

"Then God must also exist!" cried the prince.

"I am God," replied the man in full evening dress with a bow.

The young prince returned as quickly as he could.

"So you are back," said his father, the king.

"I have seen islands, I have seen princesses, I have seen God," said the prince reproachfully.

The king was unmoved.

"Neither real islands, nor real princesses, nor a real God, exist. Tell me how God was dressed."

"God was in full evening dress."

"Were the sleeves of his coat rolled back?"

The prince remembered that they had been. The king smiled.

"That is the uniform of a magician. You have been deceived."

At this, the prince returned to the next land, and went to the same shore, where once again he came upon the man in full evening dress.

"My father, the king, has told me who you are," said the young prince indignantly. "You deceived me the last time, but not again. Now I know that those are not real islands and real princesses, because you are a magician."

The man on the shore smiled. "It is you who are deceived, my boy. In your father's kingdom there are many islands and many princesses. But you are under your father's spell, so you cannot see them."

The prince returned pensively home. When he saw his father, he looked him in the eyes.

"Father, is it true that you are not a real king, but only a magician?"

The king smiled, and rolled back his sleeves.

"Yes, my son, I am only a magician."

"Then the man on the shore was God."

"The man on the shore was another magician."

"I must know the real truth, the truth beyond magic."

"There is no truth beyond magic," said the king.

The prince was full of sadness. He said, "I will kill myself."

The king by magic caused death to appear. Death stood in the door and beckoned to the prince. The prince shuddered. He remembered the beautiful but unreal islands and the unreal but beautiful princesses.

"Very well," he said. "I can bear it."

"You see, my son," said the king, "you too now begin to be a magician."[5]

If we don't believe in magic, then we can't experience what is possible only through the power of magic. If we don't believe in magic, then death comes to us and we live out our lives without real vitality, looking out at a world that seems like a collection of lifeless objects. Even other people are just glorified objects, like robots or androids, there only to meet one's needs. The boy, like the hero on a quest, wants an absolute, an answer, the Truth, a God, some firm foundation, but he discovers there is no way out of the interplay among magicians.

We are *all* magicians, but some of us have forgotten how to tune into the wild magic all around us. If we forget our childlike belief, then there are no beautiful islands in life, no enchanting partners, just places to do our business and good "catches" who function well in our overall practical scheme. To believe in magic, however, is to allow ourselves to be caught up in other beings in such a way that we enter a reciprocity with them, a shared glow of presence across boundaries, and a different kind of enlivening interconnection. Life becomes an adventure and love becomes possible. If we can dare to believe in magic, then we are already magicians.

A magician is one who isn't concerned about being "tricked" in the sense of being manipulated out of having power over others. The masculine goal is to seek such power—to be the leader, to be above others and in control of their actions. The magician has no use for this kind of power. He gives up the illusion that anyone can truly control anyone. Instead, by letting go and not worrying about being deceived by life's turns or by the actions of others, he finds in embracing the playfulness of experience itself that he can be in contact with anything or anyone. Thus, he conducts the magic that is the enlivening and emotionally touching energy that can move among all beings. By giving up his pretensions of heroic power, he is transformed into a source of empowerment among beings, who all flourish by moving into rhythmic attunement.

Nicolas, however, can never bring himself to believe in magic. He needs answers, control, something that he can be sure of. Of course, life will never be so certain—only death-in-life will get close, that place where the masculine is driven into retreat while maintaining the delusion of soaring over life. Fortunately, however, we can't utterly distance magic, or we would never feel any loss of boundaries with others. We would be here physically, but would not be "here," pierced by the presence of bird, tree, and sky, nor the smiles of others. We would become utterly "spaced out," that is to say, not partaking in any real sense of a shared space with others—the ultimate "nowhere" toward which flies the masculine defense strategy. Under extreme conditions, one can experience this state of being totally unreached by these beckonings of the world, and we recognize it as a pathological state. The fact that most of us don't approach this extreme is small comfort. Even though most of us may allow ourselves some small measure of magic in our lives—enough to survive—rare is the man who allows the world and its beings to fully nourish him with all that he could experience. Instead, most of us have the belief that there is no magic, using our belief against the power of belief as another barrier to sever us from the world and another way to cause ourselves more pain.

A very painful example of this is Hercules's disbelief that Hippolyte wants to give him her girdle as a gift of love. Since he can't believe that she is really carried beyond herself in feeling passion for him, he can't experience her love or any merging of boundaries with her. Instead, in his distrust he can only target her as an enemy to be killed. Similarly, Oedipus can't feel the magic of those who care for him, distrusts all others as motivated by scheming for their own gain, and throws away what could have been the richly rewarding connections of his life despite his bitter fate. Fortunately, as a blind beggar, he finds the magic of love, the only thing worth believing in. For this, he is honored, but his real reward was the experience of the closeness with his daughters.

Nicholas Urfe misses the point. He never understands magic—the magic of his connection to Alison, whom he abandons, still looking for an angle to gain an advantage over her. With Conchis, Urfe keeps looking for the "tricks," the "manipulations," that Conchis is using, as if all magic were just sleight of hand. However, whatever sleight of hand is used is merely the means of allowing some deeper sense of magic to occur. Conchis tries to jolt him out of his deadly seriousness. Conchis is our consciousness. Our minds are wizards. They always move about and play tricks on us— inviting us to play. Our own consciousness is trying to help us see that we won't find the absolute answer, the ultimate control—and therefore we must give up holding on to our mind's chimera—the power to figure things out. Consciousness is telling us to allow our emotions, our sensual bodies, to bring us into the connection that mind itself can be so effective in blocking. Consciousness is so acute it can reveal its own limitations in being so powerful. Consciousness is drawn to the project of control, while also whispering to us to let go.

Letting Happen versus Being in Charge

An analogous struggle happens between the archery master and Eugen Herrigal in *Zen and the Art of Archery*. At first, Herrigal is looking for all the "tricks" to get off the right shot, as if it were all a matter of technique—of manipulation. The master is upset at this and announces that he will no longer teach him, just as Conchis declares to Urfe that he is going to stop for the same reason. However, Herrigal decides to allow himself to trust. After he sticks with the process for seven years, he finally sees that there is no control: he realizes that the master's hitting two consecutive bull's-eyes in the pitch-dark archery hall is not a matter of technique or manipulation. Herrigal then experiences the need to "let go."

However, at this point, masculine consciousness must realize something further in order to let go. The hero's source of strength is his iron will. For masculinity, this iron is the core of self. Yet, the archery master wants Herrigal to see that this is his weakness. For the master, Herrigal is self-defeating, for the masculine ethos short-circuits itself. The master tells him he must no longer feel responsible for the shot, cease feeling that he has to make it happen or it will not occur. He must cease to *will* the shot. The archery master, as all Zenlike masters, is not only a trickster, ensnaring the student in his deeper tricks, not only childlike, embracing fully the process itself rather than the goal—but he is also a magician. The archery master, as all magicians, has allowed the apparent distance between himself and the world to collapse. He no longer believes in that distance—at least not seriously. It exists as a playful game. The distance is there, but only humorously, "wetly." It can also dissolve into a larger flowing presence. Thus, the master is one who "conjures" happenings—a magician.

The rain dance, the cave paintings, the kangaroo dance,

the incantation of White Shell Woman—all moments of magic—are *moments of identification*. The identification is not merely intellectual, but a *becoming* of the so-called distant in time, space, or some dimension of being—a becoming with body, emotion, rhythm, energy, bearing, sensation, attitude, and relations to other beings. When the Zen master encounters the target, he does not will an action toward that separated object through a series of manipulations. As the master seems to be indicating, Herrigal has to learn to shoot at *himself*, but not in the sense of some "inner self" locked away within a tank. Rather, he has to learn to shoot at a self that flows within target, archery hall, stretching bow, rhythm of dancing steps, and the master himself.

The master says that when Herrigal learns, he will no longer shoot but rather, "It shoots." The "It" that shoots is the circling energy flow that not only encompasses Herrigal, hall, dance, master, and bow, but in some sense also the energies of past archery masters, the smile of Siddhartha under the Bo tree, the love of Herrigal's wife, the flowers on the table in the hall, and all the other energies Herrigal can become the focus for in letting go of the shot. This is the truest sense of magic, not a trivialized sense of supernatural manipulation. The archer and the target are the same, because what one shoots at is also what one shoots with. There is a spiraling energy flow and an "empty" archer. How the shot happens when there is no one there to will it, is magic.

This brings us to the inner sanctum of masculinity. We saw that the most ancient surviving hero myth—that of Gilgamesh—is a painful struggle against the fact that death reveals that the "I"—the ego—is perishable. Gilgamesh can't tolerate the fact that Enkidu is gone and that he, too, will eventually be gone. His only recourse is to gain enough glory that his sense of himself—his ego—will live on in fame, thus defeating death's power over him. This tale is archetypal for the entire warrior mentality, for all masculinity. The "I"— the ego—is sacred. It is to be defended, to be erected, to survive unchallenged. When Jack Lucas in *The Fisher King* says, "Thank God, I'm me," he's only expressing more boldly what the hero strives for. When Rene Descartes says, "I think, therefore I am"—and means by this that nothing else can be depended upon except this inner sense of ego—he too is speaking for all masculine philosophy; he is just being more forthright about it.

It is no accident that the figures we've looked at as our own society's alternative images to the traditional masculine all suffered some trauma that shattered their sense of ego—whether the doctor diagnosed with cancer, John Dunbar, Henry Turner, Jack Lucas, or Perry. The masculine hero will never experience magic in his egocentric world. If for males to become more mature is to separate—that is, to build a more secure sense of ego as the cornerstone of self—then we will continue to work to reach a stage of death-in-life and to live in a world without magic. In 1992, the film version of *Howard's End* became very popular, but its message is still unheard. The crowning sentence of Forster's novel and the film is, "Only connect." This means that the ego, the "I" as the masculine sense of self, must be replaced.

The archery master has a different sense of time that allows a very different sense of self. The masculine obsession with "willing"—with bringing about what "I want"—will never cease with the sense in which we males live time. The trickster, the person absorbed in play, and the magician all have left behind the sense of time as a lock-step progression of past-present-future—of cause and effect as the only way things can happen. The master is not braced for a future that might betray him, as is the hero. The hero is threatened by a sense that things might stray from his direction and control. This attitude may seem bold, but it is really a bracing against possible failure, which is what the future threatens for the hero. It is another symptom of masculine distrust.

For the master, who cares not about the goal in a serious sense but only about that to which he has given his heart in sheer play, there is no future for which to prepare himself. The target itself beckons for the arrow *as its way of playing with itself.* The cosmos itself is always caught up in play. If the master can dance his dance and open himself to this magic, the arrow will be shot—it will be taken from his grasp in the proper flow, and the shot will just happen as part of his sheer presence to the world. However, in some sense, it happens *before* it happens as an expression of the end playing with itself and the master. The future and the past are within a present that plays with different dimensions of itself. This sense of an expanding present, in which other times are just places to which we step out, but remain within the present flow, is the time of magic. All time is now; the past and the future are only present in the now. This moves us beyond masculine ego to allowing ourselves to be taken into the collapse of distance, into a lightning that jumps boundaries— even boundaries in time—to feel the play in the magic of this moment. This sense of living as friends with time could have a magically healing effect on the hero. Masculinity could be freed from always trying to create a glorious future, stuck carrying the weight of the past as an "investment" that must "pay off"—never getting to just *be* in the present.

It seems a big step for us to embrace giving up the will to adopt a path of non-willing. But if we take to heart the archery master's statement, "You think that what you do not do yourself does not happen,"[6] we will have to think about doing things differently. We will see that the flowing self is no longer an agent, a doer, but is equally being acted upon; the target is as much the doer of the shot as the archer. To become the magician is to allow the world and its beings to do our actions for and with us as much as it is doing anything ourselves. This takes energy, concentration, and an openness that is itself an "action." It is not to become passive in the sense of being "inert" or "spaced out", but to experience that the self is no longer an isolated source of itself.[7]

One model that we men can turn to are the artists. There

is in our society a long tradition of male artists who have always spoken of how the object of their art worked "through them." Cezanne felt Mount St. Victoire "painted itself" through him. Valery stated that in writing his poetry, he just listened to the voices of the forest that asked to be written down. This is the magic of the world: we are linked with all beings and can always reverse our relations with any being such that we feel its presence in our own doing or being.

The male as magician cannot claim "credit" for his actions, at least not in some egoistic way that would insure the kind of distinction that Gilgamesh, Hercules, and other heroes sought as imprinting their mark against the shadow of death and human limitation. If, as a magician, I teach a wonderful class and say things that I never thought myself capable of saying and had never even imagined thinking before, or if in making love with someone with whom I have opened myself to the energy flow that overcomes boundaries and each touch has glowed with an intensity, joyfulness, and intimacy unimagined, then "I" have not done these deeds, "We" have not done these deeds, "It" has done them. We have given ourselves up to a larger flow of energy and a fittingly graceful shining forth of feeling for which we are just a conduit. If we start to monumentalize ourselves, as Gilgamesh did in his inauguration of the heroic masculine tradition, then this sense of self as the glory-bedecked doer will only barricade the flow of energy and communion, eventually exhausting the hero and leaving him—like Gilgamesh—with the bitterness of isolation and futility.

However, as men we don't have to throw away our painstakingly acquired technical mastery over the world. Each day, the Zen archer has practiced the movements of archery for hours. The hunter who draws the painting of the deer has also spent much time learning the habits and details of the deer's life. The speaker who suddenly becomes inspired and opens us all to some intimacy with each other and his subject has also studied the subject. Magic can break in at any time to the world of mundane events if we are ready for its call; however, the proficiency we males have gained in practice, such as factual knowledge or technical mastery, does not have to be antithetical to the spirit of magic, but rather the two can deepen one another and reinforce each other. The Zen archer stresses the need to let go of the will to shoot and letting the shot happen, but he assumes the student will also have worked in the more mundane realm first. The letting go and collapse of distance takes the archer far beyond archery and permeates his relationship to the rest of his life. But he also can hit the target with mastery because both dimensions, the magical and the technical, augment each other.

This is why it is particularly tragic when, in our masculine guise, we rely on technique, knowledge, and other kinds of mastery to manipulate the world in such a way as to make our skills into barriers to openness with others. *The problem is the one-sidedness*—that we depend on these skills to maintain a safe distance. Instead, these skills and knowledge could be utilized in a spirit that would let go of them as primary goals. They could be transformed into ways for kindling magic's powers of connecting with all beings. There is a need for humor about our mastery: to get wet and play with the world—albeit skillfully—but with a joy in the process and with an openheartedness to others.

The Cook Spins
the Wheel of Life and Death

Another image of the magician that has been seen to be a symbol of spiritual and psychological development is that of the medieval alchemist. Like the magic ceremonies of other cultures, the actions of the alchemists were misinterpreted as another kind of supernatural manipulation—as if they were trying to turn other elements into gold or precious materials. Carl Jung reinterpreted their work as the cooking and blending of materials, the symbolic working through of various psychic matters, with the ultimate goal being the creation of a greater and deeper sense of vitality. Jung saw the parallels with the self's need to test and fire itself, to hold and work with its contents as a "psychic vessel," to integrate and/or cast off parts of itself in alloying its own indomitable sense of aliveness.

The alchemist used fire to cook and blend the elements of the Earth. His work was understood through the metaphor of "the search for the philosopher's stone," which was misunderstood in the heroic model of the quest as a search for a supernatural life force. Perhaps some alchemists sought this; however, it also seems they realized that working with the elements of the Earth in a meditative way—slowly mixing and stirring them, being attentive to their textures, colors, and aromas, aesthetically admiring these qualities, carefully observing their transformations and combinations—was a metaphor for the magician's truest work: savoring the marrow of this world as wondrous.

Whether the alchemists were seeking the beyond or not, we can look at the magic of cooking substances not as a means of alloying something beyond the changing, interconnected Earth but as a process that might *further enmesh* us in the Earth. Looked at in this way, further metaphoric and psychic depths of magic can be found in our everyday lives right in our own kitchens. The magician's cooking may not only be an attempt to create supernatural powers in various brews, stews, or potions, but it also may represent an unleashing of the magic of connecting parts of the Earth across space and time within the process of one of our most common daily activities. This could be a help to us men in finding ways to come alive within the most mundane of settings rather than feeling that we must go on heroic quests.

Cooking has been devalued by the warrior tradition as "feminine" work—undoubtedly in reaction to the high regard with which it was held in the preceding Goddess tradition. Part of masculine common sense now is that cooking is an "unmanly" activity, and it is phobically avoided by many men. The more recent tradition of male cooks seems to be an offshoot of the renegade role some men have taken as artists who deal in magic—in this case, artists of food. By and large, though, cooking has been avoided because, like the body's emotional, sensual, and perceptual richness, like the process of sensitively making love, its power to return us to Earth is so manifest that it must be avoided by the flying boy. The two flight strategies we've seen are to invalidate such activities as "feminine" and a threat to true manhood (also labeled as "trivial") or to claim that the true value of any activity is to be found in its potential to rise above the earthly. Instead, we might look at how cookery is actually magical in its day-to-day deepening of our nourishment through working with the beings on this planet and their mutual interdependence.

Mundane cookery is already magical. Its action has several characteristics in common with the nature of magic: beings that were separate are brought into complementary relationships, undergo transformations, take on new flavors and accents, assume an identity as a larger whole, and nourish other beings. Something becomes other than it was by losing its old boundaries and entering into relationships with other beings. These other beings similarly lose their former boundaries in the process. Not only do the ingredients of the cooking process undergo transformations and form new identities (highlighted by their distinctive new flavors and sensory appearance), but the newly created dishes are changed by, and become one with, those who eat them. Those who eat the meal gain not just physiological stores of energy, but take on the emotional energies of the meal as expressed through the relationships with those who have offered the meal. Even at its most basic level then, cooking signals a connection to the earthy, to emotional energies, and to getting involved in the web of life.

However, before we explore the meaning of the cooking process in detail, we must recognize the fact that we are dealing with life and death. This is what is most striking about cooking and eating. We are not just dealing with the "materials" of the Earth, we are dealing with other living beings, with their remains—even when we use a vegetable, fruit, or spice. These ingredients were recently parts of other living beings in the web of the Earth's community.

Cooking is a way of dealing with death creatively. In some sense, we are not dealing with "remains" of living beings but rather with the "extended life" of those beings. They were all recently alive or have been kept preserved in some extended "life-giving" or "passing-along" power. Whether through drying or freezing or whatever process, their contained vitality is still there, present to be unlocked in the cooking process and passed along to other living beings. We have seen how the tradition of the masculine hero has in many ways been a reaction against the pain of death—either of our loved ones or of our own. Cooking is the magic that turns death back into life.

In a sense, the entire Earth is a wheel for turning the deaths of other beings into future lives, not just through cycles among animate beings but also through longer cycles that spiral through stages of inanimate being. However, cooking is a place where humans take direct responsibility for helping with this recycling process—and do it as a kind of play, trick, and magic. Animals and plants become things to eat we couldn't have imagined possible from their original state as ingredients, and they do so with a beauty and expression of feelings and values that bind us all together. The opposite is also true: When food is withheld from other people, from other living beings, more than their physiological needs are being denied; it is also a denial of their emotional and spiritual needs to be nourished by others. The redemption of the inevitability of death into the service of life—this kind of play with process, of ensnaring others in our wiles, and magic—is not of the puer sort. Such transformation is not achieved by transcending the Earth, but by going more groundedly into the most basic textures, smells, tastes, and colors that people hunger for. It connects us to others in an immediate, sensual way.

In his dialogue, *Phaedo*, Plato considers the different sorts of immortality to which we can aspire, despite our apparent coming to an end when we die. Plato, of course, in keeping with the masculinist, hierarchical values he espoused ("rising" above the "feminine" emotions and sensuality toward pure reason, pure being, and a home for the soul beyond the Earth) feels that we can face death and not be negated by its power only by living eternally as a pure soul—an unchanging essence detached from the body and from the "slime" of this Earth. He also considers the so-called "immortality" of remaining "alive" in some sense by nourishing other living beings and being carried on by them in some extended way. However, he dismisses this as unsatisfying to our need for human significance. If to remain at a distance from the Earth and others is painful, it is even more painful to think that the solution to life's hurt is to "remain aloft" *eternally*.

The early Vedic sages and poets, who wrote hymns more than three thousand years ago, express the sense that our existence is itself just "food" within the larger circle of death and life. From this cosmic perspective, all beings can be seen as "food," and their lives are a sacrifice or gift that nourishes other beings. As it says in the Vedas,

> FOOD is the exhaling breath; FOOD is the inhaling
>   breath of life;
> FOOD, they call death; the same FOOD, they call life.
> FOOD, the Brahmans call growing old [decaying];
> FOOD, they also call the begetting of offspring.[8]

For the early Vedic priests and poets, this mutual eating of one another in a cosmic flux captured the sense of existence as cascading, as a cosmic dance of coming into being and fading away as a discrete individual, but the dance remains. As we have seen, the heroic attitude from Gilgamesh onward has been to struggle against this irresistible flow of life forms—often falling into despair about the flux's inevitability. Rather than focus on the tragic sense of this process, the cook takes its flow and adds to its sense as a game, a universal banquet, a cosmic play. The cook seeks to nourish others in such a way that, like a beautifully thrown spiraling pass or a wonderfully moving performance of Hamlet, it can happen with grace, with a thrill, and with a sense of ennobling engagement. The cook creates flavors from this process to bring smiles to our faces and warmth to our insides that goes beyond the literal warmth of the heated ingredients.

The cook evokes the image of the male in a steamy, frothy environment, engaged in the slow stirring, the patient bringing together of elements of the organic world, engaged in the bringing forth of nourishment for others, feeling the identification with what is cooked and those who are to be nourished by it. The masterful cook's secret power is his ability to bring into his relationship with the nourishing ingredients of the Earth an appreciation of their flavor, his sensitivity to their sensual richness, and a desire to bring forth a relish, a taste for life that is also an expression of care for others. It is a celebration of the cascade of how one being brings life to others, a making of the cascade tasty, and a helping to insert others more firmly within that ongoing flow by providing the nourishment that is their fuel for being part of the parade. The cook not only expresses his own caring in his cooking, but is also a vehicle that amplifies the intrinsic caring of all living beings for others in the life and death cycle by midwifing the potency of their nourishing quality. He magically transforms the raw power of the material aspect of the continuity of life into closeness, fullness, satisfaction, beauty, and joy.

In a Zen monastery, the one who is chosen to cook is someone who is seen to be far along the path of letting go, forsaking ego, and who feels connected to all beings. He releases himself into the ingredients, into the process of cooking, and into the flow of each being nourishing others. The quality of the cook's involvement becomes part of the flavor of the dish and part of the nourishing, inspiring power of the food. We know this in other contexts, such as when we cook a special meal or a cake for our beloved or for our child and the love is expressed right within the special taste of the food. It is that caring savored in the food that the child or the lover senses and remembers long after.

The cook's care and concern provides an alternative to the romantic model of love based on conquest and possession. The figure of the lover—with whom many males have identified, besides Robert Bly's "Iron John"—is another sort of warrior. The cook challenges men to change the direction of their love. Cooking requires that the male allow his affection to take an indirect route, through the stirring, baking, selecting, and savoring of colors and tastes. It requires trusting these sensual elements. It requires trusting not only that the fruits of the Earth will allow themselves to be worked with and transformed into something pleasing and nourishing, but also that through the cooking process they will somehow express our feelings, care, and sincerity to others. It also requires coming down to the earthy, sticky, and sensitively embodied level to poke around in pots, smell rinds, mix pastes, put our hands into things, and put everything on our tongue to sample its savor for others. Finally, it is a kind of loving that creates nourishment for others without chaining their identity to masculine control. To cook for others is to facilitate them *on their own way*, to give them a gift of vitality that they will use to go in whatever direction they choose. It is an offering.

Romantic love usually includes the cloying demand that we be affirmed directly as lovable as a symbol of our great value. We have already spoken of how desperate our distanced, out-of-touch position makes us to win the regard of others. We feel the need to be the hero, the savior, the one who is necessary to life's meaning as a replacement to feeling our own connection to things and others. The model of the cook's love is a more open-spirited, playful, and magical sense of love for the sake of just nourishing the other as a mortal being—a way of loving upon which we men could build another sense of giving and caring. It is in this regard that so many men's rejection of cooking is distressing and worrisome. Cooking is one of the most elemental and simple ways to come back to the Earth and rejoin this generous web of life.

CHAPTER NINE

Coming Home, Grieving, and a Dark Star

Homecomings

The end of this book's journey is to suggest that men should end their journey, too. Insofar as we have been caught up in the masculine identity with its metallic, storming, and separatist dimensions, we have been away too long. Some of us have been very far away for a very long time, and almost all of us have been somewhat absent for some of the time. A strange thing happens when we have been away for a while: we are no longer sure that we are welcome home. I believe that we males would be welcomed back, if we took responsibility for our fate; however, this involves a certain way to come home.

I think we often feel unwelcome when we make tentative attempts to rejoin the life of the planet, but this is to be expected if we start our voyage back in any of our traditional guises. No citizen welcomes an airplane using Main Street as a landing field, or wants to see a tank rumble past the town square, or wants her home to be the site of missile impacts, or wants her capacity to listen to be overwhelmed with proclamations. In fear, under siege and manipulation, others will seemingly welcome the warrior, the hero, the monumental

263

man, but actually he is just tolerated and, behind his back, distrusted. Certainly, the film *Falling Down* gives us a startling image of D-Fens desperately trying to return home, oblivious to the terror that his masculine defenses have inspired. The last pathetic image is of D-Fens thinking he will now get his son to play with him, as a police officer uses his family's presence to maneuver into position to kill him. If we men are to return home—both to enjoy being there and worthy of being welcomed back—there are several changes that must occur to our identities.

The first change is to take responsibility for our identity instead of comparing it to others. Many of the men with whom I have spoken quickly point to women and people who are of different cultural traditions as following the same roles as those we've discussed in this book. They claim that since men are not the only ones caught in these traps, they shouldn't be expected to change. Of course, it is true that masculine defenses are used by others, but this insight doesn't help our plight. If males, having had more power through much of modern history, have successfully set up social roles and perceptions of reality, those who were part of this world—and especially those who wished to become successful within it—have probably adopted its ways as well. If we men were to give up the old ball game we've set up, most likely others would also cease to play. Whether other groups have the same problems or not is ultimately beside the point. Why shouldn't we do something for ourselves to make our lives better? Why shouldn't we take the initiative to make better the lives of those who are affected by our behavior?

Another change that we must make in order to "come home" is to stop being jealous of the neighbors. Many men are angry that women have been consolidating a new sense of awareness and purpose for themselves through the feminist movement. They feel left out. Well, it seems more hopeful and helpful to be glad that parts of the population are doing something for themselves and entering into dialogue

with us males. Now we, too, should do something for ourselves—something new, something creative, something that
takes advantage of new energies and new possibilities. We
need to avoid retreating back into the "old ways," our yearning for the "way it used to be." I have waited for an answer-
ing "men's movement" to the "women's movement," and I
am profoundly disappointed in the attitudes of those like
Robert Bly who yearn for their "absent fathers" and want to
return to a "primal maleness." Rather, I would like to see us
evolve into a new sense of who we can be.

This change in masculine attitudes—welcoming transformation rather than retreating back into the fortress—means
that homecoming is not the nostalgic yearning for the days
before the Industrial Revolution or for a return to the forests
for some "primal experience." I think, or at least hope, that
we males may undertake a true journey—a journey involving
experiences that bring us to a new place where we can make
radical changes. The man who goes away and wants to
return to some condition in the past has not really had a journey, an odyssey; he has just passed through the landscape
untouched and unchanged. This has been the puer mode of
travel.

We males can find a "movement" in ourselves by listening to the voices of other groups with new agendas. The narratives that are coming to the fore now—of women, Native
Americans, Afro-Americans, indigenous peoples worldwide,
groups that were silenced—are not tales of glory but stories
of pain endured. To learn to hear their pain and be moved by
it would allow us males to return to the oldest story of the
wandering male—*The Odyssey*—that links the ability to bear
pain with the ability to come home.

The story of Odysseus told by Homer—which became
the archetype for the hero's change into a more sensitive person so that he could finally return home—has always been an
object of contention. For Plato, this epic was the object of
scorn as he offered a new code of masculinity to replace the

older sense of men and women. They had been seen as in harmony with nature, each other, and between mind and body, reason and emotion. Instead, Plato espoused the evil of the body and emotions, the need to use detached reason to ascend above the Earth toward the light of pure being, symbolized by the sun. In doing this, he stated that poets such as Homer, in giving men the image of protagonists such as Odysseus, were *monstrously corrupting* men:

> "Listen and see. I suppose when the best of us hear Homer or any other of the makers of tragedy imitating one of the heroes deep in mourning and making a long speech in lamentations, when he shows them chanting and beating their breasts, you know we are delighted and yield ourselves; we go with him in sympathy, we take all in earnest, and praise as a really good poet one who can make us feel most like that."
> "Of course, I know."
> "But when we have a private affliction ourselves, you notice that we pride ourselves on just the opposite, if we can only keep calm and endure, believing that this is manly, and that what we praised before is womanly."[1]

Plato claims that Homer and other poets and artists are dangerous for men in appealing to that part of us that "hungers to be satisfied with tears and a good hearty cry." He explains that it is necessary for us to dry up this part of ourselves, to restrain this capacity for tears, to keep guard over the part of us that is touched by the suffering of others, and to suppress the capacity that "feels no shame for itself in praising and pitying another man who, calling himself a good man, weeps and wails unseasonably" (p. 406).

It is for the same reasons that made Plato think that Homer was a threat to the well-being of the masculine way that I think we need to turn to *The Odyssey* for help. Plato is right: what is most striking about Odysseus as he returns home from his long journey is his ability to cry, his openness with his grief for all the distance that has come between himself and those that he loves, his mourning for all the time and opportunity lost for joy with his loved ones.

However, Odysseus had a hard lesson to learn. He would not have wandered for decades, absent from home, if he had not originally turned his grief into revenge—the same problem with which we opened this book's exploration of masculinity. If Odysseus could have acknowledged his pain and grieved the loss of his crew members at the hands of the Cyclops, he could have returned home immediately. However, he took his grief and channeled it into his rage against the Cyclops. In the epic, he is driven by this rage to not only defeat the Cyclops, but also to stand on the deck of his ship and brag of his victory to the blinded beast, to boast of his superior stature in defeating him, and to taunt the Cyclops in such a way that the creature will feel more emotional pain than he already does, being maimed by Odysseus. As a result of this taunting cruelty, the gods are persuaded that Odysseus should be detained from coming home for decades. This is an important symbol for the masculine need to inflict pain in order to deal with pain. Our rage is a barrier to our homecoming.

Odysseus does change, however, in the course of his wandering. He moves beyond this old way of dealing with pain. He has an odyssey—the very thing of which we saw the puer spirit is incapable—and is transformed by the experiences he undergoes. When he finally does return home, he cries profusely when rejoined with his son, his loyal servant, his wife, and his father. Following the successive reunions with each of these people, with whom a true connection is caringly and communicatively reestablished, a time for tears of mourning and joy occurs. Odysseus even cries when reunited briefly with his dog, Argos, before the latter dies, finally content to have seen him again after twenty years. Most striking is the open acknowledgment and shared pain expressed in the reunion of father and son as

Odysseus overcomes his own "absent father" status with his son Telemakhos:

> Then throwing his arms around this marvel of a
> father Telemakhos began to weep. Salt tears rose from
> the wells of longing in both men, and cries burst from
> both as keen and fluttering as those of the great taloned
> hawk, whose nestlings farmers take before they fly. So
> helplessly they cried, pouring out tears, and might have
> gone on weeping until sundown . . .[2]

Tears of pain, of missed connection, and of becoming vulnerable to the desire for future intimacy flow in a startling expressiveness between the two men, father and son. It is this kind of encounter that is missing from many fathers and sons in the masculine father's ongoing emotional absence. The masculine father will never come home emotionally until he can cry his pain helplessly to his son, holding him close. There is no help for the pain of missed connection except the holding close in grief. Of course, it is exactly a scene like this that Plato found so monstrously corrupting to our integrity as men, and his rejection of it founded the impoverishing tradition that has remained our masculine legacy.

The picture of Odysseus weeping to return to home, weeping when he regains his son, weeping when he returns to his rightful spot, weeping over his loyal friends, and weeping at his love with Penelope, is an inspiring image for males—in stark contrast to Plato's scorn for these very passages as "womanish." The grieving man is the antidote to our manic scurrying around and above the Earth. He has been brought down from his skyward journey, been slowed down, taken the richness of the Earth to heart, and relinquished the fight against death.

The Odyssey ends with Odysseus displaying the kind of courage men need to learn. He is justifiably aggressive in defending his family from those who, while he was away, were going to rob or destroy all he had built for them. However, the men of the town are also riled up by these same usurpers and unjustly avenge themselves by attacking Odysseus and his son. Odysseus, in his turn, could have justifiably slaughtered the scoundrels in defense, but instead he stops himself in order to become aware of his choices. He sees that anger, pain, and violence will never come to an end if each man keeps repaying his hurt with further hurt. Father and son together drop their weapons and cease their hostility and revenge. Likewise, only when we men come to shed tears and stop holding onto our rage at past pain inflicted will these interlocking cycles of violation cease.

Grieving and a Different Sense of Joy

Without grieving for all that we have missed, without grieving for all the hurtfulness that has been set into motion, and without grieving for the pain of loss that is part of the fabric of life, men cannot find their way back to Earth. The roots of the word *grieving* indicate "being burdened." The world, if taken to heart, *does* bear down on us. Grieving is about feeling the weight of existence, the weight that brings us back down to a common level with all other beings. It is the way home. Grieving is a response to the world, but to be able to see what is most significant in the world necessitates that we find another kind of sight than the heroic vision.

For thousands of years, men have identified with the sun, with the power of ascent, and with the desire to be above others; yet the glare from this sun, the distance of this altitude, and our disconnection from the earthly plane blind us to the subtle glow of the process of life. We males have sought the heroic gestures that would emblazen our egos and light up the sky in our image. Yet to become part of a larger whole, we need to be able to see the variety of colors in their varying shades.

The blinding light is a spectacular display with no subtlety. We live on the Earth, whose wonder is its amazing complexity, its variety, its subtle nuances. To appreciate all the

differences and become immersed in them offers an unending play. It requires a slower, more sensually and emotionally sensitive openness, and a more immersed presence
on this planet—like Henry Turner, who turned from spectacular courtroom victories to appreciating his family skipping
across the park; like John Dunbar, who turned from seeking
glory in war to watching the mysteries of the prairie skies,
plants, and animals; like Jack Lucas, who turned from mil-
lion-dollar contracts to lying naked under the sky watching
clouds and kidding with friends. Only then can males begin
to notice a different kind of light emanating from all beings—
a light generated by the expended vitality of our all being
part of this passing dance.

Grieving makes us face our incompleteness. In grief, we
miss something or someone we held close to our heart. Now
they are gone. We grieve over the possibilities that never
came to be. We allow ourselves to feel the ways in which we
are torn in our being when others are ripped away from our
grasp. We viscerally feel our lack of control over our destiny
and the destinies of those we love.

A strange thing happens in grieving: the loss that started
this process soon brings us to feel the pains of many other
losses. Not only that, but feeling our personal griefs makes us
feel the pain of the larger cycle of tragic losses that occur
every day on the planet. All these hurts can make us feel
insignificant and helpless as a small part of a cosmic play of
people, creatures, and even inanimate objects passing away,
often so needlessly, wastefully, absurdly, or through being
violated. This is the horror that masculinity dares not face,
except as a challenge to be overcome by the hero. The hero is
looking toward some great goal to achieve that will compen-
sate for these innumerable mundane pains. However, these
losses cannot be compensated. Each loss is unique, irrepara-
ble. Grief will not let us rise above the loss and its pain.
Instead, we helplessly enter the web of impacts that is life's
process—its labyrinth.

If grieving is an open emotion, it goes beyond the boundaries of the ego to encompass the world that was its cause. It takes us out of ourselves to the web of impacts that we have identified as the debt incurred. All living beings impact each other in the process of life, which is simultaneously creation and destruction, creating both joys and pains. Grieving, when undertaken vulnerably, makes us feel how nothing is really our possession—that all is part of a process and a temporary gift we've enjoyed. It humbles us. This is quite a different feeling from the unquenchable despair at the heart of the heroic tradition so vividly expressed in the ancient image of Gilgamesh ranting inconsolably and furiously over the death of Enkidu.

The hero is unapproachable in his loss, self-enclosed in his private hell. He is bitter that the Earth has taken away from him that which he enjoyed or those whom he loved. He takes it as a personal affront—as if something has happened to him that he didn't deserve. After all, isn't he the hero, worthy of rewards, the fruits of his labor? He has *monumentalized* himself and that which he loved—whether person, position, or thing. He thought that he *owned* what he loved and that he had a right to that love. This is the plight of the pseudo–anti-hero, Bill Munny, in *The Unforgiven*. The film suggests that it is an injustice that Bill Munny is never forgiven for his violence. However, not only should he remain "unforgiven," since he has not really changed, but the source of his renewed violence is his own clinging to "unforgiveness" toward life itself! He is bitter that his wife was taken from him by death. This is not grieving—at least not in an emotionally sensitive and open manner; it is the egoistic self-pity, the masculine attempt to wrest something static, firmly possessed, and seriously deserved from life.

Sensitive grieving is responsive. It is not focused on our own ego image but on the person or thing lost—on our relationship to them and their own relationships in the world. In grieving, we feel the flowing presence of what has been and all its interconnections with the rest of the world. We don't see the person gone as our possession, as an object, but as a living presence that has been.

When in the 1990 film, *Class Action*, Jed Ward's wife of thirty-five years dies suddenly of a heart attack, he feels grief for the experiences they will never share, but he also misses and honors all that his wife stood for and achieved. He doesn't feel bitter that she has been taken from him; rather, the deeper he goes into his feelings of grief, the more he is led to feel the gift of all that she was a part. Heartfelt grieving is not only a missing but also a flowing, a connecting, a grateful acknowledgment of what has been *as precious as a being not of our making—a gift—and a life-process with its own course.* This is where joy appears in the sorrow of grief: in celebrating what this person and their relationships were, and still are, about.

In the film, Jed Ward and his daughter, Margaret, have been at an impasse throughout their entire adult lives—each misunderstanding the other, each wrapped up in their own pain. They no longer communicate in any meaningful way other than to criticize and resent the other. Jed feels that his daughter hates him. He disrespects all that she is: corporate lawyer, well off, and ambitious. Margaret disrespects Jed's past insensitivity and hurtfulness to her mother and others he loved, despite his fame as a lawyer involved in social-justice issues. For her, he is a hypocrite. The two of them are locked in an unending competition. Stella Ward, who works with poor children to help them find hope, sees both their faults and both their strengths and loves them both. After Stella dies, both Jed and Margaret are led slowly and painfully back to Stella's way of seeing things, of working things out, and into the complexities of her value system. This is what real grieving is about.

Jed and his daughter come to stand with Stella in her way of dealing with people, because grieving is part humor, part play, and part magic. Instead of monumentalizing her, they humorously and fluidly imagine where she might have gone further with the situation—not in a serious self-right-eous way, as a frozen memory, but with the smile she was capable of. We all have our own smiles about different things and in different ways, and they honor hers in grieving her. In turn, her memory allows them to enter an interplay with each other in which she is still present, despite her absence in time and space. In some very real and deeply felt way, she brings them together. This grieving, in contrast to the hero's bitter holding on to loss, is grateful and keeps the other's gifts alive.

If Bill Munny had truly grieved his wife, he would have been led into a closer, happier, and enlivened relationship with their children, with their friends, and with her estranged mother—who never understands why her daughter married him. Instead, he remains a rock—unchanging, closed within himself, and bitter—sitting by his wife's monument.

Not only do people pass away, but also periods of our life, events, and possibilities pass away. These, too, call for grieving. In *The Fisher King*, Jack Lucas does not lose anyone, but the tragedy of the murderous events in which he is impli-cated shatter his world and throw him into a long period of grief. For that first year, he remains locked into a hero's despair and frustration over the injustice that such sadness could have entered his life, and he is immobilized like Bill Munny. When he meets Perry, he begins to grieve in a more genuine way. He finds that what was good and hopeful about his life will never return, but now can be brought for-ward into a new life process. Instead of staying locked within himself in self-pity, as he did for the first year, he starts to grieve the events as a state of affairs that involved others, their actions, and their lives. He can now feel how these events can be entered into as part of the cosmic play with him that can be made into a way of connecting with others and having humor about what were his former limitations.

Henry Turner does the same thing in grieving his assault

and loss of the abilities that made possible his former career as a high-powered lawyer. These men allow life's blows to play with them in such a way that their pain also has a vein of revealing humor and becomes a way of bringing them into closer relationship with the others affected by the tragedy. Their pain is very real, but it also has a dynamic, shared, and magical quality because it is entered into fully and sensitively, thus bringing new life and transformation.

When we get beyond the hero's hardened sadness about loss that becomes self-pity, we develop the ability to hear our losses' messages about our lack of control over our destiny. The heroic paradigm tells us to stay in charge—even in the face of loss, even in the face of death. However, life's most compelling message demonstrates that this is self-defeating egoism. We might call such egoism silly if it didn't lead to so much violence and suffering for others. Death tells us: let go. Just as Keating has his students "listen to" the pictures of the dead, so we should hear the same rasp: celebrate what you are given. Pain shows us that we can't hold on. If we do, we're left with an empty husk, like Gilgamesh or Bill Munny. If we let go, we will be carried into a flowing play that contains both pain and joy.

Without feeling this grief, the magic of existence cannot be revealed and experienced. It is because we feel our insignificance that we cannot take our egos seriously. We are released from our isolation into just being a very tiny part of a larger community of people and creatures. It is because the world is fragmented that its ability to overcome these gaps through the felt identifications of its members is so wondrous—and magical. We were not put here to be gods as the masculine ethos has desired as its highest ideal. The limitations that we experience, as well as those of all other creatures and even the material world, do not ruin life or condemn us to despair. They are the source of every being finding a way to be involved in everything else. Insufficiency renders each being part of the planet-wide magic of dancing together. We are ripped open in order to be exposed to all other life forms and forces on Earth, but it is also a hurt that can be transformed into play.

The play of affirming process is not the play that comes from the puer soaring above things and refusing to take life to heart, nor does the trickster see life as a joke in this dismissive sense, nor is the magic of the true magician a manipulative sleight of hand. This play, these tricks, and this magic are the marrow of taking the Earth's daily events and flow so much to heart that their very existence gives a buoyancy even in the midst of pain. This is a joy in pain and a pain even in joy, because it brings us into the heart of a web in which life feeds death—not out of a voracious, cosmic revenge that we must in turn avenge but because in their enthusiasm to be, all lives must impact on other lives. This is what pain means, but this is also the birth of joy in community.

This is the dark star, which both contains the darker side of existence and glows from within. The glow emanates from a life with defeats, with suffering, lived in the face of death, and yet enlivened with the intrinsic wonder of entering into life's process and of experiencing interconnection across difference and distance. This is not the dazzling white sun-star that seeks to ban the mystery and reveal the secret inner springs of life and death in the hope of overcoming life's imperfections. If we men are to gain the capacity of the dark star, we will have to be able to find joy within pain by affirming process rather than seeking ultimate triumph, by taking life's blows as tricks of the cosmos rather than as personal affronts. We've seen that this is in accord with the original sense of the hero as consort to Hera, the Goddess. In this sense of the hero, the male was a protector and part of the larger natural cycle of the Earth. In this cycle, that which is alive dies but is always reborn in new forms. We males can help the planet, as well as ourselves, by abandoning the warrior's sense of masculine identity. Then we can *feel* with different people and creatures, rather than insisting that others become the same as we are.

The desert storm is the howling anger and frustration of those who seek to become like the sun but end up projecting dark violation upon others after too one-sidedly trying to become the source of illumination. This light does have its proper place in the larger cycle, but it is about time that men saw that our place is lower and more pained: mortal, yet with assent, humorously entwined and magical.

Notes

Preface

1. Robert Bly, *Iron John: A Book About Men* (New York: Addison-Wesley Publishing Co., 1990), pp. 2–3.

Chapter One: Male Pride

1. Virginia Woolf, *To the Lighthouse* (New York: Harcourt, Brace and Jovanovich, 1955), p. 159.

2. Joseph Campbell, *The Hero with a Thousand Faces* (New York: Meridian, 1956), pp. 36–38, 58. Those pages summarize the "monomyth" which is elaborated throughout the work. Campbell states, "Whether the hero be ridiculous or sublime, Greek or barbarian, gentile or Jew, his journey varies little in essential plan" (p. 38).

3. Edward Conze, trans. and editor, *Buddhist Scriptures* (New York: Penguin Books, 1959), p. 42.

4. John Briggs and David F. Peat, *The Turbulent Mirror* (New York: Harper and Row, 1989), p. 156: "In fact, all life is a form of cooperation, an expression of feedback arising out of the flux of chaos."

5. Of course, Hera, too, is in some way taking the pain of the hurt inflicted upon her by Zeus and using it to violate. We could analyze the ways in which women caught up in these cycles of violation have attempted at times to use the powers of the Earth to fight back against violation, but this is not a study of how females have been forced to deal with these hell worlds. Mary Daly's *Pure Lust* describes well how this hurt often gets passed along in a violating society. See Mary Daly, *Pure Lust* (Boston: Beacon Press, 1984) pp. 59–60.

6. See Daly, pp. 355–361.

7. See Marija Gimbutas, *The Language of the Goddess* (London: Thames and Hudson, 1989).

8. Bly, p. 3.

9. Robert Graves, *The Greek Myths*, vol. 2 (New York: Penguin, 1960), p. 126.

10. Graves, p. 117.

11. Friedrich Nietzsche, *Thus Spoke Zarathustra: A Book for All and None*, trans. Walter Kaufmann (New York: Penguin, 1978), pp. 12–13.

12. "I think too that the underworld teaches us to abandon our hopes for achieving unification of personality by means of the dream. The underworld spirits are plural. . . . Only by falling apart into the multiple figures do we extend consciousness to embrace and contain its psychopathic potentials." James Hillman, *The Dream and the Underworld* (New York: Harper and Row, 1975), p. 41. Hillman also includes a wonderful discussion of Hercules' ineptness in the underworld because of the liability of his heroic ego (pp. 110–117). The whole book complements themes in this work.

13. Bly, p. 229.

14. This is the same paradox presented so well in the image of the Zen archer by Eugen Herrigal in *Zen in the Art of Archery* (New York: Vintage Books, 1971). Herrigal, even after six years of learning with the master, can't let go of the idea that in order to hit the target, he has to want to hit the target, to try to hit the target. It is only when the Zen archer has let go of any interest in hitting the target that suddenly, almost by surprise, he hits the bull's-eye. It comes as a bonus when it is no longer what one is about! We will be discussing this at length in chapter 7.

Chapter Two: It Hurts So Good

1. A recent bestselling "men's movement" book is John Lee's *The Flying Boy* which recognizes that males defend themselves by flying away.

2. James Hillman, "Senex and Puer," in *Puer Papers*, ed. James Hillman (Dallas: Spring Publications, 1987), p. 24.

3. See p. 232 below.

4. As quoted by Martin Heidegger, *What Is Called Thinking?*, trans. J. Glenn Gray (New York: Harper and Row, 1968), p. 30.

5. Sören Kierkegaard, *Either/Or*, vol. 1, trans. David and Lillian Swenson (Princeton: Princeton University Press, 1971), p. 41.

6. "The essence of pleasure does not lie in the thing enjoyed, but in the accompanying consciousness. If I had a humble spirit in my service who, when I asked for a glass of water, brought me the world's costliest wines blended in a chalice, I should dismiss him, in order to teach him that pleasure consists not in what I enjoy, but in having my own way" (Kierkegaard, p. 30). Note both the detachment from what is enjoyed and the need to be in control.

7. Kierkegaard, p. 40.

8. In Joseph Heller's novel of the same name, "Catch-22" stated that a flier could be relieved of flying any more combat missions, if he were crazy. However, if he asked to be relieved from flying any more missions, that was an eminently sane thing to do, so he couldn't be crazy!

9. I was privileged to hear the report of extensive interviews with serial killers and the study of other interviews with them at a conference, "The Phenomenology of the Body," at Esalen Institute, Big Sur, California, in June 1991.

10. William J. Broyles, "Why Men Love War," *Esquire*, November 1984, p. 55. Further citations that follow from

this text, where it is obvious that they are taken from it, will be included with the page number(s) in parentheses.

11. See Marija Gimbutas, *The Civilization of the Goddess: The World of Old Europe* (San Francisco: HarperCollins, 1991), and Riane Eisler, *The Chalice and the Blade: Our History, Our Future* (San Francisco: HarperCollins, 1988).

12. Thomas Allen, F. Clifton Berry, and Norman Polmar, *CNN, War in the Gulf* (Atlanta: Turner Publishing, 1991), p 136. Further citations that follow from this text, where it is obvious that they are taken from it, will be included with the page number(s) in parentheses.

13. It is a rather bizarre coincidence that after I left my word processor for the day, stopping with the previous sentence, I read in the newspaper, the new Pentagon report that espoused the "air war" strategy as a paradigm for how the US should conduct future armed conflicts: to stay in the sky as much as possible.

14. I will draw on Harold Lubin's retelling of the myth in his *Heroes and Anti-Heroes: A Reader in Depth* (San Francisco: Chandler, 1968), pp. 16-31. Further citations that follow from this text, where it is obvious that they are taken from it, will be included with the page number(s) in parentheses.

15. John Barth, *Chimera* (New York: Fawcett, 1972), p. 19.

Chapter Three: The Armored Tank and the Big Missile

1. Margaret Atwood, *Surfacing* (New York: Popular Library, 1976), p. 213.

2. D.H. Lawrence, "Two Ways of Living and Dying" in *The Complete Poems of D.H. Lawrence*, ed. by Vivian de Sola and F. Warren Roberts (New York: The Viking Press, 1971), p. 675.

3. See the discussion of the power and place of this

metaphor in Catherine Keller, *From A Broken Web*
(Boston: Beacon Press, 1986), pp. 216–218.

4. *New York Times*, October 3, 1993.

5. *Ibid.*

6. *Ibid.*

7. Lawrence, p. 675.

8. Lawrence, p. 676.

9. Herman Melville, *Moby Dick, or the Whale* (Indianapolis:
Bobbs-Merrill, 1964), p. 221. Further citations that follow
from this text, where it is obvious that they are taken
from it, will be included with the page number(s) in
parentheses.

10. Allen, Berry, and Polmar, p. 212.

11. Broyles, p. 62.

12. Allen, Berry, and Polmar, p. 118.

Chapter Four: The Briefing

1. Sophocles, "Oedipus Rex," in *The Oedipus Cycle*, trans.
Dudley Fitts and Robert Fitzgerald (New York, Harvest
Books, 1969), p. 9. Further citations that follow from this
text, where it is obvious that they are taken from it, will
be included with the page number(s) in parentheses.

2. This is what Mary Daly means by "verbicide": the
destruction of the power of words to unblock us, to free
us for the deeper levels of meaning where existence is a
dynamic, interconnecting flow. See "On Lust and the
Lusty," in *Pure Lust*, pp. 1–32.

3. Daly, p. 4.

4. Allen, Berry, and Polmar, p 160.

Chapter Five: Letting Be, Finding Other Worlds, and Celebrating Interconnection

1. Woolf, p. 68.

2. Riane Eisler, pp. 16–28.

3. Marija Gimbutas, *The Civilization of the Goddess: The World of Old Europe* (San Francisco: HarperCollins, 1991), p. 399. Further citations that follow from this text, where it is obvious that they are taken from it, will be included with the page number(s) in parentheses.

4. The tale predates the third millennium B.C.'s political consolidation of Sumer.

5. Barbara G. Walker, *The Woman's Dictionary of Symbols and Sacred Objects* (San Francisco: Harper and Row, 1988), p. 95–96.

6. Eric Partridge, *Origins: A Short Etymological Dictionary of Modern English* (New York: Greenwich House, 1983), pp. 286–287.

7. Walker, p. 251.

8. Jane Ellison Harrison, *Prolegomena to the Study of Greek Religion and Themis* (New York; University Books, 1962), pp. 365–367.

9. Walker, p. 90. The Athenian coin which pictured Hercules with the tree of life and the cornucopia could no longer be explained after he was made the warrior hero. At that point, he was thought to have stolen these symbols (Harrison, p. 367).

10. Donna Wilshire, *Virgin, Mother, Crone: Myths and Mysteries of the Triple Goddess* (Rochester, Vermont: Inner Traditions, 1993), p. 34. Further citations that follow from this text, where it is obvious that they are taken from it, will be included with the page number(s) in parentheses.

11. *Ibid.*

12. Walker, pp. 16, 128.

13. Walker, p. 16.

Chapter Six: We're Kidding

1. William Shakespeare, *King Lear* (New York: Signet, 1963), p. 112.

2. Robert Moore and Douglas Gillette, *The Magician Within: Accessing the Shamanic in the Male Psyche* (New York: William Morrow, 1993), p. 167.

3. Moore and Gillette, p. 170.

4. Carl G. Jung, *The Archetypes and the Collective Unconscious* [vol. 9, part 1, in *The Collected Works of C. G. Jung*], trans. by R. F. C. Hull (Princeton: Princeton University Press, 1969) p. 267.

5. Karl Kerenyi, "The Trickster Myth in Relation to Greek Mythology," in Paul Radin, *The Trickster: A Study in American Indian Mythology* (New York: Schocken Books, 1972), p. 174. Further citations that follow from this text, where it is obvious that they are taken from it, will be included with the page number(s) in parentheses.

6. Gary Snyder, *The Back Country* (New York: New Directions, 1968), p. 125.

7. Radin, p. 22.

8. Jung, pp. 258-9.

Chapter Seven: We're Playing

1. Nietzsche, p. 268.

2. Nietzche, p. 156.

3. W. B. Yeats, "Lapis Lazuli," *The Collected Poems of W.B. Yeats* (Toronto: Macmillan, 1956), pp. 291–293.

4. Johan Huizinga, *Homo Ludens: A Study of the Play Element*

in Culture (Boston: Beacon Press, 1955), p. 8. Further citations that follow from this text, where it is obvious that they are taken from it, will be included with the page number(s) in parentheses.

5. William Shakespeare, *The Tempest* (New York: New American, 1964), pp. 103-104 [Act IV, scene 1, lines 146–158].

Chapter Eight: A Good Cook Is Hard to Find

1. Again, Briggs and Peat, in their book, *The Turbulent Mirror*, do an elegant job of summarizing these movements within science to recognize the "holographic," "non-linear" logic that is demonstrated in the world outside the over-simplified classical lab environment.

2. Archie Fire Lame Deer and Richard Erdoes, *Gift of Power: The Life and Teachings of a Lakota Medicine Man* (Santa Fe: Bear & Co., 1992), p. 17.

3. Tony Hillerman, *Coyote Waits* (New York: HarperCollins Publishers, 1990), pp. 191–192. Further citations that follow from this text, where it is obvious that they are taken from it, will be included in parentheses with the page number(s).

4. Merleau-Ponty calls this "perceptual faith." See Maurice Merleau-Ponty, *Phenomenology of Perception*, trans. Colin Smith (New York: Humanities, 1962).

5. John Fowles, *The Magus* (New York: Dell Publishing, 1973), pp. 499–500.

6. Herrigal, p. 51. Further citations that follow from this text, where it is obvious that they are taken from it, will be included in parentheses with the page number(s).

7. To be "spaced out" is actually to be that busy Herculean male, scurrying about, trying to keep the world, which is at a distance, in the order of one's bidding.

8. Heinrich Zimmer, *Philosophies of India* (Princeton: Princeton University Press, 1969), p. 347.

Chapter Nine: Coming Home, Grieving, and a Dark Star

1. Plato, *The Republic* in *Great Dialogues of Plato*, trans. W. H. D. Rouse (New York: Mentor, 1956), p. 406. Further citations that follow from this text, where it is obvious that they are taken from it, will be included with the page number(s) in parentheses.

2. Homer, *The Odyssey*, trans. Robert Fitzgerald (Garden City: Doubleday, 1963), p. 296.

Bibliography

Allen, Thomas F; Clifton Berry; and Norman Polmar. *CNN, War in the Gulf*. Atlanta: Turner Publishing, 1991.

Atwood, Margaret. *Surfacing*. New York: Popular Library, 1976.

Barth, John. *Chimera*. New York: Fawcett, 1972.

Bly, Robert. *Iron John: A Book About Men*. New York: Addison-Wesley Publishing Co., 1990.

Briggs, John and F. David Peat. *The Turbulent Mirror*. New York: Harper and Row, 1989.

Broyles, William J. "Why Men Love War." *Esquire*. (November, 1984): pp. 55–62.

Cameron, Anne. *Daughters of Copper Woman*. Vancouver: Press Gang Publishing, 1981.

Conze, Edward (ed), *Buddhist Scriptures*. New York: Penguin Books, 1959.

Daly, Mary. *Pure Lust*. Boston: Beacon Press, 1984.

DeBeauvoir, Simone. *The Second Sex*. New York: Random House, 1974.

Eisler, Riane. *The Chalice and the Blade: Our History, Our Future*. San Francisco: HarperCollins, 1988.

Fowles, John. *The Magus*. New York: Dell Publishing, 1973.

Gilligan, Carol. *In a Different Voice: Psychological Theory & Women's Development*. Cambridge, Harvard University Press, 1982.

Gimbutas, Marija. *The Civilization of the Goddess: The World of Old Europe*. San Francisco: HarperCollins, 1991.

_____. *The Language of the Goddess*. London: Thames and Hudson, 1989.

Graves, Robert. *The Greek Myths*. New York: Penguin, 1960.

Harrison, Jane Ellison. *Prolegomena to the Study of Greek Religion and Themis*. New York: University Books, 1962.

Heidegger, Martin. *Being and Time*. trans. MacQuarrie and Robinson. New York: Harper and Row, 1962.

_____. *What Is Called Thinking?*, trans. J. Glenn Gray. New York: Harper and Row, 1968.

Herrigal, Eugen. *Zen in the Art of Archery*. New York: Vintage Books, 1971.

Hesse, Hermann. *Steppenwolf*. New York: Bantam, 1969.

Hillerman, Tony. *Coyote Waits*. New York: HarperCollins,1990.

Hillman, James. *The Dream and the Underworld*. New York: Harper and Row, 1975.

_____. *Puer Papers*. Dallas: Spring Publications, 1987.

_____. *Re-Visioning Psychology*. New York: Harper and Row, 1977.

Homer. *The Odyssey*. trans. Robert Fitzgerald. Garden City: Doubleday, 1963.

Huizinga, Johan. *Homo Ludens: A Study of the Play Element in Culture*. Boston: Beacon Press, 1955.

Jung, Carl G. *The Archetypes and the Collective Unconscious* [vol. 9, part 1, in *The Collected Works of C. G. Jung*]. trans. R. F. C. Hull. Princeton: Princeton University Press, 1969.

Kapleau, Phillip. *The Three Pillars of Zen*. New York: Doubleday, 1980.

Keen, Sam. *Fire in the Belly: On Being a Man*. New York: Bantam, 1991.

Keller, Catherine. *From A Broken Web*. Boston: Beacon Press, 1986.

Kierkegaard, Sören. *Either/Or*, vol. 1, trans. David and Lillian Swenson. Princeton: Princeton University Press, 1971.

Lame Deer, Archie Fire. *Gift of Power: The Life and Teachings of a Lakota Medicine Man*. Santa Fe: Bear & Company, 1992.

Lawrence, D.H. *The Complete Poems of D.H. Lawrence*. ed. Vivian de Sola and F. Warren Roberts. New York: The Viking Press, 1971.

Lubin, Harold. *Heroes and Anti-Heroes: A Reader in Depth*. San Francisco: Chandler, 1968.

Mazis, Glen A. *Emotion and Embodiment: Fragile Ontology*. New York: Peter Lang, 1993.

_____. "The Riteful Play of Time in *The French Lieutenant's Woman*". *Soundings* (Fall, 1983), pp. 296–318.

Melville, Herman. *Moby Dick Or, the Whale*. Indianapolis: Bobbs-Merrill, 1964.

Merleau-Ponty, Maurice. *Phenomenology of Perception*. trans. Colin Smith. New York: Humanities, 1962.

_____. *The Primacy of Perception*. Evanston: Northwestern University, 1964.

_____. *The Visible and the Invisible*. trans. Alphonso Lingis, Evanston: Northwestern University, 1968.

Nietzsche, Friedrich. *Thus Spoke Zarathustra: A Book for All and None*. trans. Walter Kaufmann. New York: Penguin, 1978.

Partridge, Eric. *Origins: A Short Etymological Dictionary of Modern English*. New York: Greenwich House, 1983.

Piercy, Marge. *Woman on the Edge of Time*. New York: Fawcett, 1986.

Plato. *Great Dialogues of Plato*, trans. W. H. D. Rouse. New York: Mentor, 1956.

Radin, Paul. *The Trickster: A Study in American Indian Mythology*. New York: Schocken Books, 1972.

Shakespeare, William. *Hamlet*. New York: New American, 1963.

_____. *King Lear*. New York: New American, 1963.

_____. *The Tempest*. New York: New American, 1964.

Sophocles. *The Oedipus Cycle*. trans. Dudley Fitts and Robert Fitzgerald. New York: Harvest Books, 1969.

Tulku, Tarthang. *Time, Space & Knowledge*. Berkeley: Dharma, 1977.

Tzu, Lao. *Tao Te Ching*. New York: Concord Grove, 1983.

Walker, Barbara G. *The Woman's Dictionary of Symbols and Sacred Objects*. San Francisco: Harper and Row, 1988.

White, Terence H. *The Once and Future King*. New York: Putnam, 1958.

Woolf, Virginia. *To the Lighthouse*. New York: Harcourt, Brace and Jovanovich, 1955.

Yeats, W.B. *The Collected Poems*. Toronto: Macmillan, 1956.

Zimmer, Heinrich. *Philosophies of India*. Princeton: Princeton University Press, 1969.

Index

About the Author

Glen A. Mazis was born in 1951 and currently lives in Marietta, Pennsylvania, in a restored and converted nine-teenth-century Lutheran church. Glen received his Ph.D. in philosophy from Yale University in 1977, after writing his dissertation *Ambiguity and the Joyful Loss of Ego*. He teaches in an interdisciplinary Humanities undergraduate and master's program at Penn State Harrisburg. He has also been a profes-sor at the University of Illinois, Louisiana State University, Northern Kentucky University, Wesleyan University, and St. Lawrence University. He has published numerous essays about the body, emotions, the nature of the self, interpersonal relations, perception, film, painting, and aesthetics in *Philosophy Today, Soundings, The Semiotic Web, Semiotica, The Journal for the British Society of Phenomenology,* and others. He has also had essays included in half a dozen anthologies of Continental philosophy and the philosophy of Merleau-Ponty. Glen has written another book, a philosophical inquiry, *Emotion and Embodiment: Fragile Ontology* (Peter Lang, 1993). Glen has long been a practicing Zen Buddhist and lover of the sea, was briefly a Gestalt therapist, is a mar-athon runner, and seeks to be fully alive while here on the planet.

BOOKS OF RELATED INTEREST
FROM BEAR & COMPANY

GOSSIPS, GORGONS & CRONES
The Fates of the Earth
Jane Caputi

INNER CHILD CARDS
A Journey into Fairy Tales, Myth & Nature
Isha Lerner and Mark Lerner

ORIGINAL BLESSING
A Primer on Creation Spirituality
Matthew Fox, O.P.

STAR WARRIOR
The Story of Swiftdeer
Bill Wahlberg

SEXUAL PEACE
Beyond the Dominator Virus
Michael Sky

WHEN LIGHTNING STRIKES A HUMMINGBIRD
The Autobiography of a Healer
Foster Perry

WOMAN WITH THE ALABASTER JAR
Mary Magdalen and the Holy Grail
Margaret Starbird

Contact your local bookseller or write us:

BEAR & COMPANY
P.O. Box 2860
Santa Fe, NM 87504-2860